INSIDE
Part 2

by Kyra Anderson

www.the-amiverse.com

Website: www.kyra-anderson.com

Published by K.J. Amidon

ISBN: 978-0-9832280-7-3

1st Edition © 2014
2nd Edition © 2024

Cover Art by K.J. Amidon

Printed in the United States

Table of Contents

Dedicated to:

My friends and family who inspire me every day

R&D&Z, who put up with brainstorming sessions until the wee hours of the morning. You guys are awesome!

Beckers, for listening to me talk about this book incessantly!

Cheryl, you are my rock in turbulent times. You helped me through this darkness.

Author's Note

Welcome, Reader!

Welcome to Part Two of Inside, the continuation of the terrifying story of Lily Sandover and her fight against the Commission of the People and its leader, Mr. Dana Christenson.

As I stated in Part One, this story is not for the faint of heart or easily-offended. The story elements of this novel are meant to provoke intense and often unpleasant emotions. This is not a warning to try and sound edgy—this is to cover my bases in case some readers do not heed all the other warnings in Part One before purchasing this book.

Like all authors I ask that you suspend your knowledge of reality and step into the world created in these pages. Please remember that this is a work of fiction! Any similarities to people, places, or situations are not intentional. None of these events are meant to push political agendas, nor should anything in this book be taken as politically accurate. The politics, laws, and scenarios in Inside are 100% fiction.

Also as I stated in the first part of the novel, there will be no broad recap of what has already transpired. If you have picked up this book first, note that the first chapter in this volume is Chapter Thirty-Six. It is imperative that you read Part One first in order to have an understanding of the characters and plot.

Please remember, this is not a series, but a continuous novel.

Let us return to the dark and twisted world of the Commission of the People and the rebellion attempting to tear it down.

When you last saw Lily Sandover, she was organizing a revolution against the Commission of the People and Dana Christenson. So far, it seems the revolution is moving forward with the help of mysterious notes and angry classmates. However, Dana Christenson has a tight leash on everyone in the Commission, and they fall under his spell almost willingly, including Lily's own mother.

Chapter Thirty-Six

I spent a lot of time getting ready for the Halloween party Friday afternoon. I was no longer nervous about the pace of the rebellion. I was angry, furious at my mother and at Dana, allowing that rage to spur me into action against both of them. I eagerly prepared my costume, ready to get to work on what I was now thinking of as my revolution.

Clark brought a scarf to complete my costume as a masquerade countess. I had a corset that pushed my breasts up more than I was ever going to be comfortable with and hugged my waist so tight it was hard to breathe, along with a heavy skirt that I had to hold up to keep from tripping. The mask was peacock feathers and glitter and covered my eyes, cheeks, and forehead.

It was a costume that, no surprise, was picked out for me by my friends.

The look required considerable preparation and I needed Clark's help to tie the strings at the back of my corset and support me while I put on my shoes. Once, I caught Mark glancing in the window at us before he quickly ducked around the corner as if he hadn't been watching.

When Dana came in, however, apprehension dulled the fire of anger within me.

"Well, my goodness, Little Lily, you look royal." Dana smiled, bowing as if he were a cliché suitor. I turned away, rolling my eyes. "Can I not pay a compliment to a beautiful woman?"

"Find someone else," I sneered, reaching for the scarf and tying it around my waist.

"Clark, what are you going as?"

"A wraith," he answered, pulling up his hood to fall over his eyes.

"Who did your makeup?" Dana pressed, nodding to the pale paint that I had caked onto his face thirty minutes previous.

"Lily," Clark said, removing his hood once again.

"Nicely done," Dana said. "I just wanted to tell you two that I hope you have fun, but be sure that you're careful. You never know what can happen on nights like this. This is the night for people to be who they're not, so be sure you stay aware."

We said nothing in response.

"Well, I have a meeting in five minutes, so I'll leave you two to finish up," Dana said, stepping out the door and waving to us as he walked away.

I growled, glaring at his back as he left.

"I hate him."

An hour later, Mark pulled into the parking lot of Archangel. I busied myself studying the other costumes as people entered the club, feeling nervous butterflies in my stomach.

"Lily," Clark whispered, handing me a stack of papers we had created that afternoon with the information on where Commish Kids could meet. I put the papers in the only pocket in my skirt before sliding out of the car. Mark pulled into a parking space where he would wait until the end of the party to drive us home, at Dana's insistence. I slipped on my mask and Clark pulled up his hood before offering his hand to me.

The Halloween party was supposed to be one of the yearly highlights for the club-goers of Archangel, but there was tension throughout my body that made the party feel more like walking into an enemy camp. Everyone was dressed up, makeup and masks disguising them while the bright costumes drew attention. Many of the girls were wearing Halloween costumes that made them look older, all trying to be sexy by exposing far too much skin, many shivering as they stepped into the club.

Club Archangel had been decorated, the lights mostly orange and red with some black lights casting a milky purple color over the dancing students. There were skeletons and ghosts hanging from the ceiling— even the music was darker. The feeling was fun, yet ominous. I was surprised at how many people had their faces covered by masks or hoods. I could not recognize anyone, particularly in the darker lights.

As Clark and I were making our way through the crowd of people, I had to take a deep breath. I was about to commit an act of treason. And Dana's words were still clear in my mind.

"This is the night for people to be who they're not..."

That means you need to be brave, I scolded myself. I was sure that, as time progressed and we were more aware of our allies, I would become braver. However, tonight, my stomach was in knots and it was difficult to breathe. Of course, that could have been the corset.

"Hey!" Becca beamed as we approached the table. I stopped abruptly when I saw Todd and Taylor. When I had blinked stupidly at their costumes a few times, I started laughing.

"What the hell?!"

"What?" Todd said in a falsetto voice, waving his pom poms in my face as he bounced around in his cheerleader's skirt and sweater, the curls of his pink wig flying wildly out of control. "Are you stunned by my beauty?" He batted his glittered fake eyelashes, striking a pose.

"I told him he could try out for the squad next year," Taylor said through her football helmet, pushing one of her bulky shoulder pads back into place under her jersey.

"Does coming dressed as a jock and a cheerleader count for couple costumes?" Jill asked. "We've been trying to decide."

"I would say."

"Lily, you look gorgeous!" Devon grinned, dressed as an eighties punk rocker. I laughed when I saw his costume, pulling the lapels of his studded leather jacket and shaking my head.

"Why do you have this in your closet?" I teased.

"Oh, yeah, what about you?" He took my hand, looking me over carefully. "Wow, you look amazing!"

I never was good at taking compliments, and I was acutely aware of Jill's glaring eyes through her cat mask, so I just laughed.

"Hey, they bought this for me." I pointed to my friends.

"It's a rental!" Becca laughed. "Don't spill anything on it!"

"Can I have a dance with the beautiful lady before you get whisked away to the balcony?" Devon asked, his hand still around mine.

"Um…" I glanced at Clark. Nothing could have prepared me for the direction the conversation took.

"Wait, are you two here *together*?" Jill gasped. Before I could respond, Clark spoke.

"Well, we weren't really going to say anything…"

"What?!" everyone at the table yelped. I blinked at Clark in surprise for only a moment before trying to act natural and bringing a smile to my face.

"Way to go, Clark!" Todd grinned, giving him a thumbs up.

"Hey! Don't be a pig!" Becca scolded.

"Seriously?" Taylor pressed. I nodded, embarrassed, feeling my face flush. "Wow, that's awesome! I think you two look good together."

"So, I can't dance with her?" Devon asked with a sly smile.

"Sorry, exclusively mine for tonight," Clark chuckled—I could hear that he was also nervous about our charade.

"I'll dance with you, Devon," Jill offered.

"Alright, let's go!" Devon took Jill's hand and the four of us were engulfed in the crowd before I could completely regather myself.

"Sorry." Clark leaned in to whisper the apology as we followed Devon and Jill.

"It's fine," I assured, realizing it would be the safest way to avoid trouble between Jill and Devon. However, I was unsure if I was willing to even pretend to be dating Clark because of my feelings for Mykail.

As we were dancing, I leaned close so Clark could hear me over the thrumming music.

"How do you want to do this?"

"We should separate," he said. "You stand in one corner and I'll stand in the other."

"How are we going to know we're giving the papers to the right people?"

"Only the Commish Kids know. They'll be the only ones approaching."

The costumes were going to make it impossible to know if it was a Commish Kid approaching me, but I nodded all the same.

"We're not going up on the balcony today," he told me. "I said that I heard people were going to be here with red and blue scarves. If we go up with these," he motioned to the scarves tied around our waists, "it'll be too obvious."

"But won't they notice if we're not up there?"

"Everyone has their faces covered, no one really knows who anyone else is."

I took a deep breath, trying to calm my nerves. As I was glancing around the dancefloor for anyone who might already be approaching, I spotted Devon and Jill dancing nearby. I thought they looked good together, and even though Devon had wanted a dance with me, he seemed to be having a good time with Jill. As soon as I felt relief to have Devon's attention diverted from me, a pang of sadness hit my heart as I thought about Becca's unrequited love for Jill.

I tried to relax and return to the flow of the music, but I continued to look around the pulsing crowd, seeing flickers and flashes of golden eyes, certain that Dana was lingering somewhere in the crowd of dancing students. I closed my eyes, pretending to be immersed in the music as I tried to ignore the feeling of being watched, but with that night being our first brazen attempt at rebellion, the worry of being caught was at the forefront of my mind.

It would be just our luck to have Dana show up the first night of our treasonous activities.

After a few songs, Devon and Jill left the dance floor. Once they were gone, Clark nodded to tell me it was time to split up. With my own nod, I made my way to one of the back corners near the drinks bar, being sure to stay out of sight of my friends. I found a position where I had a wide field of vision and where it was impossible someone could sneak up behind me.

It did not take long until a costumed student approached me, taking a few moments to linger near me, studying me closely before he approached.

At first, I was extremely confused why the teenager dressed like a zombie approached me, standing silently, expectant. After two seconds of processing, my brain finally remembered why I was in the corner to begin with. I extracted one of the papers from my pocket. He nodded and extended his hand. Feeling my entire body tense in apprehension of what I was about to do, I handed him the paper and he walked away.

Through the night, I handed out fourteen papers, leaving only two in my pocket by the time the club announced they were closing. Clark rushed toward me, untying his scarf as the other students began gathering themselves for leaving the club.

"Here, give me that."

I yanked the scarf from my waist, passing it to him. Clark rushed to one of the back doors of the club—the same door we would use to leave and meet up with Mark as had become our new normal. I followed Clark, pulling off my mask. As we had planned, I slipped out of my skirt to leave me in the corset with tight black pants and my strappy high heels. Clark removed the cloak over his suit and flipped it around, exposing the red side and slipping it over my shoulders, allowing me to tie it as he fished in his pocket and pulled out fake vampire fangs, popping them in his mouth. I let down my hair, my heart racing with exhilaration as we performed the quick costume change—I even found myself smiling.

Clark looked at me, also smiling, the expression telling me that he was feeling the same excitement.

Once we were situated, he offered his hand to me and we walked to the balcony with some other Commish Kids as the club began to empty.

The meeting after the party was simple, because it was Halloween and most of the Commish Kids were unable to determine who had been gossiping. A part of me wanted to believe that the real reason they were unable to identify the gossipers was because they were too busy looking for the people with the scarves.

I felt accomplished. I felt *proud*. I was giddy at the thought of Dana knowing nothing of what was going on with the Commish Kids. I was sure he suspected given the outbursts during previous meetings, but I doubt he knew everything we were doing, and that thought was empowering.

After Clark had wrapped up the meeting, he and I slipped down the far stairs and gathered our things at the back door, scurrying out to find Mark standing by the car. He did not seem at all startled or confused by our costume change, opening the door for us as always and driving away from the club without so much as a glance in the rearview mirror.

For the first three minutes, Clark and I could not speak to one another. We were staring out opposing widows, in shock at what we had done and how well we had executed the plan. Finally, we turned to one another and burst out laughing. The giggling was hysterical and half-filled with fear, but we could not stop the outburst.

"I can't believe…" He shook his head, catching his breath.

"I *know*," I gasped. "How many do you have left?"

He fished in his pocket and pulled out five. I showed him the two I still had.

"This is really…exhilarating," he said. "Or am I crazy?"

"No, it *is*." I heaved a deep breath and started laughing breathlessly again. "I guess I'm turning into an adrenaline junkie."

We could not make conversation the rest of the drive. We were only able to laugh and shake our heads at what we had done and what it meant for our future. Even though I wanted to believe that we could succeed if we were careful enough, the larger part of me was simply happy to be doing *something*, regardless of if it would work or not. And riding the high of our success that night, I could not bring myself to be worried about how bold I felt in those moments.

As we pulled up in front of my house, Clark turned to me.

"I was thinking that you could come to my house on Sunday morning and we can go from there."

"Sounds good," I said, understanding the silent invitation to explore the addresses. "Where do you live?"

"I'll text you the address."

"Hey Clark, thanks for agreeing to this…" I said sincerely. "I really appreciate it."

"The feeling is mutual."

Mark parked the car and got out, walking to open my door for me as I untied Clark's cloak and gathered the skirt and mask.

"Clark?" I started. "Do you think this is insane? What we're doing?"

"Completely," he said strongly. I chuckled, nodding.

"Just wanted to make sure we're on the same page."

* *** *

The Saturday meeting at the Commission was not what I expected. Nothing strange happened, other than the fact that the leader of the Commission of the People was not present.

Clark's mother did not offer any explanation for Dana's absence when she told the members he would not be attending, which only served to increase my curiosity. There were so many possibilities about what he was doing that I spent the entire meeting creating as many answers as I could. The fact that Sean was also gone raised the probability that Dana was out of the Commission entirely, maybe even meeting with Leader Simon.

Whatever he was doing, the meeting passed quietly without him.

The next morning, I caught a bus to Clark's house, which was not at all far from mine, but it was in the most expensive end of the neighborhood. Even my large house was dwarfed in comparison to the mansions on Clark's street.

Clark's house was beautiful with an expansive green lawn and columns on the front of the house, making the white structure seem even taller and more stately. I stared for a moment, glancing back at my phone to be sure that I was at the correct address before I started up the gravel driveway to the front door. I saw the two cars parked out front, recognizing one as the car Mark drove with the small, white "88" painted on the back bumper. There was no one out front, making the approach to the house unnerving.

I walked up the three stairs onto the front porch before hesitantly ringing the doorbell. I heard the bells ringing inside, but no noise followed. My anxiety worsened. I had met Clark's mother, but I had never formally met his father, and I did not know if there were other people in the house besides Mark. An estate so large probably needed maids and guards at all times, but I could see no activity on the premises.

The door clicked open and a woman in a simple black dress smiled at me.

"Are you Miss Lily Sandover?"

"Yes."

"Please, come in."

Apparently, I had been right with my assumption about the maids.

I stepped into the foyer, my gaze sweeping around the two-storied cavernous room. I felt as though I had stepped into a movie with the grandeur of the paintings on the walls and the ornate railing of the sweeping staircase in front of me.

"Clark will be down in a moment," the maid said.

When another person entered the foyer from the passageway under the stairs, I jumped, but relaxed when I saw that the man in a suit and sunglasses was not Dana. Mark approached with a shy smile. While I smiled back, I was puzzled by his glasses.

When he stopped in front of me, I motioned to my own face to symbolize the glasses, hoping he understood that I was questioning why he was wearing them inside. Seeing them worried me that he would be driving us around that day and could, therefore, figure out what we were planning.

He looked at the maid, who smiled, answering his silent request.

"Sorry about Mark. He's a mute and he has sensitive eyes. Don't let the glasses bother you," she told me casually. "Would you like anything to drink?"

"…water, please," I said, realizing I could get her to leave.

"If you will wait in the living room, I will bring it to you." She motioned me to the living room which, despite the beautiful furniture, pictures, and large fireplace, had a cold and vacant aura. I gawked at the richness around the living room, Mark following me silently as the maid left us.

I had led a very privileged life, but the grandeur of the Markus home was surprising even to me, particularly because the house seemed so cold and dark despite the beautiful furnishings. The entire house looked like a movie set, perfectly designed and laid out, as if no one actually lived there.

Mark had stationed himself by the archway, silent. When I turned to look at him, my heart broke at seeing the glasses, realizing the only place he was able to take them off was in the Commission and in his own personal room—if he even had one.

"How are you, Mark?"

He remained still for a moment and then smiled, lifting his hands to give me two thumbs up, which was his common response. It never failed to put a smile on my face. I wished I could speak with him and have him understand me, and I him. I had discussed learning the experiment sign language from Mykail, but I knew it would be a long time before I could understand enough to converse with Mark.

Hesitantly, I reached a hand to my nose and brushed it with my fingers, which was the first and only thing I had learned from Mykail the previous night before we distracted ourselves with kissing. The action meant: "how are you?"

Mark seemed surprised, not immediately moving to answer, so I smiled and repeated the action to show it was intentional. He smiled again and raised his right hand to scratch his neck twice.

I'm well.

I did not have anything else to ask, but it made me happy that I could at least extend common courtesy to him.

He took one step forward, hesitant, but stopped and looked behind him as he retreated to his station. Just as I was about to walk to him, the maid came around the corner, holding a glass of water for me. She looked between us as I accepted the glass.

"Is he bothering you?" she asked. "I know he just sort of looms in the corner, but he means no harm. It's just for security." She turned to Mark. "Go on." She motioned him away rudely.

"No, it's fine," I said. "He can stay. I know him. He's been driving me and Clark around."

"Oh, I see," the maid said. "I will go see what Clark is doing and let him know that you are here." She hurried away again and I turned to Mark, motioning to him that I was sorry.

He bowed his head in response.

After a few seconds where all I could hear was the maid's heels going up the stairs, there was the sound of a door opening followed by a thud and a loud scuffle. Mark's head turned again, but he did not move from his spot. I recognized the sounds of dog's nails scraping hardwood and excited whimpers.

"Calm down, you crazy kids!" a man's voice laughed from across the foyer past the dining room. "There you go."

The sound moved quickly into the dining room and, before I knew it, there were three large, bird-hunting dogs running into the foyer. Mark smiled and dropped into a crouch as the three dogs ran to him. I scolded myself for being surprised at how warm the dogs were toward a former experiment of the Commission of the People.

One of the dogs ran to me and I dropped my hand for him to smell as he wagged his tail enthusiastically. Another one came from Mark's side and jumped up, placing his paws on my stomach excitedly as he whimpered, his tail rocking his entire body.

"Colonel! Get down!" the man's voice snapped playfully. Mark pulled the dog gently by the collar, placing him back on all fours. I laughed as I looked at the man walking across the foyer to greet me. He was obviously Clark's father—the resemblance was remarkable. He had the same dark brown eyes and tousled brown hair, and he even wore the same style of glasses.

"I'm sorry about them." He nodded to the dogs. "They don't bite, they're just too friendly." He extended his hand to me. "You must be Thomas Sandover's daughter."

"That's me. Lily."

"Lily, it's very nice to meet you, I'm Richard, Clark's father."

"It's very nice to meet you." He also had that same warm personality Clark had, even though it was obvious he was also shy.

"You, as well. Your parents have told me a lot about you." He released my hand. "My wife tells me you and Clark have become good friends."

"We have."

"I'm glad," he said. "And you know Mark, I'm sure." He motioned to Mark, who was crouching with the three dogs, holding them in place. "That's Danny Boy, Colonel, and Duke," he introduced the dogs. "I'm sorry they are so misbehaved. We don't get much company and they love meeting new people. Do you like dogs?"

"I do, but I prefer cats."

"Do you have any?"

"One," I answered. "His name is Dexter."

"They probably smell him on you, which is why they got so excited," Richard laughed. He turned. "Vanessa?" he called into the house.

It was not long before another maid came into the foyer. She stood quietly, folding her hands in front of her respectfully.

"Could you please feed them?" Richard asked, motion to the dogs.

"Of course, sir," she said, clapping to the dogs and calling them into the further recesses of the house. Mark stood when the dogs were gone, but he remained in his position as Richard motioned for me to sit down.

"I have no idea what Clark is doing," he groaned. "I hope you haven't been waiting long." He stepped out of the living room long enough to call up the staircase to Clark. He returned and sat across from me, mumbling about Clark not being hospitable. I acted as though I did not hear his complaining.

"He said that you two are going into town today," he said. I nodded. "Any special plans?"

"No," I shook my head. "Just hanging out, looking around...he was going to show me around since I'm still new to Central."

"So, is this a date?" he asked with a raised eyebrow.

"What? No!"

"Oh, come on. You two have been spending a lot of time together, you can tell me," Richard joked. "I understand how it is. You don't want drama with the parents, but I know that you two are young adults and it's only logical that you want to experiment with dating."

"What are you saying?!" Clark gasped, turning into the living room. "Dad, Lily is just a friend! Do you have to be so embarrassing?!"

"Can you blame me? This is the first girl I think you've ever even spoken to," Richard chuckled. "Of course I'm going to assume things!"

"Can't a girl and a boy just be friends?!" Clark gasped, exasperated.

"I don't know," Richard teased. "It doesn't seem to be possible in your generation."

"Oh my God, I can't believe you. Come on, Lily," he said. "We're leaving."

I tried to hide my amusement and embarrassment as I stood. Clark was making no effort to hide his self-consciousness. I would have preferred my parents tease me about dating rather than embarrass me by treating Mark as if he was some sort of rare animal.

"Is Mark driving you around?" Richard asked, following us into the foyer.

"No, we don't have a specific destination, so we're taking the bus," Clark answered casually.

"That doesn't bother Mark. You should have him drive you," Richard told us with a disapproving shake of his head.

"No, Dad, Mark doesn't need to drive me everywhere," Clark said strongly. "Let him have a day off, will you?"

"Dana will be very upset if he hears that you didn't use him," Richard told Clark with the parenting tone that all teenagers hated.

"Dana doesn't need to know everything I do," Clark said. "Let's just leave Mark alone today and let him rest. Haven't you seen how tired he is?"

"He's not tired, Clark, that's just a poor excuse," Richard said. "Where are you going that you don't want us to know about?"

"Dad, do you have to always be in my business?" Clark snapped. "Every day I go to school and then Mark drives me to the Commission and then he drives me home. Just once I want to have a weekend where I can pretend I'm a normal teenager. Is that alright? I don't need a chauffeur."

Richard hesitated a moment, then sighed.

"Alright, I'm sorry," he agreed, hanging his head. "Of course you should be a normal teenager."

"I'm sorry, Dad, it's just…I want to get away from the Commission and Dana sometimes," Clark said, his voice dropping. I hated being in those situations. Whenever one of my friends was fighting with their parents and I was nearby, I could do nothing but stand awkwardly and pretend to be invisible.

"Okay," Richard said. "When will you be back?"

"By dinner at the latest."

"Lily, would you like to join us for dinner?" Richard asked.

"Oh…um, I would have to check with my parents…" I said quietly, looking at Clark to see how he felt about me joining his family for dinner. He smiled and nodded so I smiled in turn. "If they say it's okay, I would love to."

"Great," Richard said. "Are you a vegetarian, or vegan, or allergic to anything?"

"No."

"Wonderful. Well, you kids have fun and I'll see you later tonight," Richard said. "Be careful."

"We will," we both said, walking out the door. When Clark closed the door behind us and we walked down the steps, he turned to me and cringed.

"Sorry about that…" he mumbled. "All of it."

"It's fine," I assured. "Not the first time I've dealt with parents."

"So, we want to take bus five to Main, and then bus twenty-two to Gregory Avenue," he explained, pulling out the note, which now had deeper creases and was adorned with several scribbles in different colored ink. "I figured it would be best to start downtown and move outward. We'll end at Mackay Power Plant."

We walked the distance to the bus stop with casual conversation and began our exploration of Central. The first two addresses were warehouses in the downtown area. Both were huge and in disrepair, but we could not enter them due to the high fencing topped with barbed wire that surrounded the lots. Both Clark and I agreed that they were not the best locations due to their vicinity to downtown and how many people walked by the area while we loitered.

Next, we went to an old high school that had been abandoned, but the amount of windows made the building less than ideal.

After a quick lunch at a cafe downtown, we found an old spa factory near the outskirts of the city that we were able to slip into through a hole in the fence and a loose board covering the door. Because of this, we were concerned about the possibility of other teenagers coming in to vandalize the place when we were there or that we would encounter squatters.

Because of how far away it was, we did not bother to go to the old Central junkyard. Instead, we took the bus to the closest possible stop and walked to the Mackay Power Plant, about fifteen minutes from the stop.

"This is the one that this person thinks will be the best," Clark sighed as we walked in the chilly November air. "But, if this doesn't work out, I think the spa factory might be the next best."

"I agree. I'm just worried. There was a lot of graffiti there. There might be some squatters."

"I guess we'll just have to see about the power plant," Clark sighed. "It'll probably be in bad shape as well…It's been abandoned since the Second Revolution."

Finally reaching the power plant after an uphill climb, I was shocked at just how large it was. The fence around it was still intact but the coiled barbed wire around the top was heavily rusted. The four large columns of the chimneys reached into the sky, browned with grime and age. The brick building itself still stood strong, though many of the arched windows were broken. The expansive grounds fenced around the power plant were overgrown with weeds and grass breaking sections of old cement.

"This place is huge," I said, approaching the chain-link fence cautiously.

"Let's see if we can get inside…" Clark said, pulling at one fence panel. The both of us walked in opposite directions, trying to find a weakness to slip through without climbing over the barbed wire. I walked along the fence, pulling at the panels and looking for holes in the ground or in the barbed wire above.

My phone rang just as I was about to turn to the back of the property.

"I found a spot."

I rounded the back of the building and saw that Clark had found a gap in the fence as he pulled one of the panels.

"After you," he motioned to the gap.

I glanced around to be sure we were alone, and then ducked, barely squeezing through the gap. I pushed the same panel of fence to help Clark slip through.

When we were both inside, we stood by the fence to marvel at the building. I felt daunted by the task of exploring the power plant, but another part of me had an even stronger feeling. I was not sure why it seemed obvious, but I knew, without a shadow of a doubt, that the power plant was to be the headquarters of our revolution.

"Let's check out inside," I said.

As we approached, the building grew to an intimidating height, but when we reached the walls, my heart was pounding from excitement.

"There's a door." Clark pointed.

Already partially open, we only had to push slightly to get the rusted hinges to give way and grant us access. The offices where we entered were heavily vandalized, the windows broken and graffiti, old cigarette butts, and broken bottles littering the walls and floor.

"Another popular spot..." Clark noted warily.

I moved further inside, feeling clumps of dirt crunch under my sneakers. Some of the windows had been haphazardly boarded up in an attempt to keep people out, but the graffiti and bottles were evidence of how little the place was cared for or monitored.

I stepped around some broken glass and pushed another door, my eyes widening at what I saw beyond.

"Whoa..." was Clark's response behind me.

The back of the power plant was spacious and brighter than I imagined while still grimy and run down. The windows that were not boarded over were either broken or frosted with time, muting the light. The two platforms in the plant were covered in grime, leaves scattered dead and crisp over the floor. The iron beams that were the skeleton of the structure were orange with rust and peeling paint. The red and blues and greens of the graffiti that became the new decoration were somehow befitting. The old turbines were rusted over, imposing and heavy in the room.

There were balconies lining the room five floors above the third platform, bordered with broken and boarded windows.

"This is incredible..." I whispered, walking to the staircases leading to the platforms.

"It's out in the middle of nowhere...it's huge...it looks like there haven't been vandals here in a while..."

"No wonder this was the one with two stars," I said with a chuckle, carefully kicking at the stairs before ascending them when I was fairly certain they were stable.

"Be careful, Lily," Clark's echoing voice told me. I could hear him also kicking at another staircase before ascending to explore one of the balconies lining the room.

I reached the main platform, which felt tight and constrained with the second platform so close above. The light did not reach the area, the shadows dark enough to be the perfect hiding spot.

"You can see really far into the distance from these windows..." Clark told me, his voice echoing from somewhere in the building. "And I can see across the building that there are offices with more windows, so we should be able to see from all sides."

I carefully made my way out of the shadows and to the top platform. One of the turbines was completely gone, the other left to rust in place, but the large hole in the top of the platform allowed light to fall to the main floor.

"This is amazing," I said, looking up at the windows of the decrepit building. "Why do you suppose no one tore it down?"

"Well…" Clark said, walking out of one of the offices and leaning over the railing, being sure to shake it to test its stability, "after the Second Revolution, I think a lot of the money was thrown elsewhere. An old power plant probably didn't seem important. It is out in the middle of nowhere." He looked around. "If they decide to expand the reservoir, then they'll probably tear it down."

I walked down the stairs, feeling oddly giddy.

"Well, honey, what do you think?" I teased, glancing up at Clark. He chuckled.

"Looks like this is it."

"We should explore more."

"We should be careful," he corrected. "The building is in rough condition. We can't be sure that it's entirely safe. Let's stick together."

We explored, surveying every nook and cranny of the power plant. There were several areas where the walls had tumbled into a mess of chalky mortar and fallen bricks. The doors were mostly boarded up, but if we wanted to keep the building secure as a hiding place, there were measures that would need to be taken. We knew we would have to secure windows and doors and be sure that the power plant could act as a fortress we could hide in or defend if we created too much trouble— which we planned on doing.

The situation was almost comical with the way we were looking at the potential of the space. If we weren't in an abandoned power plant thinking of breaking out human weapons from one of the most powerful organizations in the world, our scrutiny and conversation would befit a couple looking for their first home.

"There must be a basement," I said when Clark opened a door to reveal a staircase leading down into a dark space.

Using our phones as flashlights, we descended the creaking stairs into the basement, which was filled with computers and control boards, as well as more offices.

"This looks even better," he said, shining the flashlight around the room as I scanned in another direction. "We could clear this space out and let people sleep. We would have a watch at the door…it seems to be the only way in and out…"

I walked along the back wall, looking at the massive room, too excited to worry about the dark or even the consequences of what we were planning.

A brush at my ankles, however, did cause me to gasp and jump.

"What?" Clark said quickly, turning his light toward me.

"I think…something just hit my ankles…" I said, shining my phone on the ground, looking for rats. Clark scanned the floor with me, but when we saw nothing scurrying around, I shined my light in the direction the feeling had come from. At the base of the wall was a large crack. I grabbed Clark's arm, pulling him back, worried that the floor was about to sink in.

"What?" he gasped again, worried.

"I think the ground's unstable," I said, keeping my light focused on the crack so he could see it. Once his light settled on the area too, he reached one foot forward and pressed on the floor. There was no sound.

Carefully testing each step before he transferred his weight, he walked to the large crack that separated the floor from the wall. The baseboard had rotted away, so only a few splintered pieces were left around the hole that Clark was motioning his hand in front of.

"It's colder down here," he said. He held his phone out to me, which I took and shined both lights on him as he carefully put his fingers into the gap.

"Please be careful..."

Clark felt around the bottom of the wall, his fingers moving slowly and deliberately. Suddenly, his hand stopped and he hesitated.

"What?"

"There's...something metal..." He remained still, only his fingers moving over what he had found before there was a loud click and then the groan of rusted metal as the section of the wall slid backward.

I watched in fascination as Clark let go and stepped back, startled. The wall stopped moving as soon as Clark backed away, leaving a three centimeter gap between it and the rest of the wall.

"Another secret passage?" I asked, looking at Clark, surprised. "Do you think the guy who gave us these notes knew about it?"

"He knew about the passage into the records room..." Clark answered indirectly. He pressed his hands on the hidden door and pushed, but the wall only gave away another two centimeters before stopping. "It's stuck..."

I stepped to the wall and shined my light into the gap, looking behind the door. As I moved my light over the space, I saw a small bar of iron, curved and descending into the dark.

"There's a staircase..."

Clark pushed on the wall again and shook his head, shining his light down at the two tracks guiding the hidden door backward. He looked around.

"Lily, push it this way," he said, coming up next to me and putting one hand around the side of the door. I followed suit and we pulled the door away, sliding it sideways with a loud screech on the rusted tracks.

"Well...that will have to be fixed..." I said when we had moved the door out of the way, dusting my hands on my clothes

Clark stepped in first, and I followed, my eyes and light locked on the railing of the staircase.

"This can be opened from the inside," Clark said, his light showing the large handle on the back of the steel door. "What do you think they were hiding?"

"Let's find out." I took a step toward the top stair when Clark stopped me.

"Wait, Lily," he said. "Let me go first, we don't know how stable this is."

He gently placed a foot on the first grate step, shifting his weight carefully before cautiously descending the iron spiral staircase, testing the strength of the handrail and center beam as he was swallowed by the inky shadows.

"Wait until I get all the way down before you follow," his voice called to me from the shadows. I nervously waited, watching him disappear through the holes in the grate as I shined my light down. The ten seconds seemed like an eternity before I saw Clark's light shine upward and his voice called to me.

"Okay, just come down slowly. There are two stairs that are bent down here, but they're still stable."

Holding onto my phone to light my way, I carefully descended the staircase, looking only at where my feet were stepping next, worried that the creaking steel would give way with each step. I passed the two steps that were badly mangled, carefully placing my foot on the flattest areas before continuing.

When I reached the bottom, Clark was waiting, his light illuminating the dark floor in front of me.

"Are you alright?"

"Yeah." My voice cracked as I spoke. I was excited and nervous, worried my pounding heart would make its way up my throat and out my mouth. I shined my light around us, but it was swallowed by the oppressive darkness. "What the hell is this?"

"I don't know," Clark said, his light also sweeping over the shadows, turning behind us to the wall near the staircase. "There's a breaker box over here..." he said, leaving my side and stepping to the gray box on the wall. I followed hesitantly, my steps small and careful of what could possibly be on the ground. The air was musty, making it difficult to breathe and as we drew close to the wall, I was certain we were in some sort of basement.

Clark opened the box, the screeching sound piercing the air like a knife. The large switches looked rusted and unsafe, and as Clark reached forward, I panicked.

"Wait," I gasped. "We don't know if those are safe, or if they even work."

"There's only one way to find out." He reached to the switch again and flicked the first one.

There was an instant hum and Clark retreated a few steps, both of our lights sweeping the area as the hum was accompanied by a clicking sound and lights began to flicker.

Both of us looked up as bars of light blinked into life and illuminated the space in front of us.

"Holy shit..."

In front of us was another railing surrounding the balcony on which we stood. In front of the balcony was a cavernous space with walls lined with steel, bolted with large studs that were still in surprisingly good condition considering the state of the power plant above. There was a large outlined door that looked bomb-proof and three doors along the back wall, as well as another five doors on the wall where a staircase connected the balcony to the main floor.

"What is this place?" I whispered.

Clark turned back to the breaker switches, looking over each one carefully.

"Look at this," he said, motioning me over. "W Room, Bunker is the one we just turned on...Supplies...L..." He looked at me before glancing back at the other switches. "Let's go exploring." He flicked all of the switches. There was more distant humming and even loud clanking that died out after five seconds.

"Those must be water pipes, or something..." he said, answering my horrified expression at the sound.

"This is crazy...how did this person know about this?"

"Who knows..." Clark said as he started down the staircase in front of me. "Some serious research, I guess."

When we reached the concrete ground of the main domed room, my eyes were wide with amazement and, admittedly, glee.

I looked at the balcony and saw a large opening leading into another cavernous room to the left of the hallway under the balcony. The second large room had tables and shelves scattered with books and yellowed papers. I looked above the door where the slightly-faded words "Brothers of America" were painted.

"Brothers of America..." I read aloud, the words barely passing on my lips.

"Oh my God…" Clark gasped, seeing the letters. "Lily…do…do you realize where we *are*?!" I turned to him, my eyes wide. "We're in Fort Daniels…"

"No way," I murmured, glancing back at the words. "Fort Daniels was a decoy. No one could ever find it, even after the revolution ended. It was what sent the Washington System on a wild goose chase."

"This is Fort Daniels. It's exactly as it was described by Janice in *An Angel Without Wings*. The "Brothers of America" slogan, the secret location that couldn't be found…" Clark looked around. "How the hell did he *know* about this?"

"Maybe he didn't," I suggested, looking around the main bunker again. I was shaking my head in disbelief at standing in the headquarters of the Second Revolution. Thomas Ankell and his revolutionaries were said to have outfitted an old dam system to be the headquarters of their final attacks on the Washington System. They had been confined to Fort Daniels when Thomas Ankell and his followers had been surrounded on all sides by the military under control of the Washington System. And it was because of their fortified fort and the government's constant attacks on other dams in the area that turned more Americans against Washington D.C. and gave the Second Revolution the manpower needed to lead the final attacks on the old American capital.

To stand in the middle of the hidden bunker was surreal.

"Even when tortured, most of the people of the revolution had no idea where this place was. How could the person leaving those notes have known?"

I walked into the room adjoining the main bunker, Clark following me, both of us looking around in awe.

The room matched the description in *An Angel Without Wings* as the operations room. The shelves along the walls were mostly empty with only a few books and papers remaining, as well as a few scattered along the floor. On the closest table, there were large blueprints laid out, placed there recently.

My pace quickened as I walked to the table, looking over the blueprints, the top of which read "Fort Daniels."

"Clark," I called him over. He stepped to my side, looking over the blueprints before leaning over the table, surprised.

What shocked us more was the piece of paper on top of the blueprints. It was a note scrawled in handwriting that was starting to become very familiar.

"Only you two should know the exact location of this fort. Anyone that you bring here should use a different way. That was how the location was kept a secret before. Never use the same passage more

than two times if possible. There are seventeen different entrances to the fort. Some might not be safe anymore. They're marked on the blueprints."

"More than anything, I'm getting more curious…" I said. "I really want to know who this is and how he knows all this."

"It has to be someone inside the Commission," Clark declared, picking up the note and glancing over it once again. "The first set of notes had all the security rotations…he's given us the override codes for the cells…this person has intel we could never *dream* of."

"Sean?" I suggested.

"…maybe," Clark said, though he did not seem confident in the possibility. He set the note aside, returning his attention to the blueprints. "But this person obviously knew about this fort and knew we would find it."

I looked at the annotations made in the same handwriting on the blueprints, all pointing to the different passages that led in and out of the fort.

"I just…I don't even know what to do, now…" I whispered. "It's all been laid out for us. It's almost too perfect. I'm starting to think we're walking into a trap."

"I'm worried about the same thing," Clark agreed. He grabbed his phone again and took a picture of the blueprint before sighing. "But, I agree that no one else should know where this really is. I think we should explore this place a little today, see what we can, and then get the hell out of here. Next week, we'll explore some of the passages once we've located where they are and see how well we can keep this a secret until we know more about who's giving us the notes…and if we can trust them."

I agreed, taking pictures with my phone as well.

"Then we've decided that this is the place?"

"If it's not a trap, I'd say this is definitely the place," Clark said. "To think…*Fort Daniels*…"

I laughed as I glanced at the picture on my phone to be sure that I had all the details I needed.

"Let's check out the place," I declared, moving away from the table and following Clark into the main bunker.

Fort Daniels was too good to be true. We spent three hours exploring, mostly because we were too shocked at what we found and too excited to leave. A few of the rooms were offices that had plans for the city of Central and notes on the locations of the different water and sewer mains. Another area was a huge room filled with bunk beds, though there were no sheets and the mattresses were disintegrating from age.

The storage rooms were where we spent the most time. There was an artillery storage room, where bullets, grenades, and gasoline had been tucked away. The next room over was the weapons room, where guns were set securely in their cradles along the walls. They were dusty but looked functional—of course, I knew absolutely nothing about guns since they had been banned for private ownership since the formation of Central.

The third storage room had canned goods and dried food. There was no way to tell at first glance how much was still edible, but it was obvious that the room had sustained the revolutionaries for quite some time and was still well stocked.

When Clark finally glanced at his phone and realized it was nearly six at night, we hurried out of the fort, turning off all the lights before using our phones to go back up the spiral stairs and into the deserted power plant.

It was already dark, the sun setting early for the start of winter, so we had to carefully pick our way out of the power plant. Clark and I were navigating the front of the plant when both of our phones began vibrating and ringing simultaneously. Both of us stopped and looked at the screens. I had two text messages, one from my mother and one from my father.

Mom: "Are you going to be home for dinner?"

Dad: "We can't reach you or Clark. Where are you?"

"Shit…" Clark hissed.

"What?"

"My parents are freaking out," he groaned. "They sent Mark out looking for us."

"Shit," I repeated.

"Exactly. If we don't get in contact with them quickly, they'll call Dana." Clark quickly dialed his parents' phone number and pushed my shoulder gently to prompt me to keep moving. "Come on, let's go."

I led Clark out, using my phone flashlight as a guide through the darker sections of the power plant. When we were in the night air, Clark spoke.

"No, sorry, I'm sorry," he said into the phone. "We went to a movie. I turned my phone off."

That was when I glanced at my phone and texted my mother back, telling her I would be at Clark's for dinner and sorry that I didn't tell her sooner, but I was in a movie and had my phone turned off.

Fort Daniels must have jammed all the signals from our phones. I smiled, unable to help myself, thrilled that our GPS was jammed when we were in the fort, feeling very lucky considering we had both forgotten the possibility of our phones being tracked as we explored.

"No, we stuck around for the second showing. Sorry I didn't realize it was so late," Clark said as we went to the fence. "Why did you send Mark out? How was he supposed to find me?" I held the fence panel back for him. "My phone was off. He can't track the GPS." He held the panel open for me and we both started down the street at a half-jog.

"Fine, I'll go someplace and wait for him to track us," he said irritably. "Um..." He turned to me. "What did your parents say about having dinner at our house?" he asked, loud enough for his parents to hear.

"It's fine," I answered. I didn't bother to tell him that I had not asked my mother so much as told her that I would be having dinner elsewhere.

"She'll be over for dinner," he relayed. He groaned and rolled his eyes. "Oh my God, I'm out for one day and as soon as you can't reach me, you freak out. Mom, seriously, do you not trust me at all?"

I laughed quietly in spite of myself. I was sure Clark had never given his parents reason not to trust him, but the fact that we were plotting a rebellion against the Commission of the People meant they really should *not* have trusted him that day.

"Alright," he said. "We'll be back soon. We just have to find Mark...okay...bye."

He hung up the phone and groaned in annoyance.

"I swear..." he growled. "Now we have to find Mark."

"We better get out of here quickly, then," I said. "How can he track your phone?"

"He has a GPS tracker in the car," Clark said. "Speaking of which..." He turned his phone off and shook his head. "I really don't want him driving all the way out here. It's not a good idea for him to learn we've been out here."

"Not like he can ask questions or tell anyone," I said sadly.

"You like him, don't you?"

"Not in that way!" I snapped, smacking him on the arm.

"Ow! I didn't *mean* it that way!" Clark laughed. "I was just saying! You were defending him against your parents and you always greet him...I really want to thank you for that."

"Why?"

"We obviously don't talk, and he doesn't understand most of what I say, but he is a very caring person and a lot of people can't see that because they're too focused on him being different," Clark told me, putting his hands in his pockets and shivering in the cold night air. "Sometimes I just talk at him because he sits and listens, even though he doesn't understand."

"He seems to really care about you," I said. "Like an older brother."

"I've thought that, too."

We saw the bus pulling into the bus stop in front of us, so we ran and flagged the bus down, climbing on and heading into town, discussing what we were going to tell our parents about our day on the town.

When we got off the bus in the downtown area, Clark reached into his pocket and pulled out his phone, turning it back on as I pulled my jacket closer around me to fight off the encroaching chill.

"Uh...Clark?" I said quietly, my eyes widening as I saw a familiar person walking toward us.

"What?" I saw him turn the same direction out of the corner of my eye. "Mark?" I followed Clark toward the former experiment, surprised and a little suspicious. Mark took Clark's shoulders and looked him over before his covered eyes turned to me and also scanned me, assessing if we were hurt. "We're alright, we're okay," Clark said. "I'm sorry we worried you."

Mark took a deep breath and bowed his head, motioning for us to follow.

As we walked a pace behind the silent man, I turned to Clark.

"How did he know where we were?" I whispered. "Can he track my phone?"

"No." Clark shook his head. "I think he might have been walking around looking for us and it was a coincidence. Look how far away he parked."

I looked at the parking garage we were slowly approaching and sighed, guessing it was the most likely conclusion.

"Mark," Clark said when we got in the elevator and started our ascent to the seventh floor of the parking garage. Mark turned. "You should not walk in public," he said, his voice filled with worry. I looked between the two, wondering if Mark understood at all. "Someone could have seen you." Clark motioned with his hands what he meant, but even then, Mark was still, not giving any indication that he understood. When the elevator slowed, he bowed his head deeply to Clark and then motioned us to leave the elevator before him.

The drive to Clark's house was completely silent as the exhaustion of the day finally set in. After traveling around town and the adrenaline of our treasonous situation, the fatigue was threatening to overpower me. By the way Clark's head kept dropping next to me, I knew he was also fighting unconsciousness. I was nearly asleep when we finally pulled into the driveway of the Markus home.

I forced myself awake as I followed Clark to his front door.

"I'm home!" he called as he held the door open for me.

Mrs. Markus appeared from the corridor under the staircase and hastened to her son as Mark closed the door behind us.

"Oh my God, don't *do* that to us!"

"Mom, it was only six o'clock, why are you freaking out so much?" Clark groaned, rolling his eyes. "I go out once and you immediately flip out."

"What do you expect? With the way the other kids in the Commission have been acting…"

"What is *that* supposed to mean?"

Mrs. Markus drew in a deep, calming breath, shaking her head and hugging her son tightly.

"Nothing, I'm sorry…" she whispered. "Just…when you're going to turn your phone off, let us know. We worry about you…"

Chapter Thirty-Seven

"So, why do you think J.A.N.E. included the information about Thomas Ankell's private struggles with Janice in the book?" Mr. McDermott asked. I looked around the classroom as hands rose. I did not talk in class anymore, particularly about *An Angel Without Wings*. I had jumped in my seat when Mr. McDermott mentioned Fort Daniels, so I had to keep my mouth shut to avoid saying something incriminating.

"Yes, Jessica?"

"Well, the entire book has been geared toward humanizing an American hero, so showing him fighting with his wife was a way to make him appear more human to the readers."

"Very good, that's true. Even the title of the book tries to make Ankell appear more down to earth and human so that the readers can relate to him," Mr. McDermott elaborated. "Any other opinions?"

"Well, Janice was against the direction Ankell was taking the revolution and she said that his new ally was dangerous and should not be trusted, so it showed that there was a difference of opinion in the revolution that was already controversial."

"And do you know what that aspect was?" Mr. McDermott smiled mysteriously. "I know the chapter breaks off before you find out who the new ally is and what was splitting the revolutionaries apart, but does anyone have any guesses?"

Everyone looked at one another but no one voiced an opinion. I had barely been paying attention to the book as I read. I was only reading what I had to for the assignments, too wrapped up in what was going on with my own rebellion to care about the romanticized life of Thomas Ankell in the book.

Mr. McDermott closed the book and placed it on his desk, smiling.

"What was the most controversial aspect of the Second Revolution?" he asked. Again, there was silence before Becca cleared her throat.

"The cleansing of the population?" she said weakly.

"Exactly," Mr. McDermott agreed. "So, any guesses on who the new ally is?"

"Bryant Morris…" I murmured. Mr. McDermott nodded.

"Bryant Morris." He walked to the board. "There are a lot of things about Mr. Morris that remain a mystery, even today. So, let me briefly discuss what kind of man Mr. Morris was." He picked up a pen and began writing points on the board.

"Mr. Morris was the only child of a scientist who had been fired from several jobs for unethical testing," our teacher started. "His father was said to be very inattentive and Mr. Morris found himself part of a gang at a young age. It's believed that Thomas Ankell and Mr. Morris met when they were quite young but parted ways. And when Bryant Morris was sixteen, Mr. Morris saw what Thomas Ankell was doing and reached out to him to help the revolution."

"Mr. McDermott, was it Thomas Ankell or Bryant Morris who felt that the population needed to be cleansed?" Jill asked.

"The decision was not made that simply." Mr. McDermott shook his head. "Bryant and Thomas were both very young, and when the Second Revolution ended, they were only in their early twenties. They had to gain support from the people to cleanse the population before they could implement anything." He wrote a date on the board. "We know when the revolution ended, but the Commission of the People, which was responsible for the cleansing of America, was founded only seventeen months before. Does anyone know why? Any of the kids in the Commission? Do you know?"

Everyone looked around quietly, not sure. Greg finally cleared his throat.

"I'm not in the Commission, so I might be wrong, but...wasn't it because of the attack on San Antonio?"

Mr. McDermott hesitated.

"That was part of it," he said. "As you all know, even today, the Commission of the People is a very controversial institution. The attack on San Antonio, or you probably know it as the July Seventeenth Massacre, was an attempt by the Mexican drug lords to scare the revolutionaries to back off from their cleansing decision. The Commission was actually formed because of the government's silence in relation to the massacre." Mr. McDermott laughed. "How many of you knew that the Commission of the People was started by the Washington government, and not the Central government?"

I blinked, feeling my jaw drop, mirroring the surprise of my classmates.

"The Commission of the People was not founded by Bryant Morris, but by Senator Tory Genevieve, who agreed that the July Seventeenth Massacre was unfortunate but it needed to happen to straighten everyone's priorities. She founded the Commission of the People with the other Washington defectors, and as the Cleansing was approved and supported by the American people, control turned over to Bryant Morris, who ran the Commission of the People for thirty years before he died of a stroke at age fifty-three."

450

"But the Commission of the People was not originally made for cleansing the population, was it?" Kevin asked. "The Washington government was all about interracial mingling and promoting diversity, so they would have never approved the Commission of the People."

"Very true," Mr. McDermott said. "Can anyone make a guess as to what the Commission of the People was originally meant to do? What it was approved to do by the Washington System?"

Again, we all stared at one another, not wanting to speak up.

"It's okay that you don't know. The Commission is quite secretive," Mr. McDermott laughed. "Corporate crime," he answered. "It was started when an underground assassination ring was discovered. This assassination group went after white collar criminals that the police would not touch. In an attempt to appease the angry revolutionaries, the Washington government created the Commission of the People, which was powerful enough to go after corporate criminals. It was more or less based on that assassination ring."

"And that went to cleaning out the population of America as a whole?" Karmen completed.

"Yes. The Central government could not keep many of the old systems, but they changed the Commission of the People to be the ultimate secret police of America. Things have calmed down now, but the thought of the Commission really used to strike fear into the hearts of most people, even if they did nothing wrong. Now that the population is cleansed, the Commission serves to keep the peace as best it can."

"But..." I started quietly.

"What is it?" Mr. McDermott asked.

"I was just wondering about the conspiracy theory that the Commission also took previous revolutionaries after the Central government was founded as a way to keep people from spilling secrets," I said, trying to sound vague.

"Oh, yes, of course." Mr. McDermott nodded. "There were theories about that, particularly when Thomas Ankell had a heart attack and Bryant Morris was said to have had a stroke only months afterward, but these had nothing to do with the Commission. Many suspected that the Commission had become too powerful, but Leader Johnson VI, who was leader at the time of both their deaths, assured everyone that the Commission would pass into the hands of someone capable of keeping everyone under control. And as you know, with Dana Christenson as the head of the Commission, there have been no problems."

* *** *

Monday night I was unable to distract myself after my history paper was finished. I sat at dinner with my parents and we ate silently, as we had been doing for weeks. My father was always tired with his work—whatever that was, he never told me anymore—and my mother was too busy feeling sorry for herself to speak with me.

But I could not distract myself from the dread that my mother was meeting with Dana the following day.

"Dad..." I said as we were finishing dinner. "What are you doing tomorrow? Do you have a lot of work?"

"I'm afraid so." He sighed, leaning back in his chair. "I have that fundraiser tomorrow and the Europe trip is coming up. We only have a month to get everything ready."

"I thought that no one had been chosen for that trip, yet."

"The names will be announced at the meeting on Saturday, but that doesn't mean that the people who aren't going on the trip will not be doing any work."

"What is the Europe trip for, again?"

"There's been a lot of unrest in the New European Union," he explained, "and the leaders of those nations are requesting that the Commission of the People review the data and suggest a plan for stability and peace."

"You mean the Commission is expanding across the ocean?" I said incredulously. "Doesn't that mean that it's getting too powerful?"

"Nonsense, Lily," my mother chided. "Leader Simon is bringing a small delegation of people from the Commission. It's not the Commission acting on its own. Dana won't even be joining them."

I glanced at Mykail, who was sitting silently at the table, avoiding eye contact.

"Great..." I groaned. "I have to go to the Commission meetings on my own."

"No, Clark will be with you," my mother said. "You two seem to be close. Are you dating?"

"No! Mother!" I snapped, feeling my cheeks heat up in embarrassment as I tried not to look at Mykail.

"There's nothing wrong with it," she said with a smile. "I would be happy if you were dating someone. You need to start acting more like a teenager. Besides, Clark is a very sweet young man."

"Oh my God, Mom. We are *not* dating. We're just friends!"

"Alright," she said in a tone that told me she didn't believe me. I groaned and rolled my eyes.

"May I be excused?"

I waited anxiously for my parents to go to bed so I could go to Mykail's room. I did not want to talk that night, knowing tomorrow would bring nothing but pain. Even though I already knew I had lost my mother to Dana, the reality of it would be very different once she went to see him.

When my parents finally did go to bed, I silently curled up in Mykail's arms and fell into an uneasy sleep.

But sleeping made Tuesday come all too soon.

Throughout the school day, everyone was asking if I was alright. I told them yes, but I could not put up an act. I felt pain deep inside my stomach at the thought of my mother with Dana. I did not know when they were going to meet, they might have already done so, but my mind was spinning with the realization that my mother was very likely going to be unfaithful to my father. Dana had turned her against the family.

I desperately wished I had never overheard the conversation, knowing that in that situation, ignorance would have been bliss.

When I greeted Mark after school, he knew something was wrong. I tried to smile for him, but I could not even lift my head to look at him. I handed my bag to him when he outstretched his hand and he put it in the trunk before standing beside me as we waited for Clark.

I jumped when Mark placed his hand on my shoulder and squeezed once before letting go and dropping his hand back to his side. He was not looking at me, his head bent down as if embarrassed by his attempt to comfort me.

Clark walked up as I was about to thank Mark. When Clark saw my face he slowed down.

"What's wrong?"

"Nothing."

"No, seriously, what's wrong?" he asked as Mark took his backpack. I sighed and rubbed my forehead roughly.

"My mother is meeting with Dana today..." I said, barely managing to keep my voice from breaking. "...*alone*."

Clark was still for a long moment before he shook his head and stepped forward, hugging me.

"I'm sorry," he said gently, rubbing my shoulder. "Really I am."

"Please..." I said, sniffing back my tears. "Don't make me cry." I laughed brokenly, the breath straining out of me. I turned to blink the tears away and saw a very worried Mark staring at us through his glasses. "It's alright. I'm alright." I scratched my neck twice with my right hand to assure him that I was okay, but he was clearly not convinced.

After a brief hesitation, he opened the car door for us.

We were silent during the drive, but as we pulled into the gates of the Commission, Clark turned to me.

"Hey...maybe it would be a really good idea for you to just sit in the conference room and not wander around today."

I did not respond. My thoughts were elsewhere...down in the Commission...where my mother was most likely with Dana.

As we were checked in, the woman at the front desk told Clark that his mother wanted to see him, so he had to go upstairs first. He asked me if I would be okay going downstairs on my own, which I assured him I was, even though it was an automatic response and I didn't think about what he was asking before I answered.

We went into separate elevators and while he went up to his mother's office, I went into the basement with Mark. As the elevator descended, I fell further into a dark cloud where all I could think of was Dana with my mother.

When the doors opened and I stepped out, I felt my stomach tighten sickeningly. Mark followed as I moved through the now-familiar hallways to the conference rooms. I was about to walk into the nearest one when Mark stopped me with a hand on my shoulder. I turned quickly and he shook his head, pointing at the schedule by the door. Realizing I had forgotten to check, I glanced at the screen, seeing the scheduled meeting in an hour.

I walked to another conference room, being sure to check the schedule before going inside.

I was looking at the room in tunnel vision. I knew my mother was going to cheat on my father, but speculating about it was somehow worse than actually knowing. I ran my hands through my hair in frustration before shaking my head and turning to leave the conference room.

As I started to walk away from the door, Mark caught my arm. He had taken off his glasses in the elevator, so I could see the imploring look in his eyes.

"I'm alright," I assured half-heartedly, shaking my head and trying to move out of his grip. His fingers tightened just enough to be painful and I cringed, which made him release me. I stared at him for a moment and then forced a shaky smile.

"I'm okay," I repeated. He started to step forward but I held my hand up to him. "Stay here."

He hesitated, but then bowed his head and backed away, standing dutifully outside the conference room where I had placed my backpack.

I followed the curves and twists through the quiet office area, walking toward Dana's office as if my feet had a mind of their own.

Everything inside of me screamed to turn around and go back, to forget my concern about finding out the truth. I was walking toward something that would only cause me pain.

But morbid curiosity got the better of me.

I reached up and, slower than I thought physically possible, I lowered the silver handle of the door and felt the latch slip free of the confines of the door jamb.

"…appreciate all this," my mother's voice said. My entire body went cold at realizing she was already there.

"Anytime," Dana's voice was quiet, soft, flowing over his lips like water. "I want to be sure that all members of the Commission are well. I saw that you were struggling."

"I apologize…" my mother said. The door was almost open enough to see Dana's desk. I dropped to my knees, hoping that no one would walk behind me and see me spying.

"Whatever for?"

"I should have been stronger about this whole thing," she said, her voice breaking ever-so-slightly. The door was finally open enough to see them. Dana was leaning against the front of his desk, one leg relaxed as he supported his weight on his hands. My mother was sitting in one of the chairs in front of his desk. While the angle did not allow me to see her face, I saw her legs and realized she was wearing the short black dress she had always said she was too embarrassed to wear in public.

I had to wonder who was trying to seduce whom.

"You *were* strong," Dana said gently.

"It's just…don't get me wrong, I feel very privileged to be a part of the Commission of the People, but…since we joined, my family hasn't been the same."

"That's to be expected," Dana conceded. "You have been introduced to a world most would never even dream of." He reached forward, touching her jaw as he smiled that smile that made everyone weak in the knees. "But there is no need to be afraid of change. It's natural…embrace it."

The voice. The eyes. How did he know how to *do* that? How was it that even I could feel that power when it was not directed at me? It seemed to be a part of his presence, commanding the entire space around him, regardless of at whom he was directing his affections.

"How long have you been down here, Dana?" my mother asked as he slowly pulled his hand away from her face. The action was delicate, fluid, and so perfectly timed that my mother leaned forward, trying to follow his fingers. He remained close, inviting her to close the gap between them.

"What do you mean?"

I was watching a perfectly choreographed dance, but one of the participants had been told to simply react to the other. Dana knew exactly how to move, exactly how to speak and change his expression, knew which direction his eyes needed to shift and when to let the corners of his mouth move upward in the softest smile…he knew what she wanted before she even realized it. He was dancing to her presence, weaving a net that led her to react to him as he wanted.

It was captivating to watch.

"You work in the Commission all the time…down here, out of the sunlight…" My mother reached forward, her hand trembling as she brushed her fingers over the hand resting on his leg. Their faces were so close…

"I have responsibilities," Dana breathed, turning his hand so that their fingers continuously brushed one another, not intertwining or holding. "I cannot ignore them."

My mother moved forward in her seat, her other hand pressing to the lapel of Dana's suit.

"Must be stressful…" she whispered. "Shouldering all this responsibility…"

"We all have our stresses in life, Karen," Dana said. "I feel that you have an extremely stressful job, raising Little Lily and trying to keep your household together." He looked at her, his eyes changing again. "How do you manage?"

"We do what we must," she breathed, her voice sounding weak as her eyes locked with his. "We all have our own ways of relieving stress…" Her hand moved up his arm and to the back of his neck as her other hand closed around his lapel. "What about you, Mr. Christenson?" she whispered, her voice heavy with desire as she looked into his eyes. "How do you relieve your stress?"

He did not answer. He reached out with his other hand and took her chin, pulling her close and kissing her.

My stomach flipped, but another part of me was fascinated and intrigued. I wondered how Dana could so easily manipulate my mother, how he could change the conversation to make her say such things, how he was able to do this for everyone he had ever seduced in the Commission, even the men…

He pulled her out of the chair, his lips continuing to work against hers. After a few long kisses, when she had her body pressed flush to his, her hands drifted down his torso, unbuttoning the vest and pulling the shirt out from the waistband of his pants. He chuckled into the kiss and caught her hands, shaking his head.

456

"Oh no…"

"What?" she asked with a confused chuckle. He recaptured her mouth in his, pulling at his tie. Once he had released it from his neck, he wrapped her wrists in the satin fabric, smiling wickedly as she giggled.

"In this game, there are rules."

When her wrists were wrapped, he turned them both, lifting her to sit on the desk, his hands stealing up her thighs and into the short skirt of her dress as they kissed again, the action hungry and desperate.

It was when my mother hooked her legs around Dana's hips and her bound hands rested behind his neck that I closed the door, feeling the tears spring to my eyes, blurring my view of the infidelity occurring within.

I scrambled to my feet, knowing I had to get out of the hallway so that no one randomly passing would see my breakdown. I darted to the conference room, pushing past Mark and falling heavily into one of the chairs, burying my head in my arms as the tears overcame me, pouring out of my eyes, the sobs thudding from my lungs.

I don't know how long I was crying, though it could not have been long before there was a voice at the door.

"Oh, Lily…"

I looked up, blinking the tears from my eyes enough to see Clark moving toward me. What shocked me was that Mark was standing at the corner of the table, having stopped from walking to me.

Clark sat in the chair next to mine and pulled me into a hug.

* *** *

That night, I finally got the courage to lift my mattress and look through the file of experiment four-eleven forty-one—my uncle's Commission of the People file.

I had a nasty headache from all the crying earlier, which had allowed me an excuse to avoid my parents that night. Immediately after dinner, I took two aspirin and slept for an hour before waking again. I felt better, but the headache was still very present. So, I went to Mykail's room and told him through the bars of his door that I was not going to his room that night because I wanted to get rid of the headache. He told me he understood, gave me a quick kiss, and wished me goodnight.

But I was unable to fall asleep again.

Finally, I climbed out of bed, grabbed the file I had stolen from Dana's table, and sat on my floor, staring at the red stamp across the front for a few minutes before opening the folder again and beginning to read.

Subject #41141
Testing Start: October 8
Presiding: Dr. Sam Pullman

*The Commission of the People maintains the right to apprehend all individuals who threaten the peace and security of the nation of America. Individuals residing illegally or harboring individuals who are in violation of the laws set by the Cabinet of the Leader will be brought into custody by the Commission of the People. (The Code of the Commission of the People: 13-9).

Accounts for Charge:

-Harboring Illegal Residents
-Harboring Individuals Deemed Dangerous
-Assisting Criminals
-Anarchist Activities
-Risking the Safety and Security of the Nation of America
-Sedition
-Domestic Terrorism

Name: William Kaden Sandover
Height: 194 cm
Weight: 74.2 kg
Hair Color: Brown
Eye Color: Brown
Race: Caucasian
Blood Type: AB-

The first three pages of the file were extensive medical and physical notes about my uncle, detailing every possible physical aspect of his being, so I skipped through, stopping on the fourth page.

Call-in Capture – August 2, 20:00
Team Leader: Fred Bosworth
"The Commission of the People was called by the father of the suspect on the evening of July twenty-third. Upon further investigation, all allegations were found to be true. W. Sandover had been harboring illegal residents, homosexuals, and other dangerous individuals across

458

the southern border. Evidence provided proved that the suspect had been one of the leaders of 'The Coalition' terrorist group. W. Sandover had been avoiding capture by the Commission for three years and his location was unknown at the time of the call-in.

"An anonymous tip led us to his location near the southern border, where W. Sandover and six other individuals of 'The Coalition' were found in a house. Four of the individuals escaped the house, one was killed upon escape, and W. Sandover was captured trying to escape the house through a window. Another member of the Coalition, Katherine K. Laughton, was also apprehended. Upon further investigation, it has come to the attention of this team that Laughton is pregnant with Sandover's child. Her fate has yet to be decided."

My heart twisted when I read the last part of the report. Even from the short recollection, I had so many complex emotions that I did not know what to feel. My uncle had been so against the Commission that he had been a leader in "The Coalition," harboring people over the border and getting them out of the Commission's grasp. I felt proud, and knew he would approve of my current rebellion against the Commission.

However, the girl had been pregnant when she had been taken in by the Commission. Even without looking at the rest of the report I knew that her situation was going to end horribly.

I flipped the page.

Experiment Log: Day 1 – Dr. Sam Pullman

"41141 went through pre-test cleaning with no complications. For the living situation in which the subject was picked up, his health is astounding. The first test was administered with an unexpected response. S.I.D.-3 was administered at 16:17 and by 16:23, the subject was showing signs of immense pain and remained in such a state for three hours before showing any signs of muscle relaxation.

"The test appears to have failed. There were no changes in chemical or neurological reactions. The subsequent seven tests will be performed as scheduled, regardless."

Experiment Log: Day 9 – Dr. Sam Pullman

"Experiment 41141 has shown no change as a result of Test S.I.D.-3. The subject has shown the same reaction to all seven tests, which resulted in muscle tension and pain for approximately three hours followed by a coma-like state. Upon waking, the subject appeared no different than before the test was administered.

"Reports will be submitted to Mr. Bryant Morris before proceeding."

I flipped through the following seven tests. Regardless of the tests they did on my uncle, nothing about his physiology changed. His health deteriorated slightly and he got weaker, but he still remained completely human. I did not understand the tables under each entry, or the graphs and charts detailing his biological responses, but by the confused commentary of the doctors, I could tell that they were completely baffled by my uncle's response to the test.

There were notes in the margins about the experiment's outspoken attitude and how he continued to yell at the scientists and curse them until they had no choice but to gag him because he was too boisterous—even violent at times despite his failing health.

The accounts made me proud. Knowing I was from the same strong line that continued to fight the clutches of the Commission of the People was a relief. If I failed in my rebellion, at least I could continue to fight, because I had the same strength in me. Maybe I could even be immune to any tests Dana tried, and I could become the next legend among the experiments.

But I knew there was even more about my uncle to consider. He was the one who had killed Bryant Morris only to give rise to Dana. He tried to defy the Commission, but still was killed, and now most experiments did not believe he had even existed.

I closed the folder, wondering if I really wanted to know the full story behind what happened to my uncle, and wondering if it would mean anything for my own future.

Chapter Thirty-Eight

I was going into the records room for the first time that Wednesday. Clark and I spent a lot of time figuring out how to do the research while keeping Dana in the dark about what we were doing. Since the leader of the Commission had a habit of popping in on us unannounced, it was not safe for both of us to be in the records room at the same time. However, we would research faster together, thus limiting the frequency of going into the records room.

We went to Dana's upstairs office to look at his schedule.

He would return to the Commission at five from a meeting with Leader Simon, which meant we had two hours to research as much as we could together.

"Friday he's gone the whole day," Clark noticed. "He'll be with Leader Simon again." He pointed at the various meetings on Dana's schedule. "We can't risk both being in there tomorrow. What do you want to do?"

"I want to see what we can find today and then decide about Friday later."

Mark stationed himself outside the library as we set our things down at one of the tables. Clark went one way while I made my way to the secret door, carefully turning the one handle we had latched and shifting the bookshelf back, slipping inside and closing the passageway behind me. Clark was going to wander around to throw off anyone who was watching the security cameras and bring books to the table so that we could look busy when we finally did appear on the camera feeds again.

I nervously stepped down the dim hallway and opened the door at the end, pushing hard to move the filing cabinet attached to the secret door. I poked my head into the unfamiliar room. The room was plain, yet crowded. There were shelves on every wall, each on top of three filing drawers with numbers written on the front panel. The upper shelves were crammed with overstuffed binders marked with months and years.

Carefully stepping into the surprisingly cold room and pushing the file cabinet back into place, I tried to think clearly. I did not want to sneak in too often, but in order to be sure that we did not have to do so, I had to remember exactly what I needed to do there, accomplish my task, and leave as quickly as possible.

I closed my eyes, took a deep breath, counting to five before exhaling. I started forward, recalling the first experiment's number.

80111.

It took me too long to find the drawer that held the file for the first experiment. After rounding the same row of shelves twice, trying to understand how the numbers were increasing to find the drawer that would hold the file I wanted, getting very frustrated when I rounded the corner and the drawer was not the correct one, I finally turned to the next aisle, finding the properly marked drawer.

The files within reminded me of my uncle's file and my heart tightened in my chest. The files were all for people who had families, people whose lives had been ripped from them as they were changed and morphed into something else.

I thumbed through the folders, telling myself to focus only on the experiments I had been told about rather than glance through all of them in my curiosity.

I pulled out the file for experiment 80111.

The first page was different from the first page in the file I had at home.

Experiment Summary
Status – Complete
Dr. Peter Jacobs

Number: 80111
Call Name: Tara
Cell #: 3-21   Ward: 3
Age: 15
Experiment Type: Stealth-Intelligence-Defense (S.I.D.)
Abilities: strength – 13, stealth – 8; high perception in dark, reverse adhesive skin
Eligibility: Low

A sickening feeling settled within my gut at seeing someone as young as fifteen subjected to the cruel experimentations. I could feel the hot tears of anger and disgust burning my eyes. I turned the page to the medical outline and, as I was flipping to get to the summary of why she was caught, Clark rounded the corner.

"Hey, we have about an hour before we should get out of here."

"Okay." I looked up at him and cleared my throat. "Can I just say that I hate this place?"

"Me, too," he agreed, handing me a pen and some folded pieces of paper. "Write down their cell numbers so that we can find them on the blueprints."

I took the offered objects. Since we had already decided which experiments each of us were going to look into, he went to find the files for those experiments while I read about Tara's capture.

She had been born to a lesbian couple and without a Child-Rearing License. When her family was called into the Commission, her mother tried to poison Tara to keep her out of the Commission, though she survived the attempted murder. One of her mothers had been killed when she turned a knife on the Officials trying to capture them. The other one bit through her tongue in the transport car and died from ingesting her own blood shortly after they got her into the holding cells, leaving Tara to face the horrors of the Commission alone.

Once I could, I wrote down Tara's cell number, trying to keep my emotions in check as I moved onto the next experiment.

Experiment 80200 was a thirty-one year old woman named Sophia in Ward Four. She had a voice that could speak at silent and powerful frequencies that could cause painful vibrations and mechanical interference—even causing bleeding in the brain on some occasions. She had killed her abusive husband and spent five months on the run, crossing region boundaries—which was when the Commission was called in. She was finally caught robbing a bank.

Experiment 80201 was a fifteen-year-old girl, also from Ward Four, named Alexandra who had been altered for incredible strength and reflexes, but her story made the tears that had been welling in my eyes finally fall. At thirteen, she had been sold into slavery in her home country of Spain and had been bought by a corporate tycoon in America. She lived with him illegally for a year before the man was called into the Commission on charges of corporate fraud, and Alexandra was seized in the process.

The final experiment I had time to look up was 80270—Maddy—from Ward Six. She was a twenty-three year old who had a secondary skin added to hers that could absorb liquid like a sponge. She had been a college student with no previous record before being found possessing top-secret documents and delivering them to a domestic terrorist group, though she claimed she had no idea the contents of the documents.

Clark and I left the records room when our time was up and took positions around the library table, pretending to be busy with non-treasonous acts.

* *** *

After our break-in to the records room, we dared not to speak of what we had learned, still coming down from the adrenaline high.

Thursday, Clark told me about the three experiments he had looked into, confirming how horrific the injustices were for the Commission-marked criminals.

It was unfortunate that Dana was gone on Friday, because Clark and I had to leave early to go to Archangel and our research time was cut short. All the same, we both slipped into the records room where I looked at three other experiments while Clark searched for blueprints of the Commission near the front of the room.

"Lily," he whispered even though we were alone. I closed the file I had and replaced it, walking to him as he unrolled some blueprints over one of the small file cabinets. We studied the large, rolled-up papers, trying to find one that had the entirety of the Commission of the People, but each blueprint was one ward. When we realized we were not going to find a complete map, we looked at each ward to see if we could find any passages to sneak out experiments, snapping pictures on our phones for reference.

Looking over the blueprints led us to discussing how we were going to get the experiments out, a task which seemed impossible apart from walking them out the front door.

I did not get the chance to look at any other experiment files because by the time we realized we had been talking about the blueprints too long, we only had twenty minutes before we were to leave for Archangel.

Quickly cleaning up, we left the records room and, as we approached the middle table in the library, we realized how lucky our timing was when we heard the door open. It was Mark, coming in to see if we were ready to go.

I had difficulty not discussing possible plans with Clark through the rest of the night and, with the way he kept turning toward me as if he was going to say something, I could tell he was struggling with the same problem. Our minds were constantly turning over the blueprints and where the experiments were situated in order to find a way to sneak them out undetected.

Every time I started to discuss things with Clark, one of the other Commish Kids would walk too close on the balcony and I would shrink away. There were far too many people around to risk even slightly discussing our plans. The most we could discuss was that we would meet as planned with the other Commish Kids who had taken the papers from us on Saturday before the Commission meeting. That would leave our Sunday free to explore the different passages in and out of Fort Daniels.

It felt surreal to be plotting something so treasonous while surrounded by the heavy bass of the club.

I was living in a state of high adrenaline, and I could feel it emboldening me, which also meant I was becoming more daring in my relationship with Mykail. When I got home from Archangel, still riding the high of excitement I felt from the secret planning of a revolution, I changed into new pajamas that I had bought the previous week—a short, satin nightgown that I never thought I would feel comfortable wearing with matching panties.

When I walked into Mykail's room around midnight, I could not suppress my smile at the shock that crossed his features. He halted from standing, his eyes wide.

"*Well*," he said, clearing his throat, "that's…new."

I walked to him, smiling.

"Do you like it?"

"Yes," he said, looking me over. I climbed onto the bed, taking his head in my hands and kissing him as I straddled his lap.

I was definitely becoming bolder.

But he was a gentleman, and still worried about Dana finding out how close we were, so I remained frustratingly unsatisfied in my sexual desires. I wanted to have sex with him, to be daring and try new experiences. I wanted to be close to him in a way I was sure only sex could provide.

Once again that Friday night, I was sent back to my room before anything more could come of our make-out.

Saturday morning, I left a note on the refrigerator telling my parents I had a study session with some friends and that I would be back in time for dinner. I took an early bus to the park where the Commish Kids were supposed to meet, holding my version of the scribbled note to keep up appearances that Clark and I were just as confused as the other Commish Kids as to who had handed out the notes at Archangel.

I was the first one there, but Clark arrived soon after and we sat on the bench in the early morning as the first family with a child came to play in the park.

"Maybe this wasn't a good place…" I said, watching the little girl run clumsily to the swing set.

"As long as we stay in this open field and keep conversation quiet, we should be fine," Clark said, also watching the family warily. "Everyone should bring their school stuff, so we really could make it look like a study group."

"We should find a secretive way to get into the fort soon," I said. "Pretty soon the snow will keep us from meeting outside."

Clark nodded in agreement, but did not say anything in response.

"How many kids our age are in the Commission again?" I asked.

"Twenty-nine in our age group, from seniors to freshmen," he answered. "The rest are younger...a few older..."

"I'm worried that younger siblings will get involved if we move forward with our classmates."

"It's a chance we have to take," he said. "I don't like the thought either, but there is always a chance..."

The first Commish Kid showed up, causing Clark to trail off, watching the other teenager approach. It was Kelly, holding her backpack over one shoulder and looking around nervously.

"Hey, Kelly," Clark greeted.

"Hey, Clark...Lily..." She nodded to both of us, standing awkwardly next to the bench. "What are you doing here?" she asked as casually as she could manage.

"I think the same thing as you," I said, fiddling with the paper in my hands to emphasize my point.

She looked at the note in my hand and sighed, reaching into her coat pocket and pulling out the folded note as well.

"I guess so..." she said. She set her backpack down on the concrete before sitting in the empty space on the bench with us. "Do you know who gave these out?"

"No," we both said casually. I was impressed that, even though we answered at the same time, we managed to pass it off naturally.

Kelly sighed. "How do you feel about it?"

"Don't know, yet," Clark said, glancing around for more approaching Commish Kids. "We'll just have to see what people have to say."

"But this is so dangerous," Kelly hissed.

"Yeah, but..." I hesitated and then shrugged. "I think we're all a bit pissed at everything to do with...well, you know."

"Damn right," she said strongly.

When I saw the way her demeanor changed, I realized that keeping everyone angry was going to be the best way to keep everyone on my side.

The final twenty minutes before our designated meeting time passed agonizingly. By the time ten o'clock rolled around, twenty Commish Kids had shown up at the park, nervous, confused, and wondering who had given them—*us*—the papers. Clark and I played along, looking around the park even as the time to meet ticked past to see if anyone else would show up, looking for unfamiliar faces. We had all gathered on the few blankets some had brought and sat on the dried grass, huddled in blankets and coats, holding our books and bags, pretending to have a study session in the cold autumn air.

"So…what now?" Brent asked, looking around the circle.

"I don't know," Sarah said.

"Maybe we should wait a little longer…" Morgan said, her voice weak with worry as her eyes continued to scan the area.

"What the hell? Those people give us papers and then don't show up?" Dean growled. "Who was it? Someone fess up."

We all looked at one another, waiting for someone to speak.

"You two," Dean growled, pointing at me and Clark. "Do you know who told you about the people with the scarves?"

"No." Clark shook his head while I remained silent, offering a confused shrug in response.

Dean sighed, rolling his eyes. "Well, we don't need them."

"We should keep our voices down," Felicity said, looking at the few families braving the cold weather to play with their children.

"So…" Samantha said, "what do we do now?"

Everyone was nervous and worried about being caught so no one spoke up immediately. I looked around the twenty teenagers, trying to read the emotions circling the group. Most were frightened, debating whether they should be there at all. They all knew how dangerous it was to let any of the others in the Commission know that they were thinking about plotting against the Commission. If some were not fully invested in helping, they were loose ends that could be easily exploited by Dana and they could be convinced into exposing all the others who had arrived at the park that day.

"Well," I started nervously. "I guess the big question I have is…why do we want to go against Dana? I mean, I know why *I* want the Commission gone, but…what about you?"

"Why do *you* want Dana out of the way?" Ryan asked, eyeing me suspiciously. "Both of you. You and Clark are his favorites."

"Exactly why I want him gone," Clark said. "He's crazy." I nodded in fervent agreement.

"You have a lot of information on him?" Dean asked, his voice dangerous and full of anger.

"Yes," Clark affirmed. "I can get close to him, so can Lily. We can find out things about him to help us."

"That's all well and good," Matt said with a dejected shake of his head. "But this is the Commission of the People we're talking about…" He looked around nervously, trying to see if anyone was eavesdropping nearby. "How are we supposed to take it down?"

Everyone fell silent yet again. Most were too afraid to speak, worried about their own involvement in the plot. When several long seconds passed, I was about to speak, but Dean cut me off.

"We kill Dana."

Everyone turned to him quickly, even me.

"Clark, could you get close enough?" he asked. Clark blinked, too surprised to respond for several long moments.

"The man does not sleep. He has no moment where he is vulnerable enough to get close enough to kill," Clark told him sharply.

"It doesn't take much to put a bullet through someone's skull," Dean snarled.

"Where is he going to get the gun and how is he going to get it close enough to Dana?" I challenged. Killing Dana right out of the gate would not accomplish anything. It would just give rise to a new leader of the Commission and immediate exposure of our plot. I had to find a way to calm Dean down before he progressed the plan too far in a dangerous direction.

"Take one off the security," Dean said. "Steal your gift's gun when you're already down in the Commission."

"All the firearms are tagged," Clark snapped. "I will not pin anything on Mark. We'll have to find a different way."

"We can't just *kill* Dana," Anne said. "That solves nothing. We need to take out the entire organization, and to do that we have to be sure to involve the American people." She tapped the book in her hands. "Just like Thomas Ankell did."

"How do we do *that*?" Jacob asked. "It will be traced back to us in a heartbeat."

"Thomas Ankell did it over social media and the internet," Karmen said, halting her words when a man walked his dog a little too close to us. Everyone waited for the man to pass, flicking their gazes between Karmen and the man, eager for him to pass to hear the rest of her explanation. "We could do something similar with social media, or maybe even something like pop-ups and emails."

It was everything I could do not to laugh and how easily the conversation had turned the direction I wanted.

"The Censor Board could trace the messages to our computers. It would take a matter of hours for us to be found out," Cody said.

Clark straightened up next to me.

"Cody," he started, "your mom is on the Censor Board, isn't she?" Cody nodded. "What if the signal came from the CB's computers?"

"What do you mean?" several of the kids asked.

"Where would the signal *go*?" Melody asked. "There's a million different…oh," she stopped, pointing at Clark with a knowing grin. "I see what you mean."

"You mean…sending a mass message out to the people of America through the Censor Board computers?" Cody asked. At first he looked mortified, but his face eventually softened to contemplation. "I don't know…how could you do that?"

"It would depend on what kind of system they run," Melody said. "I bet if Clark and I could get in there and see what type of computers they have, we could figure something out."

"Are you good with computers?" I asked Melody.

"She's a genius," Clark answered for her.

"But how would you get into the Censor Board?" Anne pressed. "Let alone get in long enough to program something…"

"That's a good point…" Melody admitted.

"My mom gives tours to my friends sometimes," Cody said. "I could get you guys in. But…getting into the actual computer room…I'd say it would only be for three to five minutes, at most."

"We would have to know the system beforehand," Clark said, looking at Melody. "For a mass signal like that, we'd need to program things beforehand and find a way to infect the CB computers like a virus."

"Is there a way for you to get a video of the computer room?" Melody asked, looking at Cody. "Can you take a video discreetly with your phone?"

"*Maybe*…" Cody said, making a face. "I don't know. I'll have to see next time I'm at the Censor Board. I'll let you know."

"We want to do this soon," Dean said sharply. "So, try."

"I will," Cody said, unsuccessful to keep the indignation out of his voice.

"But if you take a video, try to make it a live-stream thing. Call me or Melody and use your camera, but don't record anything," Clark said. "When Dana takes the phones we check in at the Commission, he lifts all the files to keep tabs on what we're doing."

Everyone seemed much less horrified at Dana's monitoring than I was. I guess it made sense, but I was still surprised that I had not realized sooner. I was thankful Clark had the mind to handle everything on my Commission phone.

"But what message are you going to send?" Morgan pressed. "It has to be something that will get people's attention and will get them to wonder about the Commission."

Everyone started throwing out ideas, to which I listened attentively. Clark was quiet next to me, knowing we had already established our message, but interested to hear other ideas. I let the others talk, taking some aspects of their ideas and adding it to the one I already had in mind.

Finally, I spoke up and told everyone of my own idea for the message, adding in the elements from others and pretending as though the idea had just come to me during the brainstorming. Clark acted as though it was the first time he heard the idea as well, adding a few little ideas that we had already discussed when we came up with the original message. The others were soon building off the original idea, agreeing to let me make the prototype.

Once we had exhausted the topic, Matt asked the question that heightened my anxiety. I was not sure who I could trust in the group, yet, despite how enthusiastic the conversation had become.

"Even if we get the people curious, how are we going to tell them what the Commission is doing to prisoners like Miranda?" Matt asked. "You can get people curious, but they won't do anything without proof. Or without a reason."

"We have to give them a reason," Morgan said. "What about...the gifts? Show the people the different experiments."

It was so perfect, I had to fight to keep my expression neutral.

"That's risky..." Kelly murmured.

"Well, the message we're sending out is that the Commission is doing horrible things to people. What better way to prove it than to show that they are creating weapons?" Morgan said.

"That is a really good point, but who? The gift experiments?" Samantha asked. "That could be very dangerous for *us*. It could implicate us. Dana could trace each experiment to each house...he would know immediately."

Looking for ideas, gazes were darting around the circle of teens. Karmen drew in a deep breath, catching everyone's attention.

"But...I don't think there's a way to break other experiments out of the Commission..."

"We could find a way," Kelly suggested. She looked around the group, waiting for anyone to offer up ideas. I was worried the idea would be automatically shot down, certain that the other students would think it was completely impossible. Of course, I wasn't entirely sure it *was* possible. But if Clark and I did not have the support of others, we could not stage the break-out. There was no way only two of us could break out twenty-five experiments.

"Do you think it's possible?" Ryan asked, his eyes resting on Clark and me. I also turned to Clark, hoping he would phrase things in a way that would keep the others interested in the idea. He took a deep breath and picked at the blanket under him, thinking.

"I don't know…" he admitted. "I mean, it's possible that there are secret passages out of the Commission…and then there's the problem of getting the experiments out of the cells in the back…and then where to *put* them…"

"There are plenty of abandoned places around. Maybe we can use one of them," Karmen suggested.

"I think we should see if we can even get the experiments out before we decide to overtake property," Matt said. He looked at Clark and me. "Do you think you could look at the blueprints for the Commission?"

"I can try…" Clark said. "I'll have to see if I can hack into the system and get them."

"That should be our first step."

"And then what?" Dean pressed. "Sit around and wait to do something with a couple experiments?" His eyes were alight with fury. "We need more help."

"If we can get a message out to the people, that should rally them to help us," Felicity pointed out.

"Or it *won't*." Dean shook his head. "The experiments are proof of what the message is saying. We need help *before* that." He looked around again. "I say we need to break out some people in the holding cells, too. Strength in numbers."

"*What?*" Clark and I blinked at him in disbelief, speaking simultaneously.

"What?" Dean asked. "Do you really think that we can just have us and a few experiments and pull this off? We need *people*."

"But breaking even *more* people out of the Commission?" I gaped. "We don't even know if we can get *experiments* out, yet. To break them out as well as other people from under Dana's nose…I don't know if we can."

"And who would we let out?" Matt added. "There are thousands of people in the holding cells. Some of them are extremely dangerous criminals. We can't let everyone out."

"Then we research who we can let out," Felicity said.

"Don't let this become about Miranda," Matt said sharply.

"But isn't it?" Dean snapped. "Would any of us be here if she hadn't been taken?" I looked around the circle, watching their faces. They were waiting to see if anyone would say they had another reason to be there. "What Dana did to her and Julie was wrong. And we're going to make him pay. But we need as many people as we can get out in order to achieve this. Clark will look up if there is a way out of the Commission and we will go from there, but we need these people. We need Miranda."

Everyone in the circle agreed, even me, though I knew it would make the breakout that much harder. I just hoped that we would find a way out of the Commission that would allow us to get everyone to Fort Daniels. We would have to figure out so many things while also keeping the plan hidden from Dana until we had completed what felt like an impossible task.

* *** *

The Commish Kids were dark and brooding at the weekly meeting, sharing silent looks. It seemed that the ones who had not been at the earlier gathering also knew something was amiss. That worried me greatly, thinking that someone had already let slip what we were planning to one of the adults...or to Dana.

I had to constantly remind myself that the Commish Kids knew the risks of being caught involved in the rebellion, particularly after what had happened to Miranda. I was confident they would not risk their safety.

The Commission meeting was very standard, though Dana seemed distracted through the proceedings. He barely reacted when the delegation for the Europe trip was announced.

I was not surprised to hear my parents' names on the list.

They would be gone for most of the month of December. I was thrilled. The override codes that we had been given by our anonymous helper would expire at the end of December, which meant we had to break Commission prisoners out while we had the active codes, and having my parents away meant I could stay out later in the night. That, and I could spend more time with Mykail without having to stay hidden from them.

When the meeting wrapped up, Dana slipped out of the room like a shadow, which allowed everyone to leave earlier because they were not socializing with the leader of the Commission of the People.

My mother and father were talking excitedly about the Europe trip on the way home while I sat in the back of the car and thought about what I needed to do for my revolution. There was much that I needed to figure out in the following weeks before my parents left. My brain refused to be silenced, even distracting me from my late-night talk with Mykail.

"It's so busy up there," Mykail laughed, touching my temple gently as I lay on his bed, having lost my train of thought yet again.

"I'm sorry," I said, smiling apologetically. "It's just a lot to think about. Honestly, I didn't expect everything to go so well today."

"If you think about it too much, you'll think yourself in circles," he said, his fingers running through the thin hairs at my temple. "Give yourself a break. Close your eyes," I did so, "and take a deep breath…"

I tried, but found the whole exercise rather silly, giggling as I let out the breath I had taken.

"Not really working, huh?" he chuckled. He propped himself up on his elbow and one arm circled my waist. "Let's try another method."

Kissing Mykail was far more effective at taking my mind off the revolution.

I had to pull myself out of bed early the next morning and take the bus downtown, where I agreed to meet Clark. He was waiting for me with two cups of coffee, stifling yawns into his elbow as he offered me the coffee. I gratefully accepted the cup, occupying the seat next to him on the bus stop bench.

"You are a lifesaver," I said with a sleepy grin.

After we got on the bus Clark told me to turn off my phone to be sure that we could not be tracked. I did so after sending a quick text to my mother that I was turning off my phone because we were going into a museum.

Once we reached the final bus stop on the route, we walked the fifteen-minute route to the power plant, keeping our eyes out for cars and people as we moved out of the rural neighborhood.

Slipping into the power plant the same way we had a week previous, we walked back to the dark basement and made our way down the creaking spiral staircase to Fort Daniels.

"I still can't believe that we found this place," I said.

"We better find out who's sending us those notes soon." Clark rolled his eyes, descending the stairs into the main bunker.

With coffee fueling us and the lights on our now-jammed phones illuminating our path, we explored all seventeen exits and entrances to the fort. One was caved in. Another led to an active sewer line, which immediately ruled it out as a possible entrance. The other fifteen passages were in working order, and some even led to some surprising areas. One led to an underground room next to a collection of water tanks on the hill around the reservoir. Another led to the opposite face of the hill, where a door hidden behind a ridiculous amount of foliage could barely be opened enough to slip in and out. One led to a tunnel system under the city that we knew would need further exploration, and another even led to a cave system where we had to walk for five minutes through the caves just to get outside again.

By the time we had explored all the passages, the sun was setting and we were starving.

Once again, I had dinner at Clark's house, trying very hard not to fall asleep with my face in my stew.

I was completely exhausted for my classes on Monday and I even fell asleep in art class, though I was rudely awoken by my teacher, who was more worried about my health than upset about my napping.

My exhaustion also made it very difficult to deal with my friends, who were constantly asking me when Clark and I started going out.

"Well, we're not…like, going out. We're just…you know…"

I was way too tired to form a coherent thought, let alone a full sentence.

The more I was teased about being with Clark, the more I realized that I would have to come up with a reason why we were spending so much time together. Becca understood my exhaustion and she stopped teasing me, but the others were not as merciful.

Both Clark and I fell asleep in the car to the Commission. Mark woke us long enough to get to a conference room, where we promptly fell asleep again.

When I got home, I faked a headache and went to my room to do my homework, though I could not concentrate on the blurry words on the pages. I didn't *want* to concentrate. I was working on something far more important. I was going to be declaring war against the most powerful organization in the country and my opponent was Dana Christenson. Homework seemed pointless when I thought about the greater-scale operation I was organizing.

I felt bad when I fell asleep without seeing Mykail that night, but I woke up at a ridiculously early hour and slipped into his room, carefully waking him so I could talk to him before my parents woke.

"Lily?" He blinked at me, sleepy and confused. "What time is it? Is everything alright?" he asked, his eyes still partially closed. I had to force myself not to comment on how adorable he looked.

"Everything's fine," I said, feeling better after sleeping so heavily. "I'm sorry to wake you up, but I really need to talk to you about something."

"What is it?" he asked, sitting up slowly, his eyes remaining almost completely closed.

"I know that you just woke up, but I need to ask you something important," I said, sitting on his bed and folding my hands in my lap, nervous. "A lot of people…not only my parents, but people at school, think that Clark and I are dating…" I started.

"Oh, it's too early for this…" he groaned, rubbing his eyes and clearing his throat. "Okay, they think you're dating…but you're not, right?"

"No, no, of course not," I said quickly. "But I thought about it…and I think that it's the best way to explain why Clark and I are spending so much time together."

"So, you want to tell people that you're dating Clark." Mykail nodded once, his brow furrowed in drowsy concentration. "What about Dana?"

"Well, no, I won't tell Dana. Just…everyone else. But, if you don't want me to, I won't. I don't want you to worry that that means I am dating Clark. He doesn't like me that way."

"Are you sure?"

"There's no way. I mean…" I trailed off. I had no logical explanation of why Clark would not be interested in me. It was just something I *knew*.

"You might want to ask him," Mykail said, stifling his yawn. "Could save you an awkward situation later."

I looked at the sheets, now worried that Clark *could* be interested in me somehow, explaining his eagerness to help me with our dangerous rebellion. Mykail took a deep breath, putting a hand on mine.

"If he doesn't like you, and if it takes suspicion off what you two are really doing…then I'm alright with it. It will keep you safe and keep people from asking too many questions," Mykail said. "As long as you don't actually start dating him."

"Don't worry, I'm not interested in him like that."

I sat with him until he fell back asleep, apologizing for waking him up so early, and then I went to my room and got ready for school. Feeling as though I could think a little more clearly, I spent my time in art class sketching the idea for our mass email in my book, flipping to a previous picture when the teacher would walk by and look at our progress on our still-life drawings.

It was no longer possible to escape into art as I had been able to before. The revolution and going against Dana pervaded my every thought. It was like an addiction, or an obsession, something I was always turning over in my head. It was a slow process, but because of the leaps and bounds we had made recently, it was difficult for me *not* to be excited and not think ahead about everything we could accomplish.

My biology teacher pulled me aside after class and told me that my grades were slipping severely. She gave me the speech I had heard from two teachers already. They did not understand how I could go from being such a good student to a student who was sleeping in class and failing courses.

The conditioned good girl part of me wanted to care about my grades, but a bigger part of me was preoccupied with finding a way to overthrow Dana Christenson.

My biology teacher also cautiously posed the same question as my other teachers.

"Is everything alright at home?"

We went through the normal questions. I told her that I was just tired and it was tough for me to adjust to the new city. I could not tell them that I did not care about school. Everything about going to class felt like a chore, a façade I had to go through to keep everyone at bay so that they would not question what I was really doing with my time and energy.

When I walked out of the building it was snowing. I ran to the car where Mark was standing, dutifully enduring the snow. He opened the door for me to climb in the car while Clark ran to join us.

"I guess winter finally decided to show up," Clark chuckled, brushing the snow from his hair.

I could not help but feel awkward around Clark, wondering if he actually *did* like me more than I liked him. I did not want anything to complicate the already delicate situation. I was concerned that if he liked me and I rejected him, the awkwardness would come to affect our plans, putting us in more danger.

We talked about school as we went to the Commission. It was another intensive check day for the security personnel of the Commission. Josh was the one checking everyone at the door. He and Mark nodded to one another and, to my complete surprise, Josh took Mark's jacket and patted it down before quickly patting him down to be sure he was carrying nothing suspicious—ignoring the two guns that I had never noticed on Mark before.

"Why does he need to be checked?" I asked Clark.

"I think they just check them randomly." Clark shrugged. "I've seen Mark check Josh and the others before. It's just one of those random days I told you about."

Josh cleared us to go downstairs and we followed Mark to the elevators. It had become normal to go into the bowels of the

Commission and find a conference room that was not being occupied. Nothing about the routine seemed strange, and I knew that the accustomed normalcy should have concerned me.

Mark stood outside our door as Clark worked on a science paper due that week. I briefly showed him what I had done in my sketchbook and he approved, asking me where I was going to get the pictures of the people. All the photos that we had taken in the records room were put on Clark's computer and the files were encrypted until he got home and did whatever he did to keep the information safe from Dana and the Commission—this kept our phones clean and the phones that the Commission gave us clean. But we had never taken photos of any of the experiments from their files. There were pictures of them before the testing had changed them, which was where I decided we should get the pictures for our mass message.

As I was sketching and he was working on his paper, I looked up several times, trying to find the courage to ask him about his feelings for me. I kept telling myself that there was nothing to be worried about, certain that Clark did not have romantic interest in me. But as I thought over the amount of time we had been spending together and how easily he had started helping me with my idea to take down Dana, my doubts were starting to grow.

"Are you okay?" he asked with a nervous chuckle when he caught me lifting my head and turning to him to speak yet again.

"Huh? Oh, yeah, I'm fine," I said, turning back to my sketchbook, feeling embarrassment burn my cheeks.

"Are you sure?" he laughed. "You've looked up at me like you want to say something a couple times now."

I sighed and drummed the end of my pencil against the paper in front of me, using my other hand to cover the sketch, just in case the cameras were live in the conference room.

"Clark..." I finally said, keeping my eyes down, nervous. "Please...don't think I'm weird for asking this but...do you..." I sighed again and hung my head, losing my nerve.

"Do I what?"

"Do you...ugh, this is *embarrassing*," I groaned. "Don't worry about it."

"Just tell me."

"Do you...have any feelings...for me?" My voice had gotten weaker as the sentence continued so I was not sure he heard me, but with the way he stilled suddenly, I knew he had, and his reaction made me very nervous.

Then, he surprised me.

"Ugh, I was worried about this," he grumbled, putting his head in his hands and rubbing his face roughly. "I'm sorry if I made you uncomfortable during the Halloween party, I just...I don't know, I did what I thought would be the least suspicious. I'm sorry."

"Whoa, this isn't about the Halloween party."

Clark looked at me suspiciously and a little nervously.

"Then...why do you ask?"

"Clark..." I whined, feeling embarrassed and now very confused.

"Well, I can't exactly say either answer without offending or weirding you out somehow."

"What do you mean?"

"If I say yes, things get awkward between us and then our plan goes bad," he said. "But if I say no, you might think that there's something wrong with you," he said, looking at me innocently. My shoulders slumped as relief washed through me. "Which there's not."

"I won't take it that way," I assured, unable to keep myself from smiling, feeling as though I could breathe again.

"No, Lily." He shook his head. "I don't like you in that way. No need to worry."

I smiled.

"Do you have feelings for *me*?" he asked, raising an eyebrow.

"Would you be offended if I said no?"

"No," he said. "I would be relieved actually." He turned to me quickly. "Wait, that came out wrong!"

"Clark, it's okay," I said with a laugh. "I know you don't mean anything against me. I'm pretty relieved as well."

"I'm glad." He nodded with a bark of laughter. "What brought this up all of a sudden?"

"Well...I was thinking," I started, turning back to my drawing, "my friends have been asking if we're dating because we're spending so much time together. Our parents also think we're going out." I shrugged. "We could say we are so that it doesn't seem weird when we're going out on the weekends and spending so much time together."

He raised an eyebrow at me.

"Would you be okay with that?" he asked. "What if word got back to Dana?"

"We would just say it's a stupid rumor," I said. "I mean...no matter what, we're going to piss him off somehow, so we might as well try to appease as many people as possible by saying we're together."

"If you're alright with that, I'll play along."

"Are *you* alright with that?"

"I think it's a good idea," he agreed, turning back to his laptop and sighing heavily. "And it would keep my mother from pestering me about asking you out."

"Has she been doing that?" I laughed.

"Yep."

We both went back to what we were doing, but two minutes later, my brain clicked.

"Hey, Clark…have you ever had a girlfriend?"

His typing stopped, caught off guard by the question.

"…no…"

"That's okay," I said. "I've never had a boyfriend."

"Really?" he asked. "That's unexpected."

"Why?"

"You're beautiful and smart…it just seems surprising that no one would ask you out."

"Most guys our age are scared of me," I said. "What's your excuse?"

"Have we met?" he chuckled brokenly. "One, I look like this," he motioned to his face, "and two, I'm shy. I can't just walk up to girls I like and talk to them."

"Do you have anyone you like right now?" I leered teasingly. His expression immediately became defensive.

"Do *you*?"

"We're not talking about me," I said. "What was that look? You *do* have someone you like right now," I said with a smile. "Who is it? Tell me!"

"No!" he snapped, turning back to his computer, his face flushing deep crimson.

"Why not?"

"Because it's none of your business."

"What arc you, *twelve*?" I teased. "It's fine, just tell me."

"No," he said. "You'll laugh…"

"Why would I laugh?" I asked, brushing the statement off. I wanted him to trust me. I figured, maybe, if he told me who he liked, I could also tell him about my relationship with Mykail. I knew as soon as the revolution got underway, I would be unable to hide the relationship, and since Mykail wanted to remove his tracers and participate in our revolution, Clark would undoubtedly see the two of us together.

"Because it's stupid…" he said quietly, trying to disappear behind his laptop screen.

"I'm sure it's not stupid," I gently assured. "And I do mean that. You could tell me that you liked Mark and I would not laugh."

Clark glanced at me sideways, glaring playfully.

"Do you really get that vibe from me?" he asked jokingly, trying to take the attention off of the question I had asked.

"No, but I still wouldn't laugh," I said. "Come on, tell me."

"Why should I?"

"Because maybe I could help you," I said. "I could see if she likes you, too. That's the great thing about having a friend who is a girl. You can get all the inside information."

"She doesn't like me." He shook his head, looking away.

"You don't know that."

"I'm pretty damn sure."

"Please, Clark, just tell me," I said, curiosity getting the best of me. "Please, please, *please*…"

Clark groaned and rolled his eyes, hiding his face in his hands. I was reminded of the first time I saw Clark at Archangel. With all the time I had been spending with him, I had forgotten how utterly shy he was until that moment.

"…promise you won't laugh?" he pleaded.

"I promise."

He took a deep breath and, with his face hidden in his hands, he said a name, though I only caught the end of it. Despite that, I still knew immediately who he was talking about.

"…cca…"

Oh.

The situation had definitely become awkward. Clark did not know that Becca was a lesbian who was in love with Jill who was infatuated with Devon who seemed to be interested in me…

The situation was worse than I could have prepared to handle.

"See? Was that so hard?" I said with a smile, trying to stop the horrible pain in my heart at realizing Clark's obliviousness to his own situation and the situation of the girl he liked.

"*Yes*," he groaned. "Listen, *don't* tell her, okay?" he pleaded, raising his eyes to meet my gaze. "I know she doesn't have feelings for me. It's just a stupid crush, okay? *Don't* say anything. Promise me that you won't say anything!"

"I won't say anything."

Chapter Thirty-Nine

I knew that breaking the experiments out of the Commission of the People was going to be difficult, but I did not expect it to be *so* difficult. Clark and I were arguing hopelessly about the picture I had drawn to represent a simplified version of the blueprints Clark compiled together.

Our biggest problem was figuring out how we were going to get the experiments out of their cells and then get them to a location where we could break them out without tipping off the security and bringing the entirety of the Commission's security on us. The cells that we needed to open were spread out, and with how far the Commission extended, it was difficult to determine how long we would need to get everyone to the same spot where we could potentially get them out of the basement complex.

When Clark and I were sick of arguing, we finished our Wednesday with me giving him the finished sketched email message and telling him to make seven versions with pictures of different people who had been taken into the Commission. As a tribute, I also told him to use a picture of Miranda and Julie that I had obtained from Becca. It was a very sweet picture with Miranda hugging her little sister, and I knew that with the message "Why did the Commission of the People take me?" people would question who was depicted and what crime the young people could have committed.

I wanted that one to be our most widespread message.

Clark also told me that he was going to hack into the Commission computers from home and look over the prisoners of the holding cells to narrow down the cells we could reach easily, splitting up the cells between the two of us and researching the four people in each cell, deciding who would be safe to let out and who could help us with our revolution. Clark told me he would print a copy of the list and give it to me when I went to his house on Sunday.

Stifling his yawns and trying to make his tired voice stronger, Clark told me Thursday that he had spoken to Cody the previous night and knew what kind of system the Censor Board used for tracking the computers in the nation. I had to remind Clark several times that I did not speak that language and he was telling me things that just confused me. Even though I was not at all good with computers, I was invited to Clark's house Saturday before the Commission meeting for the programming of our mass message with Melody and Cody.

The reality made my heart pound, though it was not only from worry. A larger part of my apprehension was due to excitement.

Clark was exhausted from staying up all night. When the typing of my English paper was too annoying, he went to his mother's office to sleep in the quiet. Mark seemed torn about who to follow and I watched him take a few steps in Clark's direction, even though Clark told him to stay. He obeyed and returned to his position by the door of the conference room, but ten minutes later, he went in the same direction Clark had gone—I assume to check on him briefly, since he quickly returned to his position outside the conference room door.

I was alone for only twenty minutes before the door to the conference room opened and my stomach somersaulted.

"Little Lily," Dana greeted, closing the door behind him. "Long time, no see."

"Not long enough," I bit back. He chuckled, standing across the table from me. I tried to ignore him, staring at my computer, clicking my fingernails along the keyboard to mimic typing.

I saw Dana lean forward, his uncovered eyes locked on the table top. I could not see his hand, though I saw his arm moving closer. I could have sworn he was walking his fingers along the surface of the table.

I jumped when the lid of the laptop slowly closed, almost capturing my hands. Dana pulled the closed laptop away, smiling, his gaze capturing mine.

"Pay attention to me…" he cooed.

"What are you, *five*?" I groaned, making a grab for the computer. He caught my wrist.

"I haven't seen you in so long and that's all you can say to me?" He pouted, though his eyes were entirely predatory. I felt my hair rise on end and I shivered at the expression. Whether I shivered in fear or from some other feeling, I did not know.

"I didn't want to see you," I snarled as strongly as I could manage, which was not nearly strong enough.

"Really?" Dana asked, a smile creeping over his features. "Then why were you watching me with your mother last week?"

I sharply pulled my hand out of his grip, glaring, feeling the angry fire lick the sides of my belly. Dana snickered and straightened, rounding the table with careful, deliberate steps, closing the space between us until we were only separated by one chair.

"Did it excite you?" he asked. "I never took you for a voyeur, Little Lily."

"You wish," I growled. "You're the one going around and whoring yourself out."

"Whoring myself?" Dana repeated with a raised eyebrow. "Oh, darling, let me assure you, I am expensive. Most would not have the money to buy me."

"Then why are you sleeping with everyone in the Commission like a whore?"

"If an opportunity presents itself, I take it," he said simply. I blinked, unable to stop my jaw from dropping.

"Seriously?"

"Karen was willing," he said with a confident smile. "I did not force her to do anything."

"Did you ever think that maybe it would hurt my family—my *father*—if you decide to stick your dick where it doesn't belong?"

"Then where does it belong?" Dana pushed the chair between us away, taking a step closer.

"In your pants!" I snapped. "Away from the married women and men!"

"What about the unmarried ones?" I stumbled when I found my heel connecting to the metal base of another chair as I retreated. "Like you?"

"Stay away from me."

"I love when you play hard to get."

Dana lunged forward, snatching my wrist and pulling me to him. I was momentarily caught off-guard but when I felt myself connect with his hard chest, I immediately planted my other hand against his chest and pushed away. I succeeded in turning, my arm crossing over my chest as he kept a firm hold of my wrist. He laid his hand flat against my pelvis, pulling me backward toward him, pressing us together firmly as his leg slipped between mine.

I gasped and my back arched as lightning ran through my body.

"Ah...there we go..." Dana whispered against my ear. I shivered from the vibrations.

"Le...let me *go*!"

"Shh..." he whispered, the air whistling past my ear and causing my skin to tingle. I bit my lip to stop the whimper that threatened to bubble out of me. I felt his touch so acutely. His leg between mine...his hand around my wrist...his other hand against my abdomen, holding us together...his breath against my ear...It was electrifying, feeling each cell of his skin transferring a pulse to mine, feeding feelings I had been trying to ignore.

"Don't...please, stop..."

My voice was so weak I didn't recognize it.

"I'm teaching you something, Little Lily," Dana whispered, moving his head to rest against my hair, causing his breath to fan against the back of my neck. I shivered again and my eyes fluttered shut. My brain ceased function, every spark of activity that would be dedicated to thought now focused on my skin and the sparking electricity between Dana and myself.

His hand on my wrist moved to cover my hand, pressing my fingers flat against my shoulder and collarbone. My breath hitched at the movement. He put pressure over my hand and guided it downward. My eyes flashed open as I remembered the fantasy I had at Archangel. I remembered the thrumming of the music as it moved our bodies together...the electricity and need I felt being with him...the feeling in my belly that caused my body to ache with longing...

His hand pushed mine further until I reacted almost violently to the feeling of my hand brushing the top of my breast.

"Don't be frightened..."

"Stop..." I pleaded. It was too intense. Too much...

"Don't be frightened," he repeated, his voice thick with something that almost pulled a moan out of some dark part of my soul.

His hand pushed mine until it slipped under the collar of my shirt and into my bra. I felt my hand slip over my breast, his larger hand covering mine. The sound that left my mouth was more of a choked sob than a moan.

"It's alright."

"Stop...*don't*..." I tried to form a coherent sentence, my brain filled with static. My other hand was grabbing at the fabric of his jacket as his hand pressed harder into my abdomen.

"What are you thinking right now?"

I shook my head violently, feeling tears in my eyes. The intense feelings coursing through me were too strong and frightening to comprehend. Why did Dana make my body react this way? Why couldn't I control my response to him?

"Are you thinking about watching your mother with me?" he breathed against my neck as I bent forward, trying to escape. I could feel the thrumming of my heart, causing my breast to heat and pulse under my hand. "Did it excite you? Even though it was your mother you were watching?"

"No..."

"You're moving your hips, Little Lily..." he noted. He took a breath through his teeth, making a hissing sound that caused the fire in my belly to consume me. "I love your reactions...so innocent...so virginal…" His hand ghosted further down my pelvis until it was resting over my school uniform skirt just above the junction of my legs, his thumb hooking into the waistband. I felt the smooth nail of his thumb pressing into my skin. I did not understand how such a small touch over such a small area could ignite the wildfire in my veins.

"I want to change that…" he purred. "I want to change your reactions from those of a virgin to those of a powerful woman who knows what she wants…admits it to herself…" his mouth pressed to my cheekbone just below my fluttering eyelid, "and *takes* it."

This time, the moan did bubble out of me.

"You want that, don't you?" he purred, the molecules of his breath moving over my hypersensitive skin like a hurricane. "What stops you? What stops you from taking what you want?"

I was not sure how he expected me to form a coherent thought when he was touching me, speaking to me in that voice, causing every nerve ending in my body to fire until it was raw.

My eyes looked around the room, wild in their sockets, until they rested on the face of Mark, watching from the window. If my brain had been working at all, I would have registered the horrified and angry look on his face.

"Stop! Mark is—" I tried to fight Dana, but he held me tight and I faltered. "He's watching us…"

"Who can blame him," Dana's cheek ran along the side of my head, his voice heavy and powerful, "when you're putting on such a delicious show?"

"No." I shook my head again, trying to move away from him. He pushed his pelvis against my back and his leg slipped further between my thighs. My hips moved in a counter motion, providing more friction. My breath caught in my throat and a shudder racked my body from head to toe. "S-Stop, let…let me go…"

"Don't fight it…" Dana whispered. "Listen to my voice…" he breathed. "Feel me against you, feel my heat on your skin…" I bit my lip almost hard enough to draw blood to stop the sound making its way up my throat. "Succumb to it…" I shook my head. "Let it wash over you…don't fight it…surrender…"

"I…I can't…"

"Yes, you can."

"Let me go!" I snapped. My legs had the consistency of jelly and refused to support me when he did release me. I fell to my knees, feeling the room spin around me. I was shuddering violently, trying to force my body to calm down, desperately trying to kick my brain back online so I could command my limbs again.

I jumped when I heard the door open. Almost as suddenly, Dana's sharp voice pierced my ears.

"Out!"

There was a thick, two-second silence and then the door clicked shut.

I spent a few minutes breathing hard on the ground, trying to figure out why the encounter had been so intense. Every time Dana touched me, looked at me with those eyes, spoke to me with that tone of voice, I lost all sense of will and became pliant and weak. But that time had been intense, so sudden that I was frightened to my core. What could I do to stop his power over me? How could I keep my head when he tried to use his seductive power over me?

"Little Lily," he said, causing my whole body to go on alert, "why are you so afraid of the way you feel?"

"I'm...*not*..."

"Really?" Dana chuckled, not convinced. "Then why were you moaning and moving your hips like that? I can read and understand your wants better than you can. Your entire body is crying out for me every time I come near, but you fight it."

"The...*hell* it is!" I growled as strongly as I could. My voice was shaking as much as my limbs.

"No?" he asked. "Stand up, then."

I took two more deep breaths before finally forcing my legs to function, though they were unsteady and I was not sure they would be able to support me for long.

"If your body wasn't reacting to me, how do you explain that display?"

"You...you forced yourself onto me..."

"You did not push me away," he said. "Doesn't it make you curious, Little Lily? Don't you want to know? Want to feel what it's like to be connected to another person?" My blood went hot again at his words. He must have seen my reaction because his smile grew. "You do, don't you? Then why don't you succumb to it? Why don't you push me against the wall and take what you want?"

"Why would I?"

"What's stopping you?"

"People can't just be taken," I snapped.

"Why not? The Commission does it all the time."

"I'm sick of telling you how much I hate what the Commission does..." I groaned, leaning on the nearby chair, trying to pass the act off as casual even though I was trying to support the weight my legs believed to be too heavy.

"Good, because I'm sick of hearing it," he said. "When you have a legitimate argument, we'll talk about it again."

"Why do you do these things to me? To my family? To Clark and the others of the Commission?"

"I'm going to have to ask you to be more specific."

"You just come in here and molest me, you molest Clark...you seduce everyone in the Commission...because of you, my family is being torn apart..."

"It's not because of me. Well..." he tilted his head to the side, "maybe a little bit. But I am not trying to drive a wedge into your family. I don't gain anything from it." He sighed and leaned against the table, crossing his arms. "Your mother was unhappy long before I came along. I just helped her realize it."

"And what about my father? You don't think he'll find out?"

"I'm sure he will. And don't you worry, Little Lily." Dana smirked. "I'll give your father all the attention he needs."

I could not hide my cringe of disgust.

"What?" he laughed. "You don't think your father could be interested in having sex with a man?" He shook his head. "That's what everyone thinks."

"You're sick."

"No, you are," Dana told me shortly. "You've lost touch with humanity, with feeling what you should be feeling. Society has told you these feelings are dangerous."

"They *are*," I snapped. "They can hurt people. They can cause you to hurt yourself. You should know, you're always hurting people."

"People are so sensitive," Dana chuckled brokenly, rolling his eyes. "No, I couldn't possibly feel attraction to *that* person..." he said, mimicking another voice. His gaze fell on me once again. "Why can't you feel attracted to me? What's wrong with it?"

"What's *wrong* with it?" I growled. "You're much older than me, you don't listen when I tell you no or stop, you are completely insane—"

"Get some new material," he groaned, bored. "I've heard all this before. That's not the reason why you can't feel attracted to me."

"Oh, okay, because you know how I feel better than I do," I sneered.

"At this point, I believe I do. You're trying so hard to hide that animal inside of you that *wants*. It wants so many things, and you try to placate it with school, and intellect, but because you are one of those special cases, that's not enough to sate you...you want *more*." He quirked an eyebrow. "Isn't that why you love debating with me so much? Isn't that why you react the way you do when I come close?"

"I don't know why I react the way I do, but I can assure you that I feel *no* attraction to you." Even I heard the weakness of the lie.

"I'm not talking about love, Little Lily," Dana said. "I'm talking about sex. Pure and simple. Nothing more." He leaned back on his hands. "Well...go ahead. Take what you want."

I stared, not sure what he meant.

"Why are you afraid of doing so?"

"I don't want you," I growled, my voice weak with uncertainty.

"Alright." Dana sighed, standing straight. I stared at him as he started toward the door.

"Damn it, Dana, do you have any idea what it's like to be overpowered like that? To be molested and..." My voice trailed off, not sure what words were coming out of my mouth. "I bet that if you knew what it felt like, you wouldn't do it."

Dana chuckled, his hand on the door knob. He hesitated for a moment and then his hand dropped to his side. He turned back to me.

"Little Lily, I was pulled, kicking and screaming, to a testing table, strapped down, and I had a lot more done to me than you may realize," he told me bluntly. "I do know what it feels like, and I also know what it can create." He placed his hand on the door knob again and opened the door. "I'm just curious what *you* will create out of it."

With that, he left, closing the door behind him and disappearing down the hall.

As soon as he disappeared from sight, my legs gave out and I collapsed again. The door opened and Mark came in, helping me to sit in a chair. I ended up breaking down, hiding my head in my arms on the table as I cried, Mark's hand rubbing my shoulder, trying to comfort me.

* *** *

"Mykail...did they ever do anything sexual to you when you were being tested on?" I asked, my fingers lightly running up and down his arm as he held me.

"Well, that's an awkward question..." he chuckled brokenly.

"*Did* they?"

"No." Mykail shook his head. "But that doesn't mean it didn't happen to the other experiments...a lot of the girls suffer rape and assault when they are being tested on...the boys, too..." He closed his eyes and heaved a deep breath. "Why the sudden interest?"

"Just something Dana said…" I told him, my head settling back to his chest.

"You need to try and stay away from him," Mykail whispered, pressing a kiss to my head. I tried to put the memory of Dana in the conference room out of my mind, but his touch had branded me, burning my skin and permanently scarring me. I was frightened to tell Mykail about it. I did not want him to worry more about me than he already did.

"He really rattled you…" Mykail noted, reading the silence between us. "What did he do to you? Are you alright?"

"I'm alright," I told him quickly. "He just…I hate him."

"…but you find him attractive," Mykail stated quietly.

"What?"

"You heard me. You're not alone. Everyone does."

"I don't understand…" I sighed, rolling my eyes and rubbing my face. "What is this power he has over everyone? What…what is it that he *knows*? What kind of…supernatural power can he possibly have?"

"It's not power. It's charisma mixed with madness. He's completely insane, Lily."

"Generally, when someone is insane or not right in the head, you get a feeling from them… a very specific feeling…" I said. "This…it's not the same feeling."

"No one knows what Dana went through to become what he is," Mykail said. "He's never shown any symptoms of trauma, or depression…he just *is*. Something shut off something in his brain long ago. Trying to figure him out won't solve the fact that he is dangerous."

I took a deep breath, using it to steady my nerves before I sat up and looked down at him.

"Mykail, do you want to have sex with me?"

His eyes went wide and his face flushed red.

"What's with that question?"

"I'm asking if you want to have sex with me."

"Well…yes, but…not right now," he said, his eyes suspicious and worried.

"Why not?"

"Lily…it's too dangerous. Dana is more perceptive than you think, and if *he* didn't find out, then your parents would find out somehow and tell him. It's just…it's not that I don't want you, because I do. But I am worried about the consequences."

"Like pregnancy?"

"Well…Dana took care of that already," he said, lowering his gaze.

"So…if I were to pin you down," I smiled devilishly, grabbing his shoulders, turning him onto his back, straddling his waist, "you wouldn't oppose?"

"Well…I wouldn't necessarily, but…" He cringed. "Lily, I can't be on my back…"

I quickly let him up, realizing the large joints of his wings were pinned under his body at an awkward angle.

"Sorry…"

"You're getting pretty daring lately." He smiled around his cringe as he moved onto his side, his wings adjusting. "I'm sorry…I'm not trying to be difficult. I'm just worried."

"Why?" I groaned.

"I don't entirely know…" he admitted. "I guess I'm a little afraid…" He grabbed me, pulling me into his embrace again. "I'm sorry. I guess I'm just not ready yet."

"I'm not afraid," I told him. "I'm not afraid of us being together. Why are you?"

"Maybe…because I know the danger Dana poses more than you do," he murmured.

"So, it's me being stupid and ignorant," I said, unable to keep the bite out of my voice.

"That's not what I meant at all and you didn't let me finish," he said. "I was also going to say, or maybe I'm just traumatized and want to take things a little slower. I don't know."

I sighed heavily and moved away, pulling myself off the bed and walking to the door.

"Lily…" he said, not bothering to mask his annoyance.

"I just can't do this right now."

"Do what?"

"This talk, I just can't right now." I shook my head, turning to look at him as I carefully opened the door to his room. "I'm going to bed."

"Lily, I'm sorry if I said something that upset you," he said, his voice worried.

"Goodnight."

* *** *

Friday was perfect for taking my mind off of Dana and Mykail. Clark asked me if anything was wrong, but I told him I was alright. The lie was surprisingly convincing.

I had spent a lot of time mulling over my reaction to Dana and to Mykail. The time for self-reflection had left me frightened. Not of

Dana, not of my relationship with Mykail being discovered, but of myself.

Dana barely had to touch me before my entire body was on fire and I lost all sense of self. And then I was able to go to Mykail the same day and push for us to have sex. I had even pinned him down and straddled him, ignoring his worries that he was not ready to take that step. I had seen my behavior becoming bolder, but it wasn't until after my small fight with Mykail that I came to a horrific realization.

I was *bored*.

Dana was unpredictable. Exciting. He made my mind turn in different directions, foreign and unknown. He had an air of authority, and having that power close to me was intoxicating, all-encompassing, almost giving me a high. I was bored in my relationship with Mykail. While the make-out sessions were nice and they made me feel good and safe, the element of danger with Dana caused my heart to race and adrenaline to pump through me at electric speeds. I was living on a constant adrenaline high with the revolution sitting in my mind, so Mykail's plan to "play it safe" was boring me.

As I tried to pay attention in my class, I had a long talk with myself, saying that I needed to cool off before I did something stupid.

That night at Archangel, I was able to ride the high with the other teenagers as we watched Devon and his band play on the stage.

Their music was great and it made everyone scream and dance excitedly. I stayed on the dance floor the entire night, though I did get some nasty looks from Commish Kids on the balcony. Clark made an excuse for me—I didn't care what it was—before returning to our little group and shyly enjoying the music with everyone else.

Jill was screaming at Devon and the others of the band, acting even more enthusiastic because of her infatuation with him. My heart fell when I saw how Becca was watching the girl she liked be interested in someone else. I went to Becca and embraced her in a short, side-hug.

"I love you."

"Thank you," Becca said. "I'm alright."

"I can always come over and we can pig out on ice cream and chocolate."

She smiled sadly, surprising me with her pained expression as she turned to me. "Aren't you too busy?"

I hesitated, startled by the hidden meaning of the question. I opened my mouth, but nothing came out at first. I sighed and forced a smile.

"I'm sorry." I grimaced. "I'm a horrible friend. We can find time. I promise."

"It's alright," Becca said with her own forced smile. "Besides, I told you I would help you if you needed it. Just let me know."

"Well, I need you to be sure that you have plenty of chocolate and ice cream at your house, because one day soon, we will hang out and binge on junk food so that we can complain about how fat we are."

When I got home late that night, I was surprised to find my mother in the kitchen, sitting at the table in her nightgown.

"Lily," she said, startled out of her trance.

"Oh, hey, Mom," I said, surprised to see her still awake.

"You're getting in late."

I glanced at the clock on the stove. "No...this is the normal time I get in..."

"Oh, really?" my mother asked, blinking at the clock. "I didn't realize...Can you come home any earlier?"

"It's a timed bus, Mom."

"I thought Mark was taking you and Clark to the club and bringing you home afterward," she said, puzzled. If I didn't know any better, I would have thought she was drunk with her level of confusion.

"He was, but not tonight." I looked her over. "Mom, are you okay?"

"Yes," she said. I hated that tone. It was the tone that suggested that the person was not alright, but they were not even making an effort to make it sound like a good lie.

"Where's Dad? Asleep?"

"No. He's at his office. He's trying to finish some things up with Samantha before the Europe trip." It took me several long moments to place the first name of Becca's mother.

"Oh..."

"Don't worry," my mother said. "I trust your father completely."

"I'm not worried," I said sharply before I could think better of my tone. She turned to face me fully as I stared her down.

"What's with *that* tone?"

"Does Dad know?" I asked coldly. "That you've slept with Dana?"

My mother stood. "What did you say?"

"You heard me."

She was silent and still for what seemed like a very long time. I felt my skin bristle, ready for the confrontation. She was caught off-guard, and with the way her behavior had been recently, I knew this was about to turn into our first real yelling match.

"Don't you look down your nose at me, young lady."

"How can I not? When you're cheating on Dad with the man that, a few months ago, you wanted to get as far away from as possible?" I shook my head in disbelief. "What happened to you, Mom?"

"I don't owe you any explanation."

"Maybe not," I agreed, angry, "but Dad didn't deserve to be cheated on."

"Lily," my mother started, rolling her eyes, "you're only seventeen. You don't understand how it is when you get married."

"If this is the way it is, then I won't get married," I snapped. "If being married means you betray the one that you agreed to love for the rest of your life, then I never want to be married."

"Your father stopped looking at me…" my mother said. "He stopped touching me. He stopped *loving* me. Maybe he was the one who found someone new first."

"Did you ever think that it was you?" I snarled. "Did you ever think that maybe your obsession with the leader of the Commission might have put some distance between you two?"

"Don't you dare pass judgment like that!"

"I have no choice, Mom!" I barked. "When I see that you wore your sexiest dress—a dress that you never wore for Dad because you were too embarrassed—to meet Dana, and I see him tie you up like an animal before fucking you on his desk—"

I didn't have time to register the slap across my cheek before the pain spiraled through my face.

"Watch your language," my mother snarled.

"Fuck you!" I snapped, retreating quickly to avoid another slap. "Mom, when did you forget that I'm your daughter?! When did you think that I was just another person living in your house that wouldn't be hurt by what you're doing?!"

"You need to back off. It has *nothing* to do with you!"

"The hell it doesn't!" I bellowed back. "You always told me that family was more important than anything! You said that we would always stick together and support one another and never hurt one another because the family was the strongest thing we had! But as soon as you get into the Commission, you forgot that!"

"I haven't forgotten!" she snapped. "I have tried, Lily! I have tried so hard to make it so that you and your father would both be happy, regardless of how I felt or what I wanted!"

"So now it's *my* fault?!" I gasped. "*I* was the one who made you cheat on Dad?!"

"I have always denied myself, Lily!" she said, not denying my claim. "I wanted you to be happy! I wanted your father to be happy! And now I have someone who actually cares about what I need!"

"Dana doesn't give a shit what you need!" I said. "All he wants is power and control over everyone in the Commission, even if he has to tear families apart to get it."

"He's shown me that it's okay to be selfish and want something more for myself!" she yelled. "I can't take care of you and your father when I have nothing left to give. I have a hole inside of me that has grown because I have been denying what I wanted!"

I glared at her darkly, feeling the words erupt before I could stop them.

"Well, I'm glad Dana could fill your hole for you."

I walked away, heading to my room angrily as my mother stormed after me.

"Don't you dare say such things to me! I am your mother!"

"No, you're not!" I screeched, turning to face her again. "I will never forgive you for what you've done to this family!"

"I have done nothing but provide for and take care of this family, so don't you act superior to me!"

"You've torn the family apart!" I cried. "I'm telling Dad about you and Dana."

"The hell you will!" My mother grabbed my arm as I turned to walk away. I was surprised at how much the grip hurt. I cringed and tried to yank away from her.

"Let me go!"

"You listen to me," she ordered. "You will not say a word to your father, do you hear me?"

"You don't control me!" I snapped. "I will tell him because he deserves to know!"

My mother slapped me again, much harder than the previous time and I stumbled. As I stared at her, the surprised tears rising to my eyes, she pointed at me, her eyes dark and frightening.

"You say one word about this to your father and I will throw you out of this house, do you understand?"

I stared, stunned and shocked and admittedly afraid of the expression contorting her face. I darted up the stairs to my room, forcing the tears back, feeling angry and betrayed by my mother more than hurt from her physical actions against me. Of course, my face hurt, but even when I went into Mykail's room later and straddled his lap, kissing him forcefully, and his hands went to my face, my anger ran hot enough to dull the pain.

When I went to Clark's house that Saturday morning, I was still furious. But at least I had patched up the little fight I had with Mykail.

There was nothing makeup could do to cover the light bruise that painted my left cheek, so when Mark greeted me at the door the next morning, he immediately took my chin as soon as he closed the door, turning my head to scrutinize the bruise.

"I'm fine," I said, lightly pushing his hand away. He reached forward again and took my chin, but I pushed his hand away once more, feeling ashamed of the fact that, even if I tried to explain what happened, he would not understand, leaving him to worry.

Mark hesitated before dropping his hand, looking defeated. He held up his hand again, telling me to wait, and then walked out of the room. I stood awkwardly in the foyer, not sure if I should wait for Mark to return or if I should try and find Clark in the large house. Even though I had been over many times for dinner, I had never gone upstairs, so I felt that I would be intruding if I tried to find his room on my own.

As I looked awkwardly around the foyer, a voice startled me.

"Lily!" I turned quickly, frightened by the sudden voice in the quiet house. Clark was at the top of the stairs, slowly making his way down. "I was worried you had gotten lost or something."

"Yeah, sorry, slept in without meaning to," I said, a little nervous that he would see the bruise and ask me what happened. I was not ready to talk about the fight.

"Melody and Cody are already here," Clark said, a light dancing in his eyes as he reached the bottom of the stairs. "This is really working."

"Really?"

"Yeah, Cody even got us a tour of the Censor Board office." He opened his mouth to say something more as he approached, but he also caught sight of my cheek. At first he looked like he was going to ignore it, probably mistaking it for something else, but when he was closer, he confirmed it was a bruise.

"What happened?"

"Don't worry about it," I said, dropping my head.

"No, I'm going to worry about it," he said sharply, reaching forward, but I backed away. "Who did this to you? Did Dana do this?"

"No," I said. "I…my mom and I got into a little tiff last night. It's fine."

"She *hit* you?"

"Well, I did tell her to fuck off, so I guess it's justified."

"No, it's not. Shit, and the Commission meeting is tonight..."

"So?"

"*So*?" Clark blinked at me. "What are you going to do when Dana sees this?"

My heart stopped. I had not thought about that. Dana had made it clear that he was possessive over me. I still did not know what he did to the boys who attacked me outside Archangel, but they seemed afraid to even look in my direction. Even though my mother had been the one to strike me, I was not sure Dana would be willing to let the injury slide.

Mark's sudden re-entry into the foyer broke me out of my stupefied state and I backed away when he lifted a hand toward my face. I flinched, closing my eyes, surprised at the sudden cold that pressed against my left cheek. When I opened my eyes, I saw the towel-wrapped icepack he was holding to my bruised face.

I lifted my hand to the icepack as he backed away.

"Thank you, Mark," Clark said with a smile. He turned to me and shook his head with a heavy sigh. "This might get ugly..."

"I know..."

"Come on." He motioned for me to follow him. "Let's go upstairs."

I followed him to his bedroom, where Melody and Cody were sitting around his desk, arguing over something regarding programming. When they saw me, they both greeted me, though they were surprised to see me holding an icepack to my face.

"What happened?" Cody asked after the obligatory greetings were out of the way. I shook my head and rolled my eyes.

"I'm clumsy and ran into a door," I groaned. "Decided to open the door without stopping to wait for it."

Clark did not say anything to contradict my story.

I sat on Clark's bed while the three of them programmed, using a language I would never understand. I looked around Clark's mostly-bare room, surprised to find it just as cold and staged as the rest of the house. The more time I spent at the Markus' house the more I began to wonder how much time they really spent at home and how much time they spent in the Commission.

I kept the ice pressed to my face, taking it away when my cheek would get sore from the intense cold. But when it felt warmer, I would press the cool towel to my face, lost in my own thoughts, moving mechanically.

I was not sure how I was going to face my mother again. A big part of me was determined to tell my father about my mother's affair, but another part of me was afraid to do so. I wanted him to know, I wanted him to understand how Dana was tearing our family apart, and I wanted to save him the pain of finding out some other way. However, in his ignorance, he was happier.

I was also worried that Dana would somehow get involved with my father, as well.

I had to wonder about what this would do to my ability to move forward with the revolution. If my own mother was against me, I was in danger of her turning me into the Commission if she learned what I was doing. If she found even the slightest reason, with how angry she was, I was certain that she would turn me over to Dana immediately.

I also thought a lot about Dana and what his reaction would be to the bruise. I considered not telling him the truth and using the same excuse I had told Melody and Cody. But I was worried about my ability to lie to his face.

A part of me was concerned that Dana would do something harmful to my mother if he knew she had been the cause of the injury.

It frightened me when I thought of how I could turn her over to Dana. I felt nearly no sympathy for her and was a little smug knowing that Dana would punish her. Granted, I did not entirely understand his frightening possessiveness, and I was not ready to stand back and let him own me, but knowing that I could use my favorable position to get something I wanted made me feel empowered and strong.

But I did not want my mother to suffer. Despite how angry I was at her, she did not deserve to suffer because I was upset. I had to remind myself that it was just a stupid, vengeful idea that might make me feel better for a while. It was not a course of action to follow.

"Sorry, we don't mean to ignore you," Melody said over her shoulder, startling me.

"Huh?"

"We're just kind of ignoring you."

"No, it's fine," I said, taking a deep breath, rolling the now-warm icepack in the towel. "Hey, I'm going to go to the kitchen. Do you guys want snacks or anything?"

"Oh, I can get something," Clark said.

"No, it's okay," I said. "I'm going to put the icepack back. I'll bring something up. Just keep working."

Before he could protest further, I walked out the door, trying to get my mind off my spiraling thoughts. I made my way to where I knew the kitchen was, though I had never been in before. I pushed the door open and surprised Mark, who whirled around from his spot at the counter.

"Oh, Mark," I said, also surprised to see him. I felt awkward at his reaction to my entrance, not knowing if I was intruding on something.

We stared silently at one another for a few moments before he walked away from the meat he was cutting and wiped his hands on a towel, walking to me. I motioned to the icepack.

"Thank you," I said. "I was just going to put it back."

I nervously gave him the icepack when he extended his hand. When he turned to put it back in the freezer I looked around the massive kitchen. The more rooms I saw in the Markus' house, the more I was convinced that it was a movie set rather than a home. The kitchen was enormous and designed straight out of a magazine, even though it had a cold aura.

My dilemma then was finding snacks to take to Clark's room.

I was startled by a tentative tap on my shoulder. Whirling around, I saw Mark step back, surprised by my sudden movement. I let out a sigh, shaking my head.

"Sorry," I said. "Um…" I looked around the kitchen and then back to him, motioning senselessly with my hands. "Do you know where there are snacks?"

He was silent and still and, even though I could not see the confused look in his eyes, I knew he had no idea what I was trying to say. I began stupidly motioning again, trying to imitate the motion of eating.

"Snacks? Do you know where they are?"

He walked to one of the large pantries at the side of the room, opening the door for me. I saw several canisters of dried fruit, a few baskets of fresh fruit, and several bags of pretzels, chips, and other snack foods.

"Thank you." I stepped into the pantry and glanced over the selection. I started grabbing a few of the bags, struggling to hold them all until Mark grabbed a few for me, holding them as I pulled the canisters out as well, even grabbing a few apples. I decided I would put together a plate of snacks to keep myself occupied and away from the computer talk going on upstairs.

I walked to the counter next to where Mark had been cutting up cooked chicken and set some things down, taking the items that Mark had been holding.

"Thank you." I grinned sheepishly, feeling guilty about his help when he had been in the middle of something else. I looked around and motioned with my hands to make the shape of a bowl. "Do you know where the bowls are?" I asked without thinking about it.

He led me to another cabinet, opening the doors so I could choose among seven different sets of bowls. I blinked at the selection and then picked the least fancy one, worried about breaking the nicer china.

I began filling up the bowls as Mark resumed cutting the chicken. I slowly filled the bowls, occasionally glancing at Mark, wondering what he was doing. When he had finished dicing the chicken, he walked to the far end of the counter and bent down, grabbing two dog bowls from the floor and placing them on the counter before retrieving the third. At first, I felt satisfied finally understanding that Mark was feeding the dogs, but then I looked at the chicken and began to wonder what kind of special treatment the dogs received.

It was starting to occur to me that the Markus' were the stereotypical super-rich family.

I watched Mark place some chicken in each of the bowls before walking to a covered bowl and scooping some cooked wild rice in the dog bowls as well. That was when I could not help but scoff, rolling my eyes as I turned my attention back to my own task.

I finished pouring pretzels and I grabbed a cutting board.

"Knife..." I murmured, glancing around the counter. Mark grabbed one of the knives on his far left, carefully handing it to me, handle first. Just before I took it, I noticed Mark tense, hesitating. I looked up at his covered eyes, wondering what had made him so suddenly nervous. He appeared to be staring at me, frightened and still, waiting to see what I would do with the knife.

I wondered if knives reminded him of the surgery where Dana had stolen his voice, and with the visibility of the scars along his sharp jawline, I was sure Dana had roughly operated on purpose.

"I'm sorry, Mark..." I whispered, feeling saddened by the thought of Mark strapped to a table as his throat was butchered. I wondered what kind of voice he had, what his laugh sounded like, I wondered if even he remembered how his voice used to sound.

I carefully took the knife and sliced into the apple, feeling as though I had just frightened Mark. I tried to cut the apple slowly so as not to upset him further.

Chapter Forty

The morning had passed in a flash and just before it was time to get ready for the Commission meeting, the four of us discussed the plan for getting the message on the Censor Board computers. Cody could get us into the Censor Board Wednesday after school for a private tour of up to fifteen people. It was decided that we needed as many of the Commish Kids as possible on the tour to mask our actions.

Melody and Clark brainstormed how long they would need to put the message on the computer while I tried to keep up with the conversation, failing miserably.

Once we had solidified most details of our plan, Melody and Cody hurried home to get ready for the meeting. Just as Clark was turning to me to say goodbye, panic grabbed my chest, a panic that I had been trying to ignore the entire day.

"Can I go to the meeting with you and your family tonight?" I blurted.

Clark blinked, surprised by the sudden request, his mouth remaining open as he thought over my request.

"Um…"

"No, never mind, sorry."

"No, wait, Lily." He grabbed my elbow before I could walk off the porch. "It's not normally done, but…considering…" His gaze shifted to my cheek. "Let me ask my dad."

Despite the relief I felt as Clark stepped away and pulled out his phone, I was still full of apprehension. My father had not seen the bruise and I had not seen my mother since I stormed away, but the knowledge that I would have to face both them *and* Dana that night sent my stomach tossing and turning in the cavity of my abdomen, threatening to tie my insides into knots.

Clark called his father while I waited anxiously.

The conversation was short and I felt my body relax when Clark nodded to me with a smile as he wrapped up the conversation with his father.

"He said it was fine, but we have to let your family know what's going on," he said to me, pocketing his phone again. He hesitated, retrieving the phone again when he caught the expression on my face. "I'll call your mom."

As he lifted his phone to scroll for the appropriate phone number, tears threatened to overtake me with gratitude for Clark. I knew I would have to face my mother and father eventually and there was no way to avoid them at the Commission meeting, but I wanted to entertain the idea that I could put off the confrontation.

Clark left a message for my mother and then brought me back up to his room, sitting heavily in his desk chair as I resumed my seat on his bed.

"What did you and your mother get into a fight about?"

I sighed and rolled my eyes, rubbing my forehead tiredly. "About Dana. About how I saw her with him and I was going to tell my dad."

"Why would you say that?" Clark gasped. "Dana distorts everyone's thoughts. Once he has them in his grasp, they are ready to defend him to the death...even against their own family."

"I know," I whispered, forcing the tears away. "I just...I wanted to see if I had really lost her to him."

Clark bowed his head and remained silent for a long beat of silence.

"She hates me..." I said, the tears refusing to be ignored. "And I hate her...but..." I closed my eyes and pinched the bridge of my nose. "She basically said that she wished she hadn't married my dad, that she hadn't had me..." I sniffed, my voice getting weaker. "How can she even *think* that?"

Clark stood, sitting next to me and wrapping an arm around my shoulders.

"It's not like that," he said. "It's *not*. My mom says the same things sometimes, but I know it's Dana talking, not her."

"It's not Dana," I snapped angrily, pushing my tears away with the heels of my hands. "She said that to me all on her own."

"You know that Dana's influence doesn't stop when he's not in the room," Clark told me. "He brings things out in them that you would never have thought existed. That is his power." Clark's hand tightened on my shoulder. "I'm sure your mother loves you. Dana's gotten into her head and he's rattled everything around, but she still loves you. You're her daughter."

"...I don't think she sees me as anything more than another person of the Commission who lives in her house," I whispered. "And it's not like we can ever get out of the Commission. We'll never escape him...She'll think like this as long as we're part of the Commission of the People."

Clark pulled me into a hug.

I had no appetite for dinner, and while they both didn't say anything, it was obvious that Clark, who was sitting next to me, and Mark, who was standing by the door to the kitchen, were worried, watching me play with my food.

I told the Markus family that I was just not hungry because I had eaten so many snacks throughout the day. Only Clark knew I had not touched food at all.

As Mark was driving us to the Commission meeting, I felt the butterflies rise from my stomach to my throat. I had no idea what I was going to say to Dana if he saw the bruise. I was hoping he would not be at the meeting at all. He had been distracted and busy in the last few weeks, so it was possible that I would not see him. But even if I managed to avoid him that night, there was no way to be certain the bruise would fade enough by Monday when I would be at the Commission after school.

I had no idea where Mark disappeared to when we arrived, and since we were so early to the meeting, Clark's mother had several tasks before the meeting, leaving Clark and I to loiter around the tables.

"I didn't realize you got here this early," I noted.

"Yeah," Clark groaned, watching his mother speak with Dana's other advisors before dividing tasks between the advisors and her husband. "We do get here pretty early...We don't need to do anything. We can just sit and relax."

I did just that. I sat at my normal spot and picked at the lint on the table cloth. I was tired and wanted nothing more than to sleep and deal with all of this some other day. I wanted to curl up in Mykail's steady embrace where the feathers of his wing brushed my neck as the weight of the wing acted as a blanket...I wanted to feel safe.

The door opened at the back of the room and I jumped, turning to see Sean and Dana enter the meeting room. While I felt the cold fear stab at my gut and shared a worried look with Clark, Dana's advisors rushed to gather around Dana. There was a large security detail trailing Dana and Sean that had me very curious about Dana's current distractions.

"I'm sorry, Danielle," Dana said, turning to Clark's mother, his voice conveying his annoyance. "Leader Simon is about to have an aneurysm."

"I understand."

"If this had happened after the Europe trip had returned, he would not think anything of it, but now he's sure that we're going to be attacked," Dana explained. "I will not be back tonight. I'll be holding his hand until he falls asleep at the rate he's panicking."

"We'll hold down everything," Ms. Peterson, one of his other advisors, said with a chuckle.

"Thank you, Emilie." Dana flashed a smile to her. "Then, I will expect to see a full transcript of the meeting on my desk before I get back."

"It will be done," Ms. Peterson said.

"Excellent. I knew I could count on you." Dana nodded to Sean who, in turn, nodded to the security detail. Four of them bowed their heads and made their way to the elevators. Dana began following the four men as Sean fell into step behind him. The leader of the Commission reached for his lapel to pull out his sunglasses when his gaze fell on me and he halted.

"Oh, Little Lily," he said, surprised. "You're here early."

My stomach fell when he addressed me. I was sure I was going to faint from anxiety when I saw him change course and walk towards me, his hand dropping from the glasses in his pocket.

I did not stand when he stopped in front of me. I had expected to flinch away, to hide from him, to be sure that he did not see the bruise by leaning my head on my hand to hide the discoloration. I did *not* expect to turn the bruise his direction, offering it up for him to see.

Look at the bruise. See what my mother did to me. See what you made my mother do.

As if reading my mind, his eyes locked on the light bruise across my cheekbone. His face hardened and he reached forward, his hand resting against my skin with incredible gentleness. He leaned closer and suddenly, my anxiety transformed into something I wanted to find sickening…but didn't.

I was gloating, proud that I had been correct about the way he would react to the injury. He was furious. I could feel it rolling off his skin as he looked at the bruise, carefully running the pad of his thumb over the mark. I flinched more than was necessary.

"Who did this to you?" he whispered, his voice full of dark purpose that made the hair on my neck stand on end.

"No one," I said, shying from his hand half-heartedly.

"Don't lie to me. *Who?*"

I looked away, wanting him to guess—maybe that would ease whatever guilt I might have felt about turning my mother over to Dana.

Dana waved Sean and the others of the security detail away and went to his knees in front of me, meeting my eyes as I remained seated. With one hand on my right shoulder, his other hand raised back to my cheek, the pads of his fingers carefully pressing into the bruise, his eyes focused on the discoloring.

The act was so gentle and tender that I almost felt warmth tingling through my skin at the attention.

He sighed heavily, his eyes still powerful and frightening, a dark promise flashing in the molten color.

"You're not going to tell me, are you?"

I managed to shake my head, even with his eyes boring into mine. Unnerved, my eyes darted to his lips, watching them part over white teeth. This was that perfectly choreographed dance he had performed with my mother. Each muscle moved just as it needed to, not any more or less, captivating me and keeping me captive in his presence.

"Are you worried what I'll do to them?" he asked, his voice quiet, soothing, yet had a hint of danger around the edges.

I nodded.

He said nothing for a few moments, his hand resting at my jaw, his thumb stroking just below the bruise, his gaze shifting to my cheek.

"Whoever hurt you needs to pay for what they have done," he murmured. His eyes met with mine again. "You should tell me who it was…"

It took everything inside me to shake my head.

"Dana," Sean called, "we need to go."

Dana held up his hand to silence his head of security and I was momentarily distracted from Dana's flawless face. The leader of the Commission of the People held up one finger to me with the hand he had shown to Sean, his gaze never leaving mine.

"This conversation is not over." The finger came to rest on my other cheek, trailing over my cheekbone and then down the side of my face to run along my jaw, his touch barely registering on my skin. "I am sorry that I have been neglecting you, Little Lily." The familiar intoxication overtook me again, his power radiating from his very being. "I will start taking better care of you," he promised. He leaned even closer, his warm lips brushing over the bruise, not kissing it so much as feeling it with his breath.

"Friday," he told me, though I felt his lips form the word more than I heard him speak it. He backed away, rocking back on his toes to stand, his thumb passing one final time over my bruise before his hand left my skin.

I wanted to kick myself for leaning forward, chasing the touch.

Dana left the meeting room, placing the glasses on his face as he moved with Sean and the rest of his security toward the elevator.

I did not register Clark had moved until he was already at my side.

"Are you alright?"

I turned to him, startled. "Yeah…" I whispered. "Yeah, I'm fine…"

I was pretty far from fine.

504

My actions and reactions had left me terrified, questioning why I was seeking attention from Dana, why I did not flinch from his touch, why I openly showed him the bruise...

Others of the Commission of the People began trickling into the room, socializing lightly while I remained seated, Clark by my side, both of us distantly staring at the floor. I could not bring myself to lift my head, caught up in a terrifying spiral of thoughts regarding my reactions to Dana Christenson.

"Lily," Clark called my attention. I followed his line of sight to the door. My parents had just entered the meeting room.

I took a deep breath and braced myself.

"Lily!" my father called, sounding relieved as he walked to our table and hugged me. "It feels like it's been forever since I've seen you."

"Well, you've been busy," I tried to say as casually as possible to hide the shattering of my heart.

"I'm sorry about...what on earth happened to your face?" he asked, grabbing my chin and turning my head to look at the bruise.

All previous notions of what I would say when he saw the bruise vanished from my mind.

"Karen, look at this," my father called. My anger rekindled, particularly when my mother leaned close to my father to look at the bruise as though she had no idea what had caused it.

"What happened?" she asked worriedly. I opened my mouth to speak, but the intensity in my mother's eyes told me exactly what would happen if I told the truth.

"I ran into a door," I murmured, looking away from my father and pushing his hand away. "I'm alright."

"We gave her some ice," Clark said beside me. "Sorry, it happened while she was at my house."

"You should tell her to be more careful," my mother laughed lightly, backing away and calling to someone else in the room, socializing in order to avoid me.

"Thank you for taking care of her," my father said to Clark, putting an arm around his shoulders. "You have to treat your girlfriend like royalty, particularly a one-of-a-kind one like my daughter."

"Thomas," a man beckoned, motioning him over.

"Excuse me," he said, walking to the other group. Clark sent me an apologetic look while I rubbed my temples with a groan.

"I'm getting a headache..."

I avoided even looking at my mother through the meeting. I could not concentrate enough to see where on the agenda we were, so I was constantly agonizing over going home with my parents. I was so anxious to avoid them that I even debated if I wanted to ask Clark if I could go home with him, unconcerned with the suspicions and rumors that would spread like wildfire if I were to do so.

But I was desperate to avoid my mother, and to avoid spilling any secrets to my father.

The meeting passed quickly and no one questioned the whereabouts of the leader of the Commission of the People.

It took us a while to get out of the meeting room at the end of the night as the others from the Europe delegation swarmed my mother and father, discussing preparations. Eventually, when we were able to get out of the Commission, I made a show of how badly my head hurt, not wanting to speak to either of my parents. I was worried about what I might say to them, the thoughts in my head unable to coordinate themselves properly.

I said goodnight to my parents and changed into my pajamas, slipping into Mykail's room when I saw that the lights downstairs had been turned off.

"It bruised…" he noted, touching the mark on my cheek. I decided that Mykail didn't need to be slapped for touching my face, even though I was still annoyed at how much attention the bruise was getting—I could not look at his gentle, worried face and be angry.

"I'm all kinds of turned around right now," I grumbled, straddling his lap and leaning my forehead against his as his arms encircled my waist. I wanted him to hold me forever. It made me feel safe, wanted, and loved.

"You don't need to think about anything other than this moment," he whispered, lifting his forehead away from mine before running one hand through my hair and smiling. "Just be here with me. Don't be with Dana, don't be in the rebellion…just be here with me."

"I wish I could just shut that part of my brain off," I groaned. "It would be a nice break."

"Do you want to give it a try?"

"You won't do what I want to do," I said, looking him over hungrily. He hesitated, his continued apprehension causing my heart to fall again.

"Lily, your parents…"

"First it's Dana, now it's my parents…" I groaned. I was too tired to actually be angry, but I was annoyed.

"I'm sorry…" he whispered. "Really…I just…"

"I know, I know, I'm sorry," I said. "It's fine. I'm just exhausted." I kissed him lightly and smiled against his mouth. "Hold me?"

The routine was the same—fall asleep in his arms, wake up alone. I absolutely hated it. I could not wait for my parents to leave for Europe so I could wake up with Mykail's arms still around me.

I pulled my protesting body out of bed the following morning and showered, half-asleep and mentally absent. I had to leave early for two reasons. One being that I needed to meet with Clark and go to the fort. The second being the need to avoid my mother.

Clark and I took a different bus than usual, intending to start our cleaning from the first entrance we wanted the Commish Kids to use when accessing the fort. As we opened the door in the rock wall of the old reservoir drainage pipe, Clark and I discussed how to keep the fort's true location a secret from the curious Commish Kids.

It was dirty work, fixing what we had found to be broken on our previous visit and cleaning out the bunk rooms, going through the preserved food to discard anything that was no longer edible.

We were filthy by the time we left Fort Daniels. We took a bus to another part of town where Clark called for Mark to pick us up. When Mark looked us over from head to toe, confused about the dirt and grime on our clothes, I told Clark that we could not go to his parents' home for dinner in that state.

Clark gave Mark instructions by leaning forward in the car and pointing where he wanted to go on the GPS screen. We stopped in front of a mini-mall, where Clark and I found the nearest store and bought some clothes from the sale rack. We went to the bathrooms to change before going back to the very-confused Mark waiting in the car.

At dinner, Mr. and Mrs. Markus paid little attention to us, talking about other preparations that needed to be made for the Europe trip, discussing what they had talked over with the others on the delegation.

Clark and I remained silent because we were eating ravenously.

Mark drove me home and even walked me to the door, holding the bag with my dirty clothes and the printed list Clark had given me of prisoners in the holding cells. I said a tired goodnight to my mother and father, who were going over papers strewn over the table and made my way to my room, where I forced myself to take a shower even though every bone in my body screamed at me to collapse into deep slumber. But considering all the dirty work Clark and I had done that day, I knew I had to wash before surrendering to unconsciousness.

I thought I fell asleep in the shower because there was a knock at my bathroom door that frightened me and pulled me out of a half-conscious state as I sat lazily on the shower seat in the direct path of the hot water.

I irritably turned the water off and stepped out of the shower, not awake enough to deal with my parents. I looked at myself in the mirror as I toweled dry, realizing I had a few scrapes along my arm and a bruise that was forming on my knee from cleaning the fort. Coupled with the bruise on my cheek, I looked like I had been in a fight.

I opened the door once I had wrapped a towel around myself and was startled to find Mykail.

"I thought you had fallen asleep in there," he said with a grin.

"I think I did…" I droned, turning the lights off in the bathroom and stumbling to my dresser, not even thinking about the fact that I was only clad in a towel in Mykail's presence.

"How did everything go today at the fort?"

"Really well," I said, angrily attacking the tangles in my hair with the brush as I fought to stay standing. "Clark and I are going to bring some of the others there on Sunday."

"I wish I could be one of them…"

"You still have your tracers, we can't risk it."

"I know," he said. "When your parents leave on the trip, though, I want to take them out."

"Oh, God, can we not talk about that now?" I asked. I still felt nauseous when I saw the miniscule scar on my hand that reminded me of the tracers. I could not stomach thinking about cutting into Mykail when I was already half-asleep

"Sorry," he laughed.

I replaced my brush and sighed, ignoring the fact that I was still wearing only my towel, and climbed from the foot of my bed up to the pillows, lazily pushing Dexter out of the way as I collapsed in the bed.

Mykail chuckled again and walked to the side of the bed, pulling the covers out from under me.

"Come on," he urged gently. "Under the covers."

I groaned but obeyed, crawling under the blankets and feeling Mykail tuck me in. I put my head against my pillow and took a deep breath, feeling sleep envelop me eagerly as Mykail took his spot over the covers next to me and tucked a few wet tendrils of hair behind my ear.

* *** *

I had never felt fond toward school, but I never hated it as I did now.

Monday was chaotic. Clark, Melody, Cody, and I were running around the school finding Commish Kids to go with us on the tour of the Censor Board. It wasn't too difficult until I was tasked with finding four Commish Kids who were not in my class, leading me to scanning the halls rapidly between classes, hoping to spot them.

By the end of the school day, I was certain we had found fifteen people for the tour and a few more just in case some could not make it. Clark and I discussed who would be joining us as we were driven to the Commission. When we found our conference room, we quietly brainstormed how we were going to bring people to the fort that Sunday, using the underlining method in our books to communicate.

Tuesday was filled with nothing but nervous thoughts and anxiety. My mind enjoyed throwing possible hitches to our plan at me at the most inopportune times in class, leaving me flinching and trying to take deep breaths to calm down, hoping none of my classmates would see my near-panic. I felt as though I was completely out of control. I had not programmed the mass message, did not know how it worked, and had to completely rely on Clark and Melody to pull this off without putting the entire revolution at risk.

When Wednesday rolled around I could not focus, not even on my two exams. I continued to stare into space, feeling frightened and worried about what would happen after school.

Getting a message out to the people was not something we could take back, particularly on the large scale we were planning. If we managed to succeed, that was it. There was no turning back. There were many times while planning the rebellion that I had thought it was the final step and there was no turning back from my commitment, but that day was when those outside the Commission would start to learn the truth about the institution they trusted to keep them safe.

Twenty people were enough to be a nuisance. But two hundred million would be enough to bring much-needed change to America.

Mark had been informed of our tour at the Censor Board and drove us there instead of the Commission of the People, even though the Censor Board was in close proximity to the Commission.

When Mark pulled up, Dean, Melody, Cody, and Sarah were waiting for us outside.

Mark pulled into the parking lot, remaining in the car, waiting to take us to the Commission once the tour was finished. I approached the other Commish Kids, commanding the nerves in my stomach to settle.

"Are you ready?" Melody asked Clark, her voice also tight with apprehension. We were all nervous. The plan was an enormous risk and we were going up against an enemy we, unfortunately, knew all too well.

"Yes," Clark said, clearing his throat and putting his hands in his uniform pockets. He had briefly flashed the USB drive to me in the car, so I knew he was holding on to it tightly.

"How are you going to get that inside?" Sarah asked.

Melody did not say anything and Clark took a deep breath, bringing my attention to him. He put his arm around me, dropping the USB into my pocket before his hand rested at my waist.

"What am *I* supposed to do with it?"

"Don't worry," was all Clark said.

Matt and Kelly arrived shortly after, which stopped my further questions. The nerves in my stomach had every reason to be upset. I had no idea how I was supposed to sneak in the USB when I knew the metal detectors and security measures inside were meant to prevent such terrorist acts.

My anxious state grew worse as more Commish Kids turned up in front of the Censor Board. Our group rounded out to seventeen people, so two agreed to stay outside and meet with us later to discuss how it had gone.

When we decided who the fifteen people of the tour group were going to be, I steeled myself and walked inside, keeping myself in the middle of the group.

The man at the security desk looked up when we swarmed the lobby.

"Cody!" he greeted brightly. "Are these the other Commission Kids for that project you're working on?"

"Yes, sir."

"Great. If you could just sign your names on this list, we'll get you checked in. Your mother should be waiting for you."

Cody motioned to me first. I signed my name on the electronic tablet with a shaking hand. Once I stepped back, Melody pushed through the group to sign next.

"Just wait for a moment. We'll get everyone checked in before we scan you," the man at the front desk told us.

Melody and I watched as two more people signed in after us. Melody turned to the guard.

"Excuse me," she called. "Where's the bathroom?"

"Over there, around the corner." The guard pointed in a direction close to the front door.

"Thank you." She grabbed my hand and pulled me with her. I followed, trying to hide my confusion, throwing nervous glances back at the group as the other Commish Kids continued to sign in.

Once we were in the bathroom, Melody pulled me into the large handicap stall, latching the door behind us.

"What are we doing?"

"Hold this," she said, reaching into her pocket and pulling out a USB identical to the one Clark had slipped into my pocket. "Don't put it in your pocket." I held the drive in my hand, watching her unbutton her school uniform top. "Okay, give me that one." She nodded to my hand. She slipped the USB drive under her bra to rest behind the wire under her right breast.

"Will that work?" I asked skeptically.

"I'll say it was the bra wire if anything goes off in the metal detector," she said. "Can you feel it?" she asked, moving her hands out of the way. I brushed my fingers over the underwire of her bra in the same way that Mark had checked me at the Commission. I did not feel a bump when my fingers brushed over the spot where the USB was supposed to be.

"No."

"Perfect, give me the other one."

As Melody slipped the second USB under her left breast, I laughed.

"It's a good thing you've got enough to hide these under."

"Lucky me," she said, adjusting herself. "They're actually a pain. Okay, can you feel any difference between the two sides?"

I checked her once again and tucked the second USB further under the wire when I felt it. Checking her once again, I nodded.

"Good to go."

She buttoned her blouse and composed herself, slipping her school jacket on again.

"Check again."

I ran my hand along the wire once more and shook my head.

"It's fine, just don't move too much."

We walked out of the bathroom to rejoin the others. Even though we had concealed the USB, there were no guarantees that we would get away with sneaking it into the Censor Board. I took a deep breath as we rejoined the students going through the metal detector as their bags were scanned. Upon seeing us return, those at the back of the group parted to fold Melody into the middle, being sure there were enough people behind her so the guard would be pushed to get us all through and might look past some things.

I went through the metal detector with no problem and my purse came out of the scanner without incident, though the guard still placed the bag behind the counter, as we had known would happen.

When Melody went through, her bag was fine, but the metal detector beeped. Everyone in the group tensed and my heart began knocking against my ribs angrily.

"Put your jacket through the scanner and go through again," the security guard advised.

Melody took off her jacket but when she stepped through the scanner again, it beeped.

"Do you have a watch on, or anything?" the man asked, standing from behind his desk to look her over.

"No." She shook her head, double-checking herself.

The guard turned and looked at another screen as we held our breaths.

"It's around your chest...do you have a necklace on?" he asked, turning back to her.

She reached up to her neck and felt along the skin, shaking her head once again. The security guard was puzzled for a moment, scrutinizing the computer screen, so I spoke up, sounding more calm and natural than I expected.

"Is it your bra?"

Her hands went up to touch the underwire and her face lit up in realization. I knew Melody was part of the drama department, but even I was convinced that she didn't think of her bra being the cause.

"Oh, it might be," she said. "This is a new bra from that shop downtown. It might use a different kind of underwire."

"Okay, that's fine," the security guard said, turning away, uncomfortable, not bothering with a pat-down. "Next."

I tried not to let the relief show on my face. Melody picked up her jacket and slipped it back on, smiling knowingly at me as I forced a wobbly smile to my lips.

The rest of the group went through with little trouble, though Dean forgot to take off his watch and set off the alarm again.

When everyone was clear and the bags and phones were checked at the security desk, Cody led us through a door as we trailed behind him.

Cody's mother was waiting for us on the other side. I had seen Mrs. Venner once when meeting all the faces of the Commission of the People, but I had forgotten how young she looked for her age, particularly with her small height.

"Welcome everyone," she greeted. "Oh, it's nice to see all Commission kids here."

"Thank you for agreeing to give us a tour," Sarah said.

"It's no trouble at all." Mrs. Venner waved the statement away. "Why don't we get started? This room that you see behind me is the directory room. This is where all the grunt work happens…"

I remained in the middle of the group with Melody and Clark while Cody fell to the back. I was sure no one was paying attention to the tour as we were guided through the building. My heart was racing and I felt warmer than usual, sweating as we went through the heated rooms of the Censor Board.

When we reached the main computer room, Mrs. Venner smiled and lifted her hands.

"Okay everyone, hands above your shoulders so I can see them," she chuckled, walking into the room where the various computer monitors were flashing the flag of our country as the screensaver. "Do not touch anything. We can only walk down this main aisle, so squeeze together…"

We filed into the main aisle, Melody behind both me and Clark, Mrs. Venner carefully stepping over wires backwards and talking about the function of the computers and the frequency with which the Censor Board used them. I had no idea how we were going to pull off our plot, but I was thankful that every Commission Kid on the tour was aware of what we were trying to accomplish, knowing they would play along with the situation when it arose.

Melody let out a yelp and before I could turn around, I felt Clark's hands on my shoulders as he caught himself from falling forward when Melody collided with his back.

"Are you alright?" Mrs. Venner called, having halted mid-sentence to look for the source of the shout.

"Yes, sorry, I tripped," Melody called.

"Watch those wires." Mrs. Venner had to raise up on her toes to look over everyone, though I could tell by the way she was looking that she could not spot Melody.

"Oh, my earring…" Melody whispered.

"Did it fall out?" Kelly asked. We looked to the floor and Melody kept one hand on her ear as the other rose to her chest and gently worked the USB out from under her bra through the fabric of her shirt.

"I don't see it…" I murmured, pretending to look around.

"Is everything alright?" Mrs. Venner called.

"Sorry, I lost my earring. It hooked on Clark's jacket…" Melody responded, her hand falling down her torso and extracting the USB from the hem of her shirt.

"Did it roll under there?" Clark asked, motioning somewhere I could not see. We were crammed together tightly, so it was hard for me to turn and see where he was pointing.

"Oh, I see it!" Melody exclaimed. I lost sight of her for a moment as she ducked under one of the desks. No more than two seconds later she came back up, using the table to support her, and hooked her earring back in her ear. I had not been able to watch her actions, but with the small smile on her face when she stood, I was confident she had succeeded.

"I got it! Sorry!" Melody said to Mrs. Venner.

"Ow! That was my foot!" Kelly yelped as Melody stood straight.

"Okay, we should probably get out of this crowded room," Cody's mother chuckled. "Come on, follow me!"

We filed out, the adrenaline pumping through me and causing my body to quiver.

I glanced back at Clark and he smiled, nodding once.

I barely bit back my triumphant shout.

As soon as the urge passed, I almost collapsed from the release of tension and added anxiety of knowing that this really meant we were reaching out to the people of America.

The final ten minutes of the tour went by far too slowly and I was anxious to leave. I constantly fiddled with my hands and hair, trying to remain calm and hide my shaking. I wanted to ask Clark so many questions, but I chewed the insides of my cheeks, trying to keep my composure and stay silent.

When the tour finally ended, I was the first one out of the doors. Everyone gathered on the front sidewalk as I took deep, measured breaths, both hands cupped over my nose and mouth.

"Thank you, Cody," Melody said with a broad smiled.

"Well?" he asked expectantly.

The simple word had everyone turning to Melody.

"We're all set."

Everyone let out a relieved sigh and, like me, began laughing in disbelief.

We had done it. We had actually managed to infiltrate the Censor Board and send our message to the American people.

After we had calmed and finished congratulating one another and Melody, Matt grabbed our attention again.

"Clark, what did you have to tell us?"

"Oh, right," Clark bent to his shoe and pulled out a piece of paper from his sock. "Did anyone else get this in their locker?"

"No…" they chorused suspiciously.

"What does it say?" Kelly asked.

"It says that we need to meet at nine a.m. this Saturday at the Bolt Campground outside of town," he said, passing the paper around. Clark had tried his best to mimic the handwriting of the person who had been sending us notes just in case we had to cover how secretive we were being about who was really planning the rebellion.

"Who gave you this?" Dean inquired.

"It kind of looks like the handwriting on the first notes...*kinda*..." Melody said, glancing over the paper.

"I guess we need to tell everyone else," I said, taking the paper as it was handed to me, looking it over as though I had not seen it before.

"We'll meet there on Saturday then." Cody nodded to the note. "I should go, though. It will look weird if we're out here too long."

"Yeah, I need to head home," Matt agreed. "I have a paper to write."

"We better get to the Commission," Clark told me.

Saying our goodbyes, Clark and I walked through the parking lot, heading toward the familiar car where Mark was waiting. When he saw us coming, he got out of the driver's seat and opened the back door for us.

As soon as he got in the car and began to drive, I turned to Clark excitedly.

"*So?*"

"So what?" he chuckled, leaning close to whisper to me. "It's all set. She plugged it in and started the program. It will spread like a virus from there."

"When will we see it on the computers?"

"Within forty-eight hours," he answered. "It has to spread through the entire system and catalog each computer. Then it will send the message out in random waves from all the computers in the Censor Board."

I smiled and danced in my seat, hiding my face in my hands, laughing in utter disbelief. Clark laughed as well, collapsing back in his seat.

"I cannot believe..."

"I *know*!" I gasped. We met eyes again and started laughing yet again, thrilled at what we had accomplished.

"Can I hug you?" I asked.

Laughing, we hugged each other, celebrating our victory.

Chapter Forty-One

There were no words that accurately described my shock at hearing my name being called by a familiar voice as I was walking toward Mark after school on Thursday. I whirled around. Mark even stood straight from his position leaning on the car to look at the person coming towards us.

"*Dad?*"

"Hey," he greeted, wrapping his arms around me in a tight hug.

"What are you doing here?"

"I decided that I have not spent nearly enough time with you lately, so I am taking you out on the town for some quality father-daughter time," he declared. I smiled, my chest blooming with affection, but it could not overshadow the heavy worry in my heart.

"Is...is that okay? Dana said that I was supposed to go to the Commission every day after school..."

"I think Dana would understand that I want to spend some time with my daughter," my father chuckled, keeping his arm around my shoulders as we turned to face Mark. "After all, I'll be leaving for a month. I need to spend all the time with you that I can." He turned to Mark, who looked back and forth between us from behind his dark glasses. "What do you say, Mark? Can I steal my little girl?"

"Dad..." I whispered, embarrassed.

"Oh, right," my father said. "I'm sorry, Mark. I forgot you can't speak."

"Dad," I said again, "he can't really understand, either."

"Mr. Sandover?" Clark said behind us, just as surprised by my father's sudden appearance as Mark and me.

"Clark," my dad greeted. "Since I'm leaving soon, I wanted to spend some time with my little girl. Is it alright if I steal her for the day?"

"Well...I mean...of course, you should spend time with her, but...did you talk to Dana about this? He might get worried if he finds out that she wasn't at the Commission today and he doesn't know why."

"I'll call him," my father said. "Or maybe you could tell him for me. Could you do that?"

Clark looked at me, his expression showing me how worried he was about breaking bad news to Dana. I felt fear rise within me as well, worried about Clark's safety, remembering all too well what Dana had done to Clark after I was attacked outside of Archangel.

"Uh, sure..."

"Thank you." My father smiled, rubbing my shoulder. "It's cold. Come on." He guided me to our car as I threw a worried glance back at Clark and Mark.

At first, all I could think about was the torment I might have subjected Clark to by agreeing to go with my father for the afternoon, but when I started spending the "quality time" with my father, my thoughts of the Commission of the People and Dana Christenson faded away. I did not even think about how Dana and my mother had been together. I was just enjoying time with my father as I had during times before the Commission.

My father and I had always had a special relationship. While I did not like that he was in politics, and what that likely meant for my future, he tried his best to leave the politician outside whenever he got home. He was always loving and caring toward me and my mother and tried to give us everything we wanted.

We used to spend one weekend out of the month for just the two of us. When I was a child in First Tier, our time would involve activities such as playing at the park, or going to the zoo, or spending money on ice cream and candy that my mother never wanted me to have because it would make me hyper. As I had grown older, those days changed to shopping and going to concerts that my father never really liked, but it would always end with dinner at a nice restaurant and some fun times where we managed to talk about everything and nothing.

When I entered Third Tier, schoolwork got in the way of those weekends and we had them less and less. By the time we got to Central, those times had disappeared.

As my father took me shopping for some new clothes—even though he was bored and horrified by some of the things I tried on—I started to realize how much I missed those days, and how much I should have valued those times when I was younger.

After shopping for clothes, my dad was an even greater sport by going shoe shopping with me. He played along when I started trying on ridiculous shoes just to make him smile. I loved his laugh and I found myself sitting down and hugging him in between every pair of shoes. I never wanted the day to end. I always wanted to be able to wrap my arms around him and feel him kiss the top of my head. I wanted to hear him call me "sweetie" all the time and spend time with me as if we didn't have the shadow of Dana Christenson looming behind us.

After purchasing a pair of new shoes, we went to a café that my father had become fond of, though I had never been there. Where ice cream had been in our days of the past, coffee now stood in its place.

We sat on the second floor, which was mostly empty apart from one elderly gentleman in the corner falling asleep behind his tablet screen.

"Thanks for taking me out today, Dad," I said, taking a fork full of coffee cake from the piece we were sharing.

"I don't know when we stopped having these days," he said with a small smile.

"Well...I had school, and then we moved to Central..." I said slowly, looking at the cake to avoid his gaze. "I guess it just kind of happened."

"You've really grown into a beautiful young woman," my father said, looking me over with sad eyes. "It was like I blinked and suddenly you were all grown up."

"I'm not all grown up, yet," I corrected with a laugh.

"You'll be eighteen in three months," he said. "Then you graduate and go off to university, and three years from now you will be getting your driver's license..." He smiled and shook his head. "It's amazing how fast it happens...you even have a boyfriend, now."

I blinked at him stupidly before realizing he was talking about Clark. I backed away awkwardly, hiding my face behind my coffee mug.

"I'm really glad that you're willing to look past Clark's face and shy demeanor and see what a sweet guy he is," my father commented. "You make me very proud to be your father."

"Dad..." I said, self-conscious.

"Am I embarrassing you?"

"*Yes.*"

"Okay, I'm sorry, I'm sorry," he laughed, raising a hand peacefully. There was a silence that fell between us, one that I knew meant the conversation was about to get serious.

"Lily," he started.

"Uh oh..." I chuckled before I could help myself.

My father smiled, using the side of his fork to collect the final crumbs of the coffee cake, his eyes pensive.

"I want to talk to you about your mother," he started, clearly just as nervous as I felt about the subject. My anger flared and my heart broke at the same time. "I know that you two have been at odds lately." He refused to meet my gaze. "But...I need you to cut her a break."

"Cut her a *break*?" I gaped. "How the hell am I supposed to do that?!"

"I know it's a lot to ask of you right now, but—"

"No, Dad, don't you understand, she's *cheating* on you!" I snapped. As soon as the words left my mouth, I regretted them. He looked up at me sharply and I backed away, looking away from his eyes, not wanting to see his reaction, a cold dread cooling the fiery edges of my anger.

For several seconds that felt more like hours, we were still and silent.

Finally, my father heaved a sigh. I mustered the courage to look at him. His face looked resigned, saddened, and dark.

"So, it's true…"

"You didn't know?"

"I suspected," he admitted. "With Dana?"

I nodded. He nodded as well and took another deep breath, pensive.

"I'm sorry, Dad…"

"It's not something you need to be sorry for, Lily," he said. "Your mother found Dana attractive and I was not paying attention to her. I saw it coming a long time ago."

"Do…" I swallowed hard, feeling a lump harden in my throat. "Do you not love her anymore?" I barely managed to say in a choked whisper.

"Of course I love her," he said. "More than anything. But…she's fallen under Dana's spell. It's impossible to compete."

"So, you know that Dana's manipulating her."

"Lily, Dana is very powerful and very influential in many respects. It makes sense that he would be attractive to many people."

"But…there is something *wrong* with him."

"I've noticed," he agreed. "But that something is addictive, it's powerful. He's like a drug. Once you get a taste of him and his power, you keep going back. And after a few times, you realize that he's allowing you to feel what he feels every day."

"What's that?"

"Powerful…like nothing can touch you…like you're more than human, and that there will never be another struggle in your life ever again," he whispered. "Why do you think everyone falls so easily? No one wants to feel burdened. Everyone wants to be able to take what they want without consequences and hardship as he does."

"But that's not the way the world works."

"I know," he said. "Some of the others also know that, but your mother is addicted to the feeling."

"Are…are *you* addicted?" I asked worriedly.

"A little…" he admitted. "What about you?"

I thought for a moment, recalling how easy it was for him to turn me into putty at his hands.

"A little."

* *** *

It was not until I was already at school the following day that I remembered Dana saying he would meet with me after school. I had been so worried about Clark that day that I hardly realized I would be alone with the leader of the Commission that day.

My fears for Clark were confirmed when I saw him after school.

I stood nervously with Mark by the car and, when Clark walked up, he refused to lift his head and look at me.

"Hey."

"What happened?"

"Nothing, don't worry about it." He shook his head, still looking at the ground.

"Like hell," I said. "What happened? Did Dana do something to you?"

"…I don't want to talk about it," he mumbled. "Dana wanted me to remind you that he wants to meet with you in his office as soon as you arrive today."

"Clark, I'm really sorry…" I murmured. "I really didn't know my dad would show up yesterday."

"It's not anything you did. You don't need to apologize."

Mark gently placed a hand on both of our shoulders, guiding us to the back door of the car, probably in response to seeing Clark shivering in the stormy November weather.

Once seated in the car, I turned to face Clark.

"I'm so sorry, I should have told my dad that it was a bad idea not to talk to Dana first."

"Why should you need to ask to spend time with your father?" he said dejectedly. "Lily, even if you had been there, he probably would have…" He shook his head. "I don't want to talk about it."

I hugged him tightly, trying to convey how apologetic I was. It broke my heart to think that I subjected Clark to anything. Even if Clark believed that Dana would have attacked him regardless of whether or not I had been there, it still caused me pain to see him looking so broken.

Clark hugged me back before clearing his throat, backing away.

"Sorry," I said, worried I had made him uncomfortable.

520

"No, it's not that…" he said, glancing at the silent driver before turning to me and nodding his head toward Mark. "He's already agitated after yesterday. I don't want to make him more upset because I start crying or anything."

When we pulled into the Commission, we went through the normal security procedures and rode the elevator to the basement, finding a conference room as if nothing about our routine was out of the ordinary from other kids' after school activities.

When I sat at the table and pulled out my homework, Clark blinked at me.

"Lily," he said, his tone incredulous.

"What?"

"Dana said he wanted to see you when you got here."

"So?"

"So? He will come and get you if you don't go to him."

"Then let him come and get me," I snapped. "I'm fucking pissed at him. I don't know what he did to you yesterday, but I'm furious. So he can come and get me. I won't go to him just because that's what he wants."

"Lily," Clark said, his voice desperate, "don't you realize how he plays his games? If you don't listen because you're pissed about what he did to me, he will do it again and again until you do what he says."

"No, he won't."

"Yes, he will, Lily!" he said, his voice choked. "And he would do the same thing to you if I disobeyed him."

"I am going to play him right back," I said coldly. "He doesn't need to know that I am upset about what he did to you. He just needs to know that I'm upset."

"I know you're strong, but there is a certain limit you have and he knows exactly how to push it. Don't do this to yourself, or to me."

"I know what I'm doing, Clark."

I knew I would need a few minutes before I could convince myself of that fact.

I pretended to be working on my homework while an extremely nervous Clark drummed his fingers along the table, unable to focus on his own schoolwork, agitated. A part of me was very curious about what Dana had done to Clark and how I could get revenge on the leader of the Commission of the People while still playing by his rules. But another part of me was still unsure I would be able to hold my own against Dana, let alone try to manipulate him back.

I looked up, startled when I saw movement outside the windows of the conference room, more agitated than I was willing to admit to myself. Sean was speaking to Mark next to the door, placing a hand on the shorter man's shoulder before opening the door to the conference room.

"Hello Lily, Clark," Sean greeted.

"Hello," we echoed.

"Lily," he turned to me, "Dana would like to speak with you in his office. Will you please follow me?"

I glanced at Clark as I stood. His face was noticeably paler than earlier.

The head of Commission security allowed me to step outside first and then led me toward Dana's office at a slow pace. I was sure he wanted to say something to me, which was the reason for his slow progression, but he seemed uncomfortable and did not say anything until we were about to round the final corner into the hallway of Dana's office.

He stopped me, standing directly in front of me to grab my attention.

"Lily," he started, "Dana is…in a weird mood these days. Please, watch your step around him."

"What do you mean he's in a weird mood?"

"He actually has to work constantly right now and he really does not like that," Sean explained. "He's getting bored and restless since his day is structured, so he's more aggressive than usual. He's looking for some entertainment, and he's not as tactful about it as usual."

I raised my eyebrows. "You mean he normally *is* tactful?"

"Good point," he admitted. "I've been trying to keep him entertained, but he's been around me all day every day for the last two weeks and he is bored with me as well. You have no idea what bored Dana is like. Please, *please* be careful. I will be just outside if you need me."

"I'll be okay."

"Don't go in there cocky," he said, his voice stern. "He will see it as a challenge and he will tear you down."

"Okay," I said, starting to feel legitimately concerned.

"I'll be right outside," he reminded me again.

I nodded, feeling the anxiety creep into my stomach. Sean led me around the last corner to Dana's office. He knocked twice.

"Dana," he called, stepping to the side to let me in as he opened the door, "Miss Sandover is here."

"Ah, Little Lily," Dana said, turning away from his table where he was looking over some papers. He looked as impeccable as always in his expensive, well-tailored suit. His dark glasses were sitting on his desk across the room, leaving me victim to his intense, golden stare. He glanced over at Sean and nodded once.

"Leave," he bit sharply.

I heard the door close and drew in a deep breath. I decided to ignore the warnings from Sean and Clark. I was going to try and play with Dana on his level. I was going to see how well I could match him if I pushed my fear aside and let my anger fuel me.

"You didn't come to me when you were told," he said. "Didn't Clark give you my message?"

"He did," I said, surprised to find my voice strong. "But he wouldn't tell me what you did to him yesterday. He refuses to talk about it. So I didn't want to come."

"Yesterday?" Dana asked, his eyebrows furrowing. "That was nothing. I just needed to remind him that I own him, and he needs to respect me as such."

"You do not own him."

"Yes, I do," he said. "I own his future, so I do, in fact, own him." He sighed and looked at the table briefly before stepping closer to loom over me. I stayed strong, staring at him, trying to keep my expression neutral, though I did cross my arms to guard against him. He lifted his hand, his fingers brushing over my left cheek. It took everything I had not to flinch.

"It looks healed," he murmured. He pressed gently into my flesh. "Is it still tender?"

"No."

"I'm glad to see that you heal quickly," he said, his hand remaining on my face. "Are you going to tell me who hit you?"

"Why does it matter?"

"Because I will not stand for it," he said simply, as if it was an already apparent answer. "Who hit you?"

"I am willing to bet that you already know," I said, looking between his eyes as he searched my expression. "And I'm sure that you know why it happened."

He was silent and then his lips curled upward ever-so-slightly into a smirk.

"Suppose I do," he whispered. "I still want to hear you say it."

"I won't," I said as strongly as I could in the hushed tone.

"Why not?"

"Because I have no reason to. You already know. If I tell you who, you know it will make me feel guilty and, therefore, weak to your influences."

His head tilted just slightly to the side in a slow, calculated movement. I was challenging him and he was prepared to meet me full force. His mouth broke into a smile and his eyes turned dangerous and predatory.

"Then why didn't you hide it from me when I saw you on Saturday?" he questioned. "You wanted me to see it. You wanted me to know."

"Because I knew this was how you would react," I said. "I wanted to see if I was right in assuming what you would do."

"And did I meet your expectations?"

"Perfectly," I told him with a smile of my own.

"Oh, you're feeling playful today," he said, his breath moving over his teeth in a stream that carried his voice flawlessly. Rather than let it overpower me, I tried to make that energy my own and meet it with the same seductive power.

"Playful was not the word I would have used," I corrected. "I am angry, and I don't want to deal with any of your bullshit today."

"Angry? Why?"

"Many reasons. You do a lot that pisses me off."

He chuckled and backed away, a light dancing in his powerful eyes that should have frightened me. I could not let him overwhelm me. He was like an animal. As soon as he sensed that I had backed down or weakened even a little, he would pounce.

"You do a good job of that yourself," he said. He stepped closer. I refused to back away. "You are feeling feisty today, aren't you?"

"You, too, apparently," I noted. "Sean said that you're bored."

"I am."

"You've lost interest in collecting people and mutilating them?"

He groaned and rolled his eyes, slumping as his hands fell to his sides as though he had given up.

"Oh, come now, Little Lily, you were doing so well," he moaned, disappointed. "You said that you weren't going to bother me about this anymore."

"Who said I was bothering you?" I chuckled. "I was trying to point out that you're acting like a spoiled child."

He perked up, interested again. I laughed and rolled my eyes.

"You have all the power a human could ever think of. You control the ultimate law in America, and yet, you're *bored*."

"Once you reach the top, you start to wonder what's left," he said, his eyes turning back to those of the dangerous predator he had been moments before.

"What is left is what there always is," I told him. "Someone to challenge your position, ready to take over as soon as they find your weakness."

His gaze darkened. I did not think he felt threatened by me, but I was sure he was appalled that I would so openly challenge him.

"And who might that be?" he whispered, taking another step toward me, seeing if I would retreat. "*You*?" He loomed over me. "You want to take over my position, Little Lily?"

"I want to take you out of power and help all the people that you've harmed."

"What I do is for the greater good, Little Lily."

"Nothing ever justifies doing harm to another person."

"And if I didn't take these people out of society and turned a blind eye to everything while unconsciously throwing money at the problem, like the Washington System used to do, I would be harming the other people in society. Which would you rather I harm? The criminals or the good citizens?"

"Some of those people in the back *are* good citizens," I insisted. "They might be minorities, but that doesn't mean they're criminals."

"They create discontent, regardless of their morals," Dana said. "They classify people. Gay, straight, black, white, Asian…Because they cannot be seen as anything other than these classifications, they set themselves apart from others, and then we have unrest. You think that humans are so accepting, but they're not. You want to live in a world where there are no classifications, no differences between people so that everyone can go about their lives as if they were meant to live it the same as everyone else on the planet. But the fact is, you are only one of billions…and billions of people are willing to fight for their own beliefs. And, when beliefs are different, people get angry. It's safer if everyone is the same."

"But you're making people even more diverse," I pointed out. "You're taking these people on the smallest difference, and then you're creating weapons out of them. You seem to be making a brand new species with Eina. And you, *you* don't want to conform to society even when people are supposedly all the same." I scoffed. "You just take what you want regardless of how it might hurt anyone else."

Dana smiled and cocked his head to the side.

"And you?" he asked. "You want to remove me from power and bring harm to millions of people…and *I'm* the bad guy?" He laughed. "Why don't you take what you want?"

"What I want?" I growled. I had only a split second to make my decision about how far I wanted to take our game. "What, exactly," I placed my hands against his torso, "do you think I want?"

I pushed him back, guiding him until he bumped into his desk and leaned back on it, a mischievous glint in his eyes.

"I must say, I am curious to find out," he said, his eyes passing over me hungrily. My hands trailed down his vest, stopping at his expensive belt.

"You would like that, I'm sure," I chuckled. "You've taken advantage of so many people, but how many people have actually made *you* take it?"

"Not many," he admitted, still grinning.

"Something tells me you would like me to order you around and tell you what to do," I said. "Someone who doesn't put up with your bullshit..."

"You think that's something I want?"

"I think so." I smirked, feeling powerful over him for the first time. I allowed my eyes to follow the lines of his suit down to where my hands rested before dragging back up his body to meet his gaze. A few breaths passed between us before he started to move forward to kiss me. I backed away, shaking my head, my hands leaving his body.

"Unfortunately for you, that's not something *I* want."

I waited to see his reaction, but after a few silent and still moments, the phone was the thing that broke the tense atmosphere. Dana growled, leaving it to ring until the shrill sound stopped and the pager came through.

"Dana," Sean's voice called. Dana ground his teeth together, pouting before irritably turning over his shoulder to the receiver.

"*What?*"

"I need to speak with you, now."

"I'm busy."

"Sir, this is a Code Five. I need to speak with you immediately."

At this, Dana straightened and turned around to look at the phone.

"A what?"

"Code Five," Sean's voice repeated.

Dana was still for a moment and then nodded once.

"Fine, I'm putting you on hold." He hit one of the buttons on the phone before turning to me, his eyes unreadable and obviously no longer invested in our game.

"Sounds important," I said with raised eyebrows. "I guess we'll just have to continue this another time."

I turned to leave the office, but Dana's voice stopped me.

"You should be careful who you tease, Little Lily," he warned. "One might jump back and bite you."

"You should heed your own advice, Dana," I said confidently. I walked out of the room. I felt his eyes on me right up to the moment that I closed the door behind me. As soon as I heard the latch slide into place, I started walking down the hall, feeling myself slowly come back to reality.

My legs began trembling. I ducked into Clark's mother's office and collapsed against the door, sliding to sit at the bottom, my breath thudding out of me as I breathed hard, a large smile splitting my face.

I had won a small victory over Dana. I finally played him. I knew it was not to the same power that he used on other people, but I still felt triumphant, like nothing could take me down.

I did a small dance while seated at the bottom of the door, smiling like an idiot to the empty room and pumping my fists excitedly in the air.

I felt even more beautiful and powerful after I had changed into my clothes for Archangel, and as I moved through the crowds of people and danced around the floor, I was certain I was invincible.

So when I got home and checked my emails to find an email from the Censor Board that contained my message of the rebellion inside, I was on top of the world.

I knew that was the reason for Sean's call earlier. Dana knew what we had done.

It was time to play our game on a whole new level.

* *** *

"Why do you seem so proud of yourself?" Clark asked as we folded some of the old tarps that had been used to cover the bunk beds in the fort. I smiled at him in disbelief.

"You're *not*?" I gasped. "It fucking worked! Our message is out there for the people to see."

"That means Dana can see it, too," Clark mumbled. We stepped together, folding the tarp. "What happened yesterday? You had a huge grin on your face when you came back from seeing him."

"Nothing." I tried to contain my pride at the memories of my meeting with Dana. "Just had an argument with him and I think I actually held my own pretty well," I said, folding the tarp into an even smaller square before stacking it with the others as Clark grabbed the last one.

"No one has texted me about the email, but I got it and you got it, and Melody told me she got it before we left the club last night, so I think everyone knows…even the kids of the Commission who might not know entirely what's going on yet probably got it."

"You sound nervous about that."

"Well…some of the Commish Kids might be loyal to Dana."

"Even after the whole thing with Miranda?"

"Some are too afraid to go against him," Clark said. He dusted his hands off on his jeans when I took the folded tarp from him, stacking it. "And now that Dana knows about the message, he'll try harder to contain people, particularly those in the Commission."

"Well, the tighter he holds on, the less likely he is to actually have control," I said. "He's getting careless."

"No, Lily," he said. "He's getting *dangerous*. If he feels threatened, we have no idea how he'll react, so we need to be very careful and quiet. That's why we need to meet here and we need to start figuring out how we're going to get experiments out of the Commission. Especially before Dana gets more dangerous."

I walked with Clark back into the main bunker, sighing. "I really wish we had a full blueprint of the Commission…"

"I'll compile the pictures on my computer and make a full map. We might be able to see something from that."

"Clark, about the weapons in there," I said, pointing to a room where the guns lined the walls, "do you know how to use any of them?"

"Are you kidding me?" he grumbled. "Guns haven't been allowed to the public in over fifty years."

"Then how are we going to use them?"

"Hopefully someone has some knowledge. For now I say we keep the door locked and don't let any of the other Commish Kids in there…particularly Dean."

"Agreed."

After cleaning up more and making sure that we knew where we were meeting with everyone tomorrow, we headed back into town where we had a late lunch. Then I went home to get ready for the Commission meeting.

My father had been moving around in a haze since our afternoon out and my mother was clearly agitated. I did not know if my mother knew that my father was aware of her indiscretion, or if she was still trying to keep it secret. All I could do was sit by and watch the rift between my parents get larger and escape into my own little world with Mykail when it became too much. Mykail tried to get me to talk about my feelings a few times, but I kept it to myself, choosing to focus on the revolution and Dana rather than my family problems.

When we got to the Commission meeting, there was a nervous tension about the room. Dana's advisors were upset and worried, and the others in the Commission were feeding off that energy.

I relished the feeling.

I knew what the main topic of that night's meeting would be.

And from the expressions painted on the other Commish Kids' faces, it was clear they knew, as well.

As soon as the second hand passed over the twelve on the clock, the doors closed and Mrs. Markus cleared her throat at the podium.

"Ladies and gentlemen of the Commission of the People," she started, "I will now call this meeting on the night of November nineteenth in session. There was a larger list of things we planned to cover tonight, but the program has been changed." Everyone glanced at one another, nervous. Dana stood near Sean at the front of the room, waiting for Mrs. Markus to finish the introduction.

"Therefore, all things that were on today's schedule for the meeting have been moved to next week, and the only announcement I have before turning the meeting over to Mr. Christenson is that we would like the members of the party going to Europe to come here Wednesday to meet with Leader Simon."

I straightened at the news that Leader Simon was going to be at the Commission on Wednesday. If he was there when I got out of school, I could have an opportunity to see how he reacted to Dana and if he could possibly be someone willing to help us get rid of Dana and the Commission.

"Alright, I will now ask our leader, Dana Christenson, to take over the meeting," Mrs. Markus said, backing away as Dana approached the podium.

Mrs. Markus sat at her seat as Dana stood at the front of the room, Sean just behind him, watching the leader of the Commission diligently. My heart began to race. I felt anxious and exhilarated at the same time.

There were several long seconds where Dana stared at the podium, silent and still, increasing the anxiety encircling the room. In my periphery, I could see heads turning as everyone shared glances, but I refused to move my focus from Dana.

"Dana…" Sean whispered, placing a hand on the Commission leader's arm as if to wake him.

Dana jerked his arm away from Sean.

"Alright," he started, "I'm just going to say this first. I am in no mood to beat around the bush or play games, so I won't." His gaze was sharp around the room. "How many of you checked your email at some point last night?" No one moved, unsure if the question was rhetorical. "It's alright, raise your hands if you did," he urged. Slowly, everyone in the Commission raised their hands. "All of you. And based on early reports, only three of you have absolutely no idea why I'm upset." He stepped out from behind the podium, fiddling with his pocket watch, glancing at each face in the room. The expression caused me to shiver and lean back in my chair.

"A message went out yesterday," Dana continued. "To be exact, six variations of the same message. They were sent to every computer, every logged email in America, from the Censor Board. The first wave of these messages went out to roughly twenty percent of the American population at 14:42 yesterday. About two hours later, another message went to the next thirty percent of the population at 16:03, and at 17:27 yet another message went out, this was the wave that included my own computer."

Dana stepped off the edge of the platform and started walking through the tables.

"This is propaganda against the Commission of the People," he continued. To me, it looked like something was restraining him from attacking those in the room. Seeing Sean trailing him so closely, I had to wonder if Sean was sensing the same danger.

"These messages seem to be sent at random to a random selection of computers, and while the first ones were from the Censor Board, another wave that went out was supposedly sent from our computers here at the Commission."

He stopped in the middle of the room and turned abruptly, going back to the front of the room, his head twisting and his body shivering as though electricity had passed through him. He swerved again to face everyone when he was standing in front of the platform.

"As some of you may know, Leader Simon has been throwing fits over the breach in the military computers last month, and now we get a message against the Commission that is reaching all citizens in this country. That is nearly three hundred million people." His angry gaze swept over the room. "This is a problem we cannot ignore. I do not know if this is the same group, or person, who hacked into the military computers last month, and I do not know if we are going to be dealing with an insurrection, but in order to be sure that the American people are able to rest easily at night, and also to put Leader Simon at ease, the Commission is reinstating the Sweeps."

My stomach twisted. Whispers erupted through the room, everyone reacting in similar fright at the declaration.

"These Sweeps will not be as severe as previous ones," Dana said over the surprised din. "There is no need for some of the lethal tactics, but there will be heavy crackdowns on anarchist collectives and groups that might even think of mounting a rebellion. We must find this person or group and destroy them quickly before the American people panic.

"As for the content of this email message," he continued, "yes, it is anti-Commission of the People propaganda, and it is obviously propaganda, but it means that something has compromised our security here. Unless it was someone within the Commission, the information these people released should be highly guarded. So," he glanced around expectantly, "is there anyone here who would like to come forward and admit to sending this propaganda and spare us the trouble of hunting you down?"

Everyone remained deathly silent, so much so I was worried my thumping heart could be heard through the room.

"Don't think I'm stupid enough to think that it's impossible someone from the Commission orchestrated this," he near-growled. "In fact, it is most likely that this *is* someone from the Commission." He glanced around once more. "No one wants to talk?"

The silence was thick and heavy as it hung over the room.

"Clark, Lily, come here," he called.

My parents whirled to look at me and my heart stopped. When I got over the initial shock of Dana calling me, I shared a terrified look with Clark.

"Don't worry, you're not in trouble," he said, becoming impatient, motioning us up once again.

I stood, my legs quivering as I approached Dana. Clark appeared just as nervous. We approached the leader of the Commission hesitantly as he turned us to face the room and placed an arm around each of our shoulders.

"What about the young people in the room?" Dana asked, looking around before turning to me, his face dropping close to mine. "What have you heard among the young people in the Commission after the fiasco with Miranda?"

I remained silent, hoping he could not feel my shaking.

"Clark?" Dana turned his head to Clark.

I was sure I had never been so nervous in my life.

"What about you, Dean?" He looked to the back of the room, where Dean jumped to attention in his seat. "Do you know who could have done such a thing?"

"No."

"Alright, everyone, listen the fuck up," Dana sneered, standing straight, though he still kept his arms around Clark and me. "I will say this only so many times before I decide to take people into the back. Any disobedience against the Commission from its members will not be tolerated." His voice was lined with ice, causing my skin to break out in goosebumps. "Whatever personal issues you have with the Commission or me, put them the fuck behind you and realize that you are fucking with the security of the whole damn nation. Is that understood?"

I, like everyone else in the room, was frozen to the spot.

"Now," he continued, "it might not be any of you, but know this. If you sympathize with this message, or you do anything to assist these criminals in spreading this propaganda, you will not only doom yourself to a lifetime of being an experiment of the Commission, but I will take your entire family. If this is not enough to convince you of the severity of this warning, know that I am willing to take all of you and lock you up in the back and bring in a new generation of Commission members, just like what happened to Washington."

Dana leaned toward Clark and me again and I felt his smile next to my face.

"This is particularly true of the young ones in the room," he warned. "You are not exempt from any responsibilities. Miranda and Julie should have taught you that. Choose very carefully how you spend your free time outside the Commission..."

My eyes dropped to the floor, certain my heart was about to give out on me.

Dana's hand moved from my shoulder to my back and he shoved me and Clark forward. I stumbled and almost fell, but managed to catch myself before my face hit the ground. I spun around, frightened that Dana was going to hurt us, but he simply waved us away.

"Go back to your seats."

"Dana, you need to calm down," Sean whispered, putting one hand on each shoulder, trying to anchor the leader of the Commission. Dana tried to move away, but Sean followed him and, eventually, Dana threw his arms up in the air and turned around to glare at Sean, like a child throwing a tantrum.

"Get the fuck off me."

I rushed back to my seat, where my father put his arm around my shoulders protectively.

Dana's gaze scanned the room again as Sean remained close to the leader of the Commission worriedly.

"Everyone in the Commission is now responsible for handling the people that are taken in the Sweeps in their respective regions. Be prepared to send a message to the people in your regions and explain to them that we are working to find the criminals who are trying to undermine Central, and that they will be dealt with quickly, before they can cause too much trouble.

"The Sweeps will be put into effect starting at the end of the week," Dana told us. "And no one will be exempt. As far as I am concerned, you are all suspects until our investigation proves otherwise. Do I make myself clear?"

The room was silent.

"Answer me!"

"Yes, sir," we choused.

Dana's sharp eyes once again scanned the room. He looked like an animal, intimidating the other members of the pack who were not falling in line.

After a few tense moments, Sean was once again at Dana's side, trying to steer him out of the room, whispering to him.

Dana shook off his head of security and stormed through the middle of the room, between the tables, heading for the back door toward the elevators. Sean followed, calling to him as the others in the room turned away from the leader of the Commission. Sean put a hand on Dana's shoulder to stop him, but Dana turned and shoved Sean to the ground.

Those seated close let out startled yelps and backed away as Dana loomed over Sean. I could not see Sean from my position, but Dana's eyes were nearly glowing as they bore into the other man, who remained on the floor, silent and still.

Dana stormed from the room, leaving us all in stunned and terrified silence.

* *** *

Clark and I were the first ones to arrive at the Bolt Campground the following morning. We were nervous and quiet, thinking about Dana's outburst at the meeting. After the leader of the Commission had left, the room had been still for a long time before Mrs. Markus told everyone the meeting was over and we could go home.

I dared not to speak to Clark or any of the other Commish Kids until I had gotten over the shock and worry that had settled in my gut, certain the threats at the meeting had deterred other Commish Kids from our rebellion.

"Hey," Clark greeted quietly.

"Hey."

"Did you turn off your phone?"

"Yeah," I said, showing him the black screen. I sipped the coffee I had taken from the house that morning and we sat in silence, shivering in the cold November air in the campground. There was a light dusting of snow in the foothills, which made everything feel colder.

"Are you sure this is a good idea?" Clark finally whispered after an extended silence.

"A good idea? No." I shook my head. "But we need to do it."

"I don't know if anyone will even show up after what happened last night," he murmured.

"Are *you* questioning things after last night?"

"I would be an idiot not to," Clark said. "Dana was furious. He was dangerous before, but infuriated…I'm sure he could do a lot more damage."

"I thought about this a lot last night. Dana Christenson is relatively unknown to the people. No one even knows what he looks like, so if he were to show up and start commanding things to happen, I doubt that anyone outside the Commission would immediately follow orders. And besides, he has to be sure to keep the people as calm and peaceful as possible, and he can't do that by pissing people off." I leaned against the same boulder Clark was leaning against. "The people won't accept the Sweeps being reinstated. It will cause chaos."

"We already did a good job of creating chaos…"

"Hey." I turned to him. "If you're not for this anymore, then it's best if you just leave now."

"Leave?" He blinked. "And what? Pretend I don't know what's going on? That I didn't help create this mess? Be Dana's pet for the rest of my life if he doesn't decide to make me an experiment when he gets bored of me? Just like you, I'm stuck."

I watched the varying emotions play over his features, the most prominent being fear. Of course he was afraid. I was, too.

The first person showing up at the campground distracted me. Sarah smiled nervously, rubbing her hands together, half from the cold and half from anxiety.

"Hey, Sarah."

"Hey, Lily," she replied. "Clark."

"We weren't sure anyone else was going to show up," Clark said. Sarah sighed and sat at one of the picnic tables near the boulder we were leaning against. She looked at her hands as she wrung them together.

"I wasn't sure I was going to come today," she admitted. "But when I thought about it...all that happened over one little message sent to the people. A message that we don't even know how they reacted to...but Mr. Christenson is reinstating the Sweeps." She shook her head and closed her eyes. "I realized that that is not what America is anymore. Central assured the people when the Commission of the People stopped the Sweeps that the system was going to run clean...and now Dana is putting the Sweeps back into practice because he says that the people are afraid. *Dana* is the one who's afraid."

I smiled and nodded in agreement, getting up and moving to sit next to her.

"You're right. So much for the corruption-free government Thomas Ankell fought for..."

As we waited, more Commish Kids showed up—even three new faces appeared in the crowd. When fifteen minutes had passed after the agreed meeting time, Clark held up a note that he said was held down with a rock on the table, showing us where we needed to go.

Clark and I pretended to be just as confused about the scribbled map. We all discussed it thoroughly before making our way through the trees of the camp ground. Clark purposely led us on several different trails and I would correct him, telling him where we needed to go so everyone would get disoriented. That helped ensure no one could easily remember how to get to the fort.

I was apprehensive about showing others the fort, particularly since I did not know who had told us about Fort Daniels and I did not want to doom the revolution at such an early stage. But, particularly after the previous night, we needed someplace safe to plan our next move.

As we were walking, I turned around and told everyone to turn off their phones, pretending to suddenly remember about the GPS tracking. This also distracted them from the circle in the trail that led us back to the first fork, and allowed us to pass the other way without anyone taking notice.

When we finally got to the cave system where the door was, everyone was nervous about going inside. Clark put on a brave face and ventured in, pretending to be just as anxious.

We had unlocked the door previously, so we did not have to worry about a key, and it would not lead to debate about who would be in charge of the key in the group.

A few people who had lighters tried to light the hallway we entered, but the flames did little to illuminate the dark passage. Clark and I felt along the walls, remembering that we needed to confuse everyone about how to get into the fort in order to keep its location safe. The fort was built to confuse. A few small crevices to the side of the main passage led to dead ends and some led in circles, so we wandered around with the frightened Commish Kids and, just when we knew we had them agitated enough to not pay attention to where we were going, I led them down the real hall and into the main bunker, which already had the lights turned on.

For over thirty minutes, all that the others could do was run around the fort, shocked at the discovery and wide-eyed at everything within. Clark and I played along, running up the stairs to the other spiral stairs that we had taken a sledgehammer to in order to distort them further and discourage the others from finding the power plant, though they were still accessible.

"Hey, Lily, where do those stairs go?" Kelly called from below.

"Nowhere," I replied. "It looks like there was some kind of landslide or something. It's just rock and rubble at the top."

"Hey, guys, I found a note!" Cody called, entering the main bunker, holding the piece of paper aloft.

Playing surprised, Clark and I went into the main bunker as the other teenagers gathered. Cody read the note aloud, though he struggled with the sloppy handwriting.

"The location of this fort must be guarded with your life," he started. "All signals are jammed here, and there are no bugs or cameras. Use it carefully."

I had tried to match the handwriting to the original notes we had received, hoping it was convincing enough.

"How do we know Dana is not behind all this?" Matt asked.

"This is not his handwriting," Clark said, glancing at the penmanship.

"He could be changing it," Matt said.

"Have you ever seen Dana's handwriting?" Clark asked. "Look at how quick this note appears to have been written. Dana's handwriting is completely different when he writes quickly."

"But who is giving us these notes, then?" Melody pressed.

"I don't know…" I shook my head.

I wanted to know the identity of the mysterious accomplice more than anything, but another part of me did not want to know. While it was frightening to think that our helper could be anyone, even someone trying to undermine the revolution by setting a trap for us, I wanted to remain in the fantasy that it was someone we could trust completely.

Chapter Forty-Two

Monday was dedicated to studying the blueprints of the Commission of the People in an attempt to find any way to break out the experiments. After Dana's speech, there was a different feeling around the Commission. Clark and I could feel the tension and worry through the halls. I was concerned that the USB would be found at the Censor Board and pulled out, therefore stopping the distribution of our message, but Clark assured me that the program behaved like a virus. There was no way for them to stop the message without shutting down and reworking their entire system, even if the USB was removed.

Clark was more concerned about seeing Dana again than the messages being sent out.

"I hope that he's in a better mood when Leader Simon comes by..." Clark said quietly.

I straightened in my seat, remembering Leader Simon's visit.

"Is Leader Simon afraid of Dana?"

"Of course he is," Clark said, still looking at his laptop screen. "He's not an idiot."

"So, he wouldn't try to stop us, then," I continued. Clark turned to look at me, glancing at the cameras in the corners of the conference room before leaning closer.

"Speak a little quieter," he whispered. "And I don't know, to be honest."

"We could ask him."

"Ask Leader Simon if he's alright with us taking down the second most powerful man in the country?" Clark asked incredulously. "Are you insane?"

"We could ask to meet with him somewhere else."

"He's the leader of the damn country. You think he's easy to get close to?"

"He's coming here and you said he was afraid of Dana," I pointed out. "If we told him we wanted to discuss Dana, then maybe he would be willing to help us, or at least turn a blind eye to what we're doing."

"Lily..."

"He's the only authority over Dana!"

"He has no authority over Dana," Clark snapped. "Dana has been running the show for a long time, telling Leader Simon what is acceptable and what's not. Trust me, Leader Simon has no control over him."

"But he has power over other areas," I mused. "The military, the press…" Clark glanced at me sideways and I sighed, rolling my eyes. "We need to at least see if it would be a possibility."

"And risk exposing us?" he challenged. "Hell no, Lily."

I remained still in my seat, admittedly pouting, before I stood and walked to the door.

"Where are you going?"

"Bathroom," I lied.

He knew I was lying, but he did not bother to stop me. Neither did Mark as I walked down the hallway past the other conference rooms and into the hallways of the offices. I approached the door I wanted and nervously knocked before I heard a soft "come in" from within.

Slowly opening the door, I poked my head into the office and smiled at the person sitting behind the desk.

"Lily," Sean greeted, standing and moving around the desk. "How are you?"

"I'm alright," I said reflexively.

"Good." Sean stopped a few feet away from me. "What can I help you with?"

"I actually wanted to ask you a few questions…" I started nervously. He motioned for me to sit as he moved back around his desk and resumed his seat. I sat in the only other chair, not bothering to look around the simple office.

"Is this about Saturday's meeting?"

"No. Well…yeah, kind of…"

Sean sighed. "I told you Dana was getting bored, and he hates being restricted. Just when he was about to get the first problem sorted out, this popped up, and he's chained to his work again. He was just throwing a tantrum."

"A tantrum that might cost the lives of hundreds of people, if not more," I said solemnly. Sean sighed and glanced at his computer, his eyes distant.

"I tried to convince him otherwise, but…he insisted."

"Did Leader Simon have any part in reinstating the Sweeps?"

"…no," Sean reluctantly answered. "That is the first item of business for Wednesday's meeting."

"Why didn't Dana ask Leader Simon about the Sweeps? Central swore that the Sweeps would never happen again."

"Dana is throwing a tantrum and trying to get Leader Simon off his back," Sean explained. "If he can convince Leader Simon that this is in the best interest of the country, then Leader Simon would agree."

"But, if Leader Simon says no to the Sweeps...then Dana can't reinstate them, right?"

Sean hesitated.

"...in theory..."

"Dana would do it anyway," I deduced, not asking a question as much as stating a fact.

"He tends to get what he wants."

"Does Leader Simon really agree with everything Dana does down here?" I asked after a short silence.

"I wouldn't say he agrees with *everything*," Sean corrected, refusing to meet my gaze. "But...he isn't about to say anything against Dana."

I nodded slowly.

"Don't worry," he assured. "Leader Simon is not in any danger from Dana. In a few days, Dana should get over himself a little and he won't be as testy."

Hearing the light teasing tone of Sean's voice, I hesitated before asking my next question.

"Do you care about him?"

"About who? Dana?"

"Yes."

Sean was still for several moments before letting out a long breath and dropping his gaze to his desk, as if the answer would present itself on the papers in front of him.

"Why do you ask?"

"I'm just confused about the way you talk about him," I said. "You can tease him in a way I've never seen anyone else do. You also don't seem to worship the ground he walks on like everyone else. It's like you can see past that spell he casts over people."

"No." Sean shook his head. "That works on me just the same as everyone else, but I don't hunger for power. I don't want anything more than what I already have. I just want a job to do, a goal to accomplish. I don't need anything else. So I don't get as intoxicated. It also took me a long time to finally get the nerve to stand up to him as I do now."

"Do you understand him?"

"Not at all, and I don't really want to," he admitted with a broken laugh. "I don't make excuses for him, or say that what happened to him all those years ago made him what he is and, therefore, he should be forgiven for his actions. He's cruel and he can be downright evil. I know that."

"So why do you work for him?"

"Self-preservation," Sean said. "I am stuck, Miss Sandover, just like you."

"You are the one closest to him," I said, my voice dropping, worried that Dana was hiding around one of the pieces of furniture in the office. "Why don't you do something about it?"

He shook his head.

"What would that do?" he asked. "It wouldn't accomplish anything. It would only bring rise to a new leader of the Commission. And with Eina close to being done, it will be almost impossible to stop the Machine of Neutralization project, regardless of Dana's influence."

"He's almost done?" I gasped.

"He's getting close to being finished, yes," Sean confirmed. He leaned forward in his chair, laughing nervously. "And now I've said too much." His warm, comforting gaze turned to me. "Is there anything I can do for you?"

"Oh, actually, I was wondering if it would be possible for me to meet Leader Simon when he comes on Wednesday," I said innocently. "I've never met him before, and I'm not sure when I'll ever have a chance like this again."

Sean glanced at his computer and moved his mouse before turning back to me.

"Looks like you'll arrive just as the meeting is finishing…" he mused. "You might be able to catch him on his way out. I can ask him if he would be willing to stay and meet you, if you would like. We have to work with his security team, so as long as they don't have a problem with him staying a little longer, I don't see why it wouldn't be possible."

"Could you ask?"

"I will ask his security detail."

"Thank you so much!"

"You're welcome. Is that all you needed?"

"Yes, sorry, I didn't mean to disturb you," I said, standing.

"Oh, no, it's no problem," he assured. "If you ever need me, you can come here. Or just call me. My number is in your phone."

"Thank you again, Sean."

"You're welcome," he repeated. "Oh, and Lily," he called to me as I started to turn away, "try and stay away from Dana until he's in a different mood, okay?"

"Okay."

I felt guilty using Sean, but I fully planned on finding out if Leader Simon would be willing to turn a blind eye to the rebellion until we had support from the people. I did not tell anyone my secret plan, thinking about how I wanted to approach the subject with the leader of our country and how I could do so without anyone around him noticing. I did not discuss it with Clark or Mykail, knowing that they would both try to talk me out of the plan.

I spent all of my spare time on Tuesday thinking over what I would say to Leader Simon. When I was with Clark, we discussed possible ways to get to the experiments cells and sneak them out of the Commission, but without further knowledge of how long it would take for an experiment to get from one door to another, it was difficult to figure out how to override the security system, shut it down, get the experiments out of their cells, get them out of the Commission, and then hide them in Fort Daniels before Dana and the rest of the Commission discovered what we were doing. And now, thanks to Dean, we also had the holding cells to worry about.

I was thrilled when Wednesday finally came around, and was not nearly as nervous as I should have been considering the situation.

I had not seen Dana since Saturday and was unsure of his mood. If he was still in his suspicious and angry mood then it was unlikely I could execute my plan. But I held onto the hope that he would be easily distracted that day, giving me a few moments to speak with Leader Simon discreetly.

I did not say much during the drive to the Commission and went through the increased security measures that had been put in place after Saturday's meeting. Josh checked all of us, including Mark, before we were allowed into the basement. When we exited the elevators and walked through the main meeting room, we were checked by another security detail before being let further inside.

I was shaking with exhilaration. The extra security meant that Leader Simon was still there.

I walked quickly toward the door, eager to put my bags in a conference room and search for the leader of our country. But when Mark opened the door for me, I retreated a step, surprised to see Dana, Sean, Mrs. Markus, my parents, and several unfamiliar faces in the hallway.

The correct nervousness finally made itself known inside me.

I stepped cautiously toward the group. Dana was the first to notice me, turning away from his conversation with my mother and Mrs. Markus.

"Ah, Little Lily," he greeted with a wide smile.

"Dana." I nodded to him tightly, stepping away to allow Mark and Clark to step through the door. I scanned the faces of the people inching closer to the exit, trying to spot the face I had only seen on television and in pictures.

"Miss Sandover," Sean called from over someone's head, motioning me to him. I eagerly answered his beckon, squeezing through shoulders until Sean could take my hand and lead me through the crowd of diplomats and the combined security teams.

Leader Simon was speaking to my father as I approached. He was shorter than I expected, shorter than my father, and even though his suit was expensive and well cared for, making his frame intimidating, his face was very different than it appeared on news broadcasts and interviews. He seemed meek and timid, nervous about where he was. I could not help but wonder if he felt intimidated being in the Commission of the People, where Dana Christenson lurked.

"Leader Simon," Sean interjected when there was a lull in the conversation. They both turned to me and my father smiled, pulling me close and hugging me tightly with one arm. "This is Miss Lily Sandover. She wanted to meet you."

"This is my daughter, Leader Simon," my father added.

"Thomas, you didn't tell me your daughter was so beautiful!" Leader Simon smiled, extending his hand out to me. "It is a pleasure to meet you, Miss Sandover."

"The pleasure is all mine," I said excitedly. Apart from the plan I had to figure out Leader's general attitude toward the Commission of the People and Dana, I was legitimately excited to meet the leader of our country for the first time.

"Are you in Third Tier?" he asked, breaking our handshake.

"Yes, sir."

"You are...seventeen?" When I nodded again, his grin widened. "So it's the year for *An Angel Without Wings*, then, isn't it?"

"It is."

"Are you enjoying it?"

"I am," I lied. I had not been reading the book recently, particularly when I got caught up in bringing other Commish Kids to the fort and putting propaganda out through the Censor Board computers.

"Maybe not quite what you were expecting to learn about the legendary revolutionary of our country," Leader Simon chuckled knowingly.

"Nothing ever is what we expect," I said, excited and feeling myself smiling like a moron. He obviously hesitated, so I spoke again. "I mean, we just met Bryant Morris in the book, and I didn't expect the man who founded the Commission of the People to act the way the book says he did," I continued, pretending not to notice Leader Simon's tense shoulders.

"Well, some say the book is exaggerating," Leader Simon chuckled, nervous. "His intense hatred and temper, I'm sure, were embellishments."

"No, I don't think it's exaggerating," Dana disagreed, suddenly behind me. "Actually, I think it understates many things, particularly about his temper."

"Well, you would know best, Dana," Leader Simon laughed, his voice higher with tension as he spoke to the man leading the Commission of the People. "Unlike you, I never met him."

"You didn't miss anything," Dana said. He put a hand on my shoulder and I stiffened, refusing to look at him. "I see you have met Little Lily."

"Yes, she seems like a bright young woman," Leader Simon said. "You raised her right, Thomas."

"Thank you, Leader Simon," my father said with a shallow bow of his head.

"It was a pleasure to meet you, Miss Sandover," Leader Simon said. "But...I believe that we're heading out, correct?"

"Oh, actually, Leader Simon, sir," I said quickly, still keeping the excitement in my voice to mask my nerves. "I have a final paper I have to write for this semester, and I was really hoping I could ask you a few questions. I'm in over my head with the topic I chose."

"What is the paper about?" Leader Simon pressed, confused by the request.

I felt Dana's hand slip from my shoulder and I heard my mother's voice behind me, much to my relief. It was the first and only time I was pleased that my mother had demanded Dana's attention, allowing me the few moments I needed.

"Well, because we're learning about the formation of the Commission of the People in *An Angel Without Wings*, I wanted to research what Central's role, specifically the Leader's role, is in the Commission. Thomas Ankell and Bryant Morris had to create a really delicate balance, particularly with the Sweeps and the cleansing of the American population. I wanted to ask you what your role is in the Commission now and how it has transformed over time."

"My role?" Leader Simon asked, clearing his throat.

"For instance, when the Sweeps started recently, how did you know that the people wouldn't rebel against the idea? You must have some say in what the Commission does because you are the voice of the people, so I wanted to ask you what that role is in the decisions."

"Lily..." my father said in an appalled and worried tone. "I'm so sorry, Leader Simon."

"No, no, it's fine," Leader Simon said quickly. "You know, I would be happy to answer your questions, but don't you want to ask Mr. Christenson's opinion?"

"Well, sir…" I said slowly, turning to be sure that Dana was still speaking with my mother. I leaned a little closer and dropped my voice. I was thrilled that he leaned closer, instinctively understanding my intentions. "I don't really feel comfortable speaking to him about such topics…"

"Ah, yes, he can be a little overwhelming," Leader Simon chuckled, clearing his throat again and running a hand over the side of his graying hair nervously. My heart was in my throat. I knew he understood. Maybe he didn't understand entirely that I was thinking of taking down Dana and the Commission of the People, but he knew that I wanted to talk to him about the reinstatement of the Sweeps and how we both felt about them. He was clearly willing to talk to me, which meant that he was also not happy with putting the Sweeps back into effect.

My plan was going better than I could have ever dreamed.

"Well, I don't have any time today, but maybe Saturday in the early morning, around nine?" he asked. "I can have my security pick you up and bring you to Central Hall."

"Really?!" I gasped, excited and thrilled at my luck. "That would be amazing! Of course, if you're not too busy, I know you have the country to run…"

"Nonsense, it's no trouble at all," Leader Simon said with a charismatic smile. "Besides, you and your generation are the future of the country and the Commission of the People. It's a joy to meet with you and discuss your ideas and opinions."

"Thank you so much, Leader Simon, sir!"

"Everyone, we need to move out of the hallway. Leader Simon's convoy is waiting outside," one of the security guards called. The mass of people turned and began moving out of the hallway, my father stepping in between me and Dana and my mother, who were still discussing whatever my mother seemed excited about. As I took a step forward, I felt a hand on my shoulder and stiffened in surprise.

There was a voice in my ear in the next moment.

"Tonight. Eleven-thirty," Leader Simon whispered. "Be outside your house. My car will be there."

My heart stopped. I nodded once as he straightened and began to follow me out, both of us trying to keep cool and calm.

"Lily," Clark called, pushing into the crowd with Mark when he saw me. "What happened to you? You vanished."

"Nothing," I said, turning to motion back to Leader Simon. "I just wanted to meet Leader Simon. I've never met him before."

"Clark," Leader Simon greeted. "It has been so long since I've seen you." He extended his hand to the other teenager. Clark smiled, shaking his hand.

"Yes, it has, sir."

"Ah, Mark." Leader Simon grinned, releasing Clark's hand and turning to the experiment. Mark smiled nervously, his eyes averted from the leader of America as he bowed deeply.

"Dana," Leader Simon called to the head of the Commission of the People. Dana turned quickly, startled. "I will never forgive you for giving Mark away. No offense, Danielle. I'm just jealous!" he said to Clark's mother.

"You can't have him, Leader Simon!" Danielle laughed, shaking her head. "He's mine."

"I know," Leader Simon play-pouted, putting a hand on Mark's shoulder, ignoring the way the experiment flinched. "I was first in line to get him but Dana gave him to you, instead. That wasn't fair, Dana."

"He's quite special, isn't he?" Dana agreed, looking over Mark. "Everyone wanted him. Before I gave him to Danielle, seven other foreign leaders were offering large sums. I was worried if I gave him to you, someone would steal him."

I gave Mark a puzzled look, not realizing he had been so popular. While I liked Mark and he always had a way to make me smile, I was beginning to wonder what everyone saw in him as part of a security detail that I did not know.

"And because I love him too much, I wanted to keep him close by. Giving him to Danielle was my only option. I still steal him from time to time when I need him," Dana added.

Leader Simon sighed and shook his head slowly.

"I'm still jealous. I would give ten of my security detail to have him," Leader Simon said. "My wife even wanted to buy him from you, Danielle. She was willing to pay a lot of money."

"I'm not selling!" Mrs. Markus teased.

"Too bad." Leader Simon shook his head, his hand dropping from Mark's shoulder. "If you change your mind, let me know. I'd pay good money for him."

"We'll have to see if *I'm* willing to sell him," Dana laughed. "Come, your convoy is waiting."

Clark pulled me out of the group as I rapidly thanked Leader Simon again, acting excited and giggly, even though my exhilaration was far more profound.

It had worked.

I had managed to secure a meeting with Leader, made even better by the understanding that he knew I wanted to talk to him about potentially treasonous actions.

It was impossible for me to concentrate on my homework as Clark and I sat in our conference room. Clark was busy trying to find some way to get people out of their cells, getting more frustrated by the moment when no solution came to light.

We faced a large problem when it came to the humans of the holding cells. It was entirely possible that they would be frightened to see the experiments and, therefore, would compromise the entire operation. It was also difficult to figure out how to tell these people to prepare to be freed and inform them of the plan when the holding cells and the higher wards of the Commission were always under such tight security. The only probable way we could conceive to get the experiments out was through the car elevators on the far side of the holding cells, but those were heavily guarded. And the security team at the front of the Commission would see Clark and me walk into the back. If we were to disappear, or even come back when all the experiments were gone, it would not be hard to deduce who had been responsible.

As Mark drove me home, Clark and I discussed in hushed tones ways we could trick security and sneak into the Commission. Clark agreed to look at the security system to figure out how to shut down the camera feeds, as well as how long he could keep them off during our escape. He asked me to finish going through my half of the list of the holding cells and decide which prisoners we could break out by the end of the week.

Throughout dinner, all I could hope was that my parents would go to bed early enough for me to sneak out of my room and go to the front of the house to be picked up by the car that would be waiting for me.

When dinner was over, I slipped upstairs to Mykail's room, telling him that I had a report to do and that I needed to get some sleep. He agreed with a smile and a gentle kiss, saying he would see me tomorrow. I kissed him back and went to my room, where I spent the remaining two hours looking over the list of people in the holding cells.

Unfortunately, my parents were not asleep when eleven-twenty rolled around. I opened my bedroom door carefully, also worried about tipping Mykail off that I was sneaking out. I heard my parents in the kitchen talking about the Europe trip. It surprised me to hear them speaking so civilly to one another, considering the heated arguments that had plagued our house recently. I carefully crept down the stairs until I could see my parents. I watched them, my eyes darting between my mother's back and my father looking at the papers in his hands.

My eyes glued to them, I descended the final steps to the door into the garage. Slipping through the smallest opening possible, I held the handle down as I slid the door back into place before moving around the cars in the garage toward the door leading into the backyard. Closing that door just as quietly, I slipped around the far side of the house and lifted the latch on the gate open, walking into the driveway and ducking under the windows of the kitchen, making my way to the front of the house, where I sat on the sidewalk behind some of the bushes to keep from being seen by my parents.

I knew I was behaving recklessly. I did not entirely know if Leader Simon was going to understand what I wanted to do, or if he was just tricking me into revealing treasonous thoughts to him that would cause me to be put in the Commission of the People before I caused too much trouble.

I wanted to give him the benefit of the doubt, but until I knew for sure, I was not going to talk about my plans for a rebellion. I was only going to talk about how I disagreed with the Sweeps and how, as Leader, he needed to put a stop to them. I was sure that would give me a good idea of Leader Simon's stance in regards to Dana and the Commission.

Each time I saw headlights, my heart raced. When the car that was supposed to take me to Central Hall showed up and two men ushered me in, I was sure that my heart was going to come out my throat in anticipation.

I sat in the dark backseat, shivering from the chill I had caught and anxiously wringing my hands in my lap.

I had been to Central Hall before on a tour many years previous, but was still surprised by the modern building, a structure of black steel and reflective glass that lit up at night, though no one could ever see what was going on inside, despite the glassy look of the walls. The building was meant to symbolize a leap into the future and the reflected sky was meant to show the serenity and peace that Central hoped to achieve for the whole country.

It was not easy for me to get inside Central Hall. I went through rigorous security measures and when I was finally let inside the large building, Leader Simon was pacing in the foyer, waiting nervously.

"Miss Sandover," he greeted with a shaky smile.

"Leader Simon."

"I'm afraid we don't have much time," he explained, reaching his hand out to me as he motioned the security guards away. "I can only sneak away for about fifteen minutes."

"That's enough," I assured, my voice tight.

"Walk with me and speak quietly," he advised, leading me into a hallway. I did not pay attention to my surroundings, focused on the limited time frame with the leader of our country.

"Tell me the truth about what you wanted to ask me."

"I want to know why you approved the Sweeps again."

"I didn't have a choice," Leader Simon said, staring at me as we walked down another hallway. I did not know where he was leading me, but I assumed it was somewhere where we could speak privately. "Dana wanted to activate the Sweeps again. There was nothing I could do to dissuade him."

"He said that it was because you were worried about being attacked and that there was a group out there plotting to overthrow the government," I told him.

"Well, there is that," he admitted. "Several weeks ago, the military computers were hacked and very valuable information was accessed. It's entirely possible that we have a terrorist group active in the country. But when the message went out over the computers…" He sighed and shook his head, leading me around a fifth corner.

"It seemed more like the message was geared against the Commission of the People, though."

"True…"

"Do you approve of the Commission and what it does?" I whispered.

He fell silent, and after a few steps he stopped and turned me to face him.

"The Commission of the People is very important for the security of the nation," he said. "Even when nothing is wrong, it's the attack dog that we can let loose if we need to." He looked around the hallway nervously. "It's *Dana* that's dangerous. I don't know if he's running the Commission or if the Commission is running him, but the experiments and the Machine of Neutralization project…he's not protecting the peace anymore. He's trying to provoke attacks to justify these weapons and I don't know why."

"Then stop him," I hissed. He rolled his eyes.

"If I could, I would have," he groaned. "But there is nothing I can do to contain him. As soon as I try he becomes volatile and dangerous."

"He's a *monster*, Leader…"

548

"I know," he whispered. "I know…" His eyes fell to the ground and he placed a hand on my back and led me further down the hall. "Do you have any suggestions?"

That surprised me. I was not expecting the Leader of America to ask me how to get rid of the man who was supposed to be the second most powerful person in the country.

"Suggestions?"

"To appease Dana, get him to call off the Sweeps…anything?" Leader Simon asked, turning to one door and opening it, stepping inside before me. I opened my mouth to speak, but before I could, a yelp left my lips and I jumped backward at what I saw in the room.

I was in Leader's office, and sitting at his desk in front of the flag of our nation was Dana, leaning back in Leader Simon's cushioned chair, his feet on the desk, Sean standing silently behind him.

"Good evening, Greg," Dana said darkly. His eyes turned to me. "Little Lily."

"How did you get in here?" Leader Simon gasped. "My security is supposed to keep everyone out of this room unless I am in here."

"You got your security from me, Greg," Dana reminded him with a cocky smile. He tilted his head to the side. "They know who their master is."

My stomach was doing violent somersaults. I had been caught in a secret meeting with Leader Simon. I thought I was going to be sick…

"Why are you here, Dana?" Leader Simon asked, his voice shaking.

"We need to talk," he said, taking his feet off the desk and standing up, adjusting his jacket and smoothing his tie before he walked toward us. He looked me over.

"Why is she here?" he asked, raising an eyebrow at Leader Simon. "Meeting with underage girls in the middle of the night in your office is a good way to start a scandal."

"It's not like that!" Leader Simon gasped.

"It better not be," Dana growled, his voice possessive and dominating. I shivered and retreated a step, trying to keep from collapsing, my brain filled with static. "Let's talk elsewhere."

"Alright," Leader Simon agreed. He turned to me and a wobbly smile came over his face. "I'm sorry, but I will have to answer your questions another time. I will call your parents and let them know when I have some free time."

"O-okay…thank you, Leader," I said, lowering my head.

Leader Simon stepped past me and out the door while I tried to remember how to breathe.

Dana started to follow Leader Simon. I flinched away from his hand as it pressed to the side of my head. His mouth dropped to my ear, close enough that I could feel the heat of his skin.

"Did you really think I would let you pull a stunt like this?" he whispered, causing my body to lock in fear as my brain raced, desperate to figure out what he thought I was doing there and what he already knew.

He turned his head. "Don't underestimate me, Little Lily," he breathed. He came even closer to my ear, his lips brushing my skin. "I know everything…"

He gently kissed the shell of my ear and straightened, his thumb brushing over my cheek once before he brushed past me, calling over his shoulder for Sean to drive me home.

I should have known then that I was in over my head.

Chapter Forty-Three

I was quiet for the rest of the week, worried that I had exposed the entire rebellion. But even after the horrible mistake of meeting with Leader Simon, Dana made no moves to show that he understood what I had been plotting. At Archangel, others asked what was wrong, but I quickly lied, saying I was tired. At the Saturday Commission meeting, I knew I should have been paying more attention, particularly because there was a lot of information on the Europe delegation that was leaving Tuesday, but I could not focus, watching Dana and expecting at any moment to be apprehended for treason. On Sunday when Clark and I met with the other teenagers to ask what they knew about the cells of the Commission experiments, I was asked again what was wrong with me, to which I told them I was just thinking about a lot of things.

Mykail and Clark did not know what had happened. I was both too scared and too ashamed to tell them.

It was on the Sunday night news that the word went out about the Sweeps being reinstated. There were speeches from Leader Simon and the Chair of Region Affairs about the terrorist message the population had received, stating it was obvious the Sweeps needed to be reinstated to preserve the peace of America and prevent another rebellion.

Our email message was never shown on the news and little coverage was given to the message content, which annoyed me, but considering I got another one of our emails earlier that very day, I knew everyone in the country was getting the message.

Monday, the entire school was abuzz with talks of the Sweeps and the email messages. My friends at lunch were even weirder around me than usual, thinking I would turn them in due to the aggressive actions of the Commission, though they did pluck up the courage to ask me once about the Sweeps. I told them the truth and said that I had no idea how the Sweeps worked and I didn't know what else to tell them because I was just as startled.

The Commission was also abuzz with talks of the Sweeps. Almost all of the conference rooms were filled with meetings from the various small groups within the Commission, discussing the Sweeps and related protocols, as well as outlining the areas of the country where the Sweeps were going to start.

I was starting to feel like I had taken on far more than I could ever hope to handle.

The constant movement did not stop when I got home. My parents were leaving for Europe the following day and were hurriedly packing, making sure they had everything they needed for their trip, telling me a million times the rules for the house and how I needed to behave myself in their absence. I helped them pack, despite my daze, and when they were heading to bed to get some sleep before their early departure, I trudged into Mykail's room and collapsed on the bed, where he reminded me that he wanted to take his tracers out the following evening to allow the wounds as much time to heal before anyone else saw him.

Sleep was a welcome relief from the noise.

That morning, before I went to school, I said goodbye to my parents, who were loading their bags into one of the cars of the convoy that had come to pick them up. All of us were tired, so they did not repeat the house rules again, saying a simple goodbye and that they would call me every now and then to check up on me. I wished them a safe trip and the best of luck on what they were trying to accomplish, of which I had forgotten the details.

It wasn't until the middle of the school day when I realized that I would be able to sleep in Mykail's room through the night.

I was so excited by the thought that I went through the entire day with a smile on my face. That made everyone think that whatever depression I had been in the previous few days had vanished and that I was feeling better which, admittedly, I was.

But I was still irritable enough to fight with Clark about the best way to get the experiments out of the Commission. There were several cells in the holding cell area where all four inhabitants of the cell were not criminals but minorities that could be persuaded to help us in the revolution. But when we started seeing how many in the holding cells were innocent, it became difficult to decide which ones were higher priority for our cause. We wanted to help the younger captives and those with physical disabilities, but they would not have been able to help us in the same capacity as some of the well-bodied captives. Very difficult decisions had to be made.

Also, we fought about the cell containing Miranda and Julie.

Clark had found their names in a cell near the back of the holding cell area, sharing a cell with a white-collar money launderer and a man who had committed seventeen acts of armed robbery in three different regions.

As much as we wanted to free Miranda and Julie, we were not sure we could get them out while keeping the two real criminals in the cell.

Then, of course, we discussed how we were even going to get into the Commission and get the experiments out in the shortest time frame without anyone noticing.

When we were both at each other's throats and frustrated, we gave up and finished homework, preparing for the final projects and tests of the term. Break would be coming up soon, giving me a reprieve from balancing school and the revolution and I was greatly looking forward to it.

When I got home, Mykail was waiting for me in the foyer.

"Hey."

"Hey!" I grinned, throwing my arms around his neck, kissing him enthusiastically.

He smiled into the kiss.

"How was school?"

"Boring." I rolled my eyes. "But...everything is better now, knowing that I have the house, and you, all to myself." I kissed him again. "Are you hungry?" I asked, starting toward the kitchen.

"Actually...Lily..."

"What?"

"I don't know if you should really eat just yet," he said quietly, his eyes averted to his feet.

"Why?"

As soon as I asked the question, I remembered what he had told me the previous night. He wanted me to remove his tracers. My stomach flipped and my appetite disappeared.

"Oh..."

"Yeah..." he said awkwardly. "I can take the ones out of my ankles and my foot, but the wrists and my wings..." He shook his head. "I can do my left wrist, but I don't really trust myself to work a knife with my left hand."

I set my backpack against the nearest wall and took a deep breath, letting it out slowly through my nose.

"Right now?" I groaned. "I just got home...couldn't we do it another day?"

"It's going to need time to heal," he reminded me. "And I know that if I let you get out of it tonight, you'll continue to avoid it." He took my hands. "I can't help you if I can't even leave the house. Your Commission tracers will also have to be removed at some point."

"Not tonight," I said strongly.

"No, not tonight," he agreed. "But...Lily, we need to do this now. Preferably before you eat something."

I closed my eyes and nodded.

"Alright..." I whispered, barely hearing the word leave my mouth. He kissed my forehead.

"Thank you."

"What do we need?"

"I got everything together when you were at school," he said, squeezing my hand. "Come on…"

I let him lead me upstairs, feeling the nervousness eat away at my gut. I already hated needles and sharp objects. I had almost passed out when I had my tracers put in. I was not sure how I was going to handle taking out Mykail's tracers.

I found myself in his bathroom, where the matches, small knife, tweezers, gauze, and bottle of whiskey sat ominously on the counter. I glanced at the whiskey and then turned to him with a skeptical eyebrow.

"It's for sterilizing."

He closed the lid of the toilet and sat on it, his wings barely fitting in the space between the vanity and the wall.

I took a deep breath to steady my nerves and then scanned everything on the counter once more.

"I already sterilized the knife," he said, watching me stare at the objects without picking anything up. "Do you want me to do the ones in my ankles?"

"Please."

"Can you hand me the knife?"

With trembling hands, I picked up the knife, feeling the cold metal of the handle more acutely due to my anxiety.

"Will you also flick the switch on the automatic kettle?" he asked, nodding to the electric kettle filled with water he had taken from the kitchen. I pressed the button before finally handing him the knife.

He took it from me with a reassuring smile. "Breathe, Lily."

I immediately let out a breath, but I almost forgot to inhale afterward.

He raised his left foot and folded it under him to rest his ankle on the porcelain lid of the toilet.

"I think this one will hurt the most…" he murmured, looking at the tattoo of 80073 along the bottom of his instep.

"Um…w-what else do you need?" I asked weakly.

"If you could have the gauze ready, that would be good."

I closed my eyes, light-headed at seeing him steady the knife, not bothering to grab the gauze at all. I turned to where I knew the counter was and leaned against it, lowering myself into a crouch and breathing carefully, keeping my hands on the cold vanity surface.

"Lily, the cut's done and the tracer's out," Mykail said long before I was ready to open my eyes. "But I need the gauze…"

I stood, feeling my head spin, but I grabbed the gauze and turned to him. There was blood everywhere. Over his leg and running down to the tile at his feet, on the lid of the toilet, and even starting to stain the fabric of the shorts he had tried to move out of the way. The blood pouring from his foot caused me to panic and I leapt forward, taking his foot in one hand and pressing the gauze to the cut.

When my eyes turned up to his face, I was surprised to find him smiling apologetically.

"What?"

"I'm sorry, Lily," he whispered. "I don't mean to freak you out or anything…this is just something that needs to be done."

"I know…" I peeled the nearly-saturated piece of gauze away, grabbing another one to press to the wound. "Doesn't that hurt?"

"A little," he admitted. "My tolerance for pain is higher than most."

I did not respond.

Once I had wrapped his foot and sterilized the knife again, he repeated the actions on his two ankles. I was quick to cover the wounds. By the time it came to the tracers in his wrists, I was no longer as light-headed, though I was still shaking.

"Are you ready?" he asked, looking me over nervously. "Because if you're shaking that badly, I don't really want you cutting into me."

I drew in a deep breath, grabbing the knife and rinsing it off with the boiling water before grabbing the alcohol and pouring a little over the blade. As I was putting the bottle back, I glanced at it and, before I had time to think better of it, I lifted it to my lips and took two large gulps. The liquid burned and it was repulsive, but I forced it down as Mykail blinked incredulously at me.

"What the hell?"

"Oh…that was a bad idea…" I groaned, setting the bottle down with a clank.

"You need to do this quickly before that gets into your bloodstream on an empty stomach," Mykail said. "Let's get this done and get some food in you, quickly."

Not really registering the meaning of his words or his concern, I took another deep breath, carefully taking one of his wrists. My eyes were locked on the far side of his wrist, where the chip was embedded and the scar was barely visible. Focusing only on that spot, I pressed the tip of the knife to his skin.

The blood pooled and dripped onto my arm, surprising me, but I forced myself not to jump or flinch. Carefully repositioning the knife, I made another small incision and then pinched the area, seeing the tiny black chip rise to the surface.

Carefully picking it out, I got the gauze and pressed it to the wound as Mykail smiled.

"See? Easy."

"I wouldn't say easy..."

He pulled his hand away and pressed his wrist against his chest, holding the gauze against his skin as he extended his other hand to me.

"Let's get this done."

When both wrists were free of the tracers, I wrapped the wounds with gauze.

Removing the tracers from the wings proved to be easier for me, but more difficult on Mykail. His wings were very sensitive, particularly where the tracers were, which was close to where the stretched skin met with the thicker skin over the bones of his wings.

He cringed and tried very hard not to flinch when I first cut into the thick skin where only small feathers grew, but he moved, prompting us to switch positions. He turned around and rested his chest and head on the tank of the toilet while his wing stretched over the vanity, allowing me more room to move and more stability for him.

It took me a while to get through the thick skin and feathers, and then I had to search around the torn skin carefully to find the chip, which was difficult to spot since the cut was not as clean.

The second wing went a little smoother, but it was still very painful for him and I was starting to feel a little dizzy, though it was probably mostly due to alcohol.

Both wings were wrapped and, when it was over, we hugged tightly, ignoring the mess of blood around us, holding one another close.

* *** *

I knew Mykail felt better later on in the night because he was teasing me about drinking on an empty stomach and getting drunk so easily. I was sure I was not *drunk*, but I definitely felt the alcohol as the hours passed. Even though I had eaten, I was still dizzy, and a little giggly.

He did most of the cleaning in the bathroom, limping as he returned everything, carefully cleaning the blood in the bathroom while I cooked dinner, stumbling around the kitchen like an idiot.

Dinner finished, I giddily went up to his room with him, leaving the dishes in the sink, and pulled him onto the bed with me, kissing him passionately, canting my hips toward his.

He kissed me for a few minutes before pulling away and shaking his head.

"No, no," he chuckled. "You're drunk. We're not doing anything more tonight."

"I'm not drunk!"

"Go get some pajamas on and then we're going to sleep," he said, climbing off me.

"No."

"Lily, if you don't respect my wishes about not going any further tonight, then you can't sleep in here with me," he said, his tone slightly condescending, though he was smiling. "Do you want to sleep in here?"

"Yes…" I pouted.

The next morning, waking up in his arms was almost euphoric enough to overpower the pain of my headache.

But not quite.

I hid under the blankets while Mykail got me aspirin and water, smiling while I glared at him.

I still had to go to school, despite my pounding head. I slept in my first class, made an idiot of myself in English when I said something in response to a question that I had misinterpreted, and then fell asleep again in art class, only to be rudely awakened by my teacher.

When I got out of school, I was so slow that Clark had arrived at the car before me.

"Hey," I groaned, shivering at the cold.

"Hey, you look…tired," Clark noted. "What happened? Now that the parents are out of the house, you broke into the liquor cabinet?" he teased. I glared at him and his jaw dropped. "Lily!" he laughed in disbelief.

"Shut up…"

I was not in a talkative mood and I was irritable, so when I felt myself getting angry at Clark for absolutely nothing, I told him I was going to go into the records room to look for any older blueprints of the Commission that might have shown secret passages in and out of the cells.

I only looked for five minutes before taking a risk and falling asleep against one of the cabinets. I managed to sleep for about twenty minutes before my aching back and neck woke me up and I irritably said "fuck it" and left. As I was walking out of the library, though, something else tested my nerves.

"What were you doing in the library, Little Lily?"

I ground my teeth together, rolling my eyes. Of all the people I could have run in to outside the library, it had to be Dana fucking Christenson on a day where I was angry at the sun for shining.

"Research," I said, watching him approach. "For the paper I wanted Leader Simon's help on."

"Don't give me that bullshit again," Dana said, rolling his eyes as he stopped in front of me. "You look terrible."

"Thanks," I growled.

"What happened last night?" he pressed, looking me over with predatory precision, searching for clues.

"I was drinking to celebrate my parents getting away from you," I snapped.

"So this is you with a hangover," he noted. "Good to know…"

"If you'll excuse me," I said sharply, "I have a paper to write."

"No, you're not excused. We need to talk about what happened on Wednesday."

"Why?"

"Because I need to scold you for going to Leader Simon behind my back and planting ideas in his head."

"What the hell are you talking about?"

"You've already told me that you're trying to take me out of my position, and I was curious to see how you were going to attempt such a feat. I did not expect you to go to Leader Simon, but the truth is, he's off limits in our game." Dana placed his hands in his pockets, one hand clearly playing with his pocket watch. "I don't mind playing with you, but you cannot use Leader Simon. He's mine."

"You're talking about this like a fucking board game."

"With a much bigger board," he agreed. "Leader Simon is a very easily influenced man. If he begins to think that there is a way to rebel against me, I have to prove to him that he can never get away from me and, frankly, I don't have time for that right now. I have too much on my plate."

"I just wanted his opinion on a few things about the Commission and I wanted to know where he stood when it came to the decisions you make," I told him. "I need to know if he's going to be in the way of our little *game*."

Dana's smile widened despite the angry and sarcastic tone lining my voice.

"In the way?" he asked, stepping closer. "Or someone you can use against me?"

"Whichever you're more inclined to believe," I answered. "Not like I can convince you otherwise, anyway."

"Generally, no." He grabbed my arm, pulling me close and wrapping his other hand around my waist. "But I must say, I was very impressed by what you did a couple weeks ago when you were teasing me." He pressed his hand flat against the small of my back and leaned over me. "You're starting to get the idea…"

"Let me go."

"No."

"I'm in no mood to play with you right now," I snapped. "I said, let me go."

"Make me."

I reached down and grabbed at the front of his pants, pressing my fingers into him roughly. He stilled, but he did not seem worried about my hand around his genitals. I tried to ignore any strange feelings I experienced at the touch and glared at him the best I could, trying to growl.

"I will only say this once more…Let. Me. Go."

Dana smiled and the hand that had been holding my lower back slipped further down and groped me through my jeans. I tried to worm away from him but his eyes lit up and he smiled.

"You seem to be a little fuller than usual," he said. "A little swollen in the breasts and hips…" He tilted his head slightly and chuckled. "Getting close to your period?"

"None of your fucking business!" I gasped, pushing at him roughly and managing to wiggle out of his arms, rounding angrily to glare at him.

"Which means yes. No need to be ashamed. I'm certainly not disturbed."

"Why am I not surprised with your fucked-up tastes?" I growled. "Go play with someone else. I have homework."

I don't know why Dana did not follow me, but I was too irritable and my head hurt too much for me to care when he watched me go without another word.

* *** *

Thursday and Friday passed without incident, but Clark and I were getting desperate to figure out a way to break out the experiments and humans before our override codes expired.

We spent what seemed like endless hours poring over every available blueprint we had managed to get our hands on to find a way out of the Commission without being spotted. But because we had to study everything in secret, we could not brainstorm openly and that made the process even more frustrating.

Due to our frustration, we decided to meet at Clark's house on Saturday to talk about the plan of escape before the Commission meeting. Hopefully we could communicate more freely then.

Early Saturday morning, I rode the bus to Clark's house, leaving the sleeping Mykail a note telling him where I would be all day so that he wouldn't worry when he woke up to find me gone.

I was still tired from Archangel, so I stopped and picked up coffee on the way, also hoping not to arrive at the Markus home *too* early. Mark let me into the house and motioned for me to go upstairs, so I went to Clark's room.

"You didn't bring me one?" he play-pouted when he saw the cup of coffee in my hand.

"I'm sorry," I said. "I figured you would have some here."

"We do. I'm just teasing."

"What is all this?" I asked, looking over the papers strewn across the floor.

"These are the blueprints." He sighed, looking over the collage. "From the photos we took. I printed them out to look at them in a larger form and we can take them to the fort tomorrow when we meet with everyone to see if anyone knows anything more about the cells..."

"I doubt anyone will." I dropped to my knees beside Clark, looking over the photos that had been loosely taped together to make the large and confusing map of the Commission of the People. "You and Melissa and I seem to be the only ones close enough to Dana to be allowed back there at any point in time, and Melissa isn't even a part of this."

"Not yet..."

"What do you mean?"

"She is not happy about the Sweeps," he said. "She's been saying that she's getting sick of the way Dana is abusing his power. I'm waiting until I figure out if she's really serious or just temporarily upset before I tell her what we're doing."

Clark's attention turned back to the map on the floor.

"Alright, let's go over this once more," he said, pointing at the security station that led into the back of the Commission. "When Dana took you into the back, where did you go?"

"We followed this main hallway," I told him again, running my finger over the hallway that ran between the termination cells until I reached the door that led to the corridor for Wards One and Two. "And then we went straight to Ward Three. I didn't see Wards One or Two."

"That's okay," Clark assured. "None of the experiments we were told about are in those wards. Where did you go in Ward Three?"

"Down the hallway and then we turned here," I said, once again motioning to the hallways in the slightly more complicated ward.

"So, this cell," he pointed to one he had marked with a red X on the paper, "is the experiment from Ward Three we were told about." He turned to me. "You didn't see her?"

"No."

"I also need to hack into the security system and find out the cell override codes," Clark said. "There should be an emergency release code. If I can find that, it should work throughout the entire Commission."

"How many people do you think we need to pull this off?" I asked. "We don't have a lot of time, so we're going to need more than two people..."

"I think, since we have twelve experiments to break out in Ward Eight, we need at least two people in there. Then I think we need another two people in Ward Nine, one in Ward Seven, one in Wards Six and Three, and probably one in Ward Four."

"What about Ward Ten?" I asked.

"That's the highest level ward. The security around there is going to be ridiculous," he said dejectedly. "I don't even know how we're supposed to sneak all these people in to begin with. And then we have to get to everyone in the holding cells, and then get *everyone* out."

"The only two ways I see out are the elevators that lead up to the lobby, and these," I pointed at the car elevators on the far side of the holding cells that sat behind the offices of the Commission, though the only way into that area was through the expansive holding cell area. "What if we were to get everyone around security somehow, go to the car elevators and, rather than take any of them, we climb up the shaft?"

"I don't think that would really work..." Clark sighed. "Leaving aside climbing up the elevator shaft, which must be quite long due to how far underground the Commission is, we have to get them past all the security. The Commission is guarded by approximately one hundred and twenty people every day."

"But the Sweeps have started," I said. "We find out the Sweep schedule and plan this on a night where a lot of the security is out on Sweeps."

Clark seemed hesitant.

"Okay, then what about the cameras?"

"I thought you said you could shut them down."

"I can," he said. "For the Commission that's underground. The upper building is on a different security grid and if both go down, then we'll have panic and people will start to notice things. There are also cameras in the garage where those car elevators go."

I sighed heavily and rubbed my forehead.

"How long can you shut down the security in the lower part of the Commission?"

"I can shut it down for about seven minutes, but then the backup kicks in," Clark shook his head. "I mean…in *theory*. I haven't tried it yet."

"Can you shut down the backup?"

"No. That's above my pay-grade."

I groaned in frustration and leaned back on my hands.

"So, we have seven minutes to break out nearly one hundred people in the holding cells and the twenty-five or so experiments…"

Clark looked at me apologetically.

For the entire afternoon, we found the holding cells we wanted to break into and then tried to think of another way to get the experiments around the security personnel and then get everyone out of the Commission entirely.

It was beginning to look hopeless to accomplish everything without being caught, let alone in the short timeframe of seven minutes. Not only that, but we only had about two and a half weeks before the codes expired and we were not sure if we would get another set of codes from our mysterious note writer.

I called Mykail later in the afternoon and told him I would be going to the Commission meeting with Clark and that I would be back to the house later in the night. I had to be sneaky about the phone call, though, since Clark still did not know that Mykail and I were seriously involved.

After a short dinner where we ate hurriedly to rush upstairs and look at the map from another angle to see if we could find anything we missed, the time to go to the Commission meeting drew close, and Mark came to get us.

We were driven to the Commission, trying very hard not to talk about the escape plan. We figured we would have to get into the area of the car elevators and see if there was any other passage that could be used to get out of the Commission. But we would not be able to do that until the following week, so we would discuss the plan with the Commish Kids the following day and brainstorm other ideas.

I tried to pay attention at the Commission meeting, though when there was no talk of anything I was interested in, I zoned out and thought about the escape plan, working my brain around the problem to see if there was anything we could have possibly missed, running through the images of the Commission in my mind. The talk of the Sweeps did come up, but Mrs. Prescott, who was running the meetings while Mrs. Markus was in Europe, did not say anything other than that the Sweeps had already yielded some results and seventeen new people around the country had been apprehended.

We left the meeting as soon as it ended, though I did feel Dana's eyes on me as I walked to the elevators.

We got in the car and sat in silence until we had left the area where the government buildings stood. I then turned to Clark.

"I think the elevators are best," I said vaguely.

"I don't think we have another option," he agreed.

"You don't like them?"

"I don't think that they're good when a lot of people need to get somewhere," he answered just as vaguely, both of us unsure if there were bugs inside the car.

I nodded in agreement.

"But…they seem to be the best for now," I continued, trying to be vague.

"I'm worried," he admitted. "I don't know if they will work for this. And if they fail at their job…"

I fell silent.

"But we can't do anything without them."

"I know, and that's what scares me," he said. "What about emergency evacuation procedures? How do we get out if there is a problem in the building and there are only elevators?"

The thought had not crossed my mind before, but I suddenly realized that there had to be an emergency stairwell of some sort just in case there was a real problem in the basement of the Commission and everyone needed to evacuate.

"Where is the emergency exit going to be, then?"

"I don't know," he said. "Where is there room for it?"

"Around the offices," I suggested. "I think that's the only place where it could fit."

"So we need to see on Monday if we can fit it into the project," Clark said. "Maybe we'll be fortunate. If not, I guess we can…" He trailed off, his eyes glancing out the window behind me.

"What?" I asked nervously. He quickly turned to Mark.

"Mark, where are we?"

Mark did not even tilt his head to show that he heard Clark.

"Oh shit…" Clark whispered.

I looked out the window worriedly and saw that we were nowhere near our homes. We were closer to the entrance of the national park at the south end of Central. Fear grabbed at my being, choking me. Mark was driving us somewhere. All sorts of thoughts began to fly through my mind.

Does he know what we're saying?

Did he figure out about the rebellion?

Is he turning us over to Dana?

Are we being captured?

"Lily..." Clark hissed, his eyes filled with fear. I saw him nod discreetly to the door handle. I looked between him and Mark and then shifted in my seat as Clark turned to Mark.

"Mark, stop the car. I order you to stop the car!" he snapped. I carefully undid my seatbelt, preparing to throw myself out of the moving car.

Mark did not obey, and when Clark took off his seatbelt to shift forward and command Mark more forcefully, I rested my hand on the handle of the door.

"Mark!"

The doors locked and I jumped at the sound, turning to look at Mark as Clark's eyes widened.

I knew we were in deep trouble.

Mark reached up with one hand and removed his glasses, glancing in the rearview mirror at us, his eyes harsh and purposeful. I shivered and shrunk in my seat as Clark backed away from the gaze. All we could do was look at one another worriedly. A few moments later, when Mark had turned his eyes back to the road, Clark carefully moved his hand over to the door to pull on the latch above the door handle to unlock the door once again.

As soon as his hand rested on the latch, Mark made a sharp turn and slammed on his brakes, turning off the headlights and startling us both, sending us flying around the back seat since we no longer had our seatbelts.

When the car had stopped completely and we had regained our bearings, I saw that Mark was holding one finger up, telling us to wait, turned around from the driver's seat to face us in the dark car. Clark and I stared at him as his eyes darted between us. The fear in my belly was telling me to run, to get out of the car and make a break for it as quickly as my legs could carry me, but Mark reached up with his other hand and turned on the light at the front of the car, illuminating the front two seats and the radio dash.

Tearing his eyes away from us, Mark extracted a switchblade from his pocket, extending the blade and shoving it into the crack between the main dash and the black radio.

Clark took my hand and tried to pull me, telling me to open my door, but I shook my head and yanked my hand out of his.

"*Look.*"

We both watched as Mark worked the knife around the plastic and finally managed to wiggle the radio out of the dash slightly. He pressed the blade into the gap and when he lifted the tip of the knife, we both saw a small microphone on the tip, attached to a wire.

Staying completely silent, we watched Mark roll down his window and then reach into his pocket again, pulling out a lighter and burning the bug. When the plastic had melted and the wire was damaged, he flicked the blade sideways and the melted bug flew into the darkness of the surrounding woods.

Mark flicked the switchblade back and rolled the window up, putting both the knife and the lighter back into his pocket before pushing the radio back into place. Then he turned to us and pressed one finger to his lips, telling us to remain quiet.

He shifted in his seat and motioned for both of us to move to each side before he awkwardly climbed over the middle console and sat in the middle of the back seat. Pulling out his knife again, he pushed the blade into the small crack in the frosted plastic covering the light above the back seat.

Removing the cover, he stabbed the second bug planted in the light, burned it, and then tossed it out my window.

As I was rolling the window up again, he leaned to the front passenger's seat, grabbing something before sitting between us again with a notebook and pen.

In shock, both Clark and I watched as Mark opened the notebook to the first page and wrote a message to us in very familiar handwriting.

"*That won't work. You can't get everyone out by using either set of elevators in the Commission. The emergency evacuation will lead you to a parking lot where cameras feed to the National Security Council.*"

I turned to Mark, my eyes wide.

"It's *you…*"

Chapter Forty-Four

"This entire time?" Clark gawked.

"*I'm sorry I deceived you,*" Mark wrote below his other message. "*But I had to be sure that you were committed to this rebellion.*"

"How do you know all this? Everything on the notes? For that matter, how long have you been able to understand what we're saying?" Clark pressed.

"*Before I came to your family I already understood English. It's easier for me to pretend I don't understand so people will talk around me.*"

"So, you're not working for Dana?"

"*No.*" Mark underlined the word several times. "*I want him dead.*"

"I really wish you would have told us that before you drove us to a random place in the dark," I said, chuckling brokenly, placing a hand against my chest. "You scared me to death."

Mark smiled and wrote "sorry" on the paper.

"Do you know a way to get the experiments out of the Commission?" Clark asked, catching Mark's attention. "You knew which experiments we could break out, so you must have an idea for *how* we can break them out."

Mark began jotting his answer.

"*There were old blueprints in Dana's office that show secret passages between the rooms. That was how I knew how to get into the records room. There are seven other secret passages. The one that would be best to use is in the Dome.*"

"The Dome?" both Clark and I read, puzzled.

"You mean that actually exists? It's real?" Clark gasped, his expression surprised.

"Wait, what is it?"

"Remember that one set of blueprints with the huge circle that I said was never built?" Clark asked. "Apparently, it was."

"What is it?" I repeated.

Mark began writing again. "*It simulates the outside. The experiments go in there from time to time to interact with one another.*"

"Mykail told me about that..."

"*In the Dome there is an artificial stream that comes in through a pipe and is pumped into the Dome. The current is usually really strong, but when the Dome is not being used and the breakers are off, the fan for the water stops because the energy the Dome uses costs the Commission a lot of money.*"

566

"So the experiments can just swim out?" Clark said. "And into the pipeline? Where does the pipeline go?"

"It's not that simple. There is a current even when the fan is off, and there is a wall that only leaves about a meter at the bottom of the stream for someone to swim through. Against the current, that will still be difficult."

"How do you know all this?" I asked.

"I've been looking for ways to get experiments out since I got into the Commission eight years ago. Four years ago, when I came to the Markus' house, I started going out at night trying to find where the water for the stream came from."

"But how will people swim out if the current is strong?"

"My friends know that you are planning to break experiments out and they are willing to help. Two of them could swim into the pipeline and attach ropes that others could use to swim under the wall."

He motioned with his hands the act of climbing a rope after he had finished writing.

"Where does the pipeline lead?" Clark asked.

"It's a long tunnel with a few drainage exits. About seven hundred meters down the pipeline there is a ladder that leads up to the base of one of the water tanks on the hill surrounding the reservoir," Mark wrote. His handwriting was sloppy and a little difficult to read and he kept making mistakes while writing quickly, but my heart was thrumming with excitement at him sharing his knowledge.

"The same hill where you can get into the fort?" I gasped.

"No, the one next to it."

"That's almost too perfect…" I murmured. "How did you find the fort?"

"Accident," Mark wrote as he smiled. *"I went to the other water tanks and found the fort when I went down the wrong ladder."*

"We're happy you did," Clark laughed. "Does Dana know about any of this?"

Mark shook his head. *"He probably knows about the secret passageways within the Commission, but the water pipe is not marked as an entrance or exit. It's just part of the construction of the Dome. And I am sure he does not know about the fort."*

"Do you have a plan for how we can break everyone out?" Clark asked. "We want to get some out of the holding cells too."

Mark stared at him for a few moments and then back at me before he took a deep breath.

"Are you meeting with other kids from the Commission tomorrow?"

"Yes, but just a few," Clark answered. "Most are studying for finals, so not everyone could make it."

"Can I come with you to the fort and show you the plan I have?" he wrote before turning and looking at us with eyes that were so worried and wide, I would have never believed he had been diligently planning the downfall of the leader of the Commission of the People for eight years.

"Of course," I laughed. "At this point, it is mostly your plan, anyway."

"We need to break everyone out within the next few weeks," Mark wrote. *"At the beginning of the Sweeps, there are more people out of the Commission. Right now, sixty-five percent of the security has been leaving for the Sweeps. That leaves a very small amount of security in the Commission. It would be best to do this on a Sweep day."*

"Do you know when those are?" Clark asked.

"No, but I can find out. Normally, the Commission is patrolled by around two hundred security guards. It would be too difficult to get everyone out around two hundred guards."

"But you've thought up a plan, right?" Clark asked.

"Maybe." He underlined the word. *"It might not work, but I will explain it to you and maybe you can figure out how to make it happen."*

"How many people do you have that can help us from the inside?" I asked.

"About twenty," Mark wrote. *"But that will all depend on how long the security can be turned off."*

"One more thing," Clark said slowly. "Can you really not speak?"

Mark turned to him and then touched the scars on the side of his neck before shaking his head. He put his pen back to the paper.

"This is how I can communicate with you," he wrote before tapping the pen on the pad of paper.

"But you can communicate with the other experiments?" I said.

He nodded.

"Then, what do you want Mykail to do?" I asked. "He's been stuck in the house, but he wants to help."

"I don't know. He can't blend in, so it's hard for him to do anything during the day." Mark glanced at the clock in the car. *"I will drive you tomorrow to the fort and we will discuss the plan there. I need to take you both home before anyone in the Commission tries to track either of you. It's past curfew."*

Mark capped the pen before ripping the pages out of the notebook and looking at me expectantly. I blinked at him, confused and not sure what he wanted me to do. He motioned to the papers and then nodded to the door.

"What?"

He reached into his pocket and pulled out his lighter again, which allowed the gears in my brain to finally click into place. I unlocked the door and opened it, stepping out. Clark also got out, letting out a heavy sigh as he walked around the car to join us. Mark stepped away from the vehicle, flicking the lighter and burning one corner of the papers.

"This is crazy, you two..." Clark groaned.

"No kidding," I agreed. I looked at Mark. "But I have to say, it's really nice to know you're on our side."

Mark looked up at me and smiled as he moved the paper in the air, allowing the flame to grow over the paper and ink, burning our conversation.

"Wait," Clark said quickly. "If you've been able to understand all this time...then you heard all those horrible things that everyone in the Commission, even the family, calls you."

Mark spared him a glance before sighing and shrugging, returning his attention to the burning paper.

"I'm so sorry," Clark whispered.

Mark smiled to assure us everything was alright before dropping the papers on the dirt ground and crouching to watch the final corner burn, being sure that there was nothing left of the words he had written. When the paper was charred and brown, he used his foot to grind the pieces into the dirt, ensuring that any evidence was gone.

I wanted to speak even more with Mark as we drove to my house, but I remained quiet, feeling the tension slowly leave my body as I finally got over the adrenaline that had rushed through me when I thought Mark was turning us over to Dana. I was excited and thrilled that we had a strong ally. Since he was part of the security team of the Commission, he obviously had a lot of inside information that would be beneficial. And everyone, including Dana, seemed to think that he had absolutely no understanding of English, so there was no way to know what he had heard from everyone talking carelessly around him.

And, with the way he burnt the bugs in the car and the pages of the notebook, it was obvious that Mark was meticulous in covering his tracks.

It also made me realize how incredible it was that Mark had deceived everyone for eight years while plotting against the Commission of the People. Even Dana seemed convinced that Mark was not dangerous.

Mark pulled into the darkened driveway of my house and turned off the car, getting out as I opened my door, stepping into the cold night air.

The lights in my kitchen were on, leaving a dim glow in the windows of the dining room. My heart fell. Mykail was waiting for me, likely worried sick.

Clark also walked with me and Mark to my front door.

I unlocked the door and slowly pushed it open, peering in to see Mykail standing near the bottom of the staircase, his face pale.

"You had me worried sick," he gasped, hugging me tightly. I hugged him back, apologizing repeatedly, hoping the two behind me would not jump to too many conclusions about the hug.

When we parted, Mykail turned to Mark and Clark, who had quietly stepped inside and closed the door, though they did not move from the foyer.

"What's going on?" Mykail asked, looking them over. Mark reached up and removed his glasses and lowered his head in a shallow bow. Mykail also nodded in turn before his attention focused on me. "Lily?"

"Well..." I said slowly, turning to look at Mark, not sure how to tell Mykail about Mark's assistance. "Remember those notes?"

"Yes." I saw the gears click in Mykail's head and he turned quickly to Mark, who lowered his head. "It's you..." he whispered. "I thought...but...aren't you part of the Eight Group?"

Mark nodded.

"What's the Eight Group?" I asked.

"It's what we called the Asian experiments who ended up on the security detail. They're all from Ward Eight," Mykail answered distractedly, still looking over Mark with disbelief. Mykail seemed even more shocked than Clark and I had been. "I don't believe it..."

Mark reached up, scratching the back of his neck before pulling on his left earlobe.

"No, don't apologize," Mykail said quickly. "I'm thrilled, just...surprised," he admitted with a small chuckle. "How many of you can understand English?"

Mark looked thoughtful for a moment before he held up nine fingers.

"He's agreed to help us break people out," I said.

"You know how we can do it?" Mykail asked Mark. Mark sighed and scratched at the side of his jaw in what seemed like a distracted motion. "Well, it's better than nothing. Do you think it will work?"

Mark nodded and Mykail let out a short puff of breath, his eyes wide in surprise.

"Are you okay?" I asked.

"I'm just…" Mykail looked at Mark again and then shook his head slowly. "If…if there are other experiments in the Eight Group that could help…this…it could actually work…"

"You make it sound like you had no hope in accomplishing this at all," I chuckled brokenly.

"Well, I had always *hoped* it would work…but…" He looked at Clark and me again. "How? Do you know how to get everyone out?"

"He says that there's a stream in the Dome that people can swim out of," Clark explained. "What are your thoughts on that?"

"The Dome?" Mykail repeated, startled. "The river? The current is really strong…" He looked thoughtful for a moment. "I don't know. It wasn't something I ever thought of…but, *maybe*…"

Mark reached over and gently touched Clark's elbow before tapping his wrist, causing all of us to remember the time.

"Right, tomorrow," Clark agreed, giving me an expectant look.

"I'll be on the first bus over."

"Sounds good." He turned to Mykail. "Good night, Mykail."

"Good night," Mykail called back, though he seemed dazed as he lowered himself to sit on the stairs, staring at the floor with a disbelieving smile on his face. I walked to the door as Mark opened it and ushered Clark outside. Mark turned around on the other side of the threshold, opening his mouth as if he was about to tell me something.

He closed his mouth and nodded back into my house before then reaching up to his right eye, touching the inner corner with his index finger, as if wiping something away. Then he nodded once before putting his glasses back on, returning to the car.

Confused, I closed the door slowly, watching the latch slide into place as I locked it.

I walked back to Mykail, who had not moved from his seat on the stairs.

"Hey, what does this mean?" I asked, repeating Mark's action.

"Be careful."

"Oh…" I said, wondering why Mark felt that was an important message to relay.

"He's right," Mykail said, cupping his hands over his nose and mouth and letting out a heavy sigh as I sat next to him. "The more experiments like him that get involved in breaking people out, the more likely we are to be discovered."

"But no one knows that he can even understand English," I pointed out. "He's a hell of an actor."

"No kidding," Mykail said, his eyebrows shooting high. "Even most of the experiments don't know the Eight Group can understand English…well, beyond the commands they're taught." He was silent for a few moments before he turned to me. "What's his name?"

"Mark."

His eyes shot even wider and he turned to me fully.

"Mark?" he hissed. "*That's* Mark?"

"What? What is it?"

"Holy shit…" he whispered. "Mark is the best. He's the best of the Eight Group. We called him their leader, but I never knew which one he was."

"He's the best?"

"He's incredible," Mykail said. "From what I've heard, he's the fastest and the strongest and has the best aim of any of the security experiments. He's one hell of an ally."

"How many people are part of the Eight Group?"

"I don't know…maybe about twenty," Mykail said. He rubbed his forehead, shaking his head.

"What?" I asked, leaning on his shoulder.

"Nothing," he said. "I'm just a little jealous, that's all. He can work with you during the day, plan this break out…and I'm stuck here."

"No, you're not," I replied. "Your tracers are out."

"And where am I going to go with these?" he asked, jerking his thumb over his shoulder to his wings. "I'm not even sure how I'm going to leave without being noticed."

"We'll figure something out…" I assured, kissing his shoulder as he turned and kissed me on the forehead in turn. I could feel the heaviness in the air as the reality of our plan sat heavily over us. Mykail clearly was going through a storm of emotions, as his eyes remained distant on the floor even when I wrapped my arms around his.

"Hey, come with me," I said, pulling him to his feet.

"Where are we going?" he asked, smiling around the hint of sadness in his voice.

"Outside," I declared, walking to the sliding glass doors in our large living room. He hesitated but did not protest. I could feel his apprehension, but I wanted to make him feel better and I knew going outside would help.

The air was cold and I huddled into my jacket, worried that the shirtless Mykail would immediately catch a chill.

"I'll get you a coat or something," I said, turning back into the room when he smiled and caught my wrist.

"It won't do any good," he chuckled, nodding back to the wings. "Besides, I'm pretty strong against the cold."

I was about to insist that I get a blanket or something else for him, but he stepped outside, his feet resting on the cold stone patio as he drew in a deep breath, closing his eyes before moving toward the grass.

I followed, buttoning my coat to my neck and shoving my hands in my pockets once I closed the door behind us.

His feet finally hit the dying grass, his head bent back to study the stars in the sky. I remained on the edge of the patio, watching his happy expression as he stared at the sky with child-like wonderment. My chest bloomed with affection at the expression.

I left the patio to stand next to him and he put his arm around me, still keeping his eyes glued to the sky. His wing wrapped around me, and though it did not provide any reprieve from the cold, the gesture warmed me regardless.

We were silent for an indeterminable amount of time, staring at the sky as if we had never seen the stars before. Just being with him, staring at the sky and knowing how happy he was, made the moment precious. I forgot about the revolution, about Mark's warning to be careful, about Dana and the Commission of the People, and simply stared into the abyss of the stars with Mykail's presence beside me.

The feathers of his wing brushed my cheek and I flinched.

"Sorry," he chuckled, moving his wing away fluidly.

I dropped my hand from around his waist, stepping away.

"Cold?" he asked.

"No," I lied through my chattering teeth.

"Yes, you are," he laughed. "Let's go in and get some sleep."

"No, not yet." I shook my head, my curiosity winning me over. I retreated another step. "I want to see you fly."

His eyes widened, surprised by the request. Then he shook his head.

"No."

"Why not?"

"We're in your backyard! What if the neighbors see?"

"Well, the house is blocking that direction and that direction," I said, pointing to my house, "this big-ass tree is blocking this direction and the neighbors over there have their own tree," I told him. "I think you're safe as long as you don't go very high."

Mykail's head swiveled in the direction of the neighbors, confirming that it was unlikely he would be spotted, but he still shook his head.

"It's too risky," he said, starting to relent.

"Come on, I know you want to," I said. "Just quickly and not very high."

"It's not like the movies, Lily," he said. "It takes a lot of power to get me off the ground and I can't just hover a foot above the ground. I have to continuously flap my wings and if I'm not far enough off the ground, I can't stay airborne."

"I want to see you fly," I said again. "So do what you can to fly for just a few seconds without going above the house or the trees."

He looked around once more and then took a deep breath, letting it out with an excited smile.

"Alright," he agreed. "But you're going to need to stand further back."

I retreated a few further steps.

"Further."

Concerned and sure he was exaggerating, I stepped back nearly to the living room door, earning Mykail's approving nod.

I could not entirely make out his features from the moonlight and the small light that shone from the kitchen windows, but the limited light bounced off his pristine white feathers as he spread his wings to their full span. I could not breathe.

He was a beautiful sight.

I knew his wings were large, but I had never seen them at their full expanse and the sheer enormity took my breath away.

Mykail brought his wings in and crouched before jumping up and spreading his wings, angling them. With one powerful stroke, his wings beat the air and he rose higher.

The blast of wind from his wings was far more powerful than I expected, and the sudden rush of cold air knocked my breath further out of me as I stared at the powerful and beautiful creature gaining height. His wings moved with such power, and yet so fluidly, it was exhilarating to watch.

He pushed once with his wings and rose nearly to the top of the house before angling his wings and body to turn and glide to one side of the backyard, dipping low before beating the air again and turning, once again rising with the powerful wings pushing him.

I was watching him play like a child, enjoying the simple feeling of rising and falling, relishing in the ability to fly. He had told me how much he enjoyed flying, but the grace in his movements showed how much he truly loved it and how practiced he truly was with the action.

Slowly, he lowered to the ground, flapping his wings back and pushing air in my direction as he slowed his descent and planted his feet on the ground.

When his feet were touching the grass, I ran forward and threw my arms around his neck. He wrapped his arms around my waist, holding me close, laughing.

"Thank you," he said breathlessly. "I needed that."

Tears came to my eyes unbidden no matter how I tried to stop them.

He pulled away from me faster than I was willing to let go and pressed his thumbs to my cheeks, pushing the happy tears away, moving his wings around me in a protective cocoon and kissing me so gently I forgot about the chilly night.

* *** *

I was tired when I first woke, but when my brain kicked itself into gear to remember that Mark would tell us his plan for breaking people out of the Commission, I was less angry at the shrill alarm I had set the previous night.

Mykail, on the other hand, was still angry at the buzzing that rudely woke him.

He took the pillow and pulled it over his head, groaning irritably.

"Sorry," I said around a yawn, kissing the back of his hand holding the pillow. He mumbled something from under the pillow. My heart filled with the same intense feelings of love from the previous night.

It was time I admitted to myself that I was completely in love with Mykail.

I dressed quickly in something simple and warm and then darted back down the hall to see Mykail had not moved. Chuckling, I stepped forward and climbed onto the bed, kissing his hand again and pulling the pillow away, meeting no resistance.

"I'm heading out now," I said. "I'll be back later tonight and I'll make us dinner, okay?"

He did not stir. I kissed his cheek before leaving him to rest, writing him a quick note on the refrigerator to be sure that he did not feel as though I had left without saying goodbye.

I had to run to catch the first bus—the driver was kind enough to stop and let me on, even after he had started to pull away from the curb. I bounced anxiously in my seat as I watched the houses of the neighborhood pass. My thoughts were churning in my head, but I could not tell what I was thinking. I thought briefly about how happy Mykail was the previous night and how I wanted him to always wear that elated smile. I also thought about how Mark might have the insight we needed to pull off our plan. I also wondered about Dana and how we could keep him in the dark, as well as how he would react if—*when*—we broke the people out of the Commission.

I disembarked at the appropriate stop and walked down the street to Clark's house, making it there faster than usual due to my excitement.

Clark opened the front door for me but the large bags under his eyes distracted me from the broad smile on his face.

"Hey."

"Hey," I returned the greeting. "Did you not sleep at all?"

"No." He shook his head with a laugh, closing the door behind me. "Actually, Mark and I stayed up all night hacking into the Commission security system."

"Did you figure out how to shut it down?"

"I think we found a better way than my first plan," he said. "Come on, I'm making coffee."

I followed him into the kitchen, looking around for Mark.

"Where's Mark?"

"He went to take a shower. He should be out in a little bit." Clark walked to the coffee machine and poured the dark liquid into both cups. "So, here's what we found," he said as he poured. I leaned against the counter to listen. "There is a way to shut down the main system remotely. That will take out all the cameras, mic feeds…but it also requires taking out all the power in the Commission."

"*All* the power? You mean like pulling the plug on everything?"

"Kind of. The security system is secondary to the power. Mark said that the security personnel is drilled on what to do if the power and security goes out, so it's obviously happened before."

"…I'm sensing a 'but'…"

"But there is the secondary system, like a backup generator, and it will kick on automatically if the main system is down for longer than seven minutes. It will bring everything back online," Clark explained. "There's nothing we can do for that system without leaving traces."

"We only have seven minutes?"

"Yes, but there's another problem," he continued. "If an experiment is reported to be loose in the Commission, there is a failsafe that locks down the ward that the experiment is reported loose in."

"Well, as long as we just use an override code, the cells should just open, right? Without triggering that system?"

"In theory, yes," Clark said. "Mark said he would be willing to test an individual cell override code to see if the code we found works."

"But there *is* a code?"

"Yes, for emergency evacuation."

I drew in a deep breath, leaning back against the counter with the warm cup of coffee that Clark offered me clasped between my hands.

"Seven minutes, huh?"

"Mark seems confident that that will be enough time to get everyone out, as long as everyone knows beforehand," Clark said.

"Can he tell everyone?"

"He said he could," Clark said, sipping his coffee.

We stood in the kitchen, silent, drinking the hot beverage, thinking over what we were about to plan and how we could possibly accomplish everything in only seven minutes.

Just as we were finishing our coffee, Mark walked into the kitchen.

"Ready?" Clark asked. Mark nodded once and I quickly gulped down the remainder of my coffee. Clark took the cups and I stepped up to Mark.

"Good morning," I said, thrilled I could finally hold a proper conversation with him.

He bowed his head to me with a smile.

Clark rinsed out the cups and put them in the dishwasher before the three of us headed to the car. It felt a little awkward now to have Mark sitting in the front while the two of us sat in the back. I wanted to include him in our conversations, even knowing he could not respond while driving.

He did not drive us to the power plant or anywhere that we thought was close to the fort. He drove us to the zoo on the far side of town. Since it was a Sunday, the zoo was crowded with families bringing their children to see the animals.

When Mark got out of the car, Clark and I looked at one another, confused, hesitant to get out of the car.

"Uh, what are we doing here?"

Mark reached into the car again, grabbing the notepad near the passenger's seat and resting it against the car as he scrawled a quick message.

"*We're covering our tracks. If we leave the car and my tracers here, it looks like I drove you two here for the day.*"

"Leave your tracers?" I stared at the piece of paper, surprised.

He tossed the notebook and pen on the driver's seat before reaching to his right wrist and unclipping a metal band, setting it on top of the steering column. Then he slipped off his right shoe, lifting the inside sole and pulling out a plastic-covered tracer that he set under the driver's side carpet. Clark and I watched, fascinated, as he slipped his shoe back on and grabbed the notepad and pen, standing straight and locking the car.

"You *are* meticulous," I muttered. Mark smiled shyly and began to turn away from the car when Clark stopped him.

"Wait," he said quickly. "What about our tracers?"

Mark put the notebook back against the car to write.

"*Sean is the only one who has access to your tracers. He won't try to find you. Dana, though, has access to tracers for the security personnel. He can track me, and he will.*"

"And what about the car?" Clark pressed. "We can't just leave it here for seven or eight hours. Dana will notice if the car is here longer than normal."

"*After four hours, Josh will move the car to the mall.*"

"Josh?" we both asked.

"*He should be watching the car right now from the Commission computers.*" Mark wrote quickly, glancing around the parking lot before continuing his message, obviously worried about being seen. "*Josh has leave privileges as long as he's careful and he lets Sean know first. He'll check back in four hours and if the car is still here, he'll move it.*"

"You two have done this before, haven't you?" I said with a grin. He smiled as well and nodded, capping the pen and motioning to the side of the parking lot, walking around the cars to the deserted end of the zoo parking lot.

Once we left the asphalt, we went around the back of the storage buildings and along the fence of the wolf enclosure, hearing the families and children on the other side of the solid fence.

After carefully picking our way down a steep slope at the back of the zoo, we hiked to a rocky hill, which we rounded until we found a deer path that led us to the cave entrance that Clark and I had explored a few weeks previously.

"Wow..." Clark said when we entered the cave. "I have never taken that way to get here before."

Following the somewhat-familiar passageway to the underground tunnels, we were silent, feeling our way around with the limited lights of our phones. Mark, on the other hand, moved very easily in the dark, taking the correct turns to bring us into the main bunker. Mark flipped the switch for the lights as easily as if he had lived there for years.

"The others shouldn't be here for another hour. Some are taking one passage and others are taking another..." I said aloud for Mark's benefit.

He motioned for us to follow and we walked into the library-type room with the tables and dusty shelves. He set the notebook and pen on the table and opened the page, writing a quick message.

"I stole the completed blueprints of the Commission from Dana's office. I hid them in here."

"When did you do that?" I gasped, watching him walk to one of the bookshelves and pull it from the wall, extracting a large folded piece of paper from behind the shelf. As he pushed the bookshelf back into place, he held up two fingers. "Two days ago? He's probably looking for it by now."

Mark shook his head, handing the paper to Clark as he moved to write another message.

"He hasn't looked for these in two years."

Clark unfolded the blueprint and laid it flat on the table, smoothing out the creases as the three of us studied the extensive and intricate blueprints.

"It's nice having it all on one document," Clark chuckled, scanning the confusing squares etched in white on the blue paper. "And that's the Dome..." he whispered, pointing at the circle directly in front of him.

Mark grabbed his notepad and wrote a question.

"Do you know which holding cells you want to open?"

Clark and I pointed to the various cells and Mark put an X on the boxes with his pen, his eyes scrutinizing the plans. When we had finished with those in the holding cells, he went down to the different wards, marking Xs on the cells of the experiments we would break out.

I also studied the blueprints, noting the area for the offices and the main security room that led into a hallway where the termination cells stood, leading to the larger hallway that branched into the Wards One and Two. I remembered Ward Three from when Dana took me into the back. But the main hallway of Ward Three led into an even larger hallway that branched into Wards Four and Five and then into Ward Six. At the end of the larger Ward Six, there was a hallway where some unmarked cells led to the two laboratories.

On the far side of one of the labs was a large section where the words "LIVING QUARTERS" were clearly printed. There were far more rooms than I expected, and it surprised me how large the underground complex of the Commission of the People really was.

The main hallway that cut through Wards Three and Six and between the two labs led to Ward Seven, and at the end of Ward Seven there was a large room where six doors were clearly marked. One of these doors was the door to Ward Seven, while one on the left wall led into a hallway that stretched into both Ward Nine and the holding cells. Directly across from that door was another door into Ward Eight. The two other doors on each side of the empty room led into the two different sections of Ward Ten.

The final door was across from the main hallway and entered a short hallway that ended at the Dome.

"These are all the cells that we need to get to in seven minutes?" Clark gawked when Mark backed away from the blueprints. "How many people are we going to need for this?"

Mark looked over the map, his eyes lost in the Commission, pondering what he had planned before he reached for his pen and wrote a number I could have never expected.

"*4.*"

"*Four?*" Clark and I said simultaneously.

"Four people to get to all those cells?"

"*Four people breaking others out of the cells. And maybe eight people for distraction.*"

"Distraction?" I gasped. "Like a suicide mission? Send some people in there just to distract the guards?"

"*No. The distractions will come from inside.*" He moved his finger to the offices and pointed to the records room, where a scribbled note about the secret passageway between the library and the records room could be seen. "*There are three secret passageways leading into the records room. One from the library, one from Dana's office, and one from the car elevators.*"

He moved his pen and drew a line where the passageway would be in the records room.

"*If you two go through the records room passageway and into the car elevators area, you can get into the holding cells and start releasing people from the far end, getting them to run to this hallway,*" he pointed to the one that ran past Ward Nine and into the empty room connected to the Dome, "*then by the time you get done with them, you can release the experiments from Ward Nine and Ten.*"

"But for that to happen within seven minutes, we would need all the guards in this area," Clark motioned to the holding cells, "to go this direction and go somewhere where they would not see everyone running to the Dome," he pointed toward Ward Ten.

Mark nodded and then moved his pen to Ward Ten, circling three cells at the furthest end in the western side of the ward.

"What about them?" Clark asked.

"You want to turn them loose..." I whispered, understanding immediately. "Three Ward Ten experiments? You want to set them loose?"

Mark grabbed his notepad.

"When a Ward Ten is loose, all security personnel is called to that area to make sure that the experiment does not leave the ward. But if we release three on a Sweep day, there won't be enough people to contain them. Our protocol is to seal Ward Ten and be sure that the experiment does not escape. But when a Ward Ten does get out, the Eight Group specifically is supposed to take care of it."

"So?" I said, waiting for Mark to continue.

"Oh my God, that's brilliant..." Clark whispered. "Lily, if Mark tells the others of the Eight Group to go easy on the experiment, they could prolong the distraction and get the security guards out of this area," he motioned to the room where the hallway to the Dome was. "Then we can get people into the Dome and out of the Commission."

"But how can we be sure that will be believable? How will the others not know that the Eight Group aren't going easy on the Ward Ten experiments?"

"If three Ward Tens are loose, we only need to get one of them out of the ward, because then the ward locks down. At that point, we need to get the one Ward Ten into Ward Seven and that will allow the people from the holding cells and the experiments from Wards Eight, Nine, and the one in Ward Ten to get to the Dome."

Mark pointed to the first of the three cells he circled.

"This is Trisha," he wrote. *"Her stealth and strength are top-ranked in the Commission."* He moved his finger to the next cell. *"This is Cameron. He's a friend of mine. He'll know of the plan and distract any guards that will be locked in Ward Ten."* Mark pointed to the last cell. *"And this is Goliath. He's the one we're going to count on to break out of Ward Ten."*

"Why?"

"He's broken out twelve times in the last four years. Each time, he gets closer and closer to Dana's office. He's very predictable but very strong. Last time he got free, we finally brought him down in the Termination Cells area. Since then, I started telling him my plan and he said that he would be willing to fake-fight with members of the Eight Group and get as close to the offices as possible."

"Okay, well, if that works for all of these experiments, great," I said, pointing to the higher wards. "What about everyone in Ward Seven and below?"

Mark took a deep breath, putting his pen back to the paper slower than before.

"This is where we will need the fourth person," he wrote. *"I can get the experiments out of Wards Eight and Nine if I need to, but we will need an experiment to start here,"* he pointed at the lab, *"and wait for the security to run to Ward Ten before breaking out the experiments from Wards Six, Four, and Three. Then they will wait in the lab until Goliath and the Eight Group pass into Ward Six. Once that happens they will run through Ward Seven with the experiment that freed them to the Dome. Possibly, that experiment could also free the experiments in Ward Seven if we are short on time."*

"Do you have someone like that that you can trust? One of the Eight Group?" Clark pressed.

"Not one of the Eight Group," Mark wrote. *"But yes."* He pointed at one of the cells that had been marked with an X in Ward Nine. *"Griffin is a very good friend of mine. He would be perfect for this."*

"How do you know that?" I asked.

"He was the one that hacked into the military computers and scared Leader Simon. He was getting information for me about the military we might be facing if we go through with this revolution."

"You're kidding me..." I whispered.

"Wait," Clark said. "Griffin and the Ward Ten guy and the Eight Group I understand, but what about the Dome? You said that we would need to have a rope so that people can swim under the wall against the current and that you would have two of your friends do that, but if they're all fighting this Ward Ten guy...who's going to handle the ropes?"

"Once Goliath is out, we will follow protocol. There will be one member of the Eight Group at each door to contain the area." Mark pointed to the empty room with all the doors. *"The others will be fighting him. Once Goliath is in Ward Seven, the ones that are standing guard won't need to do so anymore, and they can lead everyone into the Dome and start getting them out via the stream."*

I stared at the paper, replaying everything that Mark said in my mind, my eyes moving over the blueprints, trying to see how everything flowed together. The more I thought it over, the more I saw how the plan could work. And since Mark knew inside information about the protocol of the security personnel, he would know how everyone would react to the situation as it arose. Everything would have to be timed perfectly, but it was possible.

Clark was obviously going through the same thought process. After a few minutes, he took a deep breath, letting out a broken laugh.

"Wow...it...might work..."

"There's a lot more, though. Dana cannot know that I was a part of this, or that any of the Eight Group helped. We will have to stay behind and pretend that we were fighting Goliath the entire time. We can get you and everyone else into the pipe, but after that, we have to stay in the Commission. That means you have to get everyone to the fort and you have to get their tracers out as quickly as possible and dispose of them."

"Wait, how are we going to sneak back into the Commission?" Clark asked. "We can't just disappear either."

"I can pretend to drive you home, but you can sneak in on one of Josh's cars in the car elevators and hide in the passageway until we start the plan. There's one more thing. You will both have to remove your tracers before this."

My stomach flipped.

Mark and Clark both turned to me, and I shook my head.

"Oh no, I already had to remove Mykail's tracers. I don't want to have anything to do with sharp objects and slicing into flesh," I said quickly.

"You removed Mykail's tracers?" Clark furrowed his eyebrows.

"Long story," I lied.

"We need to remove them," Clark said. "We'll just have to find a way to keep the tracers in roughly the same locations on our bodies when we're in the Commission, just in case there is a more thorough search."

Mark turned back to his notepad.

"Hand – jewelry. Foot – in the shoe. Back – bra strap."

"I don't wear a bra, Mark," Clark groaned, exasperated. I smiled before I could help myself, as did Mark.

"Pretend it's an injury and use a band aid."

"And we need to do all this in just a few weeks?" I asked.

"We need to break everyone out in the next two weeks. By the end of next week, we need to pick a day. I will go into the security computers and see when the Sweeps are and then we'll match it with Dana and Sean's schedules to be sure that they're gone, too."

"Will they be gone at the same time?"

"If Dana is out of the Commission, Sean is with him. Always."

Chapter Forty-Five

Mark slipped out of the fort before the first Commish Kids showed up and agreed only to meet with the other Commission children after the breakout to be sure that no one blew his cover accidentally before we succeeded.

Clark and I discussed with the Commish Kids the new plan, though we left out some details until we knew what day we were planning the daring escape. The seven people who came to the fort that day reacted the same way as Clark and I. They were shocked that there was a strong possibility the plan would work.

Mark was waiting for us at the mouth of the cave exit when we left later in the afternoon. He was looking over the city below as the winter sun started to descend.

Clark and I sat next to him and enjoyed the view. I dangled my feet over the edge of a large boulder and drank in the city in the sunset, trying not to ruminate on everything we were planning.

We remained silent for over an hour. The sun was gone when Mark finally stood, nodding to the road at the base of the foothills where a black car was pulling into the parking lot for a park next to the river.

"Is that Josh?" Clark asked. When Mark nodded, Clark looked at the experiment skeptically. "Do I even want to know how he has a spare key to the car?"

Mark smiled mysteriously before starting down the slope. I walked behind him, Clark falling into step behind me as we picked our way down the rocky hillside, jogging to the parking lot when there was a break in traffic.

Josh was leaning against the car, moving loose pebbles with his foot when he noticed our approach. A small smile pulled at the corners of his mouth and Mark walked to him, hugging him briefly with one arm.

A little surprised at seeing Mark affectionate, both Clark and I hesitated before getting closer. Mark's hand went up to Josh's face and he pulled on the wire attached behind Josh's ear, yanking the communication device out of his collar.

I assumed Josh rolled his eyes with the way his head moved before he said something short in a foreign language. Mark glanced at the plastic device in his hands before nodding and putting the communicator in Josh's lapel and jerking his head to us.

"Hello," Josh said. My jaw dropped.

"You speak English?" Clark and I said simultaneously.

"I understand more than I speak," he said, his accent thicker with the longer sentence. "He told you about the plan?"

"Yes," I managed to say when I got over the fact that we were speaking to one of the Eight Group members. After the silent Mark, I never thought I would be speaking to one of the Asian security experiments.

"Good," Josh said. "He asked me to translate for him, since..." he touched his throat, glancing at Mark.

"That would be a huge help," Clark said. "No offense, Mark, but writing notes takes a while."

Mark nodded, though he looked reluctant to admit it.

"But, my English is really bad...I'm sorry..." Josh admitted. "I don't get a chance to speak it."

"No, it's good," I said quickly. "Does Sean or Dana know you can speak English?"

Josh shook his head. "Sean knows I can speak a little, but he doesn't know I understand more."

Mark tapped Josh on the arm and then tapped his right wrist twice.

"Marina," Josh said. Mark nodded and reached into his pocket, grabbing his own set of keys. Josh shook his head and snatched them from Mark's hand. "I'll drive."

Mark stared at Josh through his glasses and Josh laughed.

"You drive like crazy."

Mark rolled his eyes in an exaggerated motion before opening the back door for Clark and me as Josh climbed in the driver's seat. When Mark closed the door behind us, Josh started up the car and Mark moved to the passenger's seat, climbing in last.

"Where are we going?" I asked.

"My tracers are at the marina," Josh answered, backing out of the parking space. "I'll go there, and he will drive you home."

"How long have you two been friends?"

"Since we were kids," Josh answered Clark's question. "We lived next to each other before the Commission."

"And whose idea was it to break out experiments?" I chuckled. Josh pointed at Mark and Mark pointed at Josh, then they both laughed.

"It was all of us," Josh said. "My friends, we thought about breaking experiments out for a long time."

"What stopped you before?" Clark asked.

"We needed people like you."

It was a short drive to the marina. Josh and Mark led us on foot down the aisle of the parking lot to the far corner, where a Commission van was parked. I was nervous as we approached, particularly when four people got out of the van, three men and a woman, all dressed like Mark and Josh, glasses covering their eyes.

"This is some of the Eight Group," Josh said.

"It's nice to meet you," the woman said with almost no accent, reaching forward to shake my hand. Still surprised at the way I was being greeted by the experiments I had always known to be silent, I stumbled forward to take her hand hastily. The three other men also greeted me and Clark, all with different strengths of accents.

"When we do the plan," Josh said, motioning to the other four, "this is who will help."

They nodded in affirmation.

We stood in a group awkwardly for a few moments before Mark nodded to them. Josh turned to me and took my hand.

"Lily, it was nice to see you," he said with a bright smile. "We have to go on our patrol now. We will see you later."

We said goodbye to the others as they got into the van and Mark ushered Clark and me back to the car where we sat for twenty minutes, covering our tracks in case anyone was watching the activity of their tracers.

My brain was buzzing.

The plan could actually work. I did not think of what we would do after that or how we would get the people of America to pay attention to the experiments and go against the Commission of the People. All I could turn over in my head was how we could actually get the experiments and other prisoners out of the Commission basement.

When Mark drove me home I said goodnight to them both, looking forward to getting some real sleep and waking up early to finish the homework that I should have done a long time ago and prepare for the test I had Monday.

But all thoughts of being productive vanished when I walked into the house and was greeted by Mykail, who seemed to be in a wonderful mood.

"How did it go?" he asked, taking me into his arms as I set my bag down on the kitchen island.

"Amazing," I said. I took some time to explain the plan to him in careful detail. The only part Mykail seemed skeptical about was needing only four people on the inside during the breakout. However, with his knowledge of the inside of the Commission, I could see the way his mind processed the plan. When I finished and his eyes lit up, I nodded.

"I know."

"Mark is a genius," Mykail whispered.

"Probably," I admitted with a chuckle. "Then again, he's been planning this for eight years. I guess he's had the time to really think about it."

"That means that you need to get your tracers out, though," he said. I groaned and rolled my eyes.

"I know, I know..."

Mykail took both my hands.

"Come on," he said. "Let's just do it now and get it over with."

"What?"

"I'm not giving you time to think. Let's get the tracers out now and be done with it."

"No!" I breathlessly protested.

"Lily, it has to be done."

"I'm a little concerned with how much you want to cut into me."

"Best to get this done as soon as possible," he said. "I'll get the stuff ready and I'll be sure that, this time, you don't drink the whiskey until you've got some food in you."

"Ha-ha, very funny," I groaned. He squeezed my hands.

"Look at it this way. Who would you rather have remove them? Me or Mark?"

I thought about that carefully. "Would you be offended if I chose Mark?"

He opened his mouth to say something but hesitated before laughing brokenly.

"*Yes!*"

I lowered my head in defeat. "Alright..."

"Good, come on."

Trying not to think too much about what I had agreed to, I begrudgingly followed him around the kitchen and took the things he handed me. Then, wrapping an arm around my shoulders, Mykail led me upstairs to my bathroom, where I sat on the counter, feeling my stomach twist sickly.

"I hate that the first thing I do when I come home involves some kind of improvised surgery these days," I groaned as I set down the bottle of whiskey and the gauze.

"It's only the second time."

"That's two times too many."

"Hopefully, this will also be the last time." When his hands were free, he touched my face, causing my skin to tingle as he looked at me lovingly. "Don't worry. It will be alright."

And then his lips were on mine, warm and gentle like they had been the previous night. I kissed him back, trying to distract him from removing the tracers, though I was more successful at distracting myself as my entire body heated up from the kiss.

With a gasp, Mykail separated our mouths and retreated a step.

"Nice try," he chuckled.

I blinked a few times, trying to find something to focus on.

"Huh?"

"You're trying to distract me."

"I think that was the original plan…" I admitted, though I realized it had worked on me more so than him. He chuckled and stepped forward again, pecking a kiss on my lips before grabbing the bottle of whiskey, holding it in front of me.

"What?"

"Take *one* sip," he instructed. "Don't do what you did last time."

"Are you ever going to let me live that down?" I groaned, taking the bottle and pulling the cap off irritably.

"No."

I took a small sip before passing the bottle to him. He also sipped at the strong liquid and then set the bottle aside.

I watched him wash and sterilize the knife before turning to me and nodding to my ankle.

"We'll do that one first."

I kicked off my shoes and brought my left leg onto the counter, pulling my sock off and rolling up my jeans. He went to his knees and carefully placed his hand on the top of my foot, leaning forward and kissing my ankle tenderly.

He looked around the area of my ankle, his fingers carefully passing over my skin to find the scar that marked where the tracer sat.

When he found it, he looked up at me.

"Just breathe," he whispered, his breath passing over my foot and making me shiver again. My hands found the edge of the counter, gripping the marble desperately, trying to keep calm as he lowered his gaze to my ankle.

"Deep breath," his voice traveled toward me. I didn't remember closing my eyes.

There was pressure against my skin and then the sharp bite of the metal and the warm trickle of blood as it dripped from the small wound to my heel, pooling on the vanity.

Carefully pinching the skin, I felt his fingers pluck the tracer from my ankle and then cover the wound with the gauze he had ready.

"One down."

I let out the breath I was holding and my eyes fluttered open. I watched Mykail tenderly clean the blood off my skin before placing new gauze over the wound, wrapping it gently and finally pressing a delicate kiss to the skin above the bandage. He smiled, standing straight and pecking another kiss on my lips.

"There."

"Two more," I mumbled.

He took my right hand, where the scar was still slightly visible, and ran his thumb over the rougher skin. He kissed the scar before sterilizing the knife once more.

The entire time he was removing the tracer in my hand I was staring at his face. He was handsome and beautiful at the same time. His bright blue eyes were focused on my hand and his jaw was clenched in concentration, causing the tendons to stand out under his pale skin. I could have stared at him forever.

After kissing my now-bandaged hand, he moved back to my mouth and kissed me once.

"How are you doing?"

"Okay..." I whispered. I was doing far better than I expected. Despite my fear of sharp objects and blood, I was happy. The actions that night were very intimate, full of vulnerability and trust. I was trusting Mykail not to hurt me, to respect that I had a phobia, and he was being tender, gentle, and considerate. It made my heart race in an entirely different way.

I grabbed the back of his neck with my other hand and pulled him closer, kissing him, trying to convey the complex emotions swimming within my chest.

Once again, the kiss became heated and he pulled away, though he did not leap away, hesitant in parting.

"Lily..." he breathed against my mouth. "Don't get me worked up. We still have one more."

"I know..." I whispered, grabbing him again and kissing him deeply once more as I reached down and grabbed his hands, placing them against my chest, breaking the kiss with every ounce of strength I possessed.

He stared at me for a moment before slowly unbuttoning the top button, his hands shaking just barely. He had seen me in my underwear before and he had undressed me on a few occasions, but with the intimacy of the moment, it seemed far more significant that he was the one unbuttoning my blouse.

My breath quickened and I felt my body grow warm as his eyes moved to each new expanse of skin that was revealed.

When the blouse was open, he pushed it from my shoulders, his palms flat on my skin as he moved the fabric, causing my eyes to shut and my heart to bang against my ribs. He pressed a kiss to my shoulder as he took the shirt away and dropped it to the tile floor. My head fell back, my neck weak.

His hands took my shoulders and he slowly pulled away from me, nodding once to tell me to turn around. I shakily picked my legs up and folded them under me, turning to face the mirror, embarrassed to be facing my flushed face. I took a moment to look at the two of us in the mirror—I couldn't help but think we looked good together.

He pressed his hand to my shoulder blade and then ran his fingertips up my skin, tracing the side of my bra strap before pushing it off my shoulder and down my arm agonizingly slow. He pressed his lips to my shoulder, his eyes closed.

The words out of my mouth could not have been stopped even if I wanted to stop them.

"Take it off."

His eyes opened and he looked at me through the mirror, surprised. "What?"

"Take it off," I repeated, a little stronger that time.

He glanced at the clasp of my bra. My heart was racing, almost loud enough for him to hear as my breath shuddered out of me. Mykail swallowed hard and then moved his fingers down my back, grabbing the back of my bra and releasing the two hooks.

He hesitated, holding the fabric before moving his hands to push the straps down my arms. I tried not to feel embarrassed or self-conscious as the fabric slipped away from my breasts and left me exposed to the mirror and Mykail. He looked at me in the mirror and his hands went to my shoulders, shaking more than before.

"You're beautiful."

I shivered at the sound of his voice, at how much I felt in that moment, at the closeness that we had emotionally, at how I was bare before him, at how he said I was beautiful...

He kissed my shoulder again, his fingers tracing the scar where the tracer rested. When his lips moved away from my skin, I closed my eyes so I would not be faced with the image of myself in the mirror, panting and flushed. It was embarrassing and an incredible turn on, the sensations mixing into a confusing ball in the pit of my stomach.

Mykail sterilized the knife while I kept my eyes closed, though I could both hear and feel the breath shuddering out of him. He was just as worked up as me.

I felt his fingers against my skin far too acutely, so when the knife cut into my skin, I did not feel it at all, focused entirely on his flat hand against my back, holding the skin taught as he cut. Then, I felt his fingers work the chip out before disappearing and returning with gentle care to clean the wound.

He washed his hands and covered the wound while I tried to control myself from turning around and kissing him until we both couldn't breathe.

He pushed the tape of the band aid down and then leaned forward, kissing my skin once more, as he had done with the other wounds. I lost all self-control.

I spun around on the marble countertop and grabbed his face, kissing him hungrily, as if my life depended on it. He met me with equal enthusiasm, grabbing my hips and pulling our bodies together, my breasts meeting his warm chest and causing me to release a near animal-like sound into his mouth.

He returned with his own groan as our tongues tangled and our bodies lit up like dry timber. He grabbed me from the counter and I wrapped my legs around his waist, allowing him to carry me to my bedroom and put me down on the bed, laying over me like a blanket, his wings supporting him as he covered me. I moaned into his mouth and our tongues pushed against one another, trying to decide who would control the kiss.

My brain shut off. Everything was about touch. He shifted his weight to one forearm as his other hand ran up my side to cup my breast, my back arching violently, chasing the stimulation.

His leg came to rest between mine and, instead of a whimper, Mykail swallowed the loud moan that I could not contain.

I broke the kiss to breathe, though no matter how much oxygen entered my lungs I could not catch my breath. Mykail did not allow me any time to recover, dipping his head to my neck and kissing me with open mouth kisses, trying not to leave any marks. My eyes shut, my body too focused on other sensations to keep them open.

When Mykail moved to my chest and kissed my breast before taking one of my nipples between his lips, any semblance of conscious thought I might have had was obliterated. My body was strung tighter than I had ever known. It was a delicious feeling, and yet I still craved more. One of my hands managed to find his hair and my fingers tangled in the soft tendrils, holding his head to me. His moan hummed through my skin to my spine, causing sparks of electricity to shoot through me at lightning speeds.

His hand that had been palming my other breast skimmed down my torso to the waistband of my jeans and carefully pulled the button open. I gasped and my eyes shot open, excitement spreading through me like wildfire.

After working the zipper of my jeans down, his hand slipped over my panties and cupped me intimately. A choked noise that I barely recognized as my own voice left my lips, the touch so overpowering I was sure I would faint.

His fingers began working against the fabric of my panties. Each press and push against my skin caused my sensitivity to rise higher and more cries to leave my throat.

Mykail's mouth released my nipple and kissed a path back to my mouth, swallowing the sounds I was making as his hand continued to work magic.

Suddenly, it was all too much. There was too much sensation. My muscles tensed and my legs began to shake. I felt myself cringe against the feeling, and my mouth opened again, a small plea for him to stop managing to make its way into the air. I could see the cliff I was heading toward and I was frightened to go over the edge.

"It's alright," Mykail whispered against the shell of my ear. "Let go..."

And that was it. I was flung over the edge of the cliff into all-consuming bliss. My back arched and a choked version of a moan bubbled out of my throat as my body, tightly strung, suddenly snapped and shuddered with a delicious sensation I had never known before. I was weightless and soaring for a few seconds before I came crashing down to earth, boneless and dazed.

The first thing I saw was Mykail's smiling face above me as he watched me recover.

He kissed me gently, bringing me back to reality with the touch.

"Are you alright?" he asked.

"I'm better...than alright," I managed to pant, a smile breaking across my lips. "That was..." I shook my head, unable to find the words. He chuckled quietly and kissed me once more. I swallowed hard and tried to catch my breath. "But...what about..."

"What?"

I quickly pursed my lips, knowing if I brought up sex in conversation now, he would back away and tell me it was too dangerous and that we needed to be careful and all the other excuses he had been using.

"Kiss me..." I whispered, taking his face in my hands.

He obliged, lowering himself to kiss me as I tried to find enough control of my body to reciprocate.

Just as I felt him starting to respond more heatedly to the kiss, there was a piercing ring that startled both of us. I listened carefully, not sure what I had heard, or why it was suddenly quiet.

Then it sounded again, and my brain registered the sound of the phone ringing.

Mykail rolled off me and I groaned in frustration, getting up and looking at the caller ID of the house phone, though it appeared as unavailable. Glancing apologetically at Mykail, I answered the phone, unexplainably nervous.

"Hello?"

"Lily? Hi, honey, it's Dad!"

"Dad!" I greeted. I heard Mykail chuckle at the timing for me to receive a call from my father in Europe.

It was an effective way to kill the mood.

Chapter Forty-Six

I apologized a million times to Mykail after the hour-long conversation with my father. He assured me that everything was alright and it had probably been for the best that we had stopped. I didn't agree, but Mykail refused to continue where we had left off.

It had been the first time I had had an orgasm. I had always been curious about sex and intimacy, but I had been too embarrassed to touch myself or seek answers from my more experienced friends. Now, I was worried I would become addicted to the feeling. I wanted more, and when I tried to close my eyes that night to sleep, an uncomfortable heat would pool between my legs as I thought about the intimacy earlier.

It was all I could think about and it made it extremely difficult to concentrate on anything else during school. It had been so intimate, so beautiful, and even though a part of me was embarrassed, another part of me was ecstatic.

That was when I made up my mind to finally seduce Mykail sometime that week.

After school, Mark was standing diligently in the snow, waiting for us. He opened the door to allow me to escape the weather. I said hello to him and he smiled and nodded back. Knowing Mark could understand me made me feel stupid for all the previous times I had tried to communicate with him.

Clark got in the car quickly to get out of the snowstorm, pulling his gloves off his hands and shaking the snow from his jacket as Mark climbed in the car.

"Hello," he greeted.

"Hey," I said back. I nodded to his hand. "What happened?" I asked, noting the band aid.

"Oh," he said, glancing at the wound. He pointed to the driver's seat as Mark pulled out of the parking lot. "That one happened." I saw Mark smile in the rear-view mirror.

"What do you mean?"

"He decided that I needed to take my tracers out right when we got home," Clark explained. "So he took them out."

"Really? Mykail did the same."

I thought about the statement. I doubted that the removal of Clark's tracers ended in making out and...

"Really?" Clark laughed. "That's good. Do you have a way to keep them in the same spot, yet?"

"No," I admitted. "I'm just carrying them around in my shoe right now."

I felt guilty for thinking such dirty thoughts when Clark and Mark were in the car, but thinking about the removal of the tracers had me replaying everything that happened afterward and, once again, my body was acting beyond my control. I couldn't help but notice the similarities to when Dana was near me, but this time it was all from my own brain. I really needed to learn how to control my hormones...

Going into the Commission made me remember that Clark and I had to be very careful about how we acted around Mark. I almost asked him a question, but stopped myself, even though we were alone in the elevator.

After getting into the conference room, we carefully discussed how to inform the Commish Kids who had not shown up on Sunday about the new plan. We divided up who we wanted to talk to and then decided that, on the drive home, we needed to ask Mark when we would be able to discuss things with him, when he would know the schedule for the Sweeps, and when Dana would be out of the Commission.

I wanted to ask Mark questions about the security and how many security guards were experiments, but since I could not talk to Mark in the Commission, I decided that I was going to ask Sean the questions while Clark was working on his final report like a good student.

I told Clark I was going to the bathroom and went to Sean's office, having thought through an elaborate reason for asking him such questions having to do with Miranda and Julie, asking if they would be experiments, and how it was decided which experiments would be part of the security detail.

But Sean's office was empty—the lights were on though, showing that he was somewhere in the basement. Thinking he might be in the bathroom, I decided to wait outside his door for him to return. I closed the door to his office, glancing around to see if anyone saw me, catching sight of the door to Dana's office across the hall ajar.

I hesitated, not sure if I should eavesdrop on Dana after the last time when I saw him with my mother. Curiosity got the better of me, and I was feeling very bold that day, so I crept forward.

I peeked into Dana's office, pressing my face in the small opening, barely catching a glimpse of Dana leaning against the front of his desk, twirling a pen in his hand, concentrating on the pen and ignoring Sean.

"—to stay here. It's too dangerous to have all of our resources out of the Commission at once," Sean's voice sounded within the office. I could not see him with my limited vantage point, but I knew he was close to Dana. There was a pause as Dana twirled the pen again, still concentrating on the object. "Dana, are you listening to me?"

Dana groaned and, rather than rolling just his eyes, he rolled his entire head and slammed the pen back down on the desk behind him.

"Yes, I'm fucking listening," he grumbled irritably. His head rolled forward and he stared at the floor, moving one of his shoes to press the heel to the toe of his other shoe, tapping his foot a few times. Sean moved into my field of vision, taking Dana's chin and forcing him to lift his head.

"Please, Dana, this is important."

"Everything is so damn important…" Dana pouted, looking at his feet again when Sean removed his hand.

"Dana…" Dana did not look up. "*Dana.*"

Dana let out a heavy sigh and looked up at Sean, who nodded once.

"Thank you," Sean said. "This is for your safety as well, you know."

"Oh, I can take care of myself just fine." Dana smiled, running his hands up the fabric of Sean's lapels. Sean seemed not to notice the action at all.

"You're asking for a sixty-five percent decrease in your security twice a week."

"I love it when you talk statistics," Dana cooed playfully, his hands moving from Sean's lapels to take his tie, pulling it out of his jacket and pulling him closer. Sean sighed again, seeming unaffected by Dana's advances.

"It's too dangerous," Sean said sharply, ignoring the Commission leader's hands.

"You are way too uptight…" Dana said, his hands releasing the tie and dropping down to the front of Sean's jacket, unbuttoning the two buttons and pushing the jacket apart. "It's always work, work, work with you…"

"I'm uptight, Dana, because you're compromising our security," he snapped. Dana's hand moved inside Sean's coat, his arms wrapping around Sean.

"Is that really the only reason?"

"You're making my job harder than it already is," Sean growled. I was impressed that Sean was able to ignore all the advances Dana was making. It was strange and unnatural seeing Dana try to seduce a man in such a fashion, playing the meek and playful person in front of Sean.

"Am I?" Dana whispered.

"Dana…" Sean groaned, frustrated with the unfocused leader.

"How long has it been, Sean?" Dana whispered, pulling Sean even closer until he was forced to take a step.

"You know exactly how long it's been," he answered. I felt my face go red at the implications of the question and answer. It was a very intimate and bizarre look into the relationship—whatever that was—between Sean and Dana.

"Shall we do something to help relieve the tension?" Dana murmured, leaning closer. Sean lifted his head so that Dana's was faced with his neck instead of his face.

"I would rather you focus."

Dana sighed and pressed his forehead to the collar of Sean's shirt, shaking his head.

"I would…but it's so hard not to entertain Little Lily when she's spying on me."

I fell back from the door, scrambling to my feet and running down the hall, abandoning all thought of speaking to Sean about the security of the Commission.

Dana did not follow when I ran away from his office, though I had heard him laughing as I retreated. For a long time, all I thought about in the conference room was that Dana would come in and talk about what I had seen in his office, but when he failed to find me, my thoughts calmed down and drifted back to what had been distracting me all day.

I was getting myself so worked up that I was worried I would jump Mykail in the foyer. In fact, the thought was rather appealing.

But the evening started out rather domestically. Mark walked me to the door, nodded to Mykail and then left, stopping my plan of jumping Mykail as soon as I opened the door. Mykail then approached me when the door was closed and kissed me sweetly before suggesting we make dinner together.

It was fun and easy to make dinner with Mykail helping, even though I couldn't fit between his wings and the kitchen island when he was at the sink and I teased him about it. We chatted about school and how bad my grades were and the silly things I had heard around the halls, filling him in on gossip that I had been out of touch with myself. It was so simple and seemed so profound at the same time. We had become comfortable with one another, able to talk casually, like we had known one another for years.

Over dinner, we talked about stories from Mykail's past, as well as mine, and laughed like nothing could go wrong.

"Okay, I have one," I said, finishing the last bits of salad still on my plate. "When I was eight, I was neighbors with this girl who used to bully me in school," I started my third story of the night. "At her ninth birthday party, she had a sleepover with everyone in the neighborhood, and she was bragging about all her presents and bullying me even at the party. So, when she slept, I cut all her hair off."

Mykail choked on his water, laughing as he coughed and spluttered.

"You *didn't*!"

"I did," I said, cringing. "I think I was a very angry child…I did a lot of things like that."

"Apparently," he agreed. "What happened when she woke up?"

"She screamed and cried, but no one knew who did it so I didn't get into trouble until a few months later when I finally fessed up."

"I bet that brought her down a few pegs, though."

"No, actually, it didn't," I lamented. "She got a really cute pixie cut and became the most popular girl in school. Thankfully she went to a different school as we got older and I didn't have to deal with her."

"I never understood how the schools could have a hierarchy," he said.

"Well, weren't there other children in your…family?" I said, trying to play down the fact that his family had been a drug dealing group. He nodded.

"I think we had a different kind of pecking order…"

"Oh…" I could sense that he was recalling a sadder time in his life and I immediately became awkward, not sure what to say to make him feel better. I pushed the remaining chicken around on my plate, not looking at him until he spoke again.

"It's okay, you know."

"What?"

"To ask me questions."

"You just looked really sad, that's all," I muttered, still looking at my plate awkwardly.

"It was a bad time," Mykail said with a shallow nod. "My family was always struggling, whether it was with money or law enforcement…" He shrugged and turned back to the final bit of dinner on his plate, eating slowly. "We had to do what we could for the best of the family, even if that meant doing things we didn't want to, or weren't proud of."

"Like what?" I whispered. I was unsure I wanted to hear the answer. Mykail chewed quietly and then took a deep breath, staring at his empty plate for several long, tense moments.

"Lily…" he started hesitantly. "I wasn't completely honest with you…"

"What are you talking about?"

"When...do you remember what Dana told you about me?" he asked, looking at me, his eyes trying to conceal his fear. "That I was selling my body?"

My heart fell into my stomach. He shook his head.

"I'm sorry, I really shouldn't be telling you this..."

"Well, you can't just leave it like that," I told him. "What about it?"

Mykail was obviously very nervous about continuing, so I schooled my expression in an attempt to make him more at ease. He was silent, staring at the table, wringing his hands in his lap.

"When I was twelve..." he said, "my half-brother was left responsible for the family for a year or so while my parents and my uncle went into hiding because there had been a tangle with the law enforcement. They were going to wait for things to calm down." Mykail heaved a sigh. "We fell on really hard times...We couldn't eat, we had no money..." His voice became more quiet and strained. "So my half-brother, who was the oldest of all of us at the time...he conned one of my brothers to push a different drug, while my other older brother and I..." He trailed off and reached up, pinching the bridge of his nose.

"Lily," he said suddenly, taking my hands and looking me in the eye, "I don't want to tell you this, but I think...since we're getting more...intimate, you have a right to know. I have had sex before."

"I figured," I said, trying to sound nonchalant.

"Just know that I don't really want to tell you this, but you should know," he continued awkwardly, biting his lower lip. "I made money for the family by selling my body..." he said, his voice straining over each word. "Basically, my half-brother was my pimp at that time...he would push me into cars with older women and men...anyone who was willing to pay for me...I did that for about three years, trying to get enough money with my brothers to feed our family."

A part of me wanted to be disgusted with Mykail. I wanted to ask him how he could sell himself like that, but I bit the acid words back and reminded myself of the time that Mykail had been going through. It was not fair to attack him when he had opened up and told me something so embarrassing and horrifying about his past.

"You did what you had to do to feed your family..."

"You're not angry?"

"I'm furious at your half-brother," I snarled. Mykail let out a relieved chuckle and released my hands.

"Maybe that's why my father kicked him out," he said. "I did have some infections when I came to the Commission, but they were all treated...I think it's my job as your partner to tell you about my past."

I placed a hand on his face and smiled, realizing that he only told me because he cared about me and he was behaving responsibly.

Mykail let out a nervous breath and stood, grabbing the plates.

"I'll do the dishes."

"I'm going to change into my pajamas," I declared, standing and stretching, patting my belly. "I'm gaining weight, my jeans are too tight."

"You are not gaining weight," Mykail laughed, rolling his eyes and going to the sink with the dishes. "Go change into something more comfortable."

"Want to watch a movie afterward?"

"Don't you have finals you need to study for?"

"I don't want to," I said simply, walking out of the kitchen and toward the stairs to my room as Mykail laughed behind me.

My mind was turning over what Mykail had disclosed. I knew Mykail came from a rough background, but I had not expected that he had been trafficked by his older sibling. I forced myself not to become uncomfortable, reminding myself over and over again that the reason he told me was because he cared and wanted me to know the truth about his previous sexual experiences before we became intimate.

I opened my bedroom door and let out a heavy sigh.

"Not quite the past you were expecting, was it, Little Lily?"

I screamed and leapt backward, my eyes wide as I stared at the suit-clad Dana sitting on my bed, leaning back on his hands, smiling casually, his dark glasses nowhere to be seen.

"What the fuck are you doing here?!" I bellowed. "How did you get in?!"

"You really should keep your doors locked, Little Lily," Dana chided. "Anyone could just walk right in."

"The doors *were* locked," I snapped. "I only use the front door and I always lock it!"

"Oh." Dana smiled, reaching into his pocket and pulling out a key ring. "Then I got in with my key."

"Get out of my house before I report you!" I ordered. My temper was not a matter of fighting Dana. It was primal. It was territorial.

"Who are you going to call?"

"The police!"

"I own the police."

"I am telling you now to get the fuck out of my house!"

"Lily!" Mykail rounded into my room and stopped dead in his tracks when he saw Dana. "*You...*"

"Ah, Mykail," Dana greeted, standing. "You're speaking. I guess that means you've warmed up to your new masters." He walked toward Mykail and placed a hand against the experiment's chin, forcing him to look up. "But don't forget who truly owns you..."

Mykail ground his teeth together and moved to punch Dana, but just as he swung, Dana stepped out of the way and Mykail let out a choked cry of pain, falling to the ground, his wings twitching, knocking over the lamp and clock on my bedside table as he groaned.

"Mykail!" I gasped, starting toward him, but Dana caught my arm, pulling me back and putting himself between me and Mykail.

"He's fine," he said, pointing a finger at me to scold me. "However, Little Lily, we need to have a talk."

"About what?!" I snapped, pushing at his chest unaffectedly.

"Don't think I didn't hear you two talking down there. I did enjoy all the stories about what a devious little girl you were, but the point is," his voice became icy, "he said you two were getting intimate." He shook his head, clicking his tongue. "I am very disappointed in you. I trust you to be alone in the house with him and you almost lose your virtue."

"It's none of your fucking business!"

"It is my fucking business," he snarled, leaning closer, his eyes boring into mine. "I've already told you, Little Lily. I don't like sharing."

"Fuck you, I'm not yours!"

"Oh, you are," he said with authority that sent shivers up my spine. He tilted his head slightly to the side and the shivers turned into waves of fear. "You are completely mine, you just haven't accepted that, yet."

He turned over his shoulder to see Mykail struggling to get to his feet.

"You really want to fuck *him*?" Dana chuckled brokenly. "He's just a boy, Little Lily. He's got a lot more to learn. He may have been a whore, but he knows nothing about giving pleasure to women, I can assure you."

"I'd say he knows plenty."

The words were a mistake and I knew it. Mykail blinked at me like I had levitated into the air and Dana rounded on me with fire in his eyes. I backed away. Dana pulled me into his arms, his hands hard on my body as he locked me against him.

"Don't provoke me, Little Lily," he warned. "Half the fun in having you is getting you to come to me first, but if you continue to push, I will take you right here in front of him and there will be nothing either of you could do to stop me."

His eyes revealed the promise in his words.

"Whatever pleasure you think he's given you is only a sliver of what I can show you," he whispered, his eyes changing from menacing to arousing, causing my legs to go weak. "I can take you to heights you never even dreamed existed." Dana leaned into me, pressing his mouth to my ear. "And you'll crawl to me begging for more…"

I shuddered from the tone, unable to help my response.

There was a knock that sounded from the door leading to the garage and Dana let out a breathy chuckle, standing straight and releasing me.

"That will be Sean," he said. "He's found me."

Dana looked at me and Mykail and smiled darkly.

Before I registered that he had moved, Dana took my face in his hands, kissing me deeply, overwhelming me as he pressed his weight into the kiss.

I hated to admit the feeling was electric, and I especially hated to admit that when Mykail was watching. I saw him move out of the corner of my eye, starting toward us with a growl, but Dana broke the kiss and held up a hand to Mykail, holding the remote for the disciplinary chips between his fingers.

"I wouldn't try it, little angel," he chuckled. He turned back to me. "Open your mouth," he whispered with his honey-like voice. My body shuddered, but my mouth remained shut, desperate to fight him.

"Little Lily," he whispered. "Open your mouth…"

I did not obey.

His hand moved down my back and pressed me even closer as his leg moved between mine, causing me to gasp in surprise.

As soon as my lips parted, he swooped in, tongue first, and kissed me so hard it made my head spin. I was sure I would pass out as his tongue explored my teeth and lips delicately. I never thought to bite him, too overwhelmed from the onslaught of intense sensation to command my muscles.

My eyes fluttered shut. The only thing that kept me from moaning was Mykail's proximity. I wanted to explore such sensations with him, not with Dana.

The leader of the Commission of the People broke the kiss and smiled.

"Good girl."

He turned to Mykail.

"Let's get you back to your room."

The most I could do was try not to collapse as Dana pushed Mykail down the hall to his room, shoving him in roughly and slamming the door, using his own key to lock the door.

"I will lock the other one, too, don't you worry," Dana promised. He looked over Mykail as I stumbled out of my door, trying to keep my wobbly knees from giving out on me. The leader of the Commission smirked when he caught sight of me.

"Just in case."

He pressed the button on the remote in his pocket. Mykail let out a choked scream and collapsed to the ground again.

Suddenly finding my feet again, I started forward, grabbing onto the bars and watching Mykail writhe in pain as Dana chuckled, ignoring the continuous pounding on the door to the garage.

"He'll be fine, Little Lily," Dana assured, grabbing my arm and pulling me down the stairs. I wanted to fight, but I was worried that, if I fought him, he would punish Mykail, and I could not bear to see him collapse yet again. I had forgotten about the disciplinary chips, kicking myself for not thinking to remove them as well.

"Calm down, damn it," Dana groaned, opening the door to show a flustered Sean standing in the garage. "I just got here. You're quick."

"When you vanish, I have to be," Sean said. "Good evening, Miss Sandover. I am so sorry," he said, stepping into the house. "Sir, we need to go back to the Commission."

"No," Dana snapped. "I've been cooped up there for too long and I'm going crazy. We're staying here tonight."

"What? *Why*?" both Sean and I snapped.

"We have to make sure that Mykail doesn't take advantage of having Little Lily alone in the house," Dana said, looking at Sean expectantly. The head of security groaned and rolled his eyes, closing the door behind him and shaking his head. Dana smiled triumphantly and turned to me.

"Don't worry, I will be right here," he pointed to the couches in the small living room at the bottom of the stairs, "all night to be sure that he doesn't sneak into your room when you're asleep."

"And *I'll* make sure you don't do the same," Sean added, sparing a glance at Dana. The head of the Commission made a contemptuous face at the other man before turning back to me.

"So, why don't you go upstairs, do your homework, brush your teeth, and go to bed like a good little girl?"

"Fuck you," I snarled, storming upstairs. I turned to look into Mykail's room. He was sitting against the foot of the bed, breathing hard, his eyes tightly shut, waiting for his pain to subside. I was about to open my mouth to speak when Dana's voice resonated sharply up the staircase.

"Little Lily, get your ass in your room, now!"

I flipped him off as I walked into my room, slamming my door shut angrily.

I had no intention of letting Dana stay in my house all night but I needed a few minutes to gather my thoughts. I sat on my bed, running my fingers through my hair, agitated and trying to figure out a way to get him out.

I was staring at the carpet, wanting nothing more than to go to Mykail and make sure he was alright before attacking Dana somehow. I looked at my door for a moment, seriously considering the plan before I sighed and flopped back on my bed, torn.

A small mewl startled me.

"Dex?!"

I fell to the side of my bed, looking under the bed skirt to see my cat, terrified, hiding behind the stowed suitcase.

"Oh, baby, come here, come here," I whispered, reaching under the bed and carefully extracting him, pulling him into my arms. I sat against my bed, holding him to me, stroking his fur. "Are you okay? Did he hurt you?" I asked, looking him over. "I'm sorry, sweetheart. I'm sorry…" I held him tight, both of us calming down together.

Once I regained some of my bearings, I tried to figure out how to get Dana Christenson out of my house. I paced my room, concocting a myriad of plans. My legs were tired by the time I gave up trying to figure out a way to Mykail's room without Dana seeing me. I sat on my bed, vowing that I would not sleep that night in case Dana crept into my room. When I realized he had not tried to sneak in already, I began to believe he had left—though a quick glance at Sean's car in the driveway told me otherwise.

Around midnight, I sat at my desk to do my homework, trying to keep myself awake. It was impossible to concentrate.

I was wondering what Dana was doing in my living room. Or maybe he was wandering around my house, looking through everything that my family owned. I had half a mind to storm downstairs and demand that he leave bluntly.

Before I had time to think better of it, I opened the door and started downstairs. Dana was sitting on the larger couch in the small living room, facing the fireplace, a glass of wine on the coffee table in front of him and his shoes kicked off haphazardly below his seat as he sat with his legs folded under him, an old photo album perched on his thighs as he looked at our family photos.

"You should be sleeping," he said, not lifting his gaze from the pictures.

"And you should be minding your own business and not snooping through my family album."

"There is nothing about your family I don't already know," he said, seeming disinterested as he turned the page. I looked around the room, leaning on my hands on the back of the other couch, my brain abandoning the idea of telling Dana off.

"Where's Sean?"

"He went on a walk. He'll be back," Dana answered, his eyes still downcast. He glanced over the pictures, studying every detail. "I'm surprised to see one of these old albums," he murmured. "Most families keep the electronic ones now."

I looked at the album in his hands.

"Mom used to love putting those together," I said, walking into the living room to sit on the other couch. "She used to try and get me to help, but I always thought it was such a waste of time when we could just have the electronic ones."

Dana turned another page.

"My favorite thing about albums is seeing how the style changed," he told me, his voice calm and quiet. "Makes me think about how quickly everything changes. It's refreshing knowing that change is never far away."

I watched him as he looked over the new page, trying to read his nearly-vacant expression. "Do you feel nostalgic about anything?"

He finally turned to me and shook his head slowly. "No." He looked back at the page and smiled softly. "Your father certainly had a huge smile on his face when you were born."

I studied him, surprised by his demeanor. He seemed quieter, calmer than I had ever seen him before. I still felt his power, but it was muted, as though he was partially asleep. "He must have been thrilled to have a daughter."

I looked him over, confused and admittedly curious about his change in behavior.

"You two seem to have a very special relationship."

"...we used to."

"What do you mean?"

"Ever since the Commission, things have changed," I said, turning my eyes to the album in his lap to avoid his eyes. "Nothing is what it used to be."

"How did the relationship change?"

"What do you care?"

"I'm curious," Dana said, closing the album and placing it on the coffee table. "I told you, I like noting how things change."

"You already know everything about my family, though," I pointed out. "I'm sure you don't need me to tell you."

Dana smiled, grabbing the glass of wine and sitting back in his seat. I scoffed and rolled my eyes.

"By all means, make yourself at home," I snarled coldly.

"There's no need to be hostile, Little Lily," Dana said, lifting the glass to his lips with incredible grace and power, commanding my attention to the way his wrist ever-so-slightly tilted as he tasted the burgundy liquid. "I just want to talk."

I mustered up all my courage. "What is *with* you?" I whispered. "You're...different."

"How so?"

"You're...quiet."

"I'm normally raucous?" he chuckled, lowering the glass to rest on his knee.

"No. You're normally...I don't know...not like this." I shook my head. "It's kind of like when an animal is sedated to get their shots...you seem to be running at forty percent."

Dana smiled and leaned his head back on the couch, looking at the ceiling, deciding how to respond.

"My mind is normally very busy," he said, his voice gentle. "Always buzzing, like a little bee that you can't swat away." His head rolled forward again to look at me. "But sometimes, it goes quiet...generally when I finally get out of the Commission." He looked into space for a moment. "That's why I just want to talk. I want to know how your relationship with your father changed when you became part of the Commission."

I sighed and looked around the room, trying to find a way to keep from spilling my guts to Dana. His eyes were prying and powerful as always, but they were magnetizing now, pulling me closer in a different way. I found myself relaxing, not at all worried about being alone with him.

"That's not very fair..."

"What's not?"

"That you can ask questions about my life even though you know everything about me," I said. "If I answer you, I get to ask you a question."

Dana nodded, tipping the wine glass to me before taking another sip.

"I'll go first," I said, jumping on the opportunity. I had always had a million questions buzzing in my head about Dana Christenson, but now presented with the opportunity to ask, I found I could barely think of any. "Were you a willing experiment in the Commission?"

He glanced distantly at the family photo album on the table.

"That's a little difficult to answer," he started. "At first, no. I kicked and screamed and fussed, just like all the others. But...then I started to realize how I was changing, how those barriers that had kept me from acknowledging who I was were falling...and I was able to understand better how I operated as a human. I learned more about myself on that table than anywhere else. After a while, I found myself excited to go back to the tests."

"What did they try to make you?"

"That's two questions, Little Lily," he said. "It's my turn." I grumbled irritably and slumped back in my seat. "What was it about the relationship you had with your father that made it special? That made it different from the relationship with your mother?"

"I don't know..." I mumbled. "It just...*was*." I picked at the lint on my pajamas. Dana was very quiet, waiting. I could feel his eyes, but they were gentler than usual, almost caring, even if they still made my skin prickle. "My mother was always teaching me something. Always looking for some lesson, or trying to make me a perfect woman, or...whatever it was she wanted me to be. I always had to try so hard to please her, to be the perfect daughter, the one that everyone would compliment so she would compliment me later. With my dad, he just loved me. I didn't have to be anything for him. We used to be able to go out and entertain ourselves for hours and never be bored. We were always laughing. I always felt so happy when I was with him. But now..."

"Now?"

"Now he belongs to the Commission," I finally whispered. "He's not mine anymore. I have to get permission from you just to spend the afternoon with him." The tears were beginning to rise to my eyes, but I bit them back, pursing my lips and waiting for the lump in my throat to go down before I spoke again. "And he's so busy trying to appease both my mother and me when we fight. So...he's not my father anymore. He's the peacekeeper, the one who's trying to keep things the way they were." I glanced at Dana, who was looking at me with vivid golden eyes. "But things are never going to be the way they were."

"No," Dana admitted quietly. "They won't."

"I want to go back to that time, too," I whispered. "I want my father back."

Dana nodded contemplatively, glancing down at his wine glass before he extended the drink to me.

"Would you like some?"

I blinked at the wine, and then glanced at Dana again. It was like I was sitting with a completely different person. I started to wonder if I was sitting with the human Dana had been before the Commission tested on him rather than the frightening leader of the Commission of the People. I studied his relaxed posture, the small light that played in his eyes. It was not a different look, but it was subdued, and *much* easier to handle.

Carefully, I took the wine glass from his grasp.

"Ask your question," he prompted. I lifted the wine glass to my nose and sniffed it. I stared into the burgundy liquid as I sloshed it around in the glass, pretending that I knew what I was doing as I thought of my next question.

"Do you remember your life before you were an experiment?" I asked, lifting the glass to my lips and sipping the wine.

"Of course I do."

"You said you didn't remember things from your childhood."

"Ah, well, there are certain things I don't remember. I couldn't tell you my birthday or how old I am because I don't remember. But I do remember my mother and father. I remember the little sister that died three days after she was born and made my mother terrified to try for children again...I remember how skilled my father was with a belt. That's still pretty clear in my memory."

"Abused?"

"Disciplined," Dana corrected with a small smile that made me realize he was only repeating what his father had said about beating his child. "I remember how ambitious my father was. He wanted so much for his life and his children...and how my mother refused to stand up for me when I was being hurt." He sighed and shifted his legs on the couch, stretching them out with cat-like fluidity. "But, that's ancient history." He looked at me expectantly. "Do you hate your mother for sleeping with me?"

I blinked, surprised at the bluntness of the question. I opened my mouth to say something and then stopped, closing my mouth again and sighing, shaking my head.

"I don't know..." I admitted. "I think I'm angrier about how weak she was against you. You just wave your hand, bat your eyelashes, and say the perfect sentence and everyone falls into your arms. She couldn't resist you. She was drawn to how dangerous you are. I guess no one can resist you, can they?" I said, unable to keep the disdain out of my voice.

"Some can," he said. He reached for the wine again, taking a longer sip.

"My next question…why are you so interested in me?"

He smiled, passing the wine back to me. "Because I see your potential. And I am very curious about who you will become as you mature. I can see so many incredible things in your future, and I can hardly wait for that to unfold." He tilted his head to the side, smirking. "Why are you so interested in knowing about *me*?"

"I don't know…I'm curious, I guess," I admitted. "I want to know how you can change yourself to be what everyone wants you to be…how you know what they want before they know it themselves…how you've managed to seduce so many people and they don't even think twice about turning their backs on anything they used to love or believe in because of you."

"You want to know how?" he asked with a grin. "I'm absolutely nothing, Little Lily. That's how I do it. All I am is a thought, and people read into me however they wish. It's not so much that I change myself as much as others see what they want in me." He leaned forward to take the wine from me again. "Understand something. Everything I used to be, all the feelings that I had when I used to care about others, people project those things. Whatever it is they want most out of me, they think of only that and push that on to me. They can turn a blind eye to everything else because there is that one thing that I can give them that nothing else can—a sense that they have accomplished something, fulfilled something, had power over their own lives and gained something for it." He shrugged, lifting the wine to his lips. "That's all it is."

The next question felt sharp as I spoke it. "Have you killed anyone?"

"Yes."

"Let me clarify the question," I said. "I don't mean ordered someone dead. I mean, have you ever directly killed someone?"

"Yes."

"As in shooting a gun—"

"Yes."

"Or stabbing someone—"

"Yes."

"Or beating someone to death—"

"Yes," he said again. "I have killed many people, Little Lily. I have shot, stabbed, and beaten people to death. I've even decapitated a few, and one time I even tortured someone to death."

He said it so easily, as if there was nothing wrong with the confession. I blinked at him stupidly, shocked and frightened at the same time.

"I only have one more question for you, Little Lily," he said. "You said you wanted to remove me from power, to take down the Commission of the People, more or less..." He smiled and tilted his head. "When you do that, do you plan to kill me?"

"...yes."

His smile widened.

"This is going to be a fun game, Little Lily."

Chapter Forty-Seven

I did not recall falling asleep but when I blinked my eyes open and realized I was not in my bedroom, I bolted upright, remembering the previous night and my conversation with Dana.

There was no trace of the leader of the Commission of the People in the living room. The wine glass that had been left empty on the coffee table was gone and the shoes he had kicked off below his seat had vanished along with the family photo album.

I intently listened for any sounds of movement in the house, but everything was still and silent.

I hurriedly extracted myself from the blanket but stopped when I tossed the blanket over the back of the couch, realizing Dana must have covered me after I had fallen asleep. The uncharacteristic warm action confused me as much as the conversation we had shared the previous night.

Shaking myself back to reality, I scrambled to my feet, jumping the stairs two at a time and turning the corner to Mykail's room, surprisingly nervous at what I would find.

Mykail was on his side on the bed, his eyes focused distantly at the wall.

"Mykail?"

His gaze shot to the door and he bolted upright.

"Lily," he gasped. "Are you alright?" He walked to the door and wrapped his hands around the bars. I placed my hand around his.

"I'm fine," I assured. "Are they still here?"

"No," he said. "They left about an hour ago."

"What time is it?" I asked, looking around his room as he turned to the clock.

"Seven twenty-three."

"Shit!" I gasped. "I'm going to be late!" I pulled away from the door, calling over my shoulder as I searched on my desk. "I'll unlock the door and then I have to run!"

"Lily!" he called. "It's no use! He took the key!"

"He *what*?!" I snapped, walking to his door again.

"He took the keys."

"That fucker…"

"Listen," he said, taking my hand, "I'm alright. Just get dressed and go to school and we'll figure out what to do tonight, okay?"

"I'm not leaving you in there with no food or water," I said and then cringed at the words. "That sounds bad."

"It's fine."

"Hold on, I'll be right back. I can be a little late for school."

"You have a final today!"

"Damn it..." I groaned, rolling my eyes. "Okay, hold on."

I ran down the stairs and into the kitchen, going to the pantry and pulling out two bottles of water, setting them on the table as I opened the refrigerator. I stopped at the neat handwritten note that was held to the refrigerator by the magnetic picture of our family portrait.

"Little Lily,
I enjoyed our conversation last night, though you fell asleep before we could talk more. I cleaned up the living room and made you lunch for school. It's in the refrigerator. Please be sure to eat. You are losing weight.
Regards,
Dana Christenson."

I ground my teeth together before reaching for the pen in the cup next to the refrigerator, writing my own note below his.

"Mr. Christenson,
I hate you."

I nodded once at the note, letting out a satisfied snort. I knew he would probably never see it and there was no point in having it remain on the refrigerator, but it made me happier to see my retort under his note. I tried to find something to give to Mykail to eat when I saw the brown paper bag that was sitting at my eye level in the refrigerator.

"Creepy fucker..." I pushed it aside. I grabbed a bowl of fruit salad and pushed the door shut with my foot, snatching a bag of pretzels from on top of the refrigerator.

I panicked when I saw the numbers on the microwave clock.

I rushed back upstairs, pushing everything gathered in my arms through the bars.

"Can you think of anything else you would like?" I asked, carefully maneuvering the bowl of fruit through the bars.

"No, this is fine," he assured. "You need to go so you won't be late."

"Okay," I said, leaning close to the bars and kissing him before darting into my room and finding my last clean school uniform in my closet. I grabbed my backpack and ran downstairs, grabbing my coat and shoes before running as fast as I could to the bus stop, barely catching my bus.

I was flustered all day, running around to my classes, cramming for the exam three minutes before we started it and knowing I failed as I turned my test in. I met with two other Commish Kids in between my art class and lunch and vaguely told them that we had a plan to break the experiments out and I would let them know what day it would be executed. I told the two of them what roles they had in the operation— something Clark and I had decided the previous day—and I assured them the breakout would happen in the next two weeks.

They seemed to react the same way Clark had suspected. Most of the Commish Kids joined the rebellion out of anger, but they never expected us to get anywhere with the plan. They were surprised to hear that we had a plan we thought could work, and their nerves were obvious because a real plan meant a real chance of being caught. However, they were relieved that they were not going to be inside the Commission, breaking anyone out of the cells.

That was a job for me and Clark.

The reality of that situation had yet to hit me.

At lunch, I nearly fell asleep as the tension began to leave my body from the crazy morning, allowing for more pressing thoughts to surface.

I needed to get the key back from Dana.

I thought about simply asking for it, telling him that he was the one who asked us to bathe Mykail and take care of his wings. I decided to start with that, and if it didn't work, I would go to Sean and ask him to get the key back somehow.

Mark drove me and Clark to the Commission as we talked about the people we spoke to that day and we went over the plan again quietly, asking Mark questions that he could answer with a nod or shake of his head. I had asked him the previous evening how often he checked for bugs in the car, and he wrote: "three times a day."

It eased my mind knowing he was so cautious.

Once in the Commission, I decided to immediately find Dana.

"I'm going to talk to Dana," I told Clark, setting my bag down in a chair.

"Why?"

"He broke into my house last night, that's why," I growled.

"He *what*?"

I saw Mark turn his head to look through the window into the conference room. He could hear us through the glass and was just as surprised to hear the news.

"You heard me. He broke into my house and decided to be creepy as fuck, so I want to talk to him about it."

"What is talking to him going to do?"

"It will make me feel better," I declared, walking around the table to the door but Clark stopped me.

"Lily, seriously, don't provoke him. You're feeding him more reasons to do what he does. You're giving him a reaction."

"He locked Mykail up and took the key," I told him sharply. "That means I can't take care of him. I can hardly feed him anything either because a plate won't fit in between the bars. I have to talk to him."

Clark opened his mouth to protest again, but he sighed and shook his head, understanding that I had no intention of backing down.

"I'll be fine," I said.

"Famous last words..."

I ignored him and walked out the door, where Mark's concerned face confronted me.

"I'll be alright," I repeated. He grabbed my wrist and tapped his pointer finger against my wrist once—another way to say 'be careful.'

I smiled and bowed my head to him before starting toward Dana's office.

I did not feel nervous about going to him. After the conversation last night, I did not feel I needed to be afraid of him. He had shown me that he had a calmer side.

I knocked and was met with a "come in" from inside. I took one deep breath and opened the door. Dana was at his desk, looking over a book. I recognized the diary of Bryant Morris. A part of me was very curious what he could possibly want to read in the journal when he had known the founder of the Commission of the People personally, but I tried to put that thought aside.

"Little Lily," he greeted, standing and buttoning his suit jacket as he walked around the desk to face me. I approached the desk, watching him carefully. "Did you enjoy the lunch I made for you?"

"I didn't eat it," I told him bluntly. "I wasn't sure if you had drugged it."

"Why would I do that?" he asked with an exasperated sigh.

"It seems like something you would do."

"I've told you before, I don't drug people," Dana said. "At least promise me you will eat something tonight. You look like you're losing weight, and frankly, skeletons are not at all attractive."

I rolled my eyes. "That's not what I came here to talk to you about."

"Is there a problem?" he asked, feigning innocence.

"Yes, there is," I said sharply. "You locked Mykail up and then took the keys so I can't let him out."

"Just until your parents come back and I know that he won't make any further attempts to steal your virtue," Dana assured with a dark smile.

"What makes you think I'm still a virgin?" I tested him. He smirked.

"Just a hunch. You put up a tough front, but I can tell."

"Regardless of what you think of my *virtue*, the fact remains that you took the key to Mykail's room and now I can't take care of him like you want me to," I growled. "You were the one who told us that he needs help bathing and keeping his wings clean. And how am I supposed to feed him when I can't fit a plate through the door?"

"He doesn't need a full place setting, Little Lily," Dana chuckled. "And as far as bathing him is concerned, I should have realized what a problem it would be to have you bathe him yourself. I'm sure that Mykail has been very willing to show you how he feels about you touching him."

"I have never bathed him naked, if that's what you mean," I told him shortly. "He's a perfect gentleman, not some animal."

"He's a man, Little Lily, of course he's an animal." Dana smiled, assuming the position I was beginning to see as common for him, leaning against the front of his desk.

"Just give me back the key," I ordered, holding out my hand. He shrugged, folding his arms over his chest.

"No."

"I can't take care of him if you don't give me the key."

"I'll come take care of him for you," he told me with a smirk. My stomach turned over at the thought of Dana coming to my house on a regular basis. I ground my teeth together and lowered my hand.

"What do I have to do to get the key back?"

Dana's eyebrows went high. "You're starting to sound a little more like the people I normally work with," he noted. "But you are out of your weight class, Little Lily."

"I'm not ignorant. I know what I was implying."

"Oh, really?" Dana said. "What do you think I want from you that could get you that key?" he challenged. "Do what I do. Figure out how to get what you want out of me without me knowing."

"That's not possible." I stepped forward, steeling myself to tease him again. My heart was beating fast. My body's recent taste for pleasure made me easily excited, and Dana's sparking energy made my skin tingle. "I already know you want to have sex with me."

"Eventually."

"What's the normal price for an exchange like this?" I asked, unbuttoning the button he had fixed earlier. He smiled at me knowingly.

"Depends on the person. But...the last time you did this, you left me quite unsatisfied."

"Yeah," I whispered, leaning closer, "but I bet you loved it. So many people just roll over and spread their legs for you. I bet you don't have many who actually make you work for it."

"It's been a long time since I've had to work for it, so to speak, yes," he admitted, watching my actions as I pulled the jacket away, fisting his coat pockets to feel for the key. I felt the smooth, round pocket watch he always kept on him but, otherwise, his pockets were empty.

"You strike me as the type that likes to be teased," I said, leaning even closer, sliding my hands up the front of his vest, once again feeling for pockets. When I encountered none, I slipped my hands under his jacket at his shoulders and began pushing the coat from him. I expected him to stop me, the same way he had stopped my mother from undressing him, but he remained still with a cocky smile, watching me push the jacket to his elbows, though he refused to move his hands off his desk to remove the article of clothing completely.

I was beginning to feel nervous. He had warned me before about teasing him. I was dangling meat in front of a lion, hoping he would not bite my arm off.

Still, I leaned closer, expecting him to close the gap between us and kiss me. I figured if I could distract him long enough to slip my hands into his trouser pockets, I could find the key and leave quickly before he got too excited.

But when my mouth was only a few centimeters from his, he did not move, refusing to meet me.

"Well?" I asked.

"Well, what?" he pressed, testing me, seeing how far I would go. "Are you going to continue?"

"What do you want me to do?"

"I want to see what you think up on your own." Dana grinned darkly. "If needed, I'll instruct you as you go."

My stomach twisted at the thought. Carefully, I leaned closer and flinched when our lips brushed. Even then, he did not move.

"You said that Mykail did not know anything about giving pleasure to a woman," I whispered against his mouth. "You have me intrigued..."

"Do I?"

For the first time, I initiated our kiss. Guilt settled in my chest at the betrayal. As long as Dana initiated the kiss, I could say that my body's reactions were from the unnatural power he possessed, but when my body shivered at the intensity of the kiss, I knew that it was entirely my fault.

Dana smirked against my lips and, finally, one hand came to my face, gently cupping my cheek. His fingers were insistent, holding me still as his lips carefully worked against mine, his tongue parting my lips.

He was teaching me how to kiss slowly.

I played along, groaning gently, my hands settling at his waist as I pressed my body forward, only slightly pretending to be intoxicated by our kiss.

My fingers dropped his hips and I hooked two fingers in his pockets, pressing my thumb against the bottom seam to feel for the key.

One of my hands went into his pocket as I pushed my tongue against his, trying to keep him distracted. However, my hand came across nothing at all. His pockets were empty.

Suddenly, his hand was on my wrist, his other hand twisting in the hair at the base of my neck as he broke the kiss.

"Eager little thing, aren't you?" he leered.

"I was not trying anything."

"I know," he said. "You were looking for the key. Do you really think I'm that simple? I wouldn't make it that easy for you, Little Lily." He pushed my hand deeper into his pocket. "I don't have it on me…"

"Let me go," I whispered, my fear rising in my throat to choke me.

"Why? You were the one who went reaching into my pockets. Do you have any idea what that does to a man?"

"It's not too difficult to guess," I sneered, trying to pull my hand away. I managed to get it out of his pocket and then twist it out of his grasp, but I felt the pinch of pain in my wrist. I retreated and his smirk widened, still looking completely in control, even leaning back on the desk with his suit jacket bunched around his elbows.

"I'm sure it's not," Dana said, his voice thick with something that set my body on fire. "I'll give you the key, if you really want to work for it."

"Fuck you," I snapped, backing away a few more steps.

"You're intensifying the chase, Little Lily," he told me. "I'm not the kind of man who likes to be teased too often."

"As far as I'm concerned, you're not a man at all," I snarled. "You're some kind of monster with no respect for anyone but yourself."

"Please, you give me too much credit," Dana chuckled darkly. "I don't even have respect for myself. Why do you think I'm so good at what I do?"

I stormed away, holding my left wrist, trying not to wince in pain. I threw the door open as Dana's laugh followed.

"Let me know the next time you want to search my pockets," he called. "We'll make it far more exciting."

I slammed the door behind me, shutting out his laughter.

I hated him…but I really hated myself in that moment.

I walked with my head down, rubbing my wrist as I made my way back to the conference rooms. I turned a corner and was startled by a voice.

"Miss Sandover?"

I turned to see Sean walking toward me.

"Sean," I said, relaxing a little.

"Are you alright?" he asked, glancing at my wrist. "Did you hurt yourself?"

"Not exactly…" I said, glancing in the direction of Dana's office door. Sean followed my gaze, spotting the door where my glare was directed. He turned back to me, his eyes apologetic.

"Did he hurt you?"

"He wouldn't let me go," I said, allowing Sean to pull my wrist away from my chest and rotate it to check for damage.

"He has a vice grip," Sean agreed. "He's stronger than he looks." With a sigh, he pat my wrist. "Come on, I'll get you some ice."

He led me to the break room that I had only ever been in to use the restroom. No one was there, so Sean had to turn on the lights before stepping into the room and moving toward the refrigerator as I followed quietly.

Sean opened a cabinet drawer and grabbed a bag and a cloth, reaching for the freezer to get ice.

"I want to apologize for Dana's unexpected visit last night," Sean said as he prepared the icepack. "I tried to keep him down here, but he was intent on leaving."

"How long had he been down here without leaving?" I asked, leaning against the counter next to Sean.

"He gets out every day, but he's been carted back and forth between here and Central Hall. He was getting restless," Sean explained. "I did not expect him to bother you, but when he disappeared, I figured I would try your home first."

I fell silent, thinking about the conversation with Dana the previous night while Sean was gone.

"Did you have a nice walk last night?" I asked stupidly. "I thought it was kind of cold to be outside…"

"Dana and I had a bit of a disagreement," Sean murmured, focused on his work. "I left before I pulled my gun on him."

I blinked, shocked at the confession.

"Why didn't you?"

Sean laughed, turning to me with an amused expression.

"I've pulled a gun on him before," he said. "And every time, he finds something very…*creative* to do with it." Sean turned back to the ice he was putting in the bag as I tried not to let my imagination run wild with possibilities of what Dana could do with a gun. "I wasn't in the mood for a wrestling match with him, so I walked out to cool off and calm down."

"Is he stronger than you?" I asked, looking over Sean's impressive stature.

"Yes," he said. "His body has been altered for strength and speed. He can win in a fight with anyone…hell, he might even win a fight with a bear if needed."

"And with Eina?"

Sean thought about that for a few moments. "I don't know about that, actually." He fell silent, sealing the bag and wrapping it in a towel. He turned to me as I blurted out a question I should not have asked.

"Have you had sex with Dana?"

He halted immediately, his eyes wide with shock at the question. Embarrassment burned at my cheeks and I looked away, coughing once in an attempt to dispel the awkwardness, but I made no attempt to take back the question.

The head of security was silent as he reached for my wrist again and wrapped it in the towel-covered ice. I flinched at the cold.

"Keep this on your wrist."

"I'm sorry, Sean, I shouldn't have asked…"

"It's alright," he said mechanically, but he offered no response to the question. "I hope Dana wasn't too horrible last night."

"Actually…" I murmured. He looked up at me quickly, worried. "He was…very different last night."

"Different how?"

"He was quiet…calm," I answered, seeing Sean relax at the words. "He was like a different person."

"His Dormant State," he said knowingly.

"His what?"

"That's what I call it when he gets like that," Sean explained, leaning on the counter next to me. "He kind of goes half asleep when he's like that, so I call it his Dormant State."

"Does that happen often?"

"No, not often at all. Actually, that says a lot about what he thinks about you."

"What do you mean?"

"Dana doesn't just run constantly like a machine," Sean explained. "When he's alone, he's very quiet, slow moving, and even gentle. But when someone enters the room, it's a shock to his system and he becomes...almost electric, the way you normally see him." His eyes focused back on my face. "If you can come into the room and he stays dormant, that means that he can control himself around you."

"Wait, normally when he's manipulating people and playing with people like he does, he's *out* of control?" I asked. Sean shrugged.

"He's never out of control," he corrected. "But he gets excited when someone comes near him. I guess kind of like a child given a new toy. But when he can show you his calm self that means that he's interested in more than just playing with you."

"So...he's even more dangerous?"

"Exactly," Sean said. He lifted the icepack gently off my wrist and then replaced it. "Miss Sandover...whatever game you and Dana are playing, it's going to end badly."

"Game?"

"I know Dana very well," he said, reaching into his pocket and pulling out three very familiar keys. "And I know that he's toying with you. It might seem appealing to toy back, but trust me...he always wins."

He handed me the keys.

"What can I do, though?" I asked, gripping the keys tightly in my palm.

"Stick with me, and stay with Mark," he answered. "Mark likes you. He'll protect you."

"What makes you say that?" I asked, a little worried by Sean's statement. I was not sure if Sean knew Mark's ability to understand English, or that he was planning to take down Dana alongside me and Clark, but with the way he had spoken, I was beginning to think that he might have known Mark's secret.

"Well," Sean said, lowering his head, his smile turning sad, "I'm sure he looks at you like a little sister. And since he can't see his own little sister any more, you fill that part of his life."

"He has a little sister?" I gasped.

"She's in the holding cells."

"How do you know that?"

"They have the same eyes. And Mark refused to leave her when he was being taken as an experiment. He actually attacked Dana, even biting him when Dana tried to bring her in for testing. He's very protective of her."

"But, she's still alive," I said, trying not to ask, deciding immediately that we needed to break her out of the holding cells.

"Yes," Sean affirmed. "Dana almost killed her and Mark's response was to nearly break Dana's leg. Everyone agreed that it was safer to keep her alive and safe. Because Mark is as strong and fast as he is, we keep her safe in the back. As long as Mark does his work and stays loyal, she remains alive."

My heart fell. Mark was still willing to risk going against Dana even though his little sister was being held as collateral for his loyalty. I cleared my throat, trying to keep the tears that had risen to my eyes at bay.

"What about you?" I asked. "Do you see me as a little sister? You're pretty protective."

Sean nodded.

"A little," he admitted. "My own sister died about a year and a half ago."

"Oh, I'm sorry, Sean. I didn't know…"

"It's alright," Sean said. "I knew it was coming for a while. She was very sick." He nodded down to the ice pack. "Ice that on and off for the rest of the afternoon and try not to lift anything heavy with that hand for a few days. It should feel better in no time."

Chapter Forty-Eight

Wednesday and Thursday passed and finals week rounded out with me failing just about every class. The part of me that cared about my grades was long gone and I easily ignored everything in school during finals week. I only considered it another week that brought us closer to the time when our override codes would be changed.

On Thursday, as Mark was driving us home from the Commission, he passed a piece of paper into the backseat. When I saw the message on the paper, my stomach flipped in apprehension and excitement.

"Next Thursday. 20:20"

That was when we were breaking prisoners out.

The thought that our act of terrorism would be occurring in only a week made the reality of the situation finally hit me. We were going to break out over one hundred people, or we were going to be found out and killed, or worse, taken into the back of the Commission to become experiments ourselves. I had a small panic attack in the back of the car that I tried to hide, but I was pretty sure that both Clark and Mark felt the same way as it seemed no one was able to take a deep breath.

There was a lot at stake. If we were not anxious, we were foolish.

When I told Mykail that we had a date and time determined, we started planning for Mykail's role as I cleaned the wound he had obtained on his wing from smashing the lock of his door so that it would no longer work. I knew that as soon as my parents returned from Europe, they would replace the door but Mykail and I had already made plans to tamper with the bars over his window to allow him a way out even if the doors were locked.

It was a late night project that we worked on when the neighbor's lights went out across the backyard. Mykail would help me climb to the roof below his window and then he would carefully fly to the same spot as I tried to keep myself from being thrown with the force of his beating wings.

I slept like a log Thursday night, but woke up feeling better and I went through my last day of finals week running around with excited energy, telling everyone who was part of the plan what time and day we were going through with the breakout.

Again, everyone involved had a bit of apprehension.

Clark told me what would happen with our after-school Commission trips now that school was dismissed for winter break. He explained that I would carpool with him as I had been and go to the Commission every day for practically the entire day. We were expected to bring things to entertain ourselves, though I was not sure how Dana could possibly expect us to find a way to entertain ourselves cooped up in the basement of the Commission of the People.

But I was not going to raise a fuss, knowing that being down there would allow us time to finish the final details of our plan—discreetly, of course.

That night, Archangel was abuzz with excitement at the conclusion of finals and the beginning of the five-week break before the next term.

I ignored the Commish Kids glaring on the balcony as I remained in the lower part of the club a majority of the night. Each one of the Commish Kids was in on the plan, and while there was no open opposition to the plot, there was still apprehension. No one bothered me, understanding that Clark and I were probably behind the entire plan with how we had been assigning roles and duties to everyone else.

I didn't care that they knew. In reality, it was Mark's plan, so Clark and I were also following orders.

I returned to our table near the bar, feeling adrenaline coursing through me as the bass thrummed against my ribs, my heart racing. I was smiling, feeling exhilarated and alive.

"You look happy," Jill noted, leaning against Devon. The two were in the early stages of being a couple and while a part of me was happy for them, another part of me was upset by the way their relationship was hurting Becca. She had become quiet and distant in prior weeks, blaming exhaustion for her behavior. I knew it was a broken heart.

Every chance I could, I would put my arm around her, and hug her or just pat her hand to assure her that I was there for her. She would always respond with a forced smile.

Becca went to dance with Jill while Devon disappeared with Todd to meet some friends who had just shown up, which left me alone with Taylor.

"So, how have you been? How's Clark?" she asked, smiling.

"We're fine," I said. I was still not used to the relationship questions about Clark. Girls often gossiped about their boyfriends, but I had never had anything to contribute before. As Jill and Taylor began talking about the way their boyfriends behaved, they began pestering me for information on Clark, which embarrassed me to no end. Mostly because I was really in a relationship with Mykail and when I did give information on the way Mykail was with me, I knew they were thinking of Clark.

"Have you guys done it yet?" Taylor asked bluntly.

623

"What?!"

"Oh, come on, you guys have been together for a while now. It's natural that by this point you two would be sleeping together."

"Well, we're not!"

"Geez, don't get so testy," Taylor teased. "What's the matter? Not happy with it? Or is Clark being too much of a gentleman and not giving you what you want?"

"Taylor!" I gasped.

"What? I'm not shy."

"Obviously."

"Come on, give me the details," Taylor urged. "Have you done it yet?"

I looked at my hands, taking a deep breath and then shaking my head, refusing to look her in the eye.

"Do you want to change that?" Taylor asked with a knowing smile—I could hear the smirk in her voice. I nodded slowly.

"Then, go for it!"

"But…I mean, I've never…"

"So?" Taylor said. "It will happen at some point. It's okay. You have to lose your virginity eventually."

"Doesn't it hurt?" I asked, glancing at her worriedly.

She made a face.

"A little…" she admitted. "I mean, your body isn't used to having something there and you stretch, so it hurts. You'll probably be sore for a while afterward." She drummed her fingers against the table and smiled as I shifted uncomfortably. "But, if you really like him and he's gentle, it will be worth it."

"But…what if he wants me to do other things?"

"Like what?" Taylor chuckled. "It's your first time. I doubt he'll get really creative." She looked thoughtful, lifting her eyebrows. "I'd be surprised if Clark has even *thought* of sex before, let alone knows about all the fun stuff…"

"It hurt you the first time?"

"Yeah," Taylor said. "But the second time was much better. I was a little sore, but it felt a lot better." She placed her hand on mine. "There really is nothing more amazing. At first you might wonder why everyone is making such a big deal about it, but just remember that the first time is not how it will always feel. You'll understand why it's so amazing."

I blushed and looked down at my hands, feeling nervous and yet extremely excited.

"Come on," Taylor said. "Let's go dance."

I spent the evening on the dance floor surrounded by moving bodies and humming bass. I was easily swept up in the movement, the beat dictating the way my body moved in unison with the other students. My eyes were often closed, feeling the thumping of my heart and the music, losing my breath as adrenaline pumped through my veins.

The buses came all too soon and as I sat on the bus, all I could think about was how electric my body felt. I could still feel the bass moving my blood, my skin tingling as the cool air slipped in through the gaps in my coat.

I walked quickly into my house, my thoughts jumbled and yet oddly quiet.

"Lily?" Mykail called, darting into the foyer area as I turned, smiling at him, slipping the coat off my shoulders.

"Hi, sorry I'm late."

"You're not," he told me hesitantly. "You're early…"

"Oh." I glanced at my wrist watch. "I am?"

"Yes, you normally aren't back for another hour," he said. "Is everything okay?"

"Yeah, everything's…" I stopped, my arm halfway to the coat hooks by the door. "Oh shit," I chuckled, hanging my coat up and turning to him. "I took the wrong bus."

"What do you mean?"

"Normally I have to meet with the Commish Kids after the club empties…" I said, covering my mouth, shocked I had forgotten. "Oh well, I'll just say I was feeling sick."

Mykail laughed and rolled his eyes, even though his voice was strained.

"What's wrong?" I asked, sensing his tension.

"Um…" He looked behind him and then motioned for me to follow. "Come here." I trailed after him into the kitchen. He pointed at the note left by Dana still on the refrigerator.

"Did you see this?"

"Yeah," I said, rolling my eyes.

"You saw the response?"

"The response?"

Below my message of hating Dana was another message written in Dana's neat penmanship.

"*I love you, too.*
-Dana"

"What the fuck…" I groaned, rolling my eyes again. I grabbed the paper from the refrigerator sharply and crumpled it up. "Asshole."

"You don't understand, Lily," Mykail said. "He did this at some point when neither of us saw him in the house, and I am here all day."

I stopped crumpling the note, clenching it angrily in my fist.

"He has a key."

"I know, but…" Mykail shook his head. "I'm sorry. It just startled me." He wrapped his arms around my waist, pulling me close. I relaxed and turned around, dropping the note to the floor and wrapping my arms around his neck as he pressed his forehead to mine.

"You look beautiful," he whispered.

"Thank you."

"I'm making you some dinner," he said, kissing my forehead gently. My body craved the touch of his skin and his heat as he pulled away. I tried to hold him to me, but he slipped out of my arms.

"I'll help," I offered, stepping to his side and stirring the pasta while he prepared the salad. We were mostly silent as we cooked. There was tension between us. I could not put a name to it, but I could feel it, thick and palpable, keeping alive the electricity that had been filling my body the entire evening.

We ate quietly, exchanging shy glances. It was obvious that Mykail was feeling the same electricity.

When I finished eating, he smiled and reached over, thumbing away the drop of sauce on my chin.

"I'll do the dishes," he offered.

"No, it's okay," I said. "You cooked. I'll clear."

"No, it's fine. Why don't you go change into your pajamas and wash the makeup off your face and then we can watch a movie."

"…okay."

I pecked a quick kiss on his lips before stooping to grab my shoes and take them upstairs. I closed my bedroom door behind me, my hand resting on the doorknob for several long seconds before I pulled away, moving to the bathroom.

I slipped out of my sheath dress and stepped into the shower, putting my hair up to keep it from getting wet and, therefore, losing the curls. I washed the sweat and the club from my skin, wrapping myself in a towel after the quick shower.

After wiping down the mirror, I grabbed a makeup remover cloth and removed what makeup had remained. I let my hair down and arranged it so that it framed my face in a flattering way, combing it carefully.

I took a deep breath to steady my nerves as I opened the top drawer of my dresser, pulling out the two items I had placed there a few weeks ago. The satin had been so pleasant to touch that I could only imagine what the nightgown felt like against my body and I bought it without thinking. Shedding my towel with shaking hands, I grabbed the nightgown and stepped into it before reaching for the matching panties.

I looked myself over in the full length mirror in my bathroom, surprised that my nipples were so easily visible through the deep red nightgown. I hardly recognized myself. Before I had become a part of the Commission of the People I could never have imagined myself dressing up in lingerie and trying to seduce someone.

And yet, there I was, doing exactly that.

Closing my eyes and taking a five-count breath, I prepared myself as best I could.

I stepped into the hallway and darted across the short expanse to Mykail's open door, staring at his bed for a few long seconds before crawling onto it slowly, feeling my heart fluttering in excitement and anxiety.

I felt everything acutely. The sheets on his bed were soft and smooth, and the cool air of the room made my hair stand on end. I placed myself on the bed, laying on my side, facing the door. After a few seconds in that position, I rolled onto my belly, throwing a look over my shoulder, bending my legs to point my feet in the air as I tried to imagine how the sight would look when Mykail walked in.

Deciding against the position, I turned back onto my side and propped my head up, arranging my hair and then pulling my breasts for more cleavage, bending my legs to slant my hips. I tried to force a smile, but I could feel how lopsided and nervous it looked.

I flopped onto my back with an agitated groan, starting to feel embarrassed and half-tempted to give up on the idea of seduction that night.

"Lily?" Mykail's confused voice called as he reached the top of the stairs. I bolted upright with a gasp, which must have caught his attention because he turned to look in his room first.

The look on his face when he saw me made me feel a little more confident and even more nervous simultaneously.

"Hey."

"Wha...what are you doing?" he asked with a hesitant laugh.

"Waiting for you," I said, embarrassed.

"Oh..." he said. "Lily...I really appreciate this but...I don't think—"

"No, don't say that," I said, abandoning any thought of a sexy pose and crawling to the foot of the bed, holding a hand out to him. He hesitated but stepped forward, ignoring my hand and sitting on the bed next to me, keeping his eyes averted.

"Lily…is this something you really want?"

"Why wouldn't I want it?"

"It's just…there are a lot of reasons. I'm an experiment of the Commission. Dana is bound to find out. You're only seventeen."

"Oh please, I don't care about you being an experiment, and I sure as hell don't care about Dana fucking Christenson. As for being seventeen, what time period is this? A lot of my friends have already lost their virginity and have been having sex for some time."

"But…you really should think about things like this," Mykail continued. "You deserve someone who hasn't done the things I have. Your first time…that's a big deal."

"Maybe it is, but it's *my* big deal," I said, turning his face. "It's my decision, and this is something I want." My fingers tightened on his face, forcing him to lift his gaze to me. "I'm pretty sure that I am in love with you, Mykail."

Mykail swallowed hard and closed his eyes, letting out a small breath.

"I love you, too," he told me. "Which is why I want to be sure that this is something you really want."

"It is." I leaned closer, my other hand pressing against his thigh. He flinched from the touch at first, but I pretended I didn't notice. "I want to be with you."

"Be-because there are a lot of *wrong* reasons to do something like this," Mykail said, sounding desperate to stall me. "And…and there can be consequences."

"I know," I whispered into his ear before taking his earlobe in my mouth. I could feel his resolve beginning to slip. He let out a shaky breath and licked his lips.

"Lily…"

I pressed my finger against his lips and faced him with a tender smile.

"Kiss me…"

He met my mouth, his breath hot and his pulse racing under my hands. I smiled and felt myself relax. We had made out so many times that while the kiss was electric and exciting, it was also familiar and comforting.

I took his face in both hands and guided him fully onto the bed so he covered me with his body. I did not break the kiss even as he rested on top of me, his hands on either side of my shoulders. I felt the bed dip above my head, his wings surrounding me, the large joints pressing into the bed to support him.

We continued to kiss as both his hands moved to my waist, his fingers gentle against the soft satin. The touch was electric and my body was already singing just from his fingers stroking through the nightgown.

Finally, the kiss was broken and I took in a deep breath, feeling it shudder out of me as Mykail's mouth moved to my neck, biting, his breath snaking over the wet skin. My back arched, my torso brushing his. He released another shaky breath and one of his hands traveled up my ribcage to palm my breast through the satin, my nipples standing even higher in response. His fingers moved to the thin strap, sliding it from my shoulder and down my arm while I moved to allow him to remove the strap.

He pulled down the fabric of the nightgown and his mouth went to my chest, causing me to lose any lingering doubt that might have been present.

Even though he had seen me topless before, knowing that we were going to go all the way made the experience very different and slightly embarrassing. I felt childish with how I continued to think, "This is it. I'm going all the way…" but I could not stop the revelation from repeating in my mind, sometimes distracting me from the moment.

While my rational sense was mostly destroyed by Mykail's fingers and mouth as he pushed my nightgown down to bunch at my waist, there was a part of me that was apprehensive. I tried not to psych myself out about how losing my virginity was going to hurt, but it was a small nagging concern in the back of my mind that refused to be silenced.

Mykail's mouth moved to my sternum, pressing gentle kisses as he moved between my breasts, his hands skimming down my sides to the nightgown, pushing it from my waist to my hips, his fingers pausing and flexing over the fabric of my panties before he sat up, pulling the nightgown down my legs.

Butterflies fluttering eagerly in my stomach, I lifted my hips to facilitate the removal of the nightgown, Mykail's fingers tracing over my legs as he moved the soft fabric to my ankles and set the nightgown behind him.

I tried to lower my legs, but he took my ankles gingerly, pushing them toward me to bend my knees and allowing him to settle his hips closer to mine. His eyes locked with mine as he lifted my left ankle to his mouth, pressing a kiss to the inside of my calf, closing his eyes and turning his head to kiss me in the same spot longer. The action was so tender and sweet that my heart soared and some of my embarrassment faded.

His mouth moved from my calf to the inside of my knee before he lowered my leg and his hands traced up the backs of my thighs, causing my body to shiver in anticipation and desire. My embarrassment returned when his arms hooked around my thighs and his head rested on my belly, his lips finding my belly button and pressing a tiny kiss above it.

His mouth moved to the top of my right hip, kissing and nipping at the skin above the line of the panties before his lips trailed to my other hip, repeating the same tender action.

My body lit up so fast it was painful. I let out a combination of a moan and a sob as my back arched completely off the bed. I let out a sob that sounded like his name. He kissed that part of my skin again.

"It's alright," he whispered. "I've got you."

My eyes rolled back in my head as the quiet words hummed along my spine.

His fingers moved from my lower back down to my sides, his fingers hooking into the remaining fabric and pulling the satin away.

A spark of terror ran through me and my eyes snapped open, suddenly embarrassed about being bare in front of him. My eyes met with his and my fears dissipated as quickly as they had appeared. He was looking into my eyes, the expression filled with love as his fingers slowly and delicately moved the fabric down my legs.

I let out a choked breath and my eyes closed again, my arousal going higher at the emotional connection in that moment.

Finally, I was naked, and while I should have felt embarrassed and self-conscious, his gentle smile and soft eyes made it impossible for me to feel ashamed.

"Mykail…" I called his name with a weak voice.

He moved back to my face, supporting himself on his wings again as he took my mouth in his. I felt his tongue against mine, soft but insistent, telling me that he was trying his best to control himself. It was an enormous turn on, knowing that my body had so excited him—I felt powerful and beautiful.

My hands, which had been uselessly gripping and releasing the sheets, moved to his lower back, pulling his hips over mine as we kissed. The intensity of feeling the fabric of his pants against me was too much. I let out a quiet shout that caused him to smile against my lips and push his hips into mine again, trying to elicit the same response.

I tore my mouth away, unable to focus on kissing him with the sensations rocketing along my nerves.

My hands scraped down his back, grabbing at any part of him I could. One of my hands grabbed at his back pocket and the fingers of my other hand hooked into the belt loops, trying to push the fabric away.

"Slow down..." he whispered, licking up my neck from my collarbone to my earlobe, which he took between his teeth teasingly.

"No," I whined. My brain finally scrambled a fraction of control together as the initial shockwave of intense pleasure dulled. My hands moved from their position to the front of his pants, fumbling with the button. His hips stilled. He did not make an effort to stop me, taking my chin and turning my head to kiss him again.

My fingers succeeded in getting the button undone and working the zipper down.

I moved my hands around his hips and under the fabric of his pants and boxers, pushing them down as I grabbed at the warm skin desperately.

His breath caught and his body shivered, which made me smile and my own arousal spin even higher.

Mykail's eyes locked with mine and he pulled away. My hands slipped from him as he sat up, removing his clothes.

My eyes moved hungrily over his body as he kicked the pants from his ankles. A carnal hunger grabbed at every cell of my being. I greedily studied him for the short time that his entire body was in sight.

I thought that he had leaned down to kiss me until the sudden rush of cold air against my back made me realize I had launched upright, grabbing his neck and kissing him passionately, pressing my body to his. My hand carded through his hair desperately as our mouths worked together.

He guided me back to the bed, smiling against my lips as his hand skimmed down my body. I arched into his touch, greedy for any sensation.

I stiffened when his hand rested on my thigh, running up and down the same patch of skin, soothing me. The pace was becoming torturous. My body was singing with pleasure and I desperately craved more. I groaned in frustration, trying to push my leg up so that his hand would fall where I wanted it most.

He broke the kiss, looking into my eyes as his hand finally moved upward and touched where I desperately needed.

I gasped and my body jolted but I did not break eye contact with him. He was just barely smiling, his eyes as gentle as his fingers as he touched me intimately, both emotionally and physically.

I felt the heel of his hand press to my pubic bone as one of his fingers slowly eased into me, aided by the lubrication of my aroused body.

I could not keep my eyes open. They snapped shut as a blinding bolt of pleasure ripped through me, his finger pushing deeper until his finger was not only inside me, but his palm was also pressed to my clitoris, causing continuous bolts of lightning to tear through my body.

His finger stilled for a few moments until my eyes fluttered open again. He was watching me, gauging my reaction. Gently, he pulled the finger out to the first knuckle and thrust it back in, pushing upward on the front wall, causing me to feel a pressure that was not painful, but strange.

When his second finger began to push in to accompany the first one, I could not stop my cringe at the stretch.

His hand stilled immediately and I tried to relax, nodding to assure him I was alright. Carefully, he pressed his fingers deeper. I did my best to keep my body relaxed.

Mykail kissed me, his fingers stilling once again. He waited until my focus on his lips made my body relax and allow his fingers deeper. The pressure was not something I was expecting and, as turned on as I was, I could not help but focus on the foreign feeling.

"Take a deep breath," he whispered. I did so, drawing oxygen deep into my lungs. "And slowly let it out…"

As I pushed the air out of my lungs his fingers pushed deeper, causing the last part of my exhale to become a confused, yet pleased, groan.

I shifted my hips to meet him, trying to get accustomed to the stretch of his fingers. He pulled his hand away, removing his fingers as his hips settled between my thighs.

I closed my eyes and took a deep breath in immediate understanding, trying to prepare myself for what was about to happen.

"We can stop…" Mykail's voice betrayed how much he hated to say the words. I opened my eyes and looked at his face above mine before my eyelids lowered again and I licked my lips, wrapping my arms around his waist and pulling him closer, tilting my hips.

"If you say that again, I will never forgive you," I near-panted.

One of his hands went to my thigh, pushing it to open my legs wider as he steadied himself on his wings, his other wrapping around himself as he lined himself to enter me. My heart stilled and apprehension took hold. I took a deep breath, forcing myself to calm down.

He hesitated.

"You really will never forgive me?" he asked, his eyes on my face, seeing my nervous expression.

"No, I won't," I chuckled breathlessly. My hand that had been employed scratching his shoulder moved to the side of his face. "I'm ready."

He kissed me once and began to push in.

My back arched and a choked cry managed to make its way out of me, but it was not out of an intense spiral of pleasure.

It was painful. It burned to have him pushing into me, filling me and taking my virginity. My body fell back to the bed and my head snapped to the side, my eyes tightly closed as I grit my teeth, trying to get used to the invasion.

When I thought that there was no way I could be stretched anymore and the pain was unbearable, he pushed in further.

When he was completely seated inside me, he pressed kisses to my face, his body shaking above mine.

"Don't...don't move..." I pled around my teeth.

He remained still, allowing me to scratch his shoulders and lower back as I tried to force my body to relax and accommodate him. No matter how much I tried, I could not get over the pressure and stretch. It was too painful to push aside.

My breathing finally began to slow, Mykail peppering comforting kisses over my cheek and forehead. I turned to him and kissed him fully.

"Go slow..." I breathed against his lips.

His hips pulled away from mine and the burn of my stretched skin almost made me cringe, though I bit it back to be sure that he didn't worry further. He pushed back into me, his arms and shoulders shaking as a small breath tripped over his teeth, his eyes fluttering closed. I watched his face, fascinated by the pleasure etched into his features.

The pressure was only slightly unpleasant because it was so different, but the burning and stretching was the worst, chasing away the acute feelings of pleasure and leaving behind only dull signals that made the experience tolerable.

The burning eventually ebbed and I carefully moved my hips to meet his as he continued to thrust. He moaned and my body shuddered from the sound. It was almost enough to chase away the discomfort.

Mykail began moving faster and my nails dug into his skin. There was just enough pain to keep the pleasure from overwhelming me.

The burn was still present, but my body was becoming acclimated to the sensation, I was able to focus entirely on his movements. He began moving even faster and I pushed my hips up to meet him, bringing him deeper and causing my body to tighten.

Mykail let out a moan that hummed along my spine and my body began to glow. I closed my eyes, grabbing his head and moving it from my neck to kiss him deeply. His moans caused me to shiver and pleasure began to build in my body. Before it could reach the intensity from before, his hips stilled and his body shuddered.

He collapsed with a groan and draped over me, his hips stuttering as he came inside of me. I shuddered at the intimacy of the moment, a blush blooming over my body. Though I did not orgasm, knowing that I had brought him such pleasure made me feel like I was glowing.

I kissed the top of his head, running my hands through his hair as we both collected our bearings, his breath ghosting over my chest as I held him, my heart soaring, reveling in the moment.

Chapter Forty-Nine

I felt different when I woke up Saturday morning. My body was sore all over, but the feeling was concentrated mostly in my legs and pelvis. I turned onto my back, coming face to face with Mykail, who was awake, his fingers playing over my ribcage and waist.

"Good morning."

"Morning…" I murmured.

"How are you feeling?" he asked. I smiled and stretched, trying not to wince at the sparks of pain radiating through me.

"A little sore," I admitted. His hand moved down my hip and to my thigh, his eyes scanning down my body.

"We probably should have waited until you were a little more rested," he mused.

"In that case, it would have never happened," I chuckled. "We have less than a week now."

"Shh…" He smiled, pressing a finger to my lips. "We don't need to talk about that right now."

I grinned and snuggled into the pillow, sighing contentedly. I moved my hips to turn on my other side, and while I expected the twinge of pain, I did not expect the feeling of my thighs being slightly wet and sticky. I thought I had cleaned myself up enough from the previous night before returning to bed. I furrowed my eyebrows and concentrated on the feeling.

"What is it?"

"I think I need to take a shower," I said, sitting upright.

"Is everything alright?" he asked, worried, propping himself up on his elbow.

"Yes, everything's fine," I said. "I'm just kind of…" I motioned to my sheet-covered lap, "sticky?"

His eyes widened and his breath caught in his throat. He turned away and I blinked at his reaction. At first I thought he was embarrassed, but then I realized that his reaction was something else entirely.

I guess it was pretty sexy, actually. I recalled him cumming inside me, how much pleasure he felt from me, the evidence of which was still between my legs.

"Oh…o-okay," he said as casually as he could manage.

I smiled, kissing him on the cheek before extracting myself from the sheets, trying not to cringe at the sticky, wet feeling stuck to my thighs—and probably the bedding.

"We should wash the sheets," I suggested, walking down the hall toward my bathroom, feeling only a slight twinge as I walked, ignoring my naked state.

As I stepped under the warm spray, one thought was stuck on repeat.

I did it...

It had not been as pleasurable as I had hoped, but the intimacy and connection I had shared with Mykail had been so intense it was almost painful itself. I felt the curling of warmth through my sore muscles as I recalled his voice when he moaned my name, and the way his hips fit between my legs, stuttering as he began moving faster...

I swallowed hard, trying to keep myself from craving the intimacy again. I had always expected the first time to hurt—a thought that had been amplified by my friends' constant gossip—so there was a part of me that was not sure I would feel as good as I hoped the second time. Another part of me, a *bigger* part, was more than eager to try.

A cold rush of air caught me off-guard and I spun around, surprised to see Mykail stepping into the shower, folding his wings tight into his body to fit in my large walk-in shower.

"Hey..." I whispered, my eyes traveling over him, appreciating the strong muscles of his chest and shoulders. My eyes also drank in the way his waist gently tucked into his hips and the toned muscles of his legs that guided my eyes upward toward his half-hard erection. My heart fluttered at the sight.

He trailed the backs of his fingers over my jaw as I stood still, feeling the hot water beat on my shoulders. His gaze traveled over my lips and neck, his hand leading his eyes down my shoulder and arm, dipping further toward my waist.

"I wanted to thank you," he whispered, his arms encircling me.

"For what?" I said, trying to catch my breath. Between the steam produced by the hot water and the electricity humming along my nerves, it was nearly-impossible to breathe.

"Last night," he murmured, his fingers spreading over my lower back as he pulled me close. I could not stop the moan that bubbled out of my mouth. "I'm sorry that you didn't enjoy it more."

"I enjoyed it," I protested weakly, my self-control slipping as my skin, sensitive from the hot water, was touched by his strong hands.

"Well," he whispered, pressing his head against mine, his breath at my ear, "I didn't feel you cum." I shuddered and my eyes rolled back as the short sentence crashed through my barriers. "I'm sorry...I tried to get you there."

I could hardly keep my knees from giving out on me.

"I want to try again," he said. "Right now. Just my fingers and maybe my mouth."

"Holy shit..." I gasped, my legs buckling underneath me. He held me upright. I took a few deep breaths, taking in his intoxicating scent as my heart thundered against my ribs.

"Is that okay?"

I was not sure how he expected me to be able to answer when he spoke to me like that. I could only nod furiously, clutching at him as though he was the only rock in a river of intense sensation.

"You're so beautiful," he said, his hand moving down my back to grope me, pushing my hips against his and rekindling the fire from the previous night. My hips had a mind of their own, grinding against his for any friction I could, seeking the release I had been unable to achieve.

Mykail's lips recaptured mine. I immediately grabbed his hair, tangling my fingers in the wet tendrils and trying to suck the soul out of him with the intensity of our kiss.

His fingers kneaded my skin as his other hand wrapped in my hair, gently tugging our mouths apart and tilting my head back to kiss my jaw and neck. I was useless in his arms, a creature of stimulation and pleasure, lost in the waves of his touch.

Suddenly, his hands were on my hips, turning me around, pressing my back to his front and dipping his head to my neck, nipping at the area where my neck met my shoulder. One of his hands pushed my breast upward, his fingers pinching the sore nipple, but the pain was not only tolerable, it was exciting.

His other hand cupped me, his palm resting against my pubic hair. I moaned, my knees turning to jelly. One of my hands went to his arm, while the other one wrapped in his hair, holding his head as I turned to kiss him deeply.

Two of Mykail's fingers began circling my clitoris and I arched into the touch, my moan echoing around the bathroom, though I paid no attention to the noise. I felt his erection against me and pushed back, moving my hips to give him friction, which earned me a slightly harder bite on the shoulder.

His fingers pressed harder, moving in a countering motion to my hips as his hand against my breast pinched and teased my nipple.

"Please..." I whispered.

"What?"

"I want...I want more."

Boldly, I released my hand from his hair and moved it behind me to wrap around his hardened length, surprised at the feeling of it in my hand. He stopped in his movements and let out a moan before shaking his head and grabbing my wrist, crossing it over my body so that we were both holding my breast.

"You first."

I almost collapsed again.

His fingers working me carefully, he brought me closer and closer to that cliff I had teetered on a week before and I wanted nothing more than to throw myself over the edge again. But every time my body tensed, ready to soar, he would stop, paying attention to my breast or kissing my neck to force my body back down before starting the torture again.

I finally growled in frustration, turning around and crashing our mouths together, lifting my leg to hook over his hip as his hand held my thigh.

He pulled me up and I wrapped my legs around his waist, eagerly waiting to feel him fill me again. Instead, he carefully maneuvered to his knees. Rather than feeling myself seated on his hips, I felt the cold bite of tile against my skin, hissing at the contact and breaking our kiss.

He had sat me on the seat in the shower, kneeling with my legs still looped around his waist.

Smiling confidently, he kissed me once on the lips before his head dipped to my neck, trailing kisses between my breasts. He sat back on his heels, his tongue dipping into my navel as I was left a writhing mess between the cold tiles and the stifling steam of the shower.

His hands wrapped around the backs of my bent knees and tugged gently, bringing my hips forward. Then, one of those strong hands trailed along the inside of my thigh and, as he made eye contact with me, he pushed one finger inside.

My head fell back against the tile with a dull thud, but the pain of my skull and the small burn of his finger pushing into me only intensified the pleasure, particularly when his finger crooked forward and stroked my front wall.

"Does that hurt?" he asked, kissing the inside of my thigh.

"God, no."

I felt him smile into the next kiss on my thigh and then his head moved between my legs where his finger was gently stroking my inner walls in an agonizingly sweet way.

I felt embarrassed and was about to tell him that his fingers were enough when his lips wrapped around my clitoris and his tongue pressed to the small nub. That time, the moan didn't escape me—it ripped out of me.

One of my hands interlaced with his fingers against my thigh as my other hand went to his hair, trying to decide whether to stop him or beg him to continue. The intense pleasure made me want to continue, but the embarrassment was also irritatingly present.

His tongue flicked over me as his finger not only continued to crook and stroke, but he began moving it in and out as well, intensifying the pleasure.

I sobbed, wanting more, seeing the cliff in front of me.

A second finger joined the first and I knew I would not last long. His lips and tongue worked over the sensitive flesh until my nerves were raw and my muscles were straining, begging for release.

He trapped the small nub between his lips and sucked, drawing it further into his warm mouth and my body snapped back like a catapult, sending me careening high into the air to soar for a few short moments with a choked shout before crashing back into my body, breathing heavily and shaking uncontrollably as spasms rocked my very being.

I cringed when his fingers slipped out of me. My whole body shuddered when he kissed the inside of my thigh once more before kissing me on the cheek and forehead, brushing his lips over my face to bring me back to the present.

I smiled lazily and kissed him back, my body humming in satisfaction.

"How was that?"

"Amazing..." I gasped. He stood and offered both hands to me, which I took because I was unsure my legs would support me. My knees trembled and my muscles quaked, but my hands found Mykail's biceps and held him, using him to support me as his arms circled my waist.

"...what about you?"

"Seeing you just now was enough for me."

"Really?" I whispered, one of my hands wrapping around him as he recoiled slightly from my touch.

"You don't need to do anything you don't feel comfortable with."

"I want to touch you," I told him. "I want you to make love to me..."

He kissed me and shook his head.

"Not today," he said. "You're sore. We'll wait until tomorrow. You can tell the others that you're taking a day to catch up on sleep and we can spend all day tomorrow doing whatever we want to each other..."

"Be careful." I grinned slyly. "If you give me permission to do whatever I want, I might wear you out."

"I'm glad to hear it," he said. "It means that I was good enough you want to be with me again."

"And again, and again…" I giggled. I carefully began moving my hand around him, stroking the soft skin, feeling it slide. His eyes fluttered shut and a breath fell out of his mouth, his forehead dropping to rest against mine.

"I…it won't take much…"

I felt like a goddess, or the most powerful person in the world with how easily I could excite him. I tightened my hand experimentally, my eyes dropping to watch as I sped up the pace. His fingers pressed harder against my skin and his breath thudded out of him as he continuously licked his lips, his eyes closed.

I watched his face, lost in pleasure. I locked our mouths together, moving my hand faster and feeling his hips slide in counter motions.

He gasped and our mouths broke apart. I felt him twitch, pulsing as he came on my abdomen, his breath short and eyes tightly shut.

I was so happy I was sure I was about to burst.

We stood under the spray for an indeterminable amount of time after his orgasm, holding one another, our eyes closed, basking in the afterglow, caught in our own little world where there was no revolution brewing.

* *** *

Both Mykail and I were slow moving as we washed, both trying to help one another without leaving lingering touches on soapy, hot skin. My heart was racing again by the time we turned off the shower.

Even though I had mostly recovered from the intense orgasm, my legs were still shaky and weak as I tried to remember how to walk.

Mykail toweled me dry tenderly, laughing as he rubbed my hair, causing it to fall everywhere. We giggled, giddy and happier than idiots on a honeymoon.

I finally combed my hair as Mykail went to his room to strip the bed down and wash the sheets. When I walked into my room, braiding my hair, I halted, shocked when I saw the time on the clock.

"Shit!"

I ran to my purse, rummaging through it and finding my phone, which had been on silent all night and now had three missed calls and eight text messages.

Clark: *Hey, are you coming over?*

Clark: *Are you on your way?*

Clark: *Where are you? Are you even awake yet?*

Clark: *...you're starting to scare me. Are you alright? Why haven't you answered your phone? You said you would be here an hour ago. Call or text, please.*

Clark: *Seriously, You're scaring me.*

Clark: *Mark is having a panic attack and is about five seconds away from getting in the car and driving to your house to make sure you're alright. And I'm about to go start the car for him. Please answer your phone.*

Clark: *We're in the car. I hope you're just sleeping.*

Clark: *We're pulling into your neighborhood. See you in a few minutes.*

As I hissed a few colorful curse words, I threw my towel on the bed and ran to my dresser, pulling out fresh clothes, hurriedly pulling them on as Dexter stared at me, confused by the frenzy.

I was buttoning my jeans when the doorbell rang.

"Fuck!" I snapped, rummaging through my dresser for a turtleneck to cover any marks Mykail might have left.

"I'll get it," Mykail said, sticking his head into my room.

"No! No, no, no!" I called, darting across the room faster than I have ever moved in my life.

"Why?"

"It's Mark and Clark. If you answer with wet hair and I come down with my hair wet, they'll know we were showering together!"

He looked me over as I stood in my jeans, yanking on my sweater, tugging my hair out of the collar and straightening myself up. He sighed.

"Alright. Then, I'll see you after the meeting tonight?"

"Yes. Sorry..." I whispered, kissing him tenderly. He smiled and kissed me back before pulling away when the doorbell rang again.

"You better get that before they break down the door," he chuckled, sensing the urgency.

I pecked another kiss on his lips before flying down the stairs, through the living room and kitchen and sliding clumsily to the door, fumbling with the lock just as the doorbell was rung a third time.

I threw the door open, surprising both Mark and Clark, but I was more shocked to see the snow falling behind them, making me realize I had been too wrapped up in Mykail to even look out the window at the changing weather.

"Thank God you're alright," Clark breathed, stepping over the threshold. "What happened to you? Did you just get out of the shower?"

"Yeah," I laughed nervously, trying not to let the blush creep over my cheeks as I thought about the shower again. "I was exhausted last night and I didn't feel too good, so I came home and…just sort of collapsed into bed," I rambled, motioning them both inside. "I woke up twenty minutes ago with makeup smeared all over my face and…ooh, it was bad," I finished lamely. "Sorry, I only got your texts a couple minutes ago."

"That's okay. You just had us both worried," Clark assured with a nervous chuckle. "You look a little flushed. Are you coming down with a cold?"

"No, I'm just…you know, not sleeping as much."

I could tell he didn't entirely believe me, but I just smiled and clapped my hands, rubbing them together slightly.

"So, sorry about all the concern. I'm just going to get my bag and I'll be right back."

"Okay. Where is Mykail?"

"Oh, he's, um, taking a shower I think," I made up before disappearing through the kitchen and living room, running up the stairs, mentally smacking myself for my rambling. I grabbed my bag, making sure I had everything before grabbing a hat to cover my wet hair and slipping over to Mykail's room as he pulled the fitted sheet off the mattress.

Grabbing his face, I kissed him deeply for a few seconds before darting back downstairs and joining Mark and Clark in the snow storm, heading to Fort Daniels.

I was surprised to hear that Josh and a female member of the Eight Group named Rin would be joining us to make sure we knew the procedures for Thursday.

I tried not to cringe whenever I moved a certain way that reminded me of my sore muscles. At one point Clark asked me if I was alright, to which I quickly had to explain, telling him that I must have slept wrong because my back was sore.

I wished I didn't blush so easily. He continued to ask me if I was alright, worried about me being sick despite how often I reassured him. Even though I could not see Mark's eyes through his dark glasses, I could feel his gaze on me every now and then through the rear view mirror.

We pulled into the park where we had met Josh and parked between a few other cars that belonged to families who lived near the park and had brought their children out to play in the snow.

Mark locked the car, nodding to us and motioning to the cave entrance on the hill. The climb was going to be hell with the constant reminder of last evening's activities giving me flares of pain.

"Wait," I said, glancing back at the car as we waited for the pedestrian light to change. "If Josh is there...who is going to move the car?"

"He removed the GPS last night," Clark told me, stepping into the street when the light turned. We darted across, eager to get out of the falling snow. "He'll replace it tomorrow to keep suspicion down, but today we have Josh and Rin to talk to for as long as we want. People are covering for them."

"Mark, it kinda scares me how careful you are," I chuckled. He smiled, bowing his head against the snow as he led us to where I assumed the path was. I made my way through the snow, my boots sinking to my ankles in the blanket of white and causing me to move my legs more than I wanted to. The pain in my pelvis was now constantly present.

Mark helped me up a particularly difficult section of the trail, but I could tell with the way he was looking at me, even through his glasses, that he was worried. I assured him that I was fine and ducked into the cave, shaking the snow from my coat and brushing it from the top of my hat. I shivered, watching Clark dart into the cave, shivering.

"It is getting so cold!" he complained.

We made our way down into the passage and followed the correct twists and turns to the main bunker, where Rin and Josh were sharing a casual conversation.

"Good morning," Rin said, her accent almost non-existent. I remembered her from the marina, but as she did not have her glasses on, I was able to see her natural beauty. "We were worried about you three."

Mark pinched his earlobe to apologize.

"Lily, Clark, my name is Rin," she greeted, shaking our hands. "Do you remember me? I'm part of the Eight Group."

"Yes," I said. "It's nice to see you again."

"Are any of the other kids from the Commission coming?" she asked.

"No, not today," I replied. "We've told them the date and assigned their roles, but we thought that if they came here this weekend it might be too suspicious about who is planning all this."

"Okay," she said. "We will need to decide on a day for them to go to the water towers and see where they are going to be stationed."

"We'll bring them in groups," Clark explained. "We just want to make sure Dana doesn't suspect anything."

"We have five days," Josh said, sharing a knowing look with the two other experiments. "Me and Rin went through the wards and told experiments about Thursday."

"Hiroki and Sunjin are going through the holding cells over the next few days," Rin added. She turned to Mark. "Did you talk to Griffin?"

He nodded.

"So, everyone knows about the plan on Thursday? Or, almost everyone?"

"Everyone involved," Rin affirmed. "But they don't know everything. Everyone in the holding cells is being told they are going to be broken out and told that they have to keep silent and follow your instructions. We told them that they would be swimming, also, so they won't be surprised. But that's all that's been shared."

"We should get going. We have an hour," Josh said, glancing at his watch.

"Okay, let's go." Rin turned to us. "We're going to take you to the pipe where everyone will get out of the Dome. Sean and Dana are gone for another hour, so we need to move quickly. We can come back here afterward."

Mark led us through the passage under one of the bunk beds in the larger lodging room. As we slipped into the dark passageway, Clark and I tried to make conversation.

"Were you childhood friends with these two as well?" Clark asked Rin, motioning to Mark and Josh as he turned on his phone light to illuminate the tunnel.

"No," she said. "I was brought into the Commission two years before them. I was from the South Midwest Region."

"Really?" I asked. I had assumed that everyone in the Eight Group was part of the same commune as Mark and Josh.

"Yes," Rin said. "I was in the holding cells for three and a half years before I came to the table. Once I was next to Josh, though. I remember that," she said, pointing at the shorter man.

"I remember, too."

"Next to one another in the cells?"

"No, next to one another on the tables in the lab," she corrected. "Most of the Eight Group was made around the same time. That's how we all became such good friends. I feel like I've known them my entire life. We've been through a lot together." She dropped her head as her expression fell. "Like when Hyunwoo had his throat..." she muttered, looking at Mark's back, her sentence trailing off.

"Hyunwoo?" both Clark and I tried to repeat, quickly looking at Mark. The silent experiment bent his head at the name and Josh glanced at us over his shoulder.

"That's his name."

"…does he mind if we call him Mark?" I asked with a nervous laugh.

"I think he prefers Mark, now," Rin chuckled. "Easier for everyone in the Eight Group, too, since a lot of us speak different languages."

"Why did Dana do that to him?" I asked curiously, trying to ignore the way both Mark and Josh tensed.

Rin's expression darkened further as we turned down the final stretch toward the ladder that led to the hedge-covered door in a hill by the reservoir.

"It wasn't like he was the loudest in the group. Actually, I think *you* were," she pointed at Josh, who looked sheepishly at the ground. "But he was the best in the Eight Group. He was the strongest and fastest, and when we all tried to organize an attack against Dana…Mark was the one who took the punishment when we failed."

I looked at Mark's tense shoulders as he approached the bottom of the ladder.

"Dana made us watch, telling us that the same thing would happen to us if we disobeyed further. We were not allowed to speak in our own languages…we weren't really allowed to talk to one another at all. Dana made a big show of it, too, just to scare us into obeying."

Mark stood to one side and Josh began climbing the ladder to open the door, both of them pretending that they had not heard the conversation. I felt my heart break when I barely caught sight of Mark's scars as he watched Josh get to the top of the ladder.

The open door caused a rush of cold wind and snow to careen into the tunnel, and the story ended as we climbed out into the storm, focused on our present task.

Clark and I stood in the trees, looking at the snow that fell through the branches as the other two experiments climbed the ladder. After Josh closed the door, Mark nodded to Rin, who turned to Clark and me.

"This is the entrance everyone should use since it's the closest to the water towers. The other water tower entrance has a gate," Rin said, pointing to the nearby water tanks. "Use these trees as an area to hide people as they start to go down the passage if they're moving slowly. All tracers should be removed as soon as they get into the fort. We have to destroy those as soon as possible, even though the fort has jammers."

Mark motioned for us to follow him as Rin continued explaining.

"Have one person stationed at every bend in the tunnel to guide people to the main part of the fort and two at the water towers helping people off the ladder. You should have one person standing near the hedges that is visible to everyone coming out of the pipe so they know where to go."

I glanced back at the hedges, taking note of where they were as we crossed the open expanse of the hill toward the water tanks, where Mark yanked the padlock on the gate down, unwrapping the chains that held the fence closed.

"Did you just break that?" Clark gawked.

Mark shrugged, opening the gate and walking between the two massive water tanks, the rest of us following silently.

Mark bent down to two metal panels that were also locked. Breaking the padlock with ease, he grabbed one of the heavy metal doors and pulled it open with little strain while Josh opened the other side. Below the cover was a dark drain, covered by a large, thick grate.

Both of them reaching down, Josh grabbed one end of the grate as Mark grabbed the other, struggling to move the immense iron grate out of the hole.

"Lily, always let the boys do the heavy lifting," Rin teased. I laughed, though the sound came out strange around my chattering teeth.

"Right now, the Dome is off," Josh told us, brushing his hands off. "But we need to be quiet anyway."

Mark began climbing down the iron ladder rungs into the darkness.

"Be careful," Josh told us, reaching a hand out to Clark, who grabbed his hand and carefully stepped down, grabbing the first rung and beginning his descent. I followed shortly afterward, feeling the rust on the rungs rub off on my hands as was engulfed in the encroaching black.

The ladder was a lot longer than I expected and I started to get worried when I finally caught sight of Clark's phone light at the bottom.

Mark helped me down the final few steps and then helped Rin as I looked around the large tunnel with Clark. I could hear the sound of water running distantly.

Josh finally joined us and Rin leaned over, whispering quietly to keep her voice from echoing.

"Someone will have to be standing here to guide people up the ladder, and another two people at the top to help people out," she explained. "We go down that small tunnel." She pointed to the left of the ladder, where Mark and Josh were walking.

I followed them, Clark behind me. As we crouched and made our way through the tunnel, the sound of water became louder. Moving down a slope, we drew closer to a junction.

Once we had reached the larger tunnel, I looked around, barely making out the water flowing a few feet in front of me. We were standing on a thin walkway next to the bubbling water and across the stream was another walkway. The high ceiling amplified the sound into a near roar, masking our voices.

"The water comes from there," Josh said, pointing to the nearby wall where the water was flowing from under a grated archway. He pointed down the other direction and Clark flashed the light to illuminate the other end of the tunnel. There was a short distance before a steep half-wall rose to a sharp point.

"We have to climb that," Rin said.

Mark walked to the wall first and jumped, his fingers grabbing the top of the slope and he pulled himself up, sliding down the other side. When his shoes hit the puddle of water on the other side, it was the signal for the next person to climb over.

Everyone decided that that next person was me.

Josh boosted me to grab the top of the sharp slope and I pulled myself over, trying not to cringe in pain as I hooked my leg over and sat to slide down the other side. Mark caught me and stood me up. I brushed off, looking around.

I waited for everyone to be on the other side of the wall before I asked my question.

"Why is that wall even there?" I asked. Rin laughed and looked at the obstacle.

"There used to be a grate over that whole area," she explained, motioning to Mark and Josh. "These two spent three weeks disassembling it."

"Wow, you really have spent time on this…" Clark mused, turning on his phone flashlight again.

"That's where the fan is for the Dome," Rin explained, pointing to the solid wall in front of us where the wall stopped the water, ripples showing where it flowed under. "This is what it will be like when the Commission power is cut. The Dome is not on now, so the water won't be as turbulent." She tapped Clark's shoulder and he turned around, shining his light where she was pointing. "Hiroki and Minsoo will attach ropes to those bolts where the grate was and help people to swim under the wall. When we have everyone, you will need to cut the ropes on both sides and take them with you so that we leave no evidence, just in case."

"Won't they notice the grate is gone, though?" I pointed out.

"Maybe, but that's not as bad as leaving the ropes," she admitted. "We'll get everyone into this tunnel and over the walls, then they have to get to the ladder and to the fort."

"What about the people who get out on that side?" Clark asked, pointing his light to the other walkway.

"Jump over," Josh said easily. "It's not bad. The experiments will help."

"That's true," Rin agreed. "The experiments all understand that they are expected to help because the humans will be more flustered."

I took another deep breath, my brain buzzing with information and excitement.

"Make sense?" Rin asked.

"Lily and Clark will also come through here…" Josh motioned to the water.

"Right, you'll come through last," Rin agreed. "Then Hiroki and Minsoo will come back into the Dome and we will pretend like we were fighting."

"What about their wet clothes?" I asked.

"We're going to have replacement clothes waiting in the Dome," Rin assured. "They'll be bloodied up to make it look like we were fighting longer."

"And we just follow and make sure we have everyone as we go into the fort," I said with a nod.

"Okay?" Rin's gaze passed between Clark and me. "We'll try and get to the fort as soon as possible, but we don't know what Dana will do when he realizes he has so many experiments missing. We might be stuck here for a while."

"Understandable," Clark agreed.

"Let's get back to the fort before the Dome gets turned on," Rin declared. "Oh, and also, the emergency lock down will cause the emergency lights in here to turn on," she said, motioning to the ceiling.

"There are emergency lights in here? Why?" Clark blinked.

"Repairs. This is under a lot of pressure from the earth, so emergency repairs need to be made from time to time," she explained, moving to the wall, Josh boosting her over.

Mark helped us all over the wall and then we made our way through the tunnels again, pretending that we were escaping to see how fast we could climb the ladder. Rin, Clark, and I ran ahead as Josh and Mark replaced the grate and metal doors between the water towers.

We reconvened in the strategy room of the fort, looking over the map of the Commission again as Mark took a piece of paper out of his notebook and began drawing something.

"Mark is going to deal with Ward Eight and most of Ward Nine while you are moving through the holding cells. Griffin will be dealing with Wards Three, Four, and Six at the same time. Josh and I will be following protocol when the Ward Tens are out." She turned to me. "Lily, can you break out Cody? He's in this cell." She pointed to the cell on the outside of Ward Nine that met the hall leading to the holding cells.

"Sure."

"Can you also get Tori?" Josh asked, pointing at the only marked cell in Ward Ten. "She should be the last one…"

"Okay."

"The holding cells have a different code for breaking open the cells than the experiments," Rin told me. "You will have to memorize four different codes," she pointed to the door that connected the car elevators to the holding cells. "One for this door, one for all the cells in this area," he motioned to the holding cells, "one for Cody and Tori's cells and the code to get into Ward Ten."

"Okay," I repeated, a little nervous about my ability to recall memorized numbers under pressure.

"They're seven numbers each," she told me. "Mark will write them down for you."

"Oh," I said quickly, turning to Mark, remembering something. "Mark." He looked up. "Do you know what cell your sister is in?"

This made every eye in the room turn to me in shock. Clark blinked a few times before he turned to the stunned Mark.

"You have a sister?"

"How…do you know about her?" Josh asked suspiciously.

"Sean told me," I said, worried I had brought up a taboo subject.

"We can't go out of our way for her…" Rin said solemnly.

Mark pointed to a cell we already had marked. It was on the main hallway, not at all out of the way.

"Mark," Rin said slowly. "Did *you* pick this cell?"

Mark shook his head, his eyes averted downward as he picked up his pen again.

"We should break his sister out," I said strongly.

"And we will, if you already decided on the cells," Rin agreed. "But if we had broken her out on purpose just because it was Mark's sister…Dana would know immediately he was involved." She turned to him. "Mark, can you act angry when you find out she's missing?"

Mark looked at her, exasperated, as Josh laughed.

"He's one hell of an actor," I said with a grin.

"What is that?" Clark asked, pointing to the drawing Mark had sketched.

I glanced over the drawn boxes with numbers in them, looking like the keypad of a phone.

"That's about the size of the locks," Rin explained.

"For practice," Josh added.

"I have one more question," I said, turning to Rin. "I want to bring Mykail here. He can help."

"Okay," Rin said, waiting for me to continue.

"How do I get him here?"

Everyone went silent, looking at one another, trying to see who had a plan for transporting the angel.

"...we could drive him..." Josh suggested hesitantly.

"In the van?" Rin looked thoughtful. "I guess we could."

Mark shook his head, pointing to his eye and then tucking an imaginary strand of hair behind his ear.

"Oh, right," Rin said. "Can he fit with his wings in a normal car?"

"Maybe lay down?" Josh suggested.

"Cover him?" Rin added. "That could work."

"We can try it with my parent's car in the garage," I said hopefully. "Then we'll know if he can fit."

"Okay, let's plan for that, and we'll see if it will work," Rin said. "I guess, in the meantime, all we can do is practice the codes, make sure we understand the plan, and be sure to talk to everyone involved and get them ready for Thursday."

* *** *

The Commission meeting was simple and short because Dana had a meeting with Leader Simon that diverted his time and attention. He gave short updates on the Sweeps, and then told us that the Censor Board was hard at work tracking the source of the email message, but had thus far been unsuccessful. He explained how the American people were getting restless and news casters were demanding that the Censor Board and the Commission of the People tell them what to say to the people about the messages appearing as pop-ups, emails, and sidebar advertisements.

You are going down, Dana... was my triumphant thought.

Dana's gaze continued to drift to me, and it did make me nervous that he could tell just from looking that I had had sex with Mykail, but even when the meeting was over, he did not approach me or talk to me.

I went home that night tired, yet excited to tell Mykail about the plans we had solidified.

I was more excited, though, to spend Sunday with him.

We made the most of our day alone together. I had told Clark that I was going to stay home that day because I was possibly coming down with a cold, something he had been asking me all Saturday, and he quickly agreed that I needed to rest.

While he worked with Mark on programming the blackout that would happen in the Commission on Thursday, I spent the day with Mykail.

Taylor had been right. The second time having sex was far more pleasurable than the first.

We were like honeymooners, unable to keep our hands to ourselves, regardless of where we were in the house. We drank in each other's bodies and held each other as if letting go would mean certain death. We smiled and laughed and loved every moment of that Sunday, without care of how fast it flew by.

Before I knew it, Monday arrived and Clark and I stopped at the coffee shop on the way to the Commission to meet with a small group we had texted, pretending to just hang out when we were really going over the final details of our plan. We told them where to meet Clark to go to the water towers and learn where they would be positioned. I was going to do the same with another group of Commish Kids the following evening.

Thursday drew closer and closer, and even though I should have been frightened of everything going wrong and all of us being caught and thrown into the Commission as experiments, I wasn't. I was excited, exhilarated to be playing this incredibly dangerous game with Dana, sure that we were going to win and take his prisoners out from under him, hopefully throwing him off his game.

And I was so happy to be with Mykail that I felt nothing could go wrong.

I was invincible.

Mark would slip us little notes telling us that everyone was ready to go. Clark and I would practice the codes to break into cells and continued to walk through the plan and cell numbers to be sure we both knew everything we needed to as second nature, knowing the pressure of the situation would change our ability to recall information.

On Tuesday night, after I had met with my group at the movie theater, shown them to the fort, told them where they would be positioned, and what we wanted them to do, I went home and leapt on Mykail in the living room, both of us struggling to remain on the couch as we made love.

Afterward, I went upstairs to take a shower, unable to keep the smile from my face as I washed my hair and ran soap over my body.

But when I got out of the shower, I could not stop my scream and the bolt of terror that ran through me when I glanced at the mirror.

"LL, You're so beautiful."

I knew what the "LL" meant.

"Mykail!" I cried, darting out in my towel, descending the stairs and sprinting into the kitchen.

"What?"

"He's in the house," I gasped. "He's somewhere in here. He just wrote something on my mirror."

"What did he write?"

"That doesn't matter!" I snapped. I grabbed two of the kitchen knives, handing one to him. We combed through the house, starting with my room and moving through the upstairs before going through each room downstairs, checking under beds and in closets. The leader of the Commission was nowhere to be seen.

"He must have slipped out," I said.

"Lily…" Mykail said carefully. "What if he saw us?"

"Saw us?" I asked, confused, before my brain clicked into gear. I pursed my lips and looked around the living room, feeling nervousness churn in my belly. "He didn't."

"What if he did?"

"Well," I said, looking at my feet, "you said yourself he was bound to find out sooner or later…" I walked to him, taking his face in my hands and kissing him tenderly. "I don't think he did," I assured. "If he did, I'm sure he would have no problem letting us know."

Mykail forced a smile, not nearly as confident.

"I'm not so sure about that…"

There was real fear in Mykail's voice and it angered me. I was furious at Dana—for breaking into my home, for frightening Mykail because he was in love with me, for thinking I was his, for taking people away from their families and turning them into experiments, for molesting Clark, for taking Mark's voice just to scare the other experiments…and for doing all of this while claiming it was for the best of the country.

This fucker is going down…

Chapter Fifty

"You know, when my teachers asked me what I wanted to be when I grew up, domestic terrorist was not on the list," Clark said nervously.

I glanced at him as Mark drove us away from the Commission building and rounded a corner.

"You're not getting cold feet, are you?"

"Of course I am!"

"Well, get over it!" I growled. "Everything's already in motion and Mark is glaring daggers at you because he put more work into this than anyone."

Clark glanced at Mark, who was actually glaring through the rearview mirror.

Clark drew in a deep breath to steady himself, exhaling with a determined nod.

"Good," I said. "Everyone should be getting ready to leave for their posts. Everything will be fine."

I had no guarantees that everything would work out, but I was also trying to convince myself that we would be successful. We were already heading to the designated spot to get into Josh's car and be smuggled back into the Commission, where we would wait until 20:24 exactly. That was when Clark would start the blackout, at which point we would go through with breaking one hundred and thirty-five people out of the Commission in approximately seven minutes.

We reached the spot by the river, where Clark and I scrambled out of the car at the stoplight, leaving our tracers behind. Mykail was going to move my tracers around through the evening to keep up the appearance that I was home. Melody was tasked with moving Clark's tracers every now and then as she was the closest to his house.

Clark and I watched Mark pull away from the deserted stop light in the residential area and drive away, leaving us in the snow to wait.

We were silent, running through the plan in our heads as we waited for the van to pull up to the same stoplight.

We did not have to wait long for the black Commission van to roll to the intersection, slowing as the light turned yellow. The side door slid open and Josh offered his hand, pulling us both in and closing the door.

"Ready?" he asked. We nodded. "Here." He reached to the seat in the far back, grabbing two black jumpsuits.

We awkwardly pulled the baggy jumpsuits over our clothes as another member of the Eight Group drove us back to the Commission.

My stomach was turning sickly. I was putting on a strong front for the others, but I was becoming increasingly concerned with what we were about to attempt.

Josh helped us climb into the back of the van, where a few crates were stacked, leaving only enough room for us to crouch between them and the back seat.

"Wait until I tell you it's okay," Josh instructed.

Clark and I did not look at one another as the van returned to the Commission of the People. As I contemplated how close we were, I only realized then that I had no idea what the area would look when inside. Seeing a place on blueprints was very different from standing in the same spot.

Rather than get myself worked up, I started going over the codes in my head, muttering them under my breath, tapping my fingers against my leg as I imagined typing the codes into the electronic locks.

Josh cleared his throat, signaling to us that we were close. Both Clark and I were scarcely breathing.

I felt the van dip as it drove down a hill and yellow light started to shine through the windows. I realized we had descended a ramp into an underground parking lot.

The tires moved slowly over the pavement as we turned some corners and stopped. I heard the driver's window roll down.

"Oh, you guys," an annoyed voice droned. "Alright, do you have anything that we need to check?"

"No," the driver said with a thick accent.

"What is in the back?"

"Uh...we-weapons?" the driver said, trying to find the words.

"Dirk, it's the guns for the Sweep teams," another voice said. "Don't ask them hard shit. These dumb fuckers have no idea what you're saying."

"Alright, go on," Dirk said. The car began rolling forward.

The light changed from yellow to white as we entered a very bright chamber. We felt the car give a jolt before it began to descend.

I was worried my heart was beating loud enough to give us away.

The elevator slowed and I held my breath, as did Clark. We felt the second jolt as the elevator stopped and then Josh and the driver got out of the car. Listening closely, I heard a loud clanking and then the buzz of a door opening.

"Hey!" a loud voice called happily, startling me. "It's the chinks!"

"Do you have the guns? Excellent. Just put them over there. We need the van," another voice said.

A few moments later, the back door of the van opened and the top crate next to me was removed. I ducked, frightened that it was other than the Eight Group, but Josh's voice came to me.

"One second."

I heard another conversation start at the front of the car as the driver spoke to the other two men.

"Phil," he said with a thick accent, sounding nervous. "Van broken."

"What? Where?"

My heart was in my throat as the side door of the van opened and there were sounds of panels being lifted in the floor.

"Oh, it's not broken," the man named Phil said. "But shit, there's oil everywhere…damn it. I knew we had to find a better place to keep that shit. Hey, Dave, get your ass over here and help me clean this shit out!"

Josh tapped the top of the crate in front of me and I quickly, but quietly, clambered out of the van, grabbing a crate as Clark followed suit. Josh also took one of the crates and the three of us walked around the other side of the van as the driver kept the two men occupied.

Josh led us into the main area for the car elevators and I tried not to look around. I saw three garage-looking doors on each side of the hall, the space between the two walls large enough to drive a car between. The area was brightly lit and the sounds echoed in the cavernous hallways.

Josh set his box next to a set of metal shelves on the far wall holding tools and parts for maintenance of the vans. I set my crate down as Josh darted to the side of the shelf and reached his hand behind it, clicking the latch and pushing the shelf to the side for us to sneak into the passageway. I slid in first and quickly shed the jumpsuit, handing it to Josh as Clark untangled his feet from his.

"20:24," he whispered to us, taking Clark's jumpsuit and sliding the shelf back into place.

Then we had two hours to wait.

Clark and I sat in the cold hallway between the records room and the car elevators, barely breathing, anxiously watching the minutes tick by on Clark's phone, hoping that everything would go according to plan. The timing needed to be perfect. More than anything, I prayed Dana would be gone for the entire operation, supposedly at his meeting with one of the leaders of Brazil.

I ran through the codes in my head, remembering the thirteen cells I had to find in the holding cells. Clark had twelve cells, but he also agreed he would break Julie and Miranda out while keeping the money launderer and armed robber inside the cell. I had finally won the argument, stating that if we didn't get them out Dean would do something drastic and risk the entire rebellion.

We looked at the clock on Clark's phone every three minutes, watching the time crawl by.

8:00...8:04...8:07...8:13...

When it was 8:15, Clark opened the application on his phone to gain remote access to the security. I had no idea what he was doing but watched in fascination as he navigated his way around and got ready to deactivate the mainframe.

At 8:22, we crept forward and I gently pushed the latch, pulling the shelf to the side and listening for the guards. Clark peeked around me, listening as well.

"I fucking hate being left behind on a Sweeps night," a voice droned around the corner. Seeing no one in the expanse of the hallway in front of us, Clark ducked into the car elevator room, glancing at his phone. I followed, cautiously sliding the shelf back into place. We remained where we were, knowing we were out of sight of the cameras.

8:23...

"Quit your bitching," a female voice snapped. "At least you get to go to the Northeast Region next week. I get stuck here to do Sweeps locally."

I peered at my watch, watching the second hand tick closer to the eight, and then to the nine.

"I haven't even been on a Sweep yet," a man called, further away from the other voices, standing at a different post.

"You haven't completed your training, yet, you dumbass," an older male voice called from an even further position.

Clark's thumb hovered over the button, both of us watching the second hand on my watch approach the eleven...

Three seconds before 8:24, Clark pressed the button on the touch screen.

Just as the second hand hit the twelve, the lights clicked off and the constant buzzing of machines that ran the heaters and air circulation units ceased, making a wheezing sound before silencing.

"What the fuck?" one of the voices said.

Dim emergency lights that gave off an orange glow illuminated. My brain was frozen, thinking only of the next sequence of events.

"Shit, is this another fucking drill?"

"Alright, group at post one!" the oldest guard called, his footsteps echoing as Clark and I stepped forward, pressing ourselves to the wall as we reached the intersection of the car elevator halls.

"This is bullshit," one of the men groaned.

"Oh, whatever, it's good for you, trainee," the woman teased.

"Weapon check," the older man ordered.

They clicked their weapons, checking them out of routine, when a message sounded over the one of their speakers.

"All units, be sure you gather and check your weapons."

"Unit Four, cleared," the man in the car elevators said.

"Unit Six, cleared."

Two other units called in over the speaker as I waited, my breath held.

"Unit One command," a man said. "Can you confirm our orders?"

"Not at this time."

"Holy fuck!" a voice echoed through the static of the communicator.

"Who was that?!"

"Come in. What's wrong?!"

"Talk to me! What do you see?!"

"Three Tens are out! I fucking repeat, three Tens are loose!"

"Fuck, it's not a drill!"

The four in the car elevators area turned and ran toward the door to the holding cells, yelling at one another as they burst through.

"All units to Ward Ten! We have a fourteen-four! Eight Group! Get your fucking asses to Ward Ten!"

The door remained open as Clark peeked around the corner, pocketing his phone before turning to me and nodding.

As thrilled as we both were that the plan was working so far, we were not smiling, anxious and worried. I prayed that the timing would work.

We slipped around the corner and stood at the door into the holding cells. The cavernous room was far larger than I expected. The cells had large glass doors that acted as the fourth wall to their prisoners. The people who could see us from their cells stared in shock as we darted forward when the security guards were halfway down the halls, shouting orders to one another, echoing as they screamed.

"Fucking Goliath!"

"Seventeen men down!"

"Contain the fucking ward!"

"He's already out!!"

Clark and I hid next to the cells on the main hallway on opposite sides, waiting for the guards to clear the entire area.

The people in the cell in front of me started banging on the glass. I tried to ignore them, particularly since I was leaving that group behind. I had to remind myself that a lot of them were legitimately dangerous criminals.

The soundproof glass kept their voices from reaching me, but I felt their desperate pleas all the same.

"Lily!" Clark hissed. I saw the final group of guards reach the far end of the holding cells. Circling, I darted between the cells, the faces of the frightened and confused prisoners becoming a blur as I reached the next long hallway, turning, counting to the third hallway on my left and darting down it, glancing at the top of the doors to find the cell number I wanted.

BD-2.

I looked briefly inside and nodded to the obviously-much-calmer prisoners as I typed in the override number.

"2977641," I murmured as I punched in the code. As I was typing, I heard the holding cell area go very quiet. The security guards were out.

Half of the glass slid sideways and the cell opened.

"Come on!" I ordered, leading them to the main hallway. I heard them follow and I glanced up and down the main corridor, seeing Clark lead his first group out of their cell. I ran down the main hall, eight prisoners following me.

On the third hallway on my left, I turned and motioned for them to keep running. Mark had made everyone aware of the plan, so everyone knew where to go, but I still felt like I needed to direct them.

I went to my next cell: AG-3.

Releasing the next four people, I pointed where they needed to go, quietly ushering them out of the cell before following them, continuing to ignore the other prisoners pounding on the glass, pleading to be set free. I went to the next cell, AG-4, and opened their door, adrenaline pushing me faster.

After hissing at them to hurry, I turned the other direction and ran up the hallway to another long corridor, not wanting to be in the way of the humans running toward the Dome. I did not allow my thoughts to wander to how Mark and Griffin were doing breaking experiments out, or how the Eight Group was faring against Goliath and the other escaped Ward Tens. I focused entirely on finding my next cells and freeing the captives.

I ran faster than I ever had in my life. My breath was short and I was hot from adrenaline, but I was focused—almost frightfully focused—watching the numbers and halls fly by, able to ignore the horrified and pleading faces in the cells I passed.

AL-6…AN-4…

I saw out of the corner of my eye the other humans quietly running down the middle hallway as Clark let out the prisoners from his assigned cells.

I darted across the hall, avoiding another group of people Clark had freed.

BO-5.

Back across the hall, turn at the first corner...

AP-7.

I led the group out, running down the main hall and sliding into another hallway, letting them continue on.

AS-8.

Leading them as well, I focused on numbers and hallways. No one had a face yet. I was running, racing against the clock, playing the incredibly dangerous and exhilarating game against time. The orange glow of the emergency lights only excited me further, the dark making me feel like I was moving that much faster, and making me feel that much more powerful.

Down another hall.

BU-1.

Into the main hall, down one corner and across.

AV-8.

Straight across the main hall, to the very end, stopping in front of the last cell on the left...

BW-8.

I led them, pointing to the open door as I circled into the next hall and opened cell BW-4. Leading the prisoners down the same corridor, I snapped at them to run, not sure how long we had left before the backup security system would kick on. I did not waste time looking at my watch to see how many minutes had passed, worried about getting to my last cell.

I turned down the next hallway, stopping at cell BX-2 and leading those prisoners to the main passageway, running fast, passing Clark who was freeing another cell.

I ran straight through the open door and into the room connecting the Dome and the experiment wards. I wanted to stop and listen for possible signs of trouble, but I saw a member of the Eight Group standing in the room, so I knew everything was going according to plan, since the door they were guarding was still open.

I only had to run a short distance before I caught sight of the far cells of Ward Nine, their glass doors facing the hallway. I stopped in front of the first one, quickly motioning for the humans to keep running around me.

I glanced at the teenager standing at the door of his cell before looking up above his door, my heart pounding as I checked the cell number.

Barely remembering in time that I had to use a different code, I punched in the correct number and the door slid open.

I did not wait for the experiment to move, running toward the room that connected all the wards just as another experiment darted out of the door where the member of the Eight Group was posted.

I almost halted completely when I entered the smaller orange-lit room.

There were bodies everywhere, littering the ground with blood and broken bones. They startled me, and apparently startled the people running into the room behind me from the gasps I heard.

The experiment ran in front of me, straight across the room, ignoring the bodies and running to the open door of the Dome.

I forced myself to ignore the bodies as I ran to the door marked "Ward 10 – East" and found the number pad, typing in the next code. The door slid neatly to the side.

Remembering how the ward was laid out in the blue prints, I turned left at the first corner and ran to the dead end, ignoring the confused and inquisitive looks of the observing experiments. I turned right, breathing hard and shaking with excitement. I watched the cells on my left, reading the numbers and stopping at the second cell I reached, seeing Tori waiting for me.

I typed in her number, glancing at the cell next to hers, noticing it was empty.

As I hit the last number of the code, my hair stood on end and I shivered, feeling as though I was being watched.

The door slid open and Tori darted out as I stepped back, throwing a quick look around, noting that all the cells further down the hall were empty, except for the figure I saw in the very last cell in the corner.

I was frozen, staring at the familiar face, my eyes wide as his bright hazel eyes stared back at me, his face pale and his hair matted. His chest had scabs from where the spikes had cut into his flesh the last time he was chained and his skin was marred with dark bruises.

Eina stared at me, his eyes powerful, dangerous, and predatory— a caged animal ready to pounce at the nearest opportunity.

I could not tear my eyes away, captivated by the feeling of his eyes staring me down, telling me how powerful he had become. It was clear that he was more powerful than Dana, and while that should have terrified me, it gave me hope that, one day soon, Dana's favorite experiment would kill him.

"Lily!" a female voice snapped as hands grabbed my shoulders. I whirled around, shocked out of my trance. "We have to go!"

I threw one last glance at Eina, who was still watching me, but Tori's strong hands guided me at a run out of the ward, leaving the Machine of Neutralization prototype staring after us.

Tori kept hold of my arm as we ran out of Ward Ten and into the carnage of the room leading to the Dome. She pulled me insistently, even though I wanted to stop and wait for Mark, who was running with one more experiment out of the hallway from Ward Nine. The Eight Group experiment that had been standing guard at the distorted door was gone.

Tori pulled me toward the Dome and I ran with her, stepping into the cold air of the dark Dome, trying to catch my breath. I could not see much, but I could feel how large the space was and I was particularly surprised to feel grass under my feet and smell the scent of pine.

Tori continued to pull me, ignoring my fascination and confusion, to where a member of the Eight Group stood, holding a rope next to another experiment who was extremely tall and broad with a hard face barely visible in the dim emergency lights.

"Griffin," Tori breathed in relief.

"Go, quick," he urged. She finally released my arm and grabbed the rope, lowering herself into the stream and climbing the rope to the wall, disappearing underwater. Another experiment leapt across the stream and took the other rope held by another experiment, who followed him.

"Everyone?" Griffin asked, turning to Mark. Mark nodded, breathing hard as he quickly shed his jacket to switch his clothes to the bloodied ones.

"Thank you, Mark," I whispered.

He nodded to me once and then mouthed the word: "Go."

I grabbed the rope as Griffin helped me lower myself into the water. It was frigid and I lost my breath for a few moments before I forced my muscles to work and fight against the current. Griffin got into the water behind me, startling me, but I pushed forward until I reached the wall, where I took a deep breath and ducked underwater, pulling myself along the rope. The rope moved as well, pulling me under the wall and up to resurface with a gasp, coughing as hands hooked under my arms and hauled me out of the water, Griffin's hands pushing me. I choked and wiped the water from my eyes, shivering uncontrollably as Griffin pulled himself out of the water and onto the walkway in the dimly illuminated passage.

"Okay, you two," Griffin said with a nod, turning to the two men manning the ropes, who I guessed were Hiroki and Minsoo. I watched the one across the stream use the rope to climb to the top of the half-wall and pull the knot of the rope, releasing it from the bolt before jumping across the stream.

Griffin took the rope from him and handed it to me as I rolled it up, forcing my frozen fingers to function.

Griffin seized the other rope and the two Eight Group members jumped in the stream, following the rope back into the Dome.

I watched the two of them disappear.

When the second rope was curled in Griffin's hands, he helped push me over the sloped wall before climbing up and releasing the other knot, dropping to join me on the other side of the barrier.

I started running along the passageway, motioning to Matt, who was at the junction directing people where to go.

"Go, go, that's everyone!" I snapped quietly.

"We have two minutes before the lights go back on," Griffin said behind me.

I stopped. "That really only took five minutes?"

"It's amazing what adrenaline can do, huh?" he chuckled. He guided me into the pipe and I continued walking, trying to control my shivering. I understood why Rin had made us spend hours searching every nook and cranny of Fort Daniels for blankets and clothes, knowing we would be freezing by the time we reached the fort.

There was a small crowd of people around the base of the ladder, all waiting for their chance. I could feel the winter air snaking down the tunnel and chilling all of us who were already frozen from the water.

I watched as each person followed another up the shaft to the water towers, trying not to let myself think that we had successfully managed the breakout until we were all safe in Fort Daniels. But as the last two people began making their way up the ladder before us, even the person who had been ushering people up the ladder, I began to see we had, indeed, succeeded.

Griffin helped me up the ladder since my frozen limbs refused to work efficiently. When I reached the top, Jake, another Commish Kid, grabbed my hands and hauled me out of the hole.

"Go, get to the fort," Griffin told us, climbing out, tossing the rope to me, which I failed to catch and had to stoop to pick up. Jake ran out of the gate, following the path in the snow. The clouds were covering the moon, keeping the snow from being illuminated, but I still saw the final people running to the hedges and slipping into the shadows.

Griffin strained as he moved the grate back into place. Once it was maneuvered to cover the ladder, he quickly kicked the metal doors shut and fixed the padlock to make it look like it was still locked, despite being broken.

"Come on," he urged, grabbing my hand and pulling me out of the fenced off area, closing the gate behind us and wrapping the chain around the panels before running with me through the snow, being sure to keep me from falling as my body locked up from the cold.

We reached the hedges and Griffin motioned the final Commish Kids guiding people into the tunnel, telling them everyone was out. Griffin was the last one in, shutting the doors and locking out the winter air.

He caught up to me as I walked clumsily, my teeth chattering and my body quaking.

Griffin's arm snaked around my shoulders and pulled me close.

"It will be alright," he said. "We'll get you warmed up." He rubbed my arm and walked with me, keeping me from collapsing into a shaking mess on the concrete ground. "Lily...you were amazing. We couldn't have done this without you."

I smiled, but the warmth I felt at the statement and the sense of achievement did not fight off the chill as we walked through the quiet, cold tunnel.

Griffin ascended the small ladder before me into the bunk room and then reached down, pulling me up easily. The first noise that reached my ears was a dull roar as people laughed and cheered together in the main bunker.

That noise made the reality hit.

We had succeeded.

One hundred and thirty-five prisoners were free of the Commission of the People, and our revolution was stronger.

Griffin walked into the main bunker with me where people were cheering, hugging one another, and laughing at the incredible feat we had accomplished. The smiling was infectious, and even though my teeth were chattering and my cheeks were frozen, I found myself grinning.

Clark made his way to me and threw his arms around me, spinning me once as I let out a startled squeak.

"We did it! We did it!" he chanted. I laughed and hugged him back, feeling an incredible sense of accomplishment and relief wash over me.

"You are shivering like crazy!" Clark laughed.

"Why aren't *you*?!" I gasped as he set me on my feet again.

"Everyone is cold," Griffin noted. "Rin said that there are blankets and clothes somewhere…"

"I'll show you," I offered, eager to wrap myself in a blanket as well.

"Hey, everyone!" Tori called over the crowd. "Can everyone form a line over here?" She motioned in front of her. "We're going to get blankets and dry clothes for everyone!"

The Commish Kids followed Griffin and me to get blankets and clothes as people began to form a line, though families and friends were too excited at seeing one another again to form a singular line, grouping together in a lumps, hugging one another joyously.

I walked into one of the storage rooms and began handing stacks of clothes to everyone, including Griffin. The experiment grabbed the top set of work clothes from the factory above and shoved them into my arms.

"Get changed. Go on, we got this," he ordered with a smile.

"What about you?"

"I'm not cold."

I looked him over and then took the clothes, smiling.

"Thank you."

"Go on," he repeated, jerking his head into the room. I stepped behind some crates of canned goods and stripped off my wet clothes, shivering, extremely grateful for the dry, scratchy uniform.

Gathering my wet clothes, I returned just as Griffin handed the final batch of blankets to Clark, who carried them back into the main bunker. Now that I was not so focused on how cold I was, I looked over the experiment that Mark had trusted enough to break out other experiments in our time-crunch of an escape.

He was tall and broad with tattoos on his arms and even a few on his neck. His bulging muscles were extremely impressive and his extremely short haircut made his face look fierce and frightening.

He smiled. "Better?"

"Much."

"We'll hang these up," he said, grabbing my wet clothes and walking into the main bunker, past the experiments receiving clothes and blankets. Some experiments and prisoners were holding blankets up for others to change behind while older adults helped younger teenagers get the proper fit on the dry uniforms.

I saw Dean hugging Miranda tightly as Julie hugged them both, crying. For how annoyed I got at Dean being trigger-happy and not particularly smart about what he said, I was happy to see the display.

I followed Griffin into the strategy room, where he hung my wet clothes over the back of a chair.

"You helped a lot of people today."

"So did you," I said, smiling. "So…you're Griffin."

"Sergeant Griffin Thomas," he said, extending his hand.

"Sergeant?"

"I was in the military before the Commission took me."

"What did they take you for?"

"War crimes I didn't commit," Griffin sneered. "I took the punishment for my colonel's crimes and when I tried to explain the truth, it turned into treason. In the end, we both were taken in. My colonel was killed and I ended up on the table."

"I'm so sorry…"

"It's alright." He shrugged, leaning on the table with a sigh. "Truthfully, I feel very fortunate that I was on the table when I was. It allowed me to meet Mark and the others of the Eight Group, and eventually led to this."

"How did you meet Mark?" I asked, leaning on the table with him, both of us absentmindedly watching people receive their blankets and clothes in the main bunker. "He must trust you a lot for what he asked you to do today."

Griffin looked at me, suspicious.

"How much do you know about what Mark and I did today?"

"I know that you got all these experiments out."

"And even though we killed a lot of security guards today, *humans*, you're okay with that?" he pressed.

I sighed, remembering the bodies in the orange-lit room.

"I don't know if being 'okay with it' is the right way to say it," I said, picking at my nails. "I understand it."

"Good answer," Griffin said. "Mark probably trusts me less than I trust him, to answer your question."

"What do you mean?"

"Mark does not trust easily," Griffin said. "He has an incredible ability to read people. He's careful and he's smart, and he knows how to cover his tracks. I met him not long after his vocal cords had been scarred. His neck was all wrapped up and he had bruises everywhere and all I could think about was how stupid he was to fight with Dana and the scientists…" Griffin smiled, looking at his feet. "And then I learned that, at that time, he made a fuss on purpose to draw all the attention and punishment on him and save other members of the Eight Group after their failed rebellion. Seeing that, I realized that what happened in the Commission did not dehumanize me. It made me more human than I had ever been before."

"How so?"

"In the military, we learn to follow orders, watch out for the men around us, and to protect the man to your right and your left," he explained. "We were brothers and we cared about one another. And then when trouble came into my life, they abandoned me, afraid of the repercussions. That loyalty we were supposed to have for one another vanished in an instant.

"I found out that a lot of it had to do with keeping their jobs, paying their way through school, or providing for their family..." He shook his head. "There's none of that down in the Commission. We care about each other because we have to, not for any other reason. It allowed me to connect with people in a way I never had before, horrible as it was."

I looked back to the experiments and humans who were interacting so easily, despite the knowledge that all had committed some sort of crime and a few were not even human anymore. They didn't care.

Griffin sighed heavily. "I'm worried about Mark...I don't know what Dana is going to do when he finds out about all this."

"All the experiments missing?"

"The experiments, the prisoners...all the dead security agents...the computers smashed..."

"The computers smashed?"

"I might have gotten a little carried away," Griffin admitted with a chuckle. "But it will keep them down for at least two weeks, so that buys us some time to be sure that we can't be caught. Thankfully, the security was so flustered over three Ward Tens being out that they kept getting in the way of the Eight Group. It's going to make the whole thing more believable that Mark was not involved."

"We owe him a lot..."

"Yes, we do," Griffin agreed strongly. "Incidentally, Josh told me that he has a little sister. Do you know where she is?"

"She should be there." I nodded to the group in the main bunker. Griffin leaned back on his hands.

"Good. He should get some reward for all he's doing." He sighed. "I just hope that Dana doesn't flip his shit."

"He probably will," I said, looking at my feet. "I guess I'll be able to find out a little more tomorrow...and I'm sure the Commission meeting will cover this on Saturday." I sighed and shook my head. "We just need to wait for a while, let everything quiet down, and plan our next move."

"What *is* the next move?" Griffin inquired.

"I don't know," I said. "I'll have to think it up."

"You should probably get some sleep," he told me with a nod. "The adrenaline will wear off pretty soon and you'll crash."

"...I don't know how I'm getting back home..." I said. "Mark usually drives us."

"I wouldn't expect him here any time soon," Griffin said. "I don't know much about the security protocols, and I'm pretty sure no experiment has ever actually broken out of the Commission before."

"What about four-eleven forty-one?" I asked before I could help myself. Griffin's head snapped in my direction, his eyes wide.

"How do you know about him?"

"Rumor." I shrugged. "Seems like all the experiments know him."

"Know *of* him, yes," Griffin corrected. "But I'm pretty sure he's just a story. The Commission has been around for, what, seventy years? And has been doing experiments for sixty of those years or so...if four-eleven forty-one actually existed, someone would have more solid information. Those cells are as solid as they come, and the Eight Group is damn effective at their jobs. The only experiment who could break out..." He trailed off, his eyes cast down in thought.

"Eina?"

"Yeah."

"I saw him," I said. "In Ward Ten, in the corner when I got Tori," I clarified when I saw Griffin's startled expression. "He was all alone."

"Yeah...he's gotten really sensitive lately. Last time he was in the Dome, he had to be removed because the noise of the other experiments caused him to collapse. I guess they cleared some cells around him to act as sound buffers."

"What ward are you from? Are you from Ward Ten?"

"Nine," he said. "Tori's the only Ten here." He watched Tori walk around the room, telling people where they could hang their wet clothes, getting very creative as space became more limited.

"How old is she?" I asked, surprised by her young face and skinny frame.

"Nineteen," Griffin answered. "She was taken when she was seventeen and was on the table a week later." He closed his eyes. "She's had a really tough time in the Commission, but she's extremely caring and sweet. She'll be good to lead the experiments."

"Lead the experiments?"

"Don't you know about the ranking?" Griffin asked, confused by my confusion. "There is a pecking order, and Ward Tens are at the top. Well, except for Eina. No experiment in this room would dare go up against Tori."

As Griffin finished the sentence, Tori began walking toward us, smiling.

"Lily."

"Hello, Tori," I said.

"You're even prettier than I imagined," she said. I wasn't sure how she could say that when she was so beautiful herself. She had light blonde hair that fell in natural waves and bright blue eyes that burned with excitement and power. "It's nice to finally meet you," she said, extending her hand.

"It's very nice to meet you, too."

"I'm sorry if I just sort of yanked you away back there," she said with a sheepish grin.

"No, no, no," I said quickly. "Sorry, I just kind of..."

"Yeah..." Tori nodded, lowering her head. "Eina does that to people. It would probably help if people actually spoke to him and he didn't feel like everyone was either going to run away or beat him."

"They're afraid," Griffin said. "I am, too. He scares the shit out of me."

"Well...me too, but still..." Tori murmured. She turned to me and smiled brightly. "Can I give you a hug?"

"Of course," I laughed, standing as she threw her arms around me and squeezed. I winced and then laughed as she jumped slightly.

"Thank you, thank you, thank you, thank you!" she chanted.

"You're welcome," I chuckled. "But really, this was Mark's plan, you should thank him."

"Oh, I plan to hug the life out of him when he gets here," she said with an infectious giggle. "But, it will probably be awhile and a lot of these people are pretty hungry..."

"Oh, I'll show you where the food is," I said. "We better keep an eye on our rations, though."

"We also need to start removing tracers," Griffin added, standing straight.

"Do you mind if I'm not a part of that?" I asked nervously.

"Fair enough. You've done enough for tonight."

I walked through the groups of people in the main bunker. I was startled when a group of strangers turned to me, one woman grabbing my arm.

"Thank you so much," she said, her voice breaking. She threw her arms around me, hugging me tightly as the two teenage girls and older man hugged me as well. For several long moments, I could only stand motionless, in shock, and then I smiled, hugging the woman back, feeling my heart burst. She began crying. I wasn't sure how long we

668

held each other before we broke away. I had to push the tears from my cheeks and chuckle awkwardly before nodding and smiling, turning to lead Tori and Griffin to the food and medical supplies.

I was stopped by several groups and people were thanking me left and right, hugging me and crying as I bit back my own tears of relief and happiness. I finally made it to the store room and sniffed, pointing at the food rations and medical supplies, trying to clear the lump in my throat.

Everything that we had been through in planning and executing the escape was worth it for the gratitude.

"It's okay to cry," Tori said, placing a hand on my shoulder.

"Do you want another hug?" Griffin asked.

I laughed, pushing my tears away with the heel of my hand before nodding. His huge, muscular arms enveloped me and pulled me off my feet, holding me as I giggled, the tears spilling down my cheeks against my will.

As people were fed and tracers were being removed, I hid in the strategy room, starting to feel the exhaustion as the adrenaline wore off and the release of tension racked my body, pulling me down like lead weights attached to every limb. I fought to keep my eyes open as I sat at one of the tables, watching the seconds tick by on my watch. It was approaching three in the morning when Clark gently touched my shoulder to get me to lift my head.

"We really should think about how we're getting home."

"When does the first bus run?" I asked, rubbing my face in a futile attempt to keep myself awake.

"I don't know…maybe about six or so." Clark sat next to me. "We have another problem," he said quietly, dropping his voice. "We're going into the Commission tomorrow…or today, whatever," he said, obviously exhausted himself. "Dana is going to be furious, and if we're acting this tired, he will be suspicious."

I nodded, understanding but not sure what he wanted to do about it. Even if I slept a little, it would not be enough to fight off the exhaustion of my body.

"A few of the other Commish Kids are heading home now," he said. "They're going to walk."

"What about the curfew?"

"They live not too far. They're going to stick to residential neighborhoods and back allies," Clark explained. "In about forty minutes, another group will leave as well," he added. "You and I live further away, though. We could wait for the bus."

"How do you think Mark is doing?"

"I couldn't guess," he said, troubled. "But we shouldn't expect him. If he can't get away, he won't."

"I know. I guess I'm just worried about him being found out."

"I am, too."

"Why don't we just catch the first bus and head home then?" I decided, smothering a yawn in my hand. "If Mark isn't back, then Dana can't expect us to come to the Commission."

"That's a good point," he said. "But regardless, we're going to need to load up on coffee."

"Do you really think Dana will bother us?"

"There's no telling what he'll do," Clark said. "Maybe we should catch a little bit of sleep here."

"Is everyone doing okay out there?"

"Yeah." Clark nodded, smiling and glancing behind him into the main bunker. "A bunch of people are catching up with their families and friends. Several of the experiments are meeting the humans, but they're not talking about testing or anything like that. They're just getting to know each other. Tori and Griffin are finishing taking out tracers and then they're going to assign guard duties and beds."

"Seems like they've got this handled," I said, thrilled since I was too tired to play any authoritative role.

"Seems like it," Clark agreed. "But they have to be. We can't be here all day every day."

"True." I stifled another yawn.

I must have fallen asleep shortly after my conversation with Clark finished because it was five in the morning when I jumped, sitting upright at the sound of my name. I looked around frantically and saw Griffin standing near the door of the strategy room. The fort was much quieter, but I could still hear conversations in the main bunker.

"Sorry," he said apologetically, walking closer and holding a big bottle of pills. "You will need to catch your bus soon, so I thought I would wake you up." He handed me the bottle, which I took, trying to blink the sleep from my eyes. Clark was also waking up, rubbing his eyes awkwardly around his glasses.

"What's this?" I asked, my voice thick and rough with sleep.

"It's something we used to take when we weren't allowed to sleep in the military," Griffin said. "It will keep you awake and alert, though you kind of feel like you're high if you take them too often."

"Thanks. How is everyone?"

"Good. Too excited to sleep, it seems," Griffin said, glancing toward the main bunker. "Everyone's quieted down, but they're having fun talking and just being free of the Commission."

"That's good." I looked around, tapping the big bottle of pills. "I take it Mark isn't back yet?"

"No, not yet," Griffin whispered, his eyes betraying his worry.

Worry churned in my gut, terrified that Mark and the Eight Group had gotten into trouble with Dana somehow.

"I'll bring you some water and something to eat with those," Griffin said, nodding to the pills as Clark took the bottle from under my hand and looked at the label, squinting to read it.

"I think this stuff could potentially be very dangerous to our health..."

"Not as dangerous as if Dana finds out we were behind yesterday," I said, lowering my head back to my arms, feeling the pressure of my brain against my skull.

Eating some stale crackers and taking two pills woke me up enough to return to the main bunker. A lot of people smiled at me before going back to their conversations. A few were drinking from the canteens we had filled with water that was piped into the fort. Others were nibbling on food rations. Two or three experiments were sleeping and a few freed prisoners were also resting, but with everyone in the simple clothes we had found around the Mackay Power Plant and Fort Daniels, it was difficult to tell the experiments from the humans. Everyone even had a bandage on their right foot from the removed tracers.

"How are you feeling?" a man asked. I turned to him, surprised. He was quite young with dark brown hair and eyes. I recognized him as the Ward Nine experiment I had released.

"Oh, just a little tired," I lied.

"I can imagine," he said, standing and brushing his hands off on the jumpsuit. "That was quite a feat you accomplished."

"Thanks."

"Cody," he introduced, extending his hand, which I took with a small smile.

"Lily."

"I figured you were Lily Sandover."

"People talking about me?"

"Sort of," Cody said, sticking his hands into his pockets. "Nothing bad, don't worry." He turned to the young man and woman who he had been in a conversation with. "These are my siblings, my younger brother Zane, and my older sister Candice."

"It's nice to meet you."

"The last time we saw each other was over a year ago," Cody told me. "We really appreciate what you've done for us, and for everyone else here. It was an immense risk on your part."

"I'm just happy that you are together again," I said sincerely. I looked between the siblings, trying to remember the reason that they had been brought into the Commission, but even with the pills perking me up, I could hardly remember them from my earlier research.

Just as I was about to ask, there was a clanking sound that surprised everyone. The bunker silenced and everyone turned to the source of the sound, on alert. Griffin stood, as did Tori, watching cautiously as the large door to one of the passages slid open.

At first, there was a feeling of relief, and then there was great excitement around the bunker.

"Mark!" a lot of experiments cried, jumping up and running toward the man as he walked into the fort, a nervous smile on his face. I saw a bruise on his jaw and two cuts that sliced across his temple. His suit was bloodied, the jacket torn and the tie nowhere to be seen. I was worried that he was actually harmed, but I did not know what blood was real and what had already been on the change of clothes. The very real marks on his face made me think he was truly injured.

But before I could study further, all the experiments swarmed him, thanking him over and over again, also turning to Josh, Rin, and two men of the Eight Group that I did not know.

Mark forced a smile, overwhelmed by the intense gratitude that surrounded him. Several of the humans also ran forward to thank him, having heard from the experiments that he was the brains behind the plan.

As the experiments backed away from the nervous and overwhelmed Mark, Griffin laughed and stepped forward.

"Come here, you crazy ninja!" he boomed, wrapping his arms around the smaller man and picking him up, squeezing him tightly as Mark laughed silently, cringing in the hug that looked painful. Griffin set him down. "What the hell happened to you?" he laughed. "I thought Goliath was supposed to only *pretend* to fight you." There was an underlying question in the jest.

"We had to make it look realistic," Rin laughed. As I looked over the five members of the Eight Group present, I noticed they all appeared injured and disheveled.

"What about Dana?" Tori asked, pulling away from her tight hug with Mark.

"He's furious," one of the others chuckled.

"But he doesn't suspect you?" Griffin asked hopefully.

Mark shook his head and everyone let out a long breath of relief. I turned to Clark and both of us shared the same look of happiness, thrilled that the man who had been our strongest ally was free from suspicion.

A meek voice sounded near the front of the circle around Mark and everyone turned to one small woman as she pushed through the people and launched herself at Mark, throwing her arms around his neck and pressing her face into his shoulder.

Mark's arms went around her as his eyes went wide, stunned at first before he let out a shaky breath and wrapped his arms even tighter around her, his fingers tangling in her hair and pulling her closer, his head dropping to her shoulder.

Josh and the other two men smiled at the display. My heart was soaring. Many in the circle turned and walked away with a smile, feeling as though they were intruding on a very private moment. I could not stop the happy tears that came to my eyes at the reunion between Mark and his younger sister.

After a long embrace where Mark's younger sister began crying, he broke their hug and sniffed, brushing the tears that had gathered in his eyes, pretending that he had not done so at all. His little sister laughed, her hands still on his shoulders as she also sniffed, her tears running freely down her cheeks.

Mark tenderly pushed the tears away from his sister's face, his eyes telling her that everything was alright. He hugged her once more.

When they broke apart again, Josh approached and she gasped, launching into a tight hug with him. The other two men also walked up, obviously having been friends with Mark and his sister before the Commission.

Mark scanned the dispelling circle, his eyes finally resting on me. He walked toward me and my smile widened until it was almost painful.

"Hey," I said. "I'm so glad you're okay."

Mark nodded, his eyes dropping to his feet briefly. He took a deep breath and, as he let it out, he stepped forward and hugged me tightly.

At first, I just stood there, shocked, but when his arms tightened, I wrapped my arms around his back and returned the hug. Once again feeling the tears rise to my eyes, I closed my eyes and pressed my face to his coat, squeezing him. I could feel his gratitude at what we had done for him and all the prisoners we had freed from the Commission of the People. I could feel his relief and elation through the hug.

I wanted him to understand how grateful I was, so I held him even tighter, smiling against the fabric of his coat despite my tears.

It was so quiet I almost couldn't hear it, but there was a rush of air past my ear, choked and forced past pain I could not imagine, but that made the message much more powerful, even though it was just below a whisper.

"Thank you."

Chapter Fifty-One

I was not sure what was in the pills Griffin gave us, but I felt that I could handle absolutely anything I encountered. I was fully alert as Mark drove me home. I worried that Mykail was pacing a hole in the floor, thinking we had failed and been captured by Dana.

So when we pulled into my driveway, my seatbelt was already off and I had opened the door before Mark fully stopped the car.

I ran to the front door, not bothering to close the car door behind me as I fumbled with my keys. Hurriedly swinging the door open, I left my key in the lock and ran into the house, straight into Mykail's waiting arms.

He let out a laugh and his arms wrapped around my waist, lifting me off my feet and spinning me.

"Congratulations!" he said.

"How did you know we succeeded?" I asked as he set me back on my feet.

"Because if you had been caught, Dana would have been here already to take me back," Mykail explained. "By about three a.m., I figured you had done it."

Smiling like a moron, I lunged forward and kissed him, our lips locking together desperately, both of us relieved and invigorated. I never wanted to stop kissing him.

But he finally pulled away, even as I tried to keep his lower lip in my teeth. He reclaimed his lip and then smiled awkwardly, glancing over my head, which caused me to turn to the still-open door and confront the startled faces of Mark and Clark.

My face burned hot with embarrassment.

"Uh...sorry..."

"You...you're...you two..." Clark tried to say.

I had never really meant to keep it a secret that I was in a relationship with Mykail. I had been more embarrassed about the sexual aspect and being as worried as I was with Dana finding out, I had kept our relationship quiet, even from Mark and Clark.

"Sorry," I said. "I didn't mean to keep it a secret."

"How long?"

"A while..."

"I hope you are being careful so Dana doesn't find out," Clark scolded.

"Of course," I said, choosing not to be offended, knowing he was only worried. I could hear the tension in his voice, and I knew he was worried that we were going to endanger ourselves and the revolution. I had realized that, in terms of the rebellion, Mykail was my weakness. My love and caring for his well-being would make him an easy way to get me to break. In the same way Dana kept Mark's sister to keep him loyal, I was sure that, if Dana were to harm Mykail, I could not remain strong.

My feelings for Mykail were dangerous in many ways to all of us.

Mark looked away, extremely uncomfortable and raised a hand to rub his face distractedly. He nodded to me, and while I was unable to see his eyes, I knew that he was embarrassed about what he had witnessed between us.

"I guess...we'll come pick you up?" Clark said, looking at Mark, who nodded once and turned away, leaving the foyer. As he left I could not stop the smile tugging at my mouth. Mark was not at all worried about storming into the Commission of the People and breaking out experiments from under Dana's nose, but seeing Mykail and I kiss made him so uncomfortable he had to leave abruptly.

"We'll see you in about three hours," Clark told me, glancing at his watch.

"Do you have those pills?"

"Yes," he said. "We better get going though, before someone tracks the GPS."

"Okay," I repeated. "I'll see you in a few hours."

I closed the door behind Clark as he ran through the cold December air to the car. I turned back to Mykail after I locked the door and he smiled, looking as handsome as ever.

"We did it," I whispered.

I ran into his open arms again, kissing him as though my life depended on it. My head was light by the time we finally broke away, so I knew we had been kissing for several minutes in the foyer. Mykail took my hand and led me to the kitchen.

"I have a fire going and hot chocolate."

"Hot chocolate? Not coffee?"

"Hot chocolate is more romantic," he said, walking to the warming drawer and pulling out two mugs. Handing me a delightfully warm mug, he led me to the smaller living room where the fire was roaring in the corner fireplace. It was not until that moment that I realized I was still cold. I had not taken off my jacket even after entering the house and my clothes were still damp, making me colder.

"I'm going to change."

"Okay, but hurry," Mykail said. "Your hot chocolate will get cold."

I scurried upstairs and slipped out of my cold, damp clothes, pulling out something warmer. As I was reaching for my favorite baggy sweatpants, my hair, which had the appearance of straw from air-drying in the fort, covered my face, reminding me of how filthy I was.

I jumped in the shower and washed myself in record time before pulling on my sweatpants and a shirt, rejoining Mykail in the living room. He laughed.

"Drink your hot chocolate," he said. "I was about to put it back in the warming drawer when I heard the shower running."

"I was really gross," I chuckled, plopping on the couch with my warm mug as Mykail wrapped an arm around my shoulders.

"So, everything worked out."

I nodded, a huge smile splitting across my face. He kissed me on the cheek.

"Tell me everything."

"There's not a whole lot to tell," I said. "Mark and Griffin did most of the work, along with the other members of the Eight Group—"

"Wait, *Griffin*? Not Ward Nine Griffin," Mykail said, his eyebrows furrowed in thought.

"Yes…"

"How did he get involved?"

"He's a friend of Mark's. The two seem pretty close," I explained, wondering if I had really never mentioned Griffin's name before.

"Wow…" Mykail said, his eyes turning distantly to the fire as he raised the mug to his lips and sipped the hot chocolate. I waited for him to elaborate on why he was so surprised. When he saw I was still staring, he chuckled brokenly. "I'm just surprised. Mark has a lot of friends."

"Is that a bad thing?"

"No, not at all," Mykail said. "It's just amazing. Most of the experiments I knew were terrified of the Eight Group. And here is Mark with all of these allies…"

"You never knew he was against Dana? He never came to you with his plan of breaking people out?"

"No," Mykail whispered. He looked down into his mug. "I guess that means he doesn't entirely trust me."

"Don't say that," I said, cuddling closer. "Maybe he just didn't know how to approach you."

Mykail was silent, resting his head against mine, staring ahead distantly. His silence worried me. I was sure that Mark would have told Mykail about his plan to go against Dana if presented with the opportunity. I wanted to tell him that since he was one of Dana's favorite experiments it was probably more difficult for Mark to approach him. But something about the explanation didn't sit right—Dana had also shown immense interest in Mark.

I began to question why Mark had never approached Mykail.

Mykail turned his head and kissed my temple.

"Did you sleep at all last night?" he asked, his voice strained.

I shook my head, deciding to let him change the conversation. "Only a little."

"You must be exhausted…"

"No, actually," I said. "Griffin gave us some pills and I am feeling a little hyper now."

"You're popping pills?" Mykail teased.

"He said the military uses them."

"Well, that should help you act normal when you go to the Commission today," Mykail said. I nodded, setting my half-empty mug down on the coffee table and cuddling closer, closing my eyes. "Are you cold?"

"A little," I admitted, smiling mischievously. Feeling playful and wanting to take his mind off his troubling thoughts, my fingers danced up his leg. "We have a couple hours before Mark comes to pick me up…"

"What do you have in mind?" Mykail asked.

"Well…" I plucked the mug out of his hand and set it next to mine before climbing on his lap, my arms encircling his neck. "You could help warm me up."

Mykail's head dipped under my chin and he kissed down the side of my neck, my eyes fluttering shut in response.

"How cold," he pressed a kiss to the dip of my collarbone, "are you?"

"Cold enough to want to stay close to the fire…" I murmured, my skin sparking where his fingers brushed my shoulder as he moved my shirt aside.

He began kissing down my sternum as my breath shortened.

"I guess we should celebrate," he chuckled, his breath fanning over my skin and lighting my body aflame.

* *** *

"How is this arrangement going to work, exactly?"

"What do you mean?" I asked, brushing through my drying hair as Mykail leaned against the doorframe, watching me get dressed.

678

"The fort," he clarified. "I mean, you will have to go back to school in a few weeks, and your parents will be home at the end of next week…who is watching over everyone while you're gone?"

"Griffin and Tori seem to have it under control," I said. He blinked, surprised.

"Griffin *and* Tori? Wow, talk about friends in high places." I felt guilty again, knowing that mentioning the other experiments was making Mykail wonder all the more why Mark did not include him on his list of close allies. "So, they're taking care of that, and you're planning the next move?"

"Something like that."

"I see…"

"Mykail, I'm sorry."

"For what?"

"That you feel as though you're not part of this," I said, linking my hands behind his neck. "If I could sneak you out of here, I would."

"I know," he said, his voice betraying his disappointment. I kissed him.

"I'll talk to Mark," I said. "It would at least be fair for you to go to the fort once before my parents come back."

"That's the other thing I would like to talk to you about," he said, his hand running down my arm and slipping through my fingers as I walked into my bedroom to grab my cell phone and purse. "We need to discuss how we're going to interact with each other when your parents *do* return."

I sighed as I placed my phone in the side pocket of my purse.

"I know we do," I muttered. "I just…I would rather not think about it and enjoy the time we have remaining."

"Lily, I…" Mykail stopped and shook his head. "Nothing, you're right. We should enjoy this while we can."

I looked him over. "What were you going to say?"

"Nothing." He shook his head again. "It's not important. I'm just…feeling a little useless, that's all."

I smiled sadly and walked to him, pressing my hand to the side of his face.

"I'll talk to Mark," I assured again. "I'm sure we could use your help."

"Whether you need my help or not, I can't be of any use," he told me dejectedly. "When your parents get back, I can't disappear. They'll notice."

The sound of the doorbell caused me to turn away and, even though I wanted to help Mykail feel better, I was thankful for the distraction. I pecked Mykail on the lips, promising that I would figure something out. Then we both walked to the front door, where I met a very chipper Clark.

"Ready?"

"Did you take more of those pills?" I asked suspiciously.

"...so?"

I rolled my eyes and grinned. "Where's Mark?"

"In the car." He nodded back to the driveway. "I think he's actually pretty hurt. He doesn't really want to move."

"*What*?" I stepped outside and craned my neck to look at the car, though I could only barely make out the outline of the experiment in the driver's seat.

"Lily," Mykail called, holding my coat out to me. "Go on, just ask him."

I smiled, ducking back in the house once more to kiss him, taking my coat and promising him I would be back later before leaving a very depressed Mykail at home, locking the door behind me.

"Is he okay?" Clark asked, nodding to the closed door.

"It's a little complicated..."

"That doesn't surprise me."

I got in the car and Mark smiled at me through the rearview mirror.

"Mark, are you okay? Are you hurt?"

He took a deep breath and held up his hand, holding his forefinger and his thumb close together to signify a little.

"Anything I can do?" I asked.

He shook his head.

"Where were you hurt?"

He tapped his leg as Clark climbed in the car.

"Are you sure you're okay?" I said, fixing Mark with my best mothering gaze. He nodded, putting the car into reverse.

"What do you think we should do if we see Dana today?" Clark asked.

"Hopefully, he'll be so busy we won't see him today," I groaned. "I'm too tired to deal with him, regardless of how much caffeine is pumping through me."

Mark snapped his fingers twice and reached back, pointing to the light in the middle of the car roof.

"I mean...Dana doesn't need to know that we went on a date last night," I said, sharing a purposeful look with Clark. I got a thumbs-up encouragement from Mark.

"But, what if he asks where we were? He could have seen that we were together..." Clark tried to sound natural.

"We can just tell him we were going out as friends," I said. "We should keep the information from him. We'll just tell him we were home last night, and that's all he needs to know."

Even though we had agreed to remain quiet about anything that we might have been doing last night, I was still very nervous about seeing Dana. How would he react? Would he be angry? The Eight Group had said that he was furious when he found out what happened...would that carry over to today? Would he know immediately that Clark and I were involved? Would he try to interrogate us?

I was nervous and hyper-aware of my surroundings by the time we arrived at the Commission. Though I wasn't entirely sure if the hypersensitivity was warranted concern or a side effect of the pills.

As usual, I waited for Mark to walk around the car and open my door, but I did notice the heavy limp on his right leg.

"He really is hurt," I whispered, glancing at Clark, worried.

Clark slid out of the car after me as I looked at Mark apologetically. He bowed his head, acting as though he did not understand my gaze though I knew he was trying to reassure me.

"He might not have noticed until the adrenaline wore off," Clark whispered as we walked into the lobby.

As soon as the doors opened, an amazing sense of power and an urge to gloat overwhelmed me. There were several members of the security detail behind the main counter, talking in hushed voices, looking over their tablets with intense eyes.

They turned to us when we entered, their expressions frantic. It took everything I had not to smile with pride.

One of the men whispered something to the rest of the group.

"What's going on?" Clark asked, sounding authentic with his confusion and concern.

"Nothing you need to concern yourself with," the man snapped, setting down his tablet and walking around the desk. "Random intense search day today."

Even though I knew I had nothing incriminating on me, anxiety tickled at my belly. Clark and I both stopped, worried and curious. With the way the security responded to our halt, it was obvious they had been getting the stunned reaction all morning.

"Come on..." the man said as he approached me, placing his hand on my back and gently, but insistently, guiding me.

"What are we doing with *him*?" another man asked, pointing at Mark.

"Is that Mark?" the older woman of the group inquired as she motioned me to walk to her.

Mark nodded once.

"Go to Sean," she told him clearly. "Just do basic checks on him and let him go. They're giving all of the Eight Group medical attention."

I glanced at Mark worriedly, but did not get a chance to look at his reaction before the older woman pushed me to the door behind the front desk. I walked into the office, surprised to see another group of security personnel discussing something else in hushed tones.

"Patty," the woman behind me called. A younger lady turned, her eyes glancing behind us as Clark and another member of security led him to the room. Instead of studying the woman named Patty, my eyes were drawn to the far side of the room where several stalls of black cloth had been erected. One of the stalls had another young woman standing in front of the drape while the other four were unguarded.

"Will you check her, please?"

"Sure," Patty said. Nervously, I followed as she led me to a stall and held the curtain aside. I stepped inside, unsure what to expect. Patty followed, closing the curtain and turning to me with a thin smile.

"I'll take your purse," she offered. I handed my bag to her, watching every movement. She unzipped the bag and opened it before glancing back up at me.

"Please remove all clothing."

At first, I could only blink.

"*What?*"

"It's an intense search day," she said, removing my phone and reaching outside the curtain, handing it to another person I could not see. She then resumed rummaging through the contents of my purse.

I waited for her to offer an explanation, but she did not. Nervously, I unzipped my jacket, slipping it from my shoulders and beginning to place it behind me before Patty stopped me.

"Right here," she pointed between the two of us.

I dropped the coat where she designated, pulling my sweater over my head and placing it on top of my jacket. I unbuttoned my jeans, watching as Patty abandoned her search of my purse and donned latex gloves, stooping to pick up my clothes, feeling along each seam.

I shimmied out of my jeans and placed them in the pile with my socks and shoes before I hesitantly unclasped my bra and let it fall to the ground as well, covering my bare breasts with my arms once my panties had also joined the pile of clothing.

It felt like hours that I stood there, completely naked, while every seam and pocket of my clothing was checked and my boots were inspected thoroughly.

The woman nodded to me.

"Please turn to face the wall and place your hands at the level of your ears."

Startled, it took me several seconds to obey the command but I complied, placing my hands against the cold wall with my back facing her, my stomach tumbling in my abdomen, nervous.

Her hands, still covered in the cold latex gloves, ran along my neck, shoulder blades, spine, ribs, and hips before running down each leg. After the annoyed thought that I was getting a physical, I remembered my tracers and my heart leapt into my throat. The only one that was still on my person was the one that was supposed to be in my shoulder, which I had sewn into a pouch that I could attach to the label of my bra. Realizing that she had passed over the tracer when checking my clothes eased my mind, but I wondered if she was looking for the bumps of my tracers or if she was satisfied by just seeing the scars.

Suddenly, her thumbs were pushing into my lower back, as her fingers enclosed around my hips. I gasped, cringing as the pressure became painful. My legs buckled and I tried to squirm away but she held firm.

"Sorry, have to do this," she murmured behind me.

"What?" I snarled after the released pressure allowed me to breathe again.

"Turn around."

I begrudgingly obeyed. She ran the same sweeping motions over my body down my front, passing over my clavicles, under my breasts, down my ribs, hips, and legs before she instructed me to lean against the wall. Nervous and not sure what she was going to do, I leaned my shoulders against the wall as her hands went to my hips again, her thumbs pressing hard just inside my hip bones, causing my hips to slam back into the wall as I bit my lip against the shout of pain.

Patty backed away and I caught my breath.

"What the hell?" I snapped.

"Have to make sure you're not hiding anything inside your body," she told me simply, as though it was an obvious answer. "Squat down for me."

Humiliated and unable to meet her gaze, I did as she told, my face burning hot with anger and embarrassment.

She nodded once and told me to stand. "You can get dressed now. Your phone should be coming back soon."

"This is fucking stupid..." I muttered under my breath, snatching my panties and bra from the ground.

I hurriedly redressed, refusing to lift my head as Patty scrutinized every action, increasing my anxiety no matter how I tried to ignore her.

My phone was returned as I stepped out of the stall and they told me to wait for Clark before I was allowed to leave the horrific inspection.

By the way he looked when he stepped out of the makeshift inspection area, he had also undergone the invasive inspection.

We were finally left alone when the security staff that had escorted us to the elevators were shut out by the door closing.

"Holy shit..." I let out an exasperated breath.

"Tell me about it," Clark murmured. "Were you okay with your tracers?"

"Yeah, you?"

"Yeah. Didn't check my shoes thoroughly enough to find the container."

We said nothing else during the elevator's descent.

I was expecting a lot of commotion when the doors opened but, instead, we were greeted by an eerie silence. I stepped out of the elevator, studying the dark hallway as though it was a new space.

"Is that a good or a bad sign?" I whispered.

"I don't know..." Clark admitted. "Let's just find a conference room. Maybe someone will tell us what's going on." He fixed me with a serious look, reminding me that we were not supposed to know that there was a real problem in the Commission of the People that day.

We walked through the empty meeting room. Even though the room was normally occupied with empty chairs and tables, the sight was far more ominous that day. I continued to tell myself that my knowledge of the escape was causing me to be hyper aware of the silence, but another part of me knew that there was a dark energy around the Commission of the People.

Stepping into the hallway with the conference rooms, Clark looked at the schedule of the first room.

"Canceled..." he murmured.

I looked at the darkened room and nodded with a wobbly smile.

"I guess we'll take this one."

While I was nervous at the feeling in the Commission, I was also extremely curious. I wanted to know who had told Dana that there had been a breach and how he had reacted. I wanted to know the official number of people missing, and how many guards had fallen in the ordeal.

"What are you doing today while we're stuck here?" I asked.

"I was going to try and do some of the reading we're supposed to do over break," he said. "You do remember that we start school in two weeks, right?"

"Not that soon,"

"Yes, that soon," Clark laughed brokenly.

I bit my tongue and sat at the glassy table, looking at the surface with disinterest.

I did not want to tell Clark that I remembered when school started and how much reading I had to do during break, but the truth was, I no longer cared about academic pursuits. After the thrill of the previous night, school sounded incredibly dull.

Through my entire life, I had been worshiping the country that had been painted in a way to make me proud to be a citizen of America. But when I moved to Central, I realized that the picture I had held dear, the picture of my own country, was nothing more than that—a picture. It was not the reality. The living, breathing country of America was warped and distorted, ugly in its wicked facets and policies. The Commission of the People had never been an entirely pleasant subject, but I understood it now as a festering wound in America's side, oozing and bloated with infection.

To heal the country properly, the Commission had to go.

All school did was teach me to be obedient. It had taught me how to say the pledge to the flag, how to appreciate the safety we had by telling us the horrors of other countries, it emphasized the difference between us and other countries—us versus them.

But I remembered the way the Commission prisoners had interacted once in the fort. They spoke with one another as though there were no barriers of race, sexual orientation, or language. They laughed with one another as if they had known each other for years.

The Commission of the People was the obstacle that kept people from knowing one another.

Over the previous month, when I had been in bed and unable to sleep, listening to Mykail's breathing, I would cringe when I thought back on my horror at seeing Mark for the first time. Seeing how he looked different, the way he would not speak, how uncomfortable he made me at first because he came from another way of life all felt like an embarrassing childhood memory. As I had grown fond of him, I had come to respect him more than I had respected anyone. He had been torn from his life and family, tortured, and forced into a life he should have never had, and he still stayed strong against Dana. He cared about others forced to endure the same torture. He wanted to spare even more people that fate. Rather than whine and cry, he fought back. Mark was the same, able to look past who the prisoners had been before the Commission, what they looked like, who they had fallen in love with, to see the human within.

And yet, I had still been shocked and frightened simply by Mark's appearance the first time I saw him.

I could not blame myself entirely. My parents had never shown me that there were people outside of our country that looked different. School had only mentioned them, and exaggerated drawings in history books and recovered, grainy films had done nothing to humanize other races for me. I had never been taught that human beings could be so different. I had been taught that they were different, but not human.

"Lily?"

I looked up quickly from my intense gaze at the table, turning to Clark.

"Are you okay?"

"Yeah."

"Didn't you bring your school work?"

"No."

"I feel bad that you're just sitting there staring at the table," Clark laughed. "We could watch a movie, if you want."

"No," I said. I reached for my bag, pulling out my sketchbook and some pencils. "I'll just draw."

For the first time in what felt like years, I put pencil to paper and drew things that did not involve committing acts of domestic terrorism. At first, I was frustrated because I could not focus, but before long I began drawing the one thing that came to my mind. A young man's back, bandaged from the wings that had just been attached, laying on the ground in a weakened state.

The opening door of the conference room caused me to jump out of my world of lines and shading.

Sean's smile was wobbly as he took one step into the conference room.

"Hello, you two."

"Sean," we both greeted, relieved to see it was the Commission's head of security and not Dana.

"How are you today?"

"Alright," we answered mechanically.

"Not too roughed up?"

"Roughed up?" I asked, confused, my heart jolting.

"The security at the front door," Sean clarified, looking sheepish. I felt relief spread through me but I let out a snort, reminded of the security upstairs.

"What was that all about?" I asked.

"Just one of those days…"

"Sean, are you okay?" Clark beat me in asking the question. I noticed the intense exhaustion in Sean's voice, even though he physically looked unharmed.

"Yeah, just didn't really sleep last night," he said casually. He walked forward, reaching into his coat pocket and extracting a clear bag of pills. "Clark, can you make sure Mark takes one of these twice a day?"

Clark took the bag hesitantly, glancing at the large pills as I blinked at Sean.

"What happened to him?"

"He hurt his leg. It's nothing too serious. Just some stitches."

"*Stitches?*" we gawked.

"It's alright. The doctor's just finishing up with him," Sean said. "In the meantime…have either of you seen Dana?"

The question made my anxiety worse.

"…no…"

"Did you misplace him?" Clark asked with a broken chuckle.

"No, no, I know where he is now," Sean said, showing us the screen of his phone, which made me realize that he had access to Dana's tracers. "I just…he's a little on edge today and I wanted to make sure that he didn't slip away for a few minutes to harass you."

"…Sean, what's going on?" I feigned ignorance.

"You'll find out tomorrow," he murmured vaguely, backing out of the conference room. "So, Clark, please make sure that Mark takes two of those a day, one in the morning and one at night. I will see you both tomorrow."

"Wait, Sean—"

"I'm sorry, Miss Sandover, that's all I can say right now."

* *** *

I wanted to go to the fort and see everyone on Friday, but Mark told me to wait until Sunday. Everything at the Commission was in chaos and it was entirely possible that Dana would be keeping a closer eye on us to be sure we weren't involved. Even though I was disappointed, I knew to trust Mark. I tried to get him to tell me what happened to his leg, but he put away the notebook and shook his head, effectively evading providing an answer.

"Wait," I said, tapping Mark's shoulder, "I need to talk to you about Mykail."

Mark reached back, tapping the light. I groaned and rolled my eyes, reaching a hand. He stared at it, glancing between my palm and the road before looking at me with what I assumed was a confused expression.

"Your knife," I said. He shook his head. "What? You don't trust me?" I teased.

He glanced at me once more before he shook his head again, a hint of a smile at the corner of his lips. I rolled my eyes and sat back.

"Fine…"

When we got to my house, Mark got out of the car, limping. All of us stepped inside the house as Mykail walked into the foyer from the living room.

Mykail remained quiet as I talked to Mark about bringing Mykail to the fort. Mark listened to me and then wrote how worried he was at the dangers of trying to sneak Mykail out of the house. I asked if Mark would be willing to do it once or twice before my parents returned from Europe to which he, begrudgingly, agreed. He said that he could try this Sunday and then asked if we had been able to fit Mykail in a standard size car, which I told him we could.

Mark wrote that he would let me know the next day if he thought of a way to take Mykail to the fort that Sunday.

But that did not seem to cheer up Mykail.

I could tell something was bothering him. He was quiet and distant, his eyes unfocused as he thought through whatever was gnawing at his brain. I asked him a few times to tell me what he was thinking, but he refused, continuing to stare into space. Even when I tried to distract him by kissing him, he was obviously thinking over something troubling.

I stopped pestering him, but on Saturday, the mood had still not broken and while I was determined to figure out what was bothering him, my focus had made me forget about the Commission meeting that night.

The most conversation I had gotten out of Mykail was him telling me that I needed to be careful, because he was sure that Dana was a few levels beyond furious and it would show in the meeting.

Despite the fact that I knew I should have been worried, I could not shake my pondering of Mykail's mood. I felt frustrated and, surprisingly, on the verge of tears, worried about what he was not telling me. Even when Mark wrote a quick message that he would have Josh drive Mykail to the fort the following day, I could not shake the feeling that something was very wrong.

All those thoughts were obliterated when I had to go through the rigorous security check at the Commission. Thankfully, Clark and I were there earlier than the others, so there was no line waiting to be checked. We were able to get through the embarrassing security checks with little hassle.

"What do you think?" Clark asked, worriedly rocking his chair back and forth as we waited for other Commission members.

"I don't know what to think."

My mind was rolling through all types of ideas. I had no way to predict the way the meeting would go, and I was getting more anxious by the minute.

The more confused Commission members entered the room, the more my anxiety heightened. By the time the second hand passed over the hour and the doors were shut, I was a jumpy, nervous wreck.

I threw one apprehensive glance at Clark, who returned the look. My attention then focused on Dana, who was walking toward the podium with Sean trailing close behind.

"Good evening everyone," Dana greeted. "We're going to skip the formalities tonight because we have something of great importance to discuss. I assume we all know the date and time, so let's get right down to it." He sighed heavily, stepping out from behind the podium, scanning everyone in the room. "You all noticed the increased security today. The truth is, we were breached two nights ago."

Surprised muttering broke out like a dull roar through the room. I looked around with wide eyes, acting just as surprised as the others of the Commission.

"Listen up, everyone," Dana called. "This was no small breach, either. This has the potential to become very dangerous."

I had to bite back the smile that threatened to split across my face.

"We are missing people from the back. Over eighty people from the holding cells are unaccounted for."

The muttering turned into frightened and hurried conversation. I waited excitedly for Dana to talk about the missing experiments, eager to see the reaction of the others.

"These are criminals against the nation of America. We have no leads on who broke them out or even how they managed to do so," Dana continued. "We know that the security system went down at 20:24 Thursday night, and when the secondary system kicked on seven minutes later, the criminals were gone."

"Were any of the experiments missing?" one parent called. My stomach flipped, twisting with the anticipation I was praying did not show on my face.

"No."

I felt eyes fall on me from all over the room. I wanted to scream at the Commish Kids to look anywhere else. Dana was testing the Commission, knowing that whoever had organized the breakout would know that there were experiments missing.

Most not involved in our plan relaxed, so I followed suit, looking around to show my relief about the experiments remaining contained. Thankfully, I found that only three people were looking in my direction, and they were quick to catch on to the needed act.

"That being said, we were still infiltrated, and the people released are highly dangerous," Dana continued. "These people had inside information and a lot of it. They knew how to override the system. They knew that Thursday was a local Sweep night, which meant we would have fewer security." Dana shook his head. "I am reluctant to report that we lost a lot of men Thursday night."

I tried not to cringe when I recalled the image of the dead men in the angry orange glow.

"We had fifty-seven guards on duty on Thursday," Dana started. "Of those fifty-seven, nine are in intensive care and stable, but thirty-nine are dead. Three scientists are also dead."

I was legitimately disturbed by the number. My eyes shot wide and I looked at Clark, who was just as mortified. It wasn't until that moment that I realized Goliath was not the only one responsible for the deaths— Griffin and Mark had killed several as well.

When the muttering ceased, Dana spoke again.

"While we do not know the group responsible for this, we are quite confident that they are connected with the group sending out the viral emails and programming the pop-ups over the internet. While I did not take this threat seriously before, I am now realizing my folly. I believe this is a large group of domestic terrorists hell-bent on overthrowing Central and the Commission of the People."

"We should rally the people. Tell them that these terrorist are a threat to our nation and—"

"Any more moronic ideas like that, and I will gag you," Dana growled at the man who had spoken. "The people absolutely cannot know about this. This will travel only in the elite circle, meaning the Commission will converse with Leader Simon and his cabinet, and that will be the end of it. This is highly-classified information. The way to keep the people behind us is to make it appear as though we are still infallible. Any sign of weakness, and the people will fall away from us faster than you can blink."

Dana paused for a moment, pulling out his pocket watch and rolling it in his fingers.

"Let me explain something to you," he started. "This commission is charged with the safety and security of the people. The people know that we deal with these matters very swiftly and sometimes brutally. We're the attack dog, the secret police of this nation, and that has served us very well. We are feared and respected. But as soon as that fear grows stronger than the respect, we're finished. The Second Revolution was only seventy years ago. It is still fresh in the collective consciousness of the people. Their response to fear will be violence against us, and we cannot have that."

"We have superior firepower," a woman called. "We call the army out and put down any rebellions that might be forming."

"That will strengthen the fear," Dana said. "*Again* with the moronic ideas—they outnumber us!" he barked. "Do you not remember your mothers and fathers telling you about the way the revolution spread like wildfire across the nation?! The army was called out and the people fought that much harder. Washington fell, and *we* came to clean up the mess."

Dana began pacing the platform.

"As far as the people know, there is no faction of terrorists that broke criminals out of the Commission. If we can handle this quickly and quietly, then they will go about their merry little lives, taking their children to soccer and piano recitals, and we will sit and smile as though it didn't happen. The rest of the world will never know otherwise. As soon as there is unrest in America, the rest of the world will get nervous and we will be pointing nuclear weapons at each other again as a "just in case" precaution. I will not have that."

"But, the people are bound to find out," one of the Commish Kids called. At first I was frightened that they would say something to implicate us, but I tried to calm down and trust that no one was so reckless. "I have seen the emails and the pop-ups. These guys have access to mass communication. If they really did break people out of the Commission, they are going to gloat about it, and then exploit our weaknesses."

"If new propaganda is released, then the Commission of the People will release a statement saying that it is a fear tactic from radical terrorists and that it is all a lie," Dana explained. "If the people need to be afraid of anyone through all this, it's these terrorists. And they will turn to us to tell them where their fear should be directed."

Dana waited for other people to voice questions. When no one did, he continued.

691

"We tried to trace everyone who went missing, but we cannot find their signals. We have the Sweeps teams reconvening here in Central and we will start an outward sweep. We will scan everywhere for these criminals and we will find them, *discreetly*. Until then, the papers you see before you are NDAs for the information you have heard tonight. Not even the team in Europe knows about this, yet. This is not to get out electronically. You are all signing to prove that you will not discuss this topic on any electronic medium and will not remove paper documents from the Commission. The increased security will be in effect until we find this terrorist group and neutralize them."

My blood ran cold at the word "neutralize."

Dana told everyone to sign and leave. He was agitated, pacing and fiddling with the watch in his hands. I watched him for several long moments, even as Sean walked up to him and placed a hand on his shoulder, trying to ground him before he flew into a rage.

As people began filing out, talking worriedly about what they heard, I quickly turned and signed the necessary spaces in the agreement. I stood and grabbed my purse, turning to come face to face with Clark.

"Can you believe it?" he gasped, acting in a very convincing manner.

"No," I whispered. "Do you think that's why Mark was hurt?"

"Lily, Clark," Dean said, walking up, shaking his head in mock disbelief. "It's unbelievable. I mean, how did they get people out? That should be impossible."

"How did they hack into the system? That's what I want to know," Clark said, his eyebrows high.

"How many do you think are in the sect?" Melody asked, also joining our conversation. "They killed thirty-nine people."

"There must have been fifty of them, or more," Felicity deduced. "I mean, you've seen the guards. They're *big* guys."

"May I speak with you for a moment?" a voice whispered at my ear.

I yelped and whirled around, my eyes locking on Dana. Sean was close behind. I stared at the two, noticing Dana's glasses were off, exposing the fire in his eyes.

"S-sure…"

Dana jerked his head to one of the doors, leading to a very familiar hallway that I had come to hate. I took a deep breath before I followed him, casting a worried look back at the small group of Commish Kids watching me leave. I tried to assure them with my eyes that I was alright, but I had yet to convince myself of that fact.

Seeing Sean following, though, did give me hope that I would walk out of the Commission that night.

I walked into the hallway first, trying not to notice the looming presence behind me.

I heard the door click and slowly turned around, bracing myself for the unknown reaction of the leader of the Commission of the People.

Before I could completely turn around, Dana's hand was on my shoulder. He almost violently pushed me against the wall. My head connected with a thud that temporarily stunned me, but I quickly shook it off as fear engulfed me.

"Dana! Control yourself!" Sean snapped.

"You, out!" Dana ordered, pointing to the door. His voice was not angry, but it was commanding.

"No," Sean refused, hesitant in his defiance.

"I was not asking, Sean," Dana snarled. "*Out.*"

Sean slowly backed away, opening the door and slipping out with one concerned look back at me.

When the door clicked again, my attention focused entirely on Dana's intense gaze. I was far more sensitive to the piercing glare now that I had a secret I desperately needed to keep.

I watched his face approach mine, feeling his breath fan over my lips. My head was pressed against the wall, but his strong fingers on my chin kept me from turning away as his lips brushed mine in a surprisingly chaste kiss.

The action frightened me more.

He backed away and his hand cradled my jaw, his thumb brushing over my cheek as his sparking eyes moved around my face, scrutinizing every minor detail.

"W-what?"

"I'm just in awe…"

"What the hell are you talking about?" I tried to snarl, my voice weak.

"I am just looking at you."

"Well stop," I snapped, attempting to push him away. "You said you wanted to talk, so talk, don't stare."

He captured my wrists and pinned them to the wall next to my head.

"Don't get testy with me, Little Lily," Dana warned darkly. "I have had a very trying few days and I am not in the mood."

"Well it's not my fault that you lost so many people from the holding cells," I said. "Don't take your frustration out on me."

"Not just the holding cells," Dana said, releasing my hands and retreating a step.

"Sorry, and the security guards," I added, rubbing my wrists.

"We lost experiments as well."

Now, I really had to act.

I stilled, my eyes shooting wide as my mouth dropped open.

"*What*?"

"We lost experiments," he repeated. I could tell he was watching every muscle in my body to spot any weakness in my stance, any movement that proved I was guilty.

I continued to act dumbfounded, my eyes blinking and my jaw hanging open.

"How could you let that happen?"

"Oh, you're concerned?"

"*Yes*!" I snapped. "You created weapons like that and now some of them are *loose*! How could you let that happen?!"

"I didn't hold the door open," Dana quipped. "They escaped. And we don't know how." He pointed at me. "So, I'm going to ask you what you have heard around the school and Archangel with the younger members of the Commission."

"About a plan to sneak into the Commission, murder the guards, and break people out?" I asked with an incredulous scoff.

"Yes."

"You think a Commish Kid did this?"

"I'm certain of it."

"How?" I challenged, though I was truly worried he had found proof.

"Miranda and Julie are missing, but the other two in that cell are still there. They said it was a young man who broke in. But when I showed them pictures of the young male Commission members, there were a few identified as possible suspects. The prisoners didn't get a good look."

I tried to hide the wave of nausea that washed over me. A smile quirked at the corners of Dana's lips, sensing my growing unease.

"But I don't know anything," I said, shaking my head.

"At first, I thought it was Dean, considering his ridiculous attachment to Miranda. But then I realized that there was no way he was intelligent enough to organize a large-scale breakout like that." Dana sighed. "Twenty-eight experiments slipped out of the Commission right past the guards. The cameras were down for seven minutes and twenty-three seconds. It's really a fascinating conundrum."

He tilted his head.

"How did you do it?"

My heart stopped.

"W-what?"

"How did you do it? How did you manage to sneak over one hundred people out from under my nose? Tell me. I'm really quite baffled."

"I-I didn't." My voice was weak.

His grin widened. "Oh, come now, Little Lily, I know it was you."

"No, it wasn't!" I gasped, horrified. "I didn't do it!"

"Who else could it have been?" Dana challenged. "Now, granted, your tracers showed you were at home for the time of the breakout, but I think you could have easily removed those." He took my right hand, squeezing it. "Really, I'm very curious. I was certain that my security was fool proof, and to hustle that many people out in under seven minutes...that's just fucking impressive."

"I told you, I didn't do it!"

"And why should I believe you?"

"You really think I'm stupid enough to sneak in here and let loose dangerous criminals and experiments?" I growled. "I know you would tear this country apart to find them."

"Let's hope it doesn't come to that," Dana said coldly. "And you're right, I don't believe you are that stupid. I do, however, believe that you are too caring of a person to *not* be involved. And considering the other young adults of the Commission, you are the most likely suspect."

"*How?*"

"Because you want to stage a coup, and I am your target," Dana stated. "And you are smart enough to organize something this complex."

"But I *didn't*!"

"I don't believe you."

"Then, what the hell am I supposed to say?!" I cried, my voice choked. "I didn't do it!"

"Oh, Little Lily," Dana said, looking surprised despite his amused smile, "you're terrified. Don't fret, don't fret..." He placed his hand against my cheek again. "I don't believe you, but I have no proof that you were behind this. If you really are innocent, then you have no reason to worry. I won't harm you."

"Unless you can't find anyone else?" I growled with my shaking voice.

"Rest assured, Little Lily, I will find who organized this, and they will pay," Dana promised. "Anyone involved in the breakout who puts up resistance will be put down, and those captured will be made to fill any missing experiment cells."

My heart was knocking angrily at my ribs. Dana's hand dropped from my face.

"Don't worry," he whispered, tilting his head to the side with a cold smile that made my skin prickle. "If you *are* involved, I have a special cell waiting for you…"

My blood turned cold and I shivered at the promise. My only assumption was that he had already decided what tests he wanted to perform on me. My brain automatically leapt to the conclusion that Dana had destined me to the Machine of Neutralization program.

He began walking toward the door for the meeting room.

"Keep your eyes and ears open, Little Lily," Dana said, turning back to me as I remained frozen, leaning against the wall for support. "Let me know if you hear or see anything that clears you of suspicion."

"W-what happened to innocent until proven guilty?" I barely managed to murmur.

"Leave idealism for movies and fairy tales," he said. "This is reality."

He held the door open, waiting for me. I glanced at Sean, who was standing attentively, glancing worriedly between us to be sure I was unharmed.

"Come, Little Lily," Dana said. "Mark will drive you home now."

I did not know how I kept myself from collapsing as I walked out of the hallway and into the gaze of the concerned and frightened members of my revolution. I was brave enough to glance at Dana as I passed.

He was grinning ever-so-slightly, the fire in his eyes sparking excitedly. He was thrilled, excited, bouncing and racing behind the calm exterior. He was enjoying the challenge.

Before I realized it, I was returning the same half-smile with a tense ball of excitement ricocheting in my stomach.

Chapter Fifty-Two

Sunday morning, Mykail was nervous. I, on the other hand, was excited. Due to Mykail's reluctance to tell me what was bothering him, I had given up trying to ask what was wrong. I was sure that some time in the fort would cheer him up and break the mood in which he was stuck.

Around ten Sunday morning, Clark knocked on the front door.

"Hey, can you open the garage door?"

I hurried through the house and hit the large button for the garage. As the paneled wood ascended, I ducked to glance through the widening gap. There were two cars in my driveway, one idling closer to the street. The other car's tail lights were illuminated, waiting for the garage door to open. One of our family cars had been taken to the airport for my parents' return, so there was an empty space that the car slowly backed into.

Clark was walking around the front of the house toward the garage as Mark got out of his car at the end of the driveway and also walked toward the garage.

I turned to call to Mykail only to find him standing behind me, watching worriedly, slightly pale.

"What is it?" I asked, my face falling.

"Nothing."

I wanted to press him further on the issue, but I knew he would not tell me. I stepped down the two cement steps into the garage just as Josh got out of his car.

"Good morning," he greeted with an infectious smile.

"Good morning." I turned to Mykail, who was standing completely still in the doorway. "Are you ready?"

"Are you sure this is a good idea?" he said, glancing at Mark and Clark as they walked into the garage. Josh puffed out his cheeks, thinking of the best way to respond as he looked at Mark. The silent experiment did not make any effort to communicate.

"Uh...we can't do this a lot," Josh said. "But today it's okay."

"Do you really feel that way?" Mykail near-growled, looking pointedly at Mark. I saw the muscles in Mark's jaw tense.

"Mykail," I said, startled at the sharpness in his voice.

"Mykail, we want to bring you to the fort," Josh said, clearly worried about the way the conversation was progressing.

I was beginning to get very worried that there was a much bigger problem than Mykail feeling left out of the rebellion. Seeing the fury of intense emotion in his eyes, I turned around and pushed on his chest to guide him back into the house.

"One second, please." I closed the door, leaving the other three in the garage.

I could not stop my exasperated glare.

"What is going on with you?" I asked, trying not to sound indignant.

Mykail sighed and looked around the small living room, avoiding my eyes as much as possible. That did nothing to ease my anxiety. I waited for him to speak, but he remained silent, his eyes finally dropping to the ground.

"Mykail, seriously, if there is something bothering you, I want you to tell me," I pressed as gently as I could considering my annoyance.

"I'm just..." He shook his head. "There's a lot going on in my head right now," he said, rubbing his face roughly in frustration.

"What kind of things?"

Mykail shook his head, avoiding an explanation for a few further seconds. "I just...I'm a little afraid, okay?"

"Afraid? Of being caught? Don't worry, Mark and Josh are really meticulous about covering their tracks."

"They're the reason I'm worried."

I hesitated. "What do you mean?"

"No, I don't mean that they're not trustworthy, because they are," he assured quickly, his hands fidgeting at his sides. "But...they don't trust me. And that scares me."

"Why?"

"I don't know," Mykail groaned, closing his eyes and rubbing them roughly. "I don't know. You know, it's probably nothing, I'm just being overly sensitive about it."

"No, Mykail, this is really bothering you. You've been acting weird since Friday. I want you to tell me what has you so upset."

"You wouldn't understand..."

I felt more offended by his statement than I should have.

"What wouldn't I understand?"

"There's just some things that you wouldn't understand, okay?"

"No, not okay," I said. "I have always been very honest with you, Mykail, but now it seems like you can't trust *me*."

"I do trust you, but you really would not understand."

"Why not?"

"Because you've never been on the table before," he snapped. He let out a defeated sigh and hung his head. "Relations between the experiments are complicated. You generally need to stay with your group of people. For Mark and Josh, the Eight Group is their group. And…if Mark is such good friends with Griffin and Tori, then…his group is a lot bigger…I didn't really have a group…now, Mark doesn't trust me. I'm an outsider on this, Lily, no matter how you look at it."

My heart broke at the pain in Mykail's voice. He was right, I did not understand the norms of interacting among the experiments, but from the way he was fretting over it, I was able to appreciate that it was far more complicated than I originally thought.

I pressed my hands to his face, lifting his head to look at me.

"Listen," I said, "Griffin told me that Mark does not trust easily, but he's still bringing you to the fort. He's risking Josh today, too. If Mark really didn't trust you, he would have no problem refusing to bring you to the fort."

Mykail sighed and looked back to the ground.

"Mykail," I said, "remember how long it took for Mark to come to me and Clark? He was testing us, too. But when he saw he could trust us, he opened up. He's giving you the chance to prove that you are trustworthy." I smiled gently. "So, can you be a little more open to the idea? Instead of expecting him to trust you right off the bat, give him some time."

Mykail sighed, nodding reluctantly. I kissed him on the cheek.

"Okay, let's go."

I returned to the garage, keeping a hold of Mykail's hand as I peeked around the door.

"Is it okay to bring him out?"

Mark glanced around outside to be sure no one was watching. Josh said something to Mark who turned to the house across the street and studied the windows. Josh opened the back door of the car as Clark moved to block the narrow space between me and the car, looking out the open garage door with Mark.

Mark nodded to me over his shoulder, so I pulled Mykail out, who ducked low as Clark did his best to block the view of the experiment darting to the car, slipping into the back seat in a crouch, his wings folded tight. He maneuvered his legs into the space behind the driver's seat and rested his head on his hands, laying down so that his wings were barely out of sight.

Taking the large tarp we had practiced covering him with, I passed it to Mykail, allowing him to take the edge and pull it over the top part of his wings as I covered the larger feathers and his feet.

When he was completely shielded from view, Josh closed the door. With the tinted windows of the Commission car, I could only make out the faint outline of something being in the back seat, though I would have never been able to see it was a person.

I walked to the front of the car and stood next to Clark as everyone looked at the front windshield to be sure that the back seat didn't look suspicious.

Satisfied, Mark nodded to Josh, who got into the car and pulled out of the garage. After telling Clark I would meet them out front, I ducked into my house, grabbing my bag, checking to be sure that I had the container with my tracers before running to the front of the house, briefly leaning down to stroke Dex as I made my way to the front door and out into the December cold.

I hurried to the idling car, where Mark was waiting to close the door behind me. We smiled at one another as I got in the back seat with Clark.

"Is Mykail alright?" Clark tried to ask light-heartedly.

"Uh…" I watched Mark walk around the car to the driver's seat. "Sort of…I'll tell you later."

Clark looked confused, and his look of confusion turned to one of concern when he saw that I was not telling him because Mark was within earshot. I smiled, trying to assure him that everything was alright. I did not want Mark to know that Mykail was agitated about not being trusted. I did not want Mark to feel any pressure about accepting Mykail and, if I was honest with myself, I was a little disturbed by Mykail's behavior. Mark's previous warning for me to be careful and his reluctance to bring Mykail to the fort made me wonder if Mark was paranoid, or if there was a reason for legitimate concern.

I distracted Clark by asking Mark if he was alright, and then asking Clark to confirm if the experiment was actually well following the stitches.

"He won't show me the wound on his leg, so I don't know," Clark said, glaring playfully at the driver. "I guess we'll just have to take his word for it. I did give him the painkillers last night and this morning, though, so at least he's not limping as much."

"Mark, are you sure you're alright?"

He nodded again.

"You're not lying to me?"

He shook his head.

"You better not be," I warned. "I will tell Griffin and Tori if I need to."

Mark laughed silently.

We drove to the industrial part of town, pulling into some old warehouses I remembered looking at when Clark and I were trying to find a place as the base of our rebellion. Those days of awkwardly exploring, unsure if we would be able to complete such a feat, seemed so far in the past now that we had accomplished what we thought we couldn't.

Mark put the car in park, leaving the engine running as he got out to signal to Josh. I turned in my seat and watched through the back window as Josh maneuvered the car through the narrow space between Mark's car and the wall of the nearby darkened warehouse.

The other Eight Group member exited the car and walked to the three graffiti-decorated dumpsters in front of our car. I watched, curious as they both pushed one dumpster to separate it from the other two.

Mark then motioned for the two of us to get out.

I stepped closer to the two dumpsters, shivering as I hid my mouth in my collar, scanning the area between the rancid dumpsters. A square grate extended from the edge of the building. Josh removed the cover with little strain.

"Clark," I laughed, motioning him closer, "this is one of the ones that we thought was blocked," I told him, pointing. "Remember? We could get the grate to move a little, but not enough to get out."

"The dumpster was over it," he realized.

Josh turned to me as he brushed his hands off on his pants.

"Check that way," he said, pointing the direction the cars were facing. I obeyed, scanning the alleyway for anyone who might see us sneak Mykail out of the car. Josh turned to Mark and said something with a concerned tone. Mark hesitated and stepped close to the open hole, studying it. I was not sure Mykail could fit with his wings, which also clearly concerned Josh and Mark.

Mark nodded and looked at us before nodding to Josh once more.

The smaller member of the Eight Group opened the car door and offered his hand to Mykail, telling him to keep the tarp over him. Mykail stumbled clumsily out of the car and hurried to the space between the two dumpsters, which effectively blocked him from view. Mark helped Mykail down the drain, being sure his wings did not catch on anything as he descended. He waited until Mykail had his footing on the iron rungs of the ladder before releasing him, Mykail swiftly descended with the tarp into the drain. I smiled, heaving a sigh of relief. Josh closed the door to his car and turned to me.

"Show him where to go," he said. "We'll meet you at the fort."

I went down the ladder next, meeting Mykail at the bottom, who was smiling, exhilarated by the sneaking around. Clark joined us and Josh replaced the grate with a loud clang.

"We did it," I said triumphantly.

"Now, we just have to remember how to get back..." Clark laughed brokenly, looking down the pipe where only a small amount of water trickled in a steady stream. "We only took this way once and that was a long time ago."

Navigating the tunnel was more difficult than I remembered. Clark and I argued about which ways to take toward the fort and continued to get turned around in the false tunnels that led nowhere. Clark and I were getting into several heated arguments while Mykail teased us about being an old married couple.

By the time we finally stumbled into the correct passage, I was disoriented and had no idea how I would be able to make my way back to the grate when we left. After fifteen minutes of walking, listening to the resounding echoes of the dripping water as it trickled down the middle of the gargantuan pipe, we finally made it to the blast door that led to the secondary passage into the fort.

Thrilled to be going in the right direction, the three of us quickly made our way through the smaller passageway and to the door for the dry storage room. We startled one girl who was pulling a box off a higher shelf. I heard a crash and a colorful curse before I saw her, picking up the large box that had burst at the side, causing the packages of salt to escape and litter the floor.

"Sorry," I said, helping turn the box on its side, stuffing the packets back inside.

"No, it's fine," she said with a giggle. She glanced at me—she looked to be only fifteen. "Oh my God, you're Lily," she gasped, a smile breaking out over her features.

"Yeah," I said. "What's your name?"

"Katrina," she responded. "You probably don't remember, but you broke me out of my cell."

"I don't remember you exactly, sorry," I chuckled, embarrassed.

"No, I understand," Katrina said quickly. "It's still great to see you again!" She released the box and lunged forward, hugging me. I struggled to maintain my balance but hugged her back regardless. I looked up at the amused faces of Clark and Mykail as they approached.

"The others will be happy to see you!" Katrina grinned broadly as she backed away and stood. She took my hand and helped me to my feet. She stopped abruptly when she saw Clark and Mykail. Her eyes went wide and she stepped back unsteadily, her eyes focusing on Mykail's wings.

"Oh my God..."

"This is Clark, and this is Mykail," I introduced.

"Are you…are you real?" she murmured. Mykail smiled shyly and looked at his feet, nodding. "You're…you're an *angel*?"

"No, just an experiment of the Commission," he corrected.

"Can I—" She extended her hand, motioning to his wings. He nodded and she stepped closer, cautiously reaching her hand out to stroke his feathers. I watched with a smile. I could tell that Mykail was extremely uncomfortable and nervous about the attention, but I was sure that he was concerned he would frighten her more than anything. She was enthralled by his appearance, a thrilled light dancing in her blue eyes.

"Whoa…" she whispered. She let out a breathy laugh as her hand retreated. "Sorry. I didn't mean to be so creepy. I'll take you to the others."

Reclaiming my hand, Katrina pulled me to the main bunker, where there was a fair amount of activity as groups talked to one another, accomplishing different tasks for the day. A few were washing clothes in a large tub while another group was cleaning up what was left of their morning meal.

"Griffin! Tori! Mark!" Katrina called happily, catching everyone's attention. I was thrilled to see that most of the faces lit up when they saw me and then turned to a look of awe when they saw Mykail. Many started forward in surprise, surrounding us, which made me backpedal against the wall, Mykail ducking back into the storeroom, looking quite frightened.

"Alright, everyone, back up!" Tori ordered lightly, pushing her way to the front of the group. "Let them breathe! You'll get your chance to meet Mykail in a minute."

Everyone obeyed, retreating while I turned to Tori.

"Welcome back," she said, hugging me tightly.

"Thank you!" I returned the embrace. "Seems like you have everyone pretty well organized here."

"Oh, we get along well, that's all," Tori downplayed, greeting Clark with another hug. She looked beyond us to Mykail, who had his eyes nervously averted to his feet. "Hello, Mykail."

"Hello, Tori," he murmured.

"Come out here," she said, motioning for him to step forward. Katrina got out of the way, mingling with the group that had formed a semi-circle around us. Clark and I parted and Mykail took Tori's outstretched hand.

"It's alright," Tori said. She turned to the excited crowd. "Everyone, this is Mykail, who I told you about last night. I'm sure that he would love to talk to all of you, but you can't crowd him." Tori

703

looked at him with a small, sad smile. "He's been through a lot, so please be respectful. He will also be helping with our rebellion."

Tori looked over the heads to the strategy room door.

"Griffin! Mark!"

A few seconds later, Griffin pushed the large door to further open, walking away from the strategy room to join the group around Mykail.

"Mykail, it's been a long time," Griffin said as the crowd parted for him. Mykail looked very nervous around Griffin, more so than being around Tori. He even retreated a step.

"Hello, Griffin."

"No need to be shy here," Griffin said, walking to Mykail's other side so that the winged experiment was flanked by both Griffin and Tori. "Alright everyone, clear a path."

They started forward as I turned my attention to the strategy room. There were two suit-clad figures watching the others in the main bunker. Mark was leaning against the wall, his arms folded as he scanned the moving group. Josh was standing in the opening of the doorway, turning his head to briefly speak to Mark. Mark turned his head, listening to his friend, but he did not move to respond. It was when he turned back to the group around Mykail that I felt the churning of fear in the pit of my stomach. Mark looked troubled and upset. While his face was not creased with thought, his eyes were cautious and guarded. Whatever Josh said only seemed to increase his anxiety.

I started toward him and his eyes locked on me from the movement. A small smile quirked at his lips and he waved at me with one hand. I hesitated in stepping closer, getting the feeling that he was trying to keep me away.

Josh said something else and Mark sighed heavily, but still did not offer any form of answer.

I walked to them anyway, where I received warmer greetings from Josh than Mark.

"We were going to look for you," Josh teased. "It took you a long time!"

"We got lost," I said with a sheepish smile. "Everything okay?" I asked, looking between him and Mark, trying to sound casual.

"Yes," Josh said, though I could tell the word was forced. He turned to Mark and reached over, hitting him in the arm, snapping something in their native language. Mark flinched away from the touch and sighed, smiling at me and nodding.

"I don't really believe you guys," I tried to tease. Josh laughed nervously and Mark's smile dropped.

"Everything's okay," Josh said, giving me two thumbs up.

I turned to look at Mykail surrounded by people.

"He's popular," I chuckled.

"He's the only one who is an obvious experiment," Josh explained, also watching the commotion.

"Mark, can I ask you something?" I said, turning to him, though he was still staring intensely at the enthusiasm in the bunker. He nodded once, only flicking his eyes to me briefly. "If Mykail had been in the cells during the breakout, would you have let him out?"

Josh quickly turned to Mark, which worried me further. Mark turned his gaze to me, but did not make any effort to communicate. He stared, guarding something behind his eyes. My anxiety peaked angrily. For several long, agonizing moments I was staring into his dark eyes, trying to understand what he was feeling. Though he offered me no explanation, I understood his answer.

He would have left Mykail in the Commission.

"Lily, why?" Josh asked, clearing his throat to catch my attention.

"Mykail is worried about being an outsider...that he wasn't part of your group of friends, and that scares him," I elaborated. "How did you choose who to let out?"

"It was difficult," Josh said. "We had to leave a lot of people..."

I tried to take comfort in that, but my anxiety refused to be completely quelled.

"*Do* you trust Mykail?"

Mark looked at me briefly before glancing at Mykail and finally over at Josh. He took a deep breath through his nose, his gaze focused distantly on the ground before he turned to me, lifting his hand to his right eye and pretending to wipe something away with his index finger.

Be careful.

My heart plummeted, halting the blood in my veins.

Mark did not trust Mykail.

What scared me most was the understanding that I was more inclined to believe Mark's judgment than trust the man I had fallen in love with.

Chapter Fifty-Three

As I suspected, the outing to the fort had cheered Mykail up considerably. I, on the other hand, had grown ill at ease. I did my best to hide my anxiety from Clark and Mykail, but since they continued to ask if something was wrong, I was clearly not succeeding.

After I had gotten over the initial shock of Mark not trusting Mykail, I began to seriously evaluate my emotions. I trusted Mark implicitly and I respected him immensely. I was debating passing off Mark's distrust as paranoia, but I couldn't help but wonder if there was something he could see that merited concern. I wanted to kick myself for so easily becoming suspicious of Mykail and tried to remind myself how often Mykail had helped me plan for Dana's downfall.

While I was trying to sort out my feelings, I was reminded of the New Year approaching that Wednesday, and the day after meant the return of my parents.

Monday, I was nervous around Mykail. I tried my best to hide it. I told him I was feeling depressed that my parents would be returning and that school would be starting again, meaning that I was not as free as I had been during the break, but he could see I was lying. He did not press me, but I could see the knowing light in his eyes.

As we made love that night, I almost had a panic attack, thinking about how Mark did not trust Mykail and what that could mean for us as a couple. Mark knew more about the Commission than anyone else, which meant he probably knew more about Mykail than I ever could. Josh had said it was not an easy decision determining who to break out, but there had been no doubt in Mark's eyes. He would have left Mykail behind.

Thankfully, Dana was busy cleaning up the mess of the breakout and, therefore, did not bother Clark and me at the beginning of the week. The Commission of the People was going to be "closed" for the New Year, which allowed me the entire day with Mykail, watching the New Year's parade on television while drinking hot chocolate and watching the snow fall outside. We savored the time together. Even though I was seriously questioning if I could trust Mykail, I cuddled with him, made love with him, and spent all the time I could with him because, the following afternoon, my parents would be home and we would have to pretend as though we were not in love, and not plotting the downfall of the most powerful organization in the world.

The day ended all too quickly.

I had allowed that Wednesday to be the day that I dismissed all my concerns and pretended that everything was normal.

Thursday, though, there was a tight ball of apprehension in the pit of my stomach. It felt as though I was saying goodbye to my life, the feeling almost identical to the one I had when moving to Central. My parents were returning from Europe only to be greeted by the heightened security and the order to be on the lookout for anything suspicious, which meant I had to be more than cautious, even in my own home.

Hearing the garage door open almost made me cry.

Mykail took my hand and squeezed it before standing from the couch and quickly making his way to his room, slowly pulling the door closed as much as he could, considering that the lock was still bent out of shape.

I took a deep breath and waited on the couch in the small living room until I heard the car engine turn off. I heaved myself to my feet and walked to the door, taking another deep breath before I opened the door.

"Lily!" my father boomed. I had to admit that I was thrilled to see my father's smiling face. He released the handle of his suitcase as I stepped into the garage. He gathered me in his arms and I hugged him tightly, some tears escaping my eyes. "I missed you so much!"

"I missed you more," I murmured.

"Oh, sweetheart, don't cry," my father said, backing away and thumbing the tears away from my cheeks. "We're home now."

"Don't I get a hug?" my mother asked.

I was less enthused to see my mother.

However, I smiled and nodded, hugging her tightly. For that moment, it felt as though my mother was the mother I remembered, the woman not having an affair with the man I had sworn to kill, and not the woman who was hurting my father with her infidelity. I was genuinely relieved to hug her again.

"Seems like you missed us."

"Of course I did," I said, sniffing and pushing new tears away as I walked to the back of the car and helped them unload suitcases. I complained about them buying rocks in Europe with the weight of the luggage. They told me it was all papers from the trip and souvenirs.

I helped them unpack in the master bedroom, reveling in the illusion that we were a normal family once again.

"How was Europe?" I asked. I was not really interested in what they had done in Europe as much as I wanted to keep the old feeling alive for as long as possible.

"Amazing," my father said.

"When we weren't in conference, we toured all the old castles and buildings that survived the wars. You remember doing that, right?"

"Not really," I chuckled. "I was eleven when you took me to Europe."

"We'll have to go again," my mother declared, turning to my father with a large smile. My heart soared. My mother was looking at my father with love in her eyes. I allowed myself to hope that they had reconciled and rekindled their relationship on the trip.

However, unlike before, my father was the one not interested. He smiled thinly at her before grabbing more clothes from his suitcase on the other side of the bed.

"What was the food like?" I asked, striking up mundane conversation to avoid the awkwardness between them. My mom prattled on about the food and the funny stories that she remembered, trying to engage my father in conversation as much as possible. What had started as feeling like a normal family again turned into the feeling that I was being used as an excuse to speak to one another.

My mother then abandoned the idea all together and pulled me aside, showing me the clothes and trinkets she had bought for me in Europe. I feigned interest, smiling and thanking her as necessary. I was hesitant, remembering how our relationship had been before she left. I wanted to believe that she was trying to make up for the way things had been, but considering my father's distance, I was not sure *our* bond was her main goal.

My father was more than willing to speak and interact with me, hugging me, telling me how much he missed me and how often he thought of me while he was gone. But his interaction with my mother was limited at best.

It was concerning to witness.

As the laundry was going and we had finished storing the suitcases in the garage, my mother glanced up the stairs and gasped.

"We didn't greet Mykail!" She ran up the stairs, my father and I following at a slower pace.

"Mykail, we're home!" my mother greeted in a high falsetto, as if she was speaking to a puppy she was expecting to run to the gate. She reached for the door and stopped. "Lily, what happened to the door?"

"Oh," I said, pretending to be indifferent, "I did something really stupid. I accidentally hit the discipline remote and when I heard him I opened the door and one of the spasms caused his wing to smash into the door."

"Lily! How could you?" my mother scolded.

"It was an accident!" I defended. "I accidentally set my purse down on the remote. I didn't mean to."

"Did you tell Dana so he could come fix the door?"

"Yes," I lied. "Mykail's okay, though. He was a perfect gentleman while you were gone."

Mykail stood and smiled shyly when my mother entered the room. She walked to him, opening her arms.

"Thank you for being so well-behaved while we were gone," my mother cooed, hugging him awkwardly. "Come downstairs. We can make some dinner."

Just as the family had done before they left, my mother and I made dinner together while my father checked messages on his laptop and Mykail sat quietly, looking at the floor, wringing his hands.

As we sat down to dinner, the other topic of conversation came up.

"You went to the Commission meetings on your own, then?" my father asked, looking at me with a smile. I nodded, my mouth full of food. "How did that go?"

"Fine."

"Anything exciting?" my mother asked.

I stopped chewing immediately, my heart stopping. I was not sure if I was supposed to mention anything to my parents about the breach at the Commission or if I should wait until they met with Dana.

"Uh…" I said stupidly, forcing my throat to work and swallow the food so I wouldn't choke. "Um, when do you see Dana?"

"…we're going to meet him tomorrow," my father answered suspiciously. "Why?"

"Something…kind of bad happened…" I said. "Dana didn't want to tell the Europe party until you were back in the country."

"Something bad? How bad?" my mother gasped.

"Well…" I said, toying with the remaining food on my plate, "…pretty bad."

"For God's sake, Lily, you can't just say that. What happened?" my father pressed.

"I'm not sure if I should tell you or wait for Dana to tell you."

"We're seeing him tomorrow. We won't have time to tell anyone or do anything Dana wouldn't approve of before we see him," my father insisted. "What happened?"

"Uh, do you remember those pop-ups?"

"I still get the emails," my mother grumbled. "I thought they would have fixed that by now."

"Well, Dana thinks that the same group broke into the Commission and broke out a bunch of people from the holding cells."

"People are missing from the Commission?" my mother gawked. I nodded slowly, looking at Mykail, who was also acting surprised, as though hearing the information for the first time. My parents looked at one another in disbelief before turning back to me.

"No one saw anything? There are cameras and guards all over the place!"

"From what he told us, a lot of guards were killed, and the security system was down for seven minutes. By the time they got the system back online, it was over and all those people were gone."

"Are there any leads?" my mother asked.

"I don't know," I said. "I haven't seen Dana since Saturday, and the break-in happened a week ago. All I know is that security is a lot tighter now."

"That is terrifying...to think, a terrorist group that has access to the Commission..." my father muttered.

"I guess it's a small miracle that the experiments weren't broken out as well," my mother said with her eyebrows high.

I glanced at Mykail, who looked at me briefly before we turned away and played our ignorant parts.

* *** *

I was not worried about my parents meeting with Dana and learning more about the breakout because, while Dana suspected I was involved, he had no proof. I knew he wouldn't say anything to my parents. The game was between the two of us. The bulk of my anxiety was directly linked to Mykail. I went to the Commission Friday with Mark and Clark, where Clark once again tried to get me to tell him what had been bothering me, but I still told him it was nothing and that I was overthinking our revolution.

I wanted to pull Mark aside and ask him for greater details on why he did not trust Mykail, but I was so worked up, the thought of confronting the leader of the Eight Group made my anxiety much worse.

Therefore, when I got home, I texted Becca and asked if she wanted to see a movie in order to enjoy our last Friday of freedom before school started. I did not entirely expect her to answer, since it had been so long since we had spoken, but she texted me back only ten minutes later and told me that she would meet me at the movie theater near the river.

Telling my parents I was going to a movie, I took the bus to the center of town, where I walked to the river and sat on a bench outside

710

the theater, looking over the low water tumbling over the rocks. I was huddled in my scarf, my hands shoved deep into my pockets as I bounced my legs, trying to stay warm. Light snow was falling, but most of the snow on the sidewalks and streets had been cleared or had melted, so nothing was sticking to the wet surfaces.

I glanced up and down the walk, looking for Becca. I spotted a couple walking with their arms linked, smiling at one another. They were not talking or making a big fuss like most of the couples my age did. They were walking quietly, occasionally throwing shy smiles at the other. I wished that I could have that type of relationship with Mykail. We would never be able to stroll down the river in public, holding hands and smiling at one another. And now that I was worried about trusting Mykail, I was not even sure if I could call Mykail my boyfriend anymore. The realization made my heart ache.

More than anything, it still frightened me how easily my thoughts changed and how quickly I became paranoid about Mykail.

"Hey, sorry to keep you waiting," Becca said, suddenly at my other side.

I jumped in surprise. She smiled warmly and I returned the grin, thrilled to meet with her after so long. I had not realized I was in such desperate need for a friend until that moment. A big smile broke out over my face and I leapt to my feet, throwing my arms around her. She let out a surprised laugh as she hugged me back.

"I missed you, too."

I pulled away, trying to pass my sniffle off as the result of cold weather.

"So, do you have a movie you want to see? I don't really know what's out right now…"

"Well…we *could* see a movie," Becca said. "But you can't really talk in a movie."

My eyes went wide at how easily she had sensed that I needed to talk to someone. Her smile widened. The tears came to my eyes though I tried to hold them back. I sniffed again and cleared my throat.

"Do you have any idea how much I love you?" I said, my voice breaking. Becca hugged me again, weakening my barriers further and causing the tears to flow.

She took my hand and led me to the coffee shop across the street, which was crowded with people enjoying their Friday evening. After ordering something hot in an attempt to stop the violent shivering of my body, Becca and I took a back corner table, where we had to sit close to hear one another over the din.

"So…what's the problem? Is your plan not going to work?"

"No, it's not that—hold on." I reached into my purse and pulled out my makeup bag, opening it quickly.

"You look fine, hun," Becca teased.

"Not that," I said. "Can you turn off your phone for me? Make it seem as though we went to a movie?"

"Sure…" As Becca reached for her phone, I began rifling through my makeup bag, looking for the gift Griffin had given me on Sunday. Finally finding the black compact-looking object, I set the makeup bag on the table. I opened up the compact, using my nail file to pry the mirror off the back.

"What are you doing?" Becca whispered, watching me set the mirror aside. I pressed a button on the side of the three-button panel. The small screen lit up blue, flashing the number one. I hit the middle button twice to get the number to three and then held the far right button until the number stopped flashing. "What is that?" Becca pressed.

"A scrambler," I said. "If there are any bugs around this table, this should jam the signal."

"Where the hell did you get *that*?"

"Some friends…" I close the compact, replacing it in my makeup bag and shoving everything into my purse again. "Actually, we did it. We succeeded."

I was sure that Becca's eyes could not get wider.

"You…you already—? It worked?"

"Yes. A week ago. Over one hundred people."

"Holy shit…" Becca whispered. "That's incredible. And you got away with it? I assume so, since you're sitting here now."

"Yeah."

"Well then, you should be *celebrating*!" Becca grinned. "I mean, I know you still have a lot to worry about, but right now, you shouldn't be this upset."

"It's not about breaking everyone out," I murmured, wrapping both my hands around the warm mug in front of me, trying not to make eye contact.

"What's the problem, then?"

I sighed and attempted to hide behind my mug as I lifted it. When I glanced over the steaming liquid at her, she was waiting patiently for an explanation.

"You know, we broke out humans…and experiments…"

"People like Mykail?"

"Yeah, basically. Clark and I worked with a few other experiments on this plan and they told us which experiments were safe." I tapped my forefinger against the cup. "These experiments, well, particularly one, I really trust his opinion."

"What's his name?"

I opened my mouth, but hesitated, not wanting to reveal Mark's name, even if I did trust Becca and I had the scrambler working.

"Uh...let's just call him Dex."

Thankfully, Becca just laughed and played along. "Okay, Dex."

"But...he doesn't trust Mykail."

"Why not?"

"I don't know," I said, my eyes locked on the table. "He more or less said that if Mykail had been in the cells when we broke everyone out...he would have left Mykail behind."

"Okay, so 'Dex,'" she enclosed the name in air quotations, "doesn't trust Mykail and you don't know why. What's the problem?"

I worried at my bottom lip with my teeth.

"Um...things...got a little complicated since the last time you saw Mykail," I said awkwardly.

"What do you mean?"

"I...I mean, he and I..." I sighed and hung my head, my cheeks burning hot.

Becca leaned back in her chair.

"You're not dating Clark at all, are you?" she deduced. "It's Mykail."

I nodded, closing my eyes, thankful I had not had to say anything aloud.

"You're in love with him?"

I looked at her, feeling the tears come to my eyes and a raw ball of emotion jam into my throat as I tried to keep my composure.

"...I thought I did..."

"What does that mean?"

"I mean...as soon as I found out that 'Dex' didn't trust him...I didn't really trust him, either. And that scares me."

"You don't trust Mykail at all?" Becca looked at me skeptically. "You obviously trusted him enough to...I mean, I only assume that you..."

"We did," I confirmed.

"So, you still trust him," she declared with a nod.

"Not as much as I did...or as much as I *should*," I said. "I mean, I trusted him without question and then as soon as 'Dex' says that he doesn't trust him..."

"Don't be afraid, be aware," Becca told me. "Remember those guest speakers that came to the school to talk to us about danger awareness back in Second Tier? They went to every school…They said to always trust that inner instinct when something feels wrong and get away from the situation. So just follow your intuition."

"You don't think I'm a horrible person for doubting him so easily?"

"Lily, considering his past and what you're involved in, I don't think you're horrible. I think you're smart." Becca reached across the table and took my hand. "Don't beat yourself up thinking that you should feel a certain way. If you trust Dex more than you trust Mykail, there is nothing wrong with that."

"No?"

"Trusting someone is not a bad thing, even in your position. Obviously, you trust him more than you trust the person you're in a relationship with, which means he must have done something to earn it."

"I guess so…"

"Is that what has you so worked up?"

"Ugh, it's everything," I groaned. "I mean, what we did caused a lot of panic, then I started having my trust issues with Mykail, and then to top it off, my parents came back from Europe, so I have to be super sneaky again."

"How are your parents doing?"

"Oh my God," I lamented. "My mom is having an affair and she—"

"She's having an affair?! How do you know?"

"I saw her with the other man," I told her vaguely. She leaned back in her chair, her eyes still wide. "What's wrong?"

"I think my mom is having an affair, too, but I don't know for sure."

"You're mom?" I repeated, leaning forward. "Why do you think that?"

"She and my dad have been fighting a lot. I've never heard them fight before, and now every night they're arguing about one thing or another. My mom is saying that my father doesn't pay enough attention to her and he blames her work for her not being around more often…then he accused her of being unfaithful…but…"

"Parents fight and stay stupid stuff all the time," I said, rolling my eyes. "I doubt she's having an affair."

"She's always on the phone with someone, giggling like a schoolgirl," Becca said, her expression defeated.

I dropped my gaze to the table top.

"That doesn't necessarily mean anything," I said. "Does your dad seem unhappy?"

"Yeah," Becca said. "He's always moping around, looking at old pictures..." Becca's face became creased with suspicion and fear. "I'm pretty sure she's having an affair. I can't explain how I know. I just do."

I sighed, taking her hand and squeezing it gently.

"Unfortunately, there is nothing we can do about it. Our parents can do whatever they want and we have no way to stop them."

"I'm sorry you saw your mom with the other guy."

"And I'm sorry that you're going through this, too," I said. "I'm so sorry."

Becca squeezed my hand.

* *** *

I had stayed out very late with Becca—past curfew. So, when I snuck into the house, my parents were waiting for me in the dining room. They drilled me about where I had been and I told them the truth—that I was at a cafe with Becca—and they told me to never frighten them in such a manner again before sending me to bed.

I went directly to my bedroom, avoiding Mykail's door like a child. I slipped into my room to put on my pajamas, exhausted and desperate for sleep.

A part of me did feel guilty for avoiding Mykail in such an immature way, but I did not feel ready to speak to him. That, and I *was* physically exhausted. I was feeling the cumulative exhaustion of the past week catch up with me rapidly and I fell into unconsciousness huddled securely under my blankets without much difficulty.

When I woke the following morning, my head was pounding angrily and I was shivering like a leaf. I groaned, realizing that I was sick. While I knew I was not in horrible health, I did not want to move, and being stuck inside the house all day, sleeping, sounded like a wonderful idea. My mom came to check on me when I did not come downstairs for breakfast and quickly brought me some soup and medicine, being quite attentive, as if I was six years old again.

"You should rest for the rest of the weekend," she declared, setting my soup in front of me and running her hand over my hair. "You don't want to start school feeling sick."

I wanted to ask her why she was suddenly being so kind when we had seemed set on killing one another before she left for Europe. But I did not want to start another fight, so I just quietly thanked her. I took the opportunity to catch up on some much-needed sleep, as well as to read most of the assigned reading I had meant to do weeks before.

It felt good to not do anything that day, and with my parents home, it gave me an excuse not to see Mykail. I knew I was acting silly, but I wanted more time to work through my feelings so I would not say something rash when I saw him.

But when my parents went to the Commission meeting, leaving me behind, there was nothing stopping Mykail from coming into my room.

I heard my door latch click and I felt my heart jump into my throat. I wanted to kick myself for being so paranoid, but I was too worked up to scold myself.

"Hey…" he said when he saw me on my bed, my school book resting against my lap.

"Hey."

"I was getting worried about you," he said, sitting on my bed, reaching a hand out to take mine. "Are you feeling any better?"

"A little," I said. "I guess everything kinda caught up to me."

"Understandable. You have been on the go for a long time now. You needed the rest." He squeezed my hand lovingly. My heart fluttered, and I found myself relieved at the feeling. Slightly more relaxed now that I felt I was behaving what I considered normal, I smiled genuinely.

"I'm sorry if I worried you."

"I just hate having to be so careful now that your parents are home. I had to pretend like I didn't want to burst in here and cuddle with you until you went to sleep."

"You wanted to cuddle with me?" I teased.

"Of course. I hope you didn't feel like I was neglecting you, or anything."

"No, of course not," I said. "I know how careful we have to be now." I pecked a quick kiss on his lips. "And I'm sorry I can't take you with me tomorrow."

"It's okay," Mykail assured, tenderly tucking a strand of hair behind my ear before placing his hand against my cheek. "Just don't push yourself so hard that you become sick again."

"Okay."

"Mind if I sit with you?" he asked, moving so that he was lying on his side next to me. I smiled, picking up my book and pretending to read it. In reality I was listening to his breathing, thrilled that I still felt in love with him, despite the fact I did not trust him as much as before.

Chapter Fifty-Four

"Okay, how are we going to do this?" Clark asked, glancing around the massive circle in the bunker.

"Anyone have any ideas?" Tori asked.

I was excited as I studied the massive group we had finally coordinated into a circle around the perimeter of the main bunker. Since everyone in the fort had had time to settle into a routine of living, it was time to get to know one another. Tori was calling it a therapy-support group, where everyone could talk about their family, their past, how they got into the Commission, as well as what had happened to them since. I knew it was going to be an emotionally heavy day with tears and painful stories, but I was hungry for information about the people I had helped free from the Commission of the People.

There was an awkward silence before everyone started laughing nervously.

"What if we took one of the old tennis balls and threw it to one another and that person has to talk?" Griffin suggested.

"Why are there tennis balls down here?" Clark laughed.

"Who knows."

"Wouldn't that…kind of single some people out? Like, you'll only choose someone you know?" one of the younger girls asked.

"Well…I don't know how else we could do this," Tori said with a laugh.

Josh, who was sitting next to Mark, five people away from me and Clark, looked at two others from the Eight Group nearby, asking them a short question only they could understand. Mark's face broke into a huge smile. The other two started laughing as Josh smiled broadly.

"What?" Griffin asked.

"There is a game we used to play," Hiroki said. "We pass the ball and each person counts one, two, or three numbers, and whoever has to say the number thirty-one is the loser."

"What happened to the loser?" Cody called.

"It was a drinking game."

"So, we pass the ball around and each person that has it has to count…and whoever reaches thirty-one has to speak," Griffin concluded. "After a while, if they've already spoken, they will pass the ball to whoever is next to them."

"Sounds like a good system," Tori agreed, getting to her feet to retrieve the tennis ball.

"Seriously, why are there tennis balls down here?" I laughed.

Not long after she disappeared, Tori returned with a faded, worn tennis ball. Sitting back in her spot of the circle, she looked at Griffin next to her and at the girl on her other side. "Clockwise?" she asked, motioning to the girl.

"…how does this work again?" she giggled, not understanding the game, looking at the Eight Group members.

"Tori counts up to three numbers, and then passes the ball, then you count four and up and pass it, and then that person counts more, but no more than three numbers," Hiroki explained, motioning his hands. "And we stop at thirty-one."

Now clear on the rules, Tori started the count.

"One."

"Two, three."

"Four."

"Five, six, seven."

The ball slowly made its way in my direction as everyone counted.

I was beginning to worry that I would be the first singled out. Realizing that I might have to speak made me realize that I had nothing to tell. I did not have a story of how I was brought into the Commission. Out of the entire group, six Commish Kids were seated, looking just as anxious about speaking of our privileged lives in front of those who suffered the Commission torture.

The ball stopped two people away from me. The teenage boy stared at the tennis ball, his hands shaking, not saying the final number.

"Just take your time," Griffin said.

"Why do I have to be first?" he grumbled with a wobbly smile. We chuckled nervously. It had been a stretch to get everyone to agree to the exercise. However, executing the plan was very different.

The boy was becoming quite distressed when Tori smiled, sitting on her heels and lifting her hand.

"Okay, because it will be hard to get going on this, I will offer myself up and start with my story," she said. The boy with the tennis ball visibly relaxed. Tori took a deep breath, steadying herself.

"Hello, everyone," she greeted. "For those of you who don't know who I am, my name is Tori Gilligan, and I am nineteen years old. I was born in Fairfield in the North-East Region. I had a younger sister named Tiffany. She was ten when I was captured," she started. "The Commission took me because I was in love with a girl named Brianna." Tori looked down at her hands. "When I was fifteen, I came out to my mother, and she said she had always known, and she still loved me. She agreed to protect me. She never told my father, because he would have turned me in immediately. So, for two years she protected me, even after I had fallen in love with Bri, who sat next to me in my geometry class." Tori's smile turned sad. "But, someone in our school saw us together and reported it to the school board, who reported it to the Commission. We were both taken and separated. I never saw her again, but…I heard that she died on her second day on the table.

"I was put in a holding cell with a serial rapist, who insisted that the reason I liked girls was because I had never been shown real love by a man…and he took it upon himself to 'teach' me," Tori continued. "But, I was only in that cell for a month before the Commission pulled me out and started experiments on me. And that's how I got here." She looked around the circle, her gaze settling on the young man holding the tennis ball.

"Your turn," she said. "It's alright to take your time."

He forced a smile and nodded once, looking at the tennis ball he was rolling over his thigh.

"I also liked people of my own sex," he said quietly. "I never told my parents, but…they turned me in when they found me kissing my friend Luke behind our house. Luke was never called into the Commission," he added. "My name is Andy, by the way. Andy Korra and I'm eighteen years old. I was taken into the Commission nine months ago."

He passed the ball to the person between me and him and counted "one." The person he was handing the ball to hesitated in taking it, waiting for more of Andy's story. When he did not continue, the girl took the ball and counted "two."

"Three, four," I said, passing the ball to Clark.

"Five."

And around the circle the tennis ball continued.

Grace was the next to speak. She was twenty-seven and had been taken into the Commission because she was a citizen of Canada, yet did not know so. Her mother had crossed the northern border into the North-Midwest Region when pregnant, and Grace had been born in America. She had been raised believing she was a citizen until her own child was born and Central could not find her name as a legal citizen. Her child was eight months old when she was taken into the Commission of the People.

She cried telling her story. The woman next to her hugged her, comforting her as she tried to speak. Many people were in tears.

Grace ended her story with a small joke, saying that the people who signed off on her marriage and child-rearing license probably lost their jobs as her investigation progressed.

719

The tennis ball made its way around the circle once more, stopping with a very young girl, who moved the ball nervously back and forth in her small hands.

"My name is Sydney Tate, I'm thirteen years old—" my heart plummeted, "—and I am an experiment for the Commission. My parents came from the northern border when I was eight and we were all caught by Border Patrol. My mom died three years ago and my dad is in the holding cells."

She passed the ball on, seeming oblivious to the sympathetic eyes surrounding her.

The next to speak was Biren, a twenty-one-year-old who had been a student in his home country of India when his parents died from illness. An archeologist in the area at the time had agreed to take Biren to his home in America and adopt him, but Biren only lived for a month in the man's home before someone reported them and Biren was taken into the Commission as an illegal.

Sonya, the next girl to speak, had been a woman sold into a sex-trade on a small island in East Asia where she was later sold as a bride to a wealthy man in America. As soon as she had arrived in the country, she had been taken into custody, as was the man. She had been in the Commission for nine of her twenty-four years of life.

Tara was another young experiment, only fifteen years old, who had been born to two mothers in a remote town in the South-East Region. She was born from a donor, though she had never known who he was. She was also an illegal birth, born without the proper permit. As such, she had been raised inside and taught never to look outside and never leave the house. When she was seven, she went out into the street to play with some of the other neighborhood children and that was how her parents were caught.

Her recollection of the night of the capture was horrific.

"I remember my moms were arguing, and one of them ran to get me and forced me to drink something that made me really sick. It was some sort of cleaner. She had tried to poison me so that I would not have to live in the Commission. I was really sick when the Commission van came. One of my moms was hit in the head with a club and killed before she even got to the van...my other mom bit through her tongue and died of blood loss. When I got to the Commission, they thought I would die, too, but I guess they were able to save me...which is when they decided that I would be a good experiment for the Commission, because I was strong enough to survive."

While there was a very dark feeling settling over everyone at the horrible stories of capture and torture, there was also a very profound and beautiful feeling of trust and understanding that was strengthening. No one tried to psychoanalyze anyone else, or tell them that they deserved what had happened. Everyone was there to support, not to judge.

Victor was the next to tell his story.

He tossed the ball around in his hands, staring at it pensively before he shook his head.

"My name is Victor Peterson and I am thirty years old. I was taken into the Commission seven years ago..." He trailed off and took another deep breath. "There is something I want to say. I think that all of you are very strong and incredible people for how you have endured everything you've been through in your lives, and I feel as though I don't really belong with such amazing people." He bowed his head. "As far as I'm concerned, none of you really committed any crimes...I was taken into the Commission because I was a criminal. I was an arms dealer of illegal weapons. I sold to domestic terrorist groups...and when they were caught, so was I."

"You still belong here, Victor," Tori said.

"I'm a criminal."

"In the eyes of the Commission, we all are," she told him with a reassuring smile. "You sold weapons to a domestic terrorist group? Were they anti-Central?"

He nodded.

"Then you're okay in my book," Tori laughed. We all chuckled in agreement.

"Victor," Griffin called, "we all are domestic terrorists now. You belong here just as much as everyone else."

"And Victor," a young man across the circle called, "I am sorry if we ratted you out."

"Was it you?" Victor laughed.

"Do you two know each other?" Griffin asked.

"I might as well go," the young man shrugged. I recognized him as Cody. "I'm Cody, and this is my sister Candice, and my brother Zane. We were part of a terrorist group called the Central Citizens Liberation Front."

"I did sell to you a few times," Victor said with a nod. "But I was ratted out by a minor league player."

"You were in the CCLF?" Griffin gaped.

"We were born into it," Zane elaborated. "We're probably the only ones who survived the raid. The Commission found us in our camp one night and killed all the men and women who were able to fight back and captured anyone else."

I had heard of the Central Citizens Liberation Front. It had been one of the largest domestic threats to America since the foundation of Central. The CCLF had not opposed the Second Revolution, but had disagreed with the radical reconstruction tactics of Thomas Ankell and Bryant Morris. Thirty years previous, there had been a large push to eliminate the group and while it seemed that they had vanished, the group had really moved into the wilderness, living off the land and trying to attack large corporations that supported Central, particularly the Commission of the People. There had been a bust seven years ago that had led to the capture of the main faction of the group.

Passing the tennis ball once again, it moved past Tori and Griffin and fell into the hands of another young experiment named Patricia.

"My name is Patricia and I am fourteen years old," she started. She was adorable, with bright hazel eyes and kinky dark brown hair that continued to fall in her face as she averted her eyes to the ground. "I was born in the holding cells. I don't know why my mom was there, but I've heard it was because she had me without a permit and my father was not an American."

Deciding that was enough, she passed the ball as Griffin reached his hand behind the person sitting between them, placing his hand on Patricia's head, smiling.

We heard stories of gays and lesbians, as well as people who had crossed from the northern border from the middle region of Canada, which had been locked in bloody civil war for nearly a decade. There were stories of people who had been slaves in their countries and sent to America when the wealthy bought them for their pleasure, like exotic pets, emulating the gift system of the Commission of the People.

I listened tearfully to the story of David, Jeremy, and Lauren. Lauren had escaped a life of abuse and illegal sex slavery in her home country and stowed away on a boat bound for South America, where her darker complexion would be less noticeable among the locals. However, the trading ship hit a storm and was severely damaged, so it docked in the peninsula of the South-Eastern Region of America. David, who had worked on the docks, found her in the cargo hold and agreed to hide her with his brother, Jeremy. They had been trying to find a way to send her safely to South America when their neighbor caught sight of Lauren through the window and called them into the Commission.

Hope was an experiment who had been called in for harboring seventeen Commission criminals across the northern border with fake papers by using her home in the North-East Region as the final stop in a long train of safe houses that helped Commission victims escape. It appeared that all of the people harboring others and helping them escape the Commission had been quickly pulled out of the holding cells and put on the table as experiments.

The ball finally made its way into the hands of a familiar face.

Minsoo looked around.

"Um...I am Minsoo...but my name is now Sam..." he said with extremely broken English. He sighed heavily. "My English is...very bad..." He turned to Hiroki and said something, extending the tennis ball to him.

Hiroki looked at Griffin and Tori.

"Is it alright if I tell the story?"

"Sure," Griffin agreed.

"He's the best at English," Josh declared.

"I guess that this is really the story for Hyunwoo—Mark—Woobin—Josh—Minsoo," he pointed at his friend next to him before pointing to two other people in the circle, "Ichiro—or Jacob—Keiko and Eun, Hyunwoo's younger sister. And my story, too. I'm Hiroki, but you can call me Dale if that's easier." He moved the tennis ball in his hands, not looking up for several long moments. "We are part of the Eight Group, which handles security inside the Commission. We were brought in eight years ago, and we are all from Ward Eight," he continued awkwardly. "We were all living in a place that had been bombed during the Second Revolution. Our families had been trapped in the country when the war started and they hid there for three generations. We all grew up there, but...almost nine years ago..."

Hiroki looked at Mark and Josh, who were both looking at the ground, along with Mark's sister. I blinked, confused and wondering why Mark looked so ashamed.

"There was a girl named Mana who went outside our community. None of us had ever been beyond the fence...but she decided that she wanted to see what was on the outside." Hiroki closed his eyes. "Of course, because of the way she looked, she was called into the Commission. She managed to avoid the van the first time, and when she came back home...she had endangered the rest of our community."

I studied the present members of the Eight Group. Mark's younger sister leaned against her brother, who wrapped his arm around her in comfort.

"What did you do?" Zane pressed.

"The older members of the community agreed to sacrifice her in order to protect everyone else. When the van came by, they pushed Mana out and locked her out of the community so that she would be caught while the rest of us hid until we were safe." Hiroki glanced at

Mark and Josh. Mark did not turn to him, but Josh looked at Hiroki before nodding slowly.

"But...Hyunwoo couldn't let Mana be sacrificed like that," Hiroki continued, his voice strained. "So, he went after her. And Woobin followed."

I quickly turned to Mark and Josh, surprised.

"They saved Mana, and killed the five Commission men in the van."

"You must have loved her," Tori whispered, looking over at Mark, having never heard Mark's past before. Mark looked up at Tori, though his eyes remained distant. "What happened to her?"

"She was killed when the Commission raided the community," Hiroki answered. "It was only a week after she had been saved. Everyone knew it was coming."

"Was she your wife?" Grace inquired, looking at Mark.

Mark shook his head. Josh spoke for his friend.

"Older sister."

Even more admiration grew within me at the story. Mark was completely dedicated to his family. Sean had said that the only way Dana could keep Mark in line was to keep his younger sister as collateral. To hear that he killed for his older sister, even when he knew it would endanger him, made me realize just how loyal he could be to those he loved.

There was a silence that followed where everyone looked at one another, communicating the same surprise at Mark and Josh endangering the hidden community and leading to the largest contribution of members to the Eight Group.

Griffin cleared his throat and leaned forward, glancing at Mark.

"So..." he started slowly, "you're the middle child?"

Mark laughed silently, closing his eyes as the others of Mark's old community also laughed.

"And the only son," Tori noted. "You've come a long way, Mark."

Mark lowered his head further, shaking his head, refusing to look up despite the amusement on his face.

The tennis ball began making its way around the circle once again.

Dean, who was sitting next to Miranda, got the tennis ball next, but he passed it to her, saying that he was a Commish Kid and had no story to tell. Miranda took it and sighed worriedly.

"My story is pretty short..." she began. "I was a Commish Kid also, but...Dana Christenson omitted a lot of my story from the Commission meetings." She sighed again and closed her eyes. "The truth is, when I was brought into the Commission, everyone was told that it was because my little sister and I had been smuggling across the border. The truth is that I am a criminal, but not for any kind of trafficking. I was pregnant when I was captured."

That did not seem to surprise most of the people in the circle, but the Commish Kids straightened, shocked by the confession.

Miranda took Dean's hand.

"We were not going to tell my parents. I did not want to get an abortion. I wanted to have the baby."

"But you are so young…" Griffin said.

"I know." Miranda nodded sadly. "I knew, logically, that there was no way to keep the baby. But the truth is," she closed her eyes, "I was born as a legacy into the Commission of the People and I hated what Dana did to the people he captured. I never said anything. I was afraid. I knew I was stuck there for life, and I vowed that I would not subject any children to growing up in a place without compassion and respect for human life. But…when I found out I was pregnant…I really wanted to have a child with Dean."

Dean wrapped an arm around her and held her close.

"Dana did find out about my pregnancy, but instead of following the laws and going through the abortion procedure, he imprisoned me in the Commission of the People holding cells. And then he took my little sister because she was the only other one who knew the truth." Tears rose to Miranda's eyes. "I…I don't know why Dana…" She looked at Mark. "Mark, you're close to Dana. Do you know why he framed me?"

Slowly, the experiment shook his head, reluctant to admit that he did not know.

"You're not…still…" Tori questioned, looking over Miranda expectantly.

Miranda shook her head.

The tennis ball moved once again, bringing more stories of victims who had been wronged by the Commission of the People. I remembered when Clark and I were looking through the extremely long list of people locked in the holding cells and deciding who to break out, the stories had sickened me. I had been horrified that just because some of these people loved differently, or had been victims of their parent's treason against the country, or been slaves sold from other countries, or believed in a higher power, or even had only disagreed with the way the government was run, they were locked away forever. And no one batted an eyelash.

If the people of America could hear the stories, if they were forced to look at people one-on-one and hear of the horrible ordeals they had suffered through, they would wonder why it was that the Commission thought they were dangerous. In the post-Secondary Revolution America, 'victim' had come to mean 'criminal,' 'different' had come to mean 'dangerous,' and anything that wasn't in line with everyone else's way of thinking was simply 'wrong.'

Seeing everyone open up to one another, take comfort in and provide comfort to the same people who had comforted them made me realize that we had strength over the Commission. We could see past skin color, facial features, love styles, and thought processes and connect on the basic human level of wanting to be accepted and loved.

There was laughter and tears through the stories of the Commission criminals. We all cried with Ivo, who took comfort in Griffin's understanding of how war time could leave a soldier with PTSD and how the government abandoned his needs and led him to living on the streets until, in a traumatic panic, he killed someone who tried to mug him. When he realized what had happened, he killed those who pursued him, terrified and traumatized.

We laughed with Griffin, who tried to light-heartedly tell us his story, joking about the way he was brought into the Commission and the way he felt about his capture.

We all wanted to comfort and fight for Celina, who had been a student intern in Central and was repeatedly molested by the cabinet member for whom she was interning. She ended up accidentally killing her by pushing her down in an attempt to escape another molestation and causing her to hit her head on the corner of the desk. As she cried, explaining how sorry she was that she had killed a Central Official, many crowded around her and held her close, telling her that she was not to blame.

We heard about Nicki, who had been a lesbian married to a man she did not like and fell in love with her co-teacher abroad, continuing the relationship when her co-teacher came to visit America and was caught by the Commission. We listened to the heart-wrenching story of Meg, who had been fourteen in an illegal brothel owned by her uncle and captured by the Commission when she was sixteen. PTSD had caused her to kill her holding cell mate when he had come onto her, which eventually led her to becoming an experiment.

Some of the experiments, such as Park, Jenny, and Typhen were actual criminals. Those three had been in a drug cartel and had killed Commission members by blowing up one of the vans. Sophia turned to a life of crime when she killed her abusive husband and spent years running from the police and the Commission to eventually be caught robbing a bank. Benjamin had had sex with a male prostitute on

American soil when he was in the country as a delegate from his own country and was apprehended and taken into the Commission.

The humans were as diverse as the experiments, telling heartbreaking and terrifying tales. Some were criminals, though we had been sure to keep the truly dangerous criminals in the holding cells. Many were just victims of the rules of the Commission of the People and who qualified as 'dangerous minorities.' There were a few that had been apprehended for disagreeing with the Central government, some had been refugees from other countries trying to find a better life, others had fallen in love with people that the Commission deemed unacceptable, and there were a few who simply worshiped God.

Yet, despite the diversity, everything felt harmonious in the bunker that day.

Chapter Fifty-Five

I was back in my blue school blazer and it was suffocating.

The school bus was stuffy and too loud. I was hypersensitive to every noise and bump in the road. As much as I tried to quell it, I was angry and upset at the people around me who were gossiping trivially over winter break flings, parties, and trips. A part of me wanted to turn around and yell at the students to shut up and that no one cared. I wanted to tell them that I had become a criminal over the break. That I had infiltrated the most powerful organization in the world and broken out criminals of America to organize a rebellion, showing how insignificant their parties and relationships were in comparison.

Everything in our microcosm of the real world seemed insignificant. I wanted nothing more than to be in the fort, planning our next move, exchanging ideas on how to take down the Commission of the People.

Instead, I was in classes that no longer seemed important. Becca was the only one who did not ask me what was wrong. She understood I was feeling out of place, as if she also knew I belonged in the fort rather than a classroom.

Even Mr. McDermott's class, despite the fascinating subject material, seemed dull. I was bouncing my leg, staring out the window at the overcast day, waiting for the snow to start falling again so I could watch something move.

"How was your break?" Mr. McDermott asked, leaning against his front table, tapping the digital copy of An Angel Without Wings against his palm. There was a chorus of enthusiastic answers.

"Did anyone travel?"

A few raised their hands.

"Great." He smiled devilishly. "But, you still had time to read the seventy-nine pages, right?"

Everyone laughed. Even I managed a small grin.

"Just a little bit of light reading," Mr. McDermott teased. "I know that these chapters were definitely not easy to get through. This is the darkest point in the book, but—obviously, since you are sitting in this classroom today—things got better." He reached behind him on his table and grabbed his tablet. "But, before we talk about this lovely, sunshine-filled part of the book, just a few reminders. In case you forgot, you have your term paper due in March. And your final exam for this," he waved the book, "will be at the beginning of April. The reason I do this is so that you have April, May, and June to fill out your university applications and decide where you're going." He smiled broadly. "That's right, you're almost out of here!"

And moving into a bigger jail...I groaned internally.

"Also, I know I asked you for your rough drafts on Friday, the fourteenth, but then I remembered that we don't have school on the fourteenth. It's the Liberation Parade." Mr. McDermott laughed at his memory lapse.

My brain focused on that sentence as though I was a predator that had caught sight of its prey moving in the brush. My entire body went on alert.

"What?" Becca asked, surprised by my sudden movement.

"The Liberation Parade?" I said. "That's on the fourteenth?"

"Yeah..."

"So, we're going to move those rough drafts to the following Wednesday, okay?" Mr. McDermott announced. "Don't forget, if you have any questions, come talk to me as soon as possible."

My breath had stuck in my throat. I had to resist every urge not to squeal and do an excited dance in my seat. My brain was racing beyond my control as I saw the plan unfold in front of me. My eyes searched abstractly in the wood grain of my desk as I thought through everything I had ever seen on television for the Liberation Day Parade. I knew I would have to meticulously plan and I would have to make sure that Griffin, Tori, and Mark all agreed, but I had figured out our first strike back against the Commission of the People.

"Now, I know that this was a very difficult section of the book, which is why I gave you the entire break to read it," Mr. McDermott continued. "What was the hardest part for you guys to read?"

Several hands went up, causing me to snap back to the present, even though my mind was still working over something completely unrelated.

"Yes?" Mr. McDermott pointed to someone.

"The part where Thomas found Diana, Paul, and George hanging from the tree was horrible to read," one of the girls in the front said. "I mean, Paul was only six years old and the army mutilated him and then hung him upside down from a tree. That's just sick."

"It is, that's very true," Mr. McDermott agreed whole-heartedly. "There are three incidents in the book that mention such mutilation of the members of the Second Revolution. Was the one with Paul the hardest for most of you?"

Everyone nodded, including me. Even though I had only skimmed through the pages, I remembered feeling sick when I read, in vivid detail, about the three bodies hanging from the tree. Now that I had seen a dead body from our breakout from the Commission, the imagery hit far closer to home.

"That's understandable," Mr. McDermott said. "J.A.N.E. does not spare the details of how these people were mutilated and displayed. That's part of what makes this book so difficult." He grabbed the remote from his table, turning to the front board.

"I am going to show you the images of these three mutilated attacks. If you have a weak stomach, or want to leave the room, I understand and I will come get you when the pictures are gone." He watched the circle in the middle of the screen turn as the images loaded. "There are a few reasons I show you these pictures. These are the same scenes that are described in the book, and they are the ones that, as you read, were used to outrage the public into joining the Second Revolution movement. Also, as you know, J.A.N.E. is an anonymous writer, so these pictures make it even more difficult to pinpoint who J.A.N.E. actually was because it is possible that the writer was able to describe such vivid detail from looking at the pictures revealed to the public."

I shifted nervously in my seat. I had become sensitive to the imagery concerning the dead since seeing the room filled with fallen security guards. I was worried I would have to be one of the students who left.

The first picture flashed up on the screen and most of the girls gasped and looked away. Even the boys cringed and shied away from the brutal image.

I remembered the scene in the book describing Janice, wife of Thomas Ankell, finding the body of their friend Kyle Brodie tied to the flagpole of the local community college, naked and beaten to death. His skin was purple and red, marred with gashes from where the nails had been on the end of the boards that had beaten him.

"This is Kyle Brodie," Mr. McDermott said, clicking the picture to show another large photo that was made of three angles of his dead body, including the one with the sign reading "Traitor of the U.S.A." hanging around his neck.

"Now, Washington said that this was a plant, and that the people of the Second Revolution killed one of their own for trying to defect, and that the United States Military had nothing to do with his death. Does anyone know how people were able to tell that the army had committed this crime?"

There was a silence before Taylor raised her hand.

"Taylor."

"The sign says 'Traitor to the U.S.A.,' but Thomas Ankell said in many speeches that the country had not been united in over a century and that when the government was replaced, the states would be done away with and he would create the nation of America."

"Exactly," Mr. McDermott said. "Ankell never referred to the country as the United States of America. He personified the country only as 'America,' never as the U.S.A."

He clicked to the next picture.

"Heather and Vanessa Smith were the second mutilations mentioned in the book. By the way," he turned to us quickly, "don't think that these were the only instances where the Washington Army mutilated members of the Second Revolution. The reason why we focus on these three is because they were the ones that Thomas Ankell used as examples most. They were among the most heinous of crimes committed against the revolutionaries."

One girl left the room. A few of the others in the classroom were looking at their desks, trying not to look at the bodies but unwilling to leave the room. My eyes followed every nasty cut and slice across the pale skin in morbid fascination.

"These two sisters were torn apart with the use of the machetes that the army used when cutting through jungles and underbrush in other countries. After they were cut up, the sisters were left as roadblocks for over a month on the major highway leading between former Utah and Colorado, which is where Thomas Ankell was at the time. As you may recall from your years of study on the Second Revolution, the entire country was afraid to leave their homes when the revolution really started, and many never crossed state lines. Those who did were demonized as sympathizers of the Second Revolution by the Washington System, so the army blocked all entry to the state on major highways. The Smith sisters," he motioned to the bodies on the black pavement, "were left as warnings to those who sympathized with Ankell."

Mr. McDermott moved to click the button for the next picture but he stopped and turned to the class.

"The next picture is the one with Paul and the others, so if you feel that you cannot handle it, I suggest you leave now."

Two students did leave. I was tempted, but stayed, curiosity outweighing my fear.

"Okay," Mr. McDermott nodded when the door closed, showing the next picture in vivid, distressing color. My stomach flipped and I turned away, closing my eyes, but the image was burned into my retinas. Paul was hanging between Diane and George from a tree branch next to a road. Diane was closest to the trunk, and as a runaway at age seventeen, I was sure that she had been beautiful in life. Now, she was hanging from the tree with one arm extended stiffly above her head, the rope cutting under her arm and around her neck, holding her in a crooked suspension. She was naked, her body covered in blood, feces, and flies as her glassy eyes stared coldly into space. George, on the other side of Paul, was hanging from his neck, both his arms twisted angrily behind his back, broken in multiple places, his body also defiled in the same manner. However, his eyes were not staring into space, for there were two gaping, bloody holes in place of a glassy gaze.

Paul was defiled and hanging upside down from one foot, causing his other leg to fall to the side, showing that there was no care in displaying his dirty, mutilated body. As a child, his dead face filled me with horror and disgust. I could not understand how someone could do such horrors to a child.

"As you know, these were all orphans that Thomas took into the revolution when their orphanage burned to the ground in the riot of San Francisco. Thomas Ankell never allowed them to fight in the war, but when they were out gathering food, they were killed by the Washington Armed Forces. This was the single act that brought the most support to the Second Revolution and tripled the strength of Ankell's force."

Mr. McDermott clicked off the projector and walked outside the classroom to retrieve the students who had left, bringing them back in with apologies.

"Okay, no more pictures today," he said, resuming his position at the front of the room as the students returned to their desks. "The ultimate question is…why did Washington allow this to get out?" He looked around the silent classroom expectantly. "Why would Washington, who had already limited press coverage and silenced most people from talking about the Second Revolution, allow these stories to become so widespread that the people would be allowed to know about them?"

There was still no answer.

"Come on…get off your break brain and turn your school brain back on. Try to think of it from Washington's perspective. What do they gain from this?"

I looked at Becca and the others around me, trying to see who would speak first. No one did, all doing the same thing I was doing by looking around to see who would talk.

"Do you think they believed it would turn people away from the Washington System?" Mr. McDermott prompted.

"I don't see how they could think it *wouldn't*," Felicity said. "I mean...the Washington military is doing these horrible things to people, to *children*. Of course the people would side with Ankell."

"Right," Mr. McDermott said. "So, why did they do it?"

No one spoke.

"They were desperate," Mr. McDermott answered. "They had a revolution that was growing bigger and bigger by the day and they were desperate for *any* results. So, they allowed these stories to be published." He set his copy of the book down and thought about how to continue. "Thomas Ankell and his force were using guerilla warfare, and even though the Washington military outnumbered the revolutionaries, they were unable to defeat them because the attacks were at night, they were done in places where the larger tanks and guns would have caused immense civilian casualties, and Washington did not want any civilians dead because they did not want to run the risk of people turning against them due to the casualties." Mr. McDermott pursed his lips. "They did not want to risk that, so why did they think that these photos were okay?"

There was a long silence before Ben raised his hand and started to answer hesitantly.

"Well...I don't know about the other two, but you said that Washington tried to pin the death on Thomas Ankell and his group..."

"Exactly!" Mr. McDermott said. "They were trying to demoralize the enemy. Understand this very thoroughly. They were trying to pin Thomas Ankell as someone who did not care for human life, someone that could not be trusted. Now, obviously, they missed their mark entirely, but there was another reason for mutilating members of the Second Revolution, and that was to try and get them to give up. Washington wanted Ankell and Morris to lose their will to fight because they were tired of seeing their comrades dead. This is very important in this kind of warfare. It is not exclusive to this war. It happens all around the world in all different wars. That's why they say war is hell."

* *** *

For the rest of the day, I was perfecting my plan for the Liberation Parade. I was practically bouncing in my seat as I waited for the clock to move to the right position, signaling the end of the school day.

I was excited to see Mark after school. He smiled at me and took my backpack, as was our tradition, and I got in the car to avoid the chill. I wanted to tell Mark my plan, but I knew that Dana would have replaced the bugs in the car with his increase in security measures. Therefore, as I waited for Clark, I grabbed the notebook that Mark had by the passenger's seat, ripping one of the pages out and using the pen in my purse to scrawl a quick message.

As Clark got in the car, I capped the pen.

"It is *so* cold," Clark said around his chattering teeth. "How are you?"

"Okay." I extended the paper to him.

I have a plan. Can we meet tonight?

"How are you?" I asked casually.

Clark nodded, pointing at the driver's seat, where Mark was getting in the car.

"Can't complain," he answered. I sat forward as I laughed, extending the paper in front of Mark.

"I am not looking forward to having homework again," I groaned, keeping up with our casual conversation as I handed Mark the pen for a response.

"Tell me about it," Clark agreed. "But, at least this is our last year. And then off to university."

"Yay…" I groaned. "Same game, different building."

Mark passed the paper back to me.

Eleven. Lily's house.

I showed it to Clark who nodded as he laughed at my sarcastic statement. Mark extended his hand again, so I handed him the note. He ripped off the portion used to write the short message before returning the rest of the paper to me. I watched with wide eyes as Mark put the two-statement conversation in his mouth and began chewing it as he turned the car on.

Clark was just as surprised. I was still impressed at how careful Mark was despite already knowing his meticulous care.

Mark drove us to the Commission where we went through the new security measures before going through the routine of finding a conference room. Clark was a good student, pulling out his homework while I pretended to read, fine-tuning my plan, Mark standing dutifully outside the door.

Sean came into the room in the early evening.

"Miss Sandover," he said, motioning for me to follow him.

"What is it?"

"Dana wants to speak with you," he said. "Don't worry, you're not in trouble," he added when he saw my horrified expression. "He should be getting out of his previous appointment now and he asked me to bring you to his office."

I glanced at Clark and then nervously stood, walking to Sean and sending Mark a semi-reassuring smile. I wanted to ask Sean a bunch of questions about how the investigation into the missing prisoners was going and what kind of mood Dana was in, but I said nothing, unable to find the courage.

We were at Dana's office door far too soon. I took a deep breath as Sean opened the door and motioned me in.

Stepping in, I saw that Dana was not alone. There was an overweight man standing on the other side of Dana's desk, his suit jacket off as he straightened his tie. The stranger whirled around, his eyes wide with horror. I stopped in my tracks and blinked at him before turning to Dana, who was perfectly composed, as usual, sitting in his chair, looking at the surface of his desk pensively. He looked up when he heard me walk in, his uncovered eyes focusing on me with hawk-like intensity.

"Little Lily," he said. "Monsieur Debord, if you will pardon me. My head of security will see you out."

"Yes, of course," the man mumbled with his thick accent, grabbing his jacket hurriedly and scurrying past me, avoiding eye contact as he slipped out the still-open door, which closed behind him.

As soon as the door shut, Dana sighed and rolled his eyes, reaching for his desk drawer and opening it as I walked closer. He opened a container from the drawer and pulled out a white mint, popping it between his perfect teeth and sighing, throwing the tin of mints on the desk and leaning back in his chair.

"It's going to take forever to get that taste out of my mouth..."

I cringed.

"You're disgusting," I snarled. "With him? *Really*? Whoring yourself out to old, fat, foreign guys now?"

Dana shrugged and took a breath through his nose, slowly exhaling as he drummed his fingers along the arm rests of his chair, looking distantly around his office before he finally focused on me, finding his train of thought.

"How was school today?"

"What are you? My father?"

"No," Dana said, extracting a letter from the papers on his desk, turning it to me. "But you might not graduate with your current grades."

I studied the piece of paper, seeing the official letterhead of my school above the graph of my grades.

"Why do you have this?"

"All of your records are open to the Commission. You should know that," Dana said. He leaned back in his chair, clicking his tongue against the roof of his mouth, playing with the mint. "If you keep these grades, you won't graduate."

"What do you care?"

"You're in the Commission. I need to make sure my people look educated." Dana said. "It is in my best interest if you don't fail in your last year of Third Tier." He motioned to the seats in front of his desk. "Sit."

I lowered myself into one of the chairs, watching as his tongue rolled the mint, pressing it to his teeth and to each cheek.

"After all those wonderful years of being in the top one percent, you're suddenly sliding at an alarming rate," he noted. "Is there anything you want to talk about?"

"What are you now, my guidance counselor?" I scoffed.

"Something like that," Dana said, though the statement did not sound like a joke. "Your parents are home, what's that like?"

"You didn't see how they were when they got back?"

"I did, but I can assure you, I see something very different than you."

"What do you mean? What do you see?"

"Oh, come now, that's no fun," Dana chuckled. "Besides, I'm not talking about how *they* were. I want to know how you're handling it."

"They're my parents, of course I'm happy to have them back."

"Has your mother been kinder to you?"

"Yes..." I answered hesitantly. "Did you say something to her?"

"No, I've hardly spoken to her since she left," Dana said. "But I figured that she would act differently when she returned. What about your father?"

"What about him?"

"Does he still seem like the peacekeeper?"

I opened my mouth and then stopped, thinking carefully about the atmosphere in my house since my parents' return.

"No..." I admitted, a little surprised at the realization.

"So, things aren't as turbulent anymore?" Dana continued. I shook my head slowly. "Great. Then you can pull those grades up and graduate."

I rolled my eyes. "My grades have nothing to do with what's going on in my family."

"No?"

"No," I repeated. "I don't care about school."

"You don't care about your future?" Dana raised an eyebrow.

"Why should I?" I asked sharply. "You own my future."

"I do," Dana affirmed. "Which is why I want you to graduate. I am making an investment in you."

"An investment?"

"In a manner of speaking."

"I thought you wanted to have me locked up in the back so you can make me into some experiment," I snarled.

"Ooh, that would be fun, too," he said, standing and walking to the front of his desk, leaning against the front edge and crossing his arms. "But you need to learn a little more before I can really have fun with you. You're still so simple, so direct in your behavior. I need you to be keener, and just a little more discreet."

"What is *that* supposed to mean?"

"You think you know how to play me, Little Lily," Dana said. "And while, right now, you might have me confused about your involvement in the breakout, you have not done anything to clear my suspicions."

"I don't know how to," I defended. "I didn't do anything."

"And see, if you were smarter, you would find a way to make *me* believe that," Dana said with a smile. "But you don't believe it, so how can I?"

"What?" I snapped, standing. "How can I not believe that I wasn't involved when I *wasn't* involved?"

"You tell me."

I let out a short pant of disbelief.

"I must say, Little Lily, you are making fine progress," Dana complimented darkly. "You're more commanding, far more in control of your desires." He smiled knowingly. "Did you have a little help breaking down some barriers?"

"What are you implying?"

Dana grabbed my arm, pulling me to him, his hands locking around my lower back as I fell against him. I tried to push away from his chest, but his hands were hard on my body. One of his hands reached down to palm me through my skirt while the other hand held me close. I shivered, but managed to push away, squirming out of his grasp and glaring at him from a safer distance.

"Stop *doing* that!" I barked.

"You're not a virgin anymore," Dana noted. "Congratulations."

"What gave you that idea?"

"You didn't notice the difference?" Dana asked, his eyebrows high. "You need to sharpen up, Little Lily. You pushed away from me. You still shivered when I touched you, but there was a time when my touch intoxicated you and all your barriers fell immediately. Now that you know what a man can offer, the anticipation factor has greatly decreased."

I blinked, surprised at his ability to read something so easily, and my inability to notice sooner.

"You're telling me that all those times you were touching me, coming onto me and seeing what I would do…that was just to see if I was still a virgin?"

"Yes."

"You're unbelievable."

"Thank you."

"I did not mean that as a compliment."

"I took it as one regardless." He leaned back on his hands. "The fact that you're not a virgin anymore makes me more suspicious that you were involved in our breach of security."

"What does that have to do with anything? How would my being a virgin change anything?"

"Virgins are timid, more filled with fear, whether they acknowledge it or not. But I know your type, Little Lily. You get a taste of something and you start wanting more, and that makes you understand better your desires, your limits, your powers…and you start learning how to get what you want without letting your fear cloud you."

"I am still afraid," I corrected. "I am afraid that you are going to control the rest of my life. I'm afraid that if I do one thing wrong, you will take me in the back and mutilate me into something that should never come into being. I mean, how can you blame people for wanting to break out of the Commission? How can you not expect some sort of uprising from these people that you are capturing and torturing?"

"I do expect it," Dana contradicted. "I expect it, and I am prepared for it."

"How can you pass it off like that?!" I snapped. "Those people are just like the people of America. They just want to live their lives!"

"So I should let murderers and rapists go free?"

"No, they should be punished for their crimes, but not tortured and mutilated!"

"Why not?" Dana shrugged. "They do that to others. It might as well be karma."

"What about the people who believe in God?"

"What *about* them?" Dana chuckled. "Believe me, since the ban on religion, the country has been much better off."

"What's so wrong with wanting to believe that there is a higher power?"

"Do *you* believe in God?"

"Well…no…I…" I glared. "I don't know. Maybe there is some higher power."

"If there is, he is long dead." Dana shook his head with a broken laugh. He spread his arms wide. "*I* am the higher power, now."

"You think you're God? Creating these monsters in your little confined area? Seeing what you can create?"

"No, of course I'm not God. Why would I want to have all those people begging me to explain why they have problems? I am simply a creation of my environment, just like you. Only my environment was very different. I was created by the humans who have fear of something they believe is higher in power. Something they *fear*. Humans are masters at living their lives in complete fear; fear of death, fear of loss, fear of hardships, fear of a higher power…fear that one day, something might happen to upset their trivial routines and they will have to work a little harder than before. It's the same fear that leaks into their governments and churches—their so-called higher powers—and infests like the plague. Fear of losing power, of stepping on a few toes for a greater result, fear of the people they govern…and then the people become afraid of the very government that they've created, seeing the wound that they are too lazy to clean. Everyone is too afraid to stand up and take responsibility for the monster."

He smiled, tilting his head to the side.

"You can blame the government all you want, but *you* are the one who is willing to tolerate it, deal with it, let it breed and infect like a virus. You are the one truly at fault. But, as history has proven, you," he pointed at me, "are also the most dangerous force."

"*Me*?" I echoed. "I'm just one person…"

"True," he admitted. "But one person with an idea can turn into thousands of people with a revolution."

I was silent, staring at him with wide eyes.

"You think that these Commission escapees are going to try and make a revolution?" I whispered incredulously.

"They've already started," Dana said. "The pop-ups, the emails…believe me, the gears are already turning. There has been a forty-one percent increase in people searching for things related to the people captured by the Commission of the People. The populace is curious, and that is very dangerous for me, because that quickly turns into fear."

"You have a thing for fear."

"It's the only emotion every human feels the same way," Dana stated. "But fear quickly turns into anger, which is what makes a revolution thrive. Another revolution will take its course. It's just a matter of time. Anger will always lead to change. Then, hope will rebuild what anger tore down. That hope turns into contentment, and will eventually lead to laziness, which will bring problems and anger and around and around we go in the never ending dance of coexistence."

"And you?" I said. "Where do you fit in?"

"I fit in wherever I need to fit in," he said. "I've told you before. I am only what people make me out to be."

"*How*?" I hissed. "How can you just…turn off everything inside you that was once human? Don't you feel fear at all?"

"Not yet," Dana admitted. "Maybe one day. I'm still looking for the thing that frightens me. That way, I can learn how to overcome that as well." Dana leaned forward. "Why don't you take the first step and let go of your fear of *me*?"

"No."

"Why not?"

"Because I don't want to become like you."

"Yes, you do," Dana chuckled. "Everyone does. Everyone wants to be this powerful, this in control…I'm sure you know the feeling. The feeling of running free, following only your instinct and your gut, being completely controlled by your nature. You probably felt it when you were breaking everyone out of the Commission cells…"

"I told you, I didn't do it."

"It was exhilarating, wasn't it? How would you like to feel that all the time?"

"I have no idea what you're talking about," I snapped. "How would you expect me to break out all those people, kill all those guards…all in less than seven minutes?"

"Well, *obviously* you had help." Dana rolled his eyes. "By my calculations, though, you could have probably done this with…five people?" He looked at me, expecting me to correct him.

"Five people?" I barked. "*Five*? You're telling me that you were infiltrated by only five people and you got kicked in the ass this hard?" I laughed heartily, shaking my head. "Oh, Dana, you're way off your game."

Dana grinned, showing all his teeth. I was enraptured in our game. He knew I was gloating. There was a cocky part of me that wanted to correct him, to tell him that we managed it with only four people, but the more rational part of my brain immediately stamped out the desire.

"You're enjoying this," he noted.

"I am," I said. "Seems you're not as powerful and in control as you think."

"Oh, I am," he corrected. "More than you know."

"I don't see it."

"Because you're not looking the right way," Dana said. "For instance, if you were looking correctly, you would see that I am incredibly aroused by your defiance."

"Maybe I did see it," I shrugged, "and I'm just teasing you." I began walking toward the door. "Besides, I figured you would have been satisfied sucking your fat French friend's cock."

"Don't get it backwards," Dana laughed. "It is a rare occasion that I go on my knees."

I opened the door and threw a cocky look over my shoulder.

"In my experience, you don't always have to be on your knees." I slipped out the office door and closed it behind me, grinning broadly and walking confidently back to the conference room.

* *** *

Thankfully, my parents were still trying to recover from their long time in Europe, so they went to bed early. I stayed up, trying to complete my homework, though I could not focus. A part of me wanted to get it done, to pull my grades up and get into university, but there was a dark, angry part of me that told me not to. I needed to rebel against Dana, against his plan for me. I needed to focus on only doing the opposite of what Dana wanted for me.

A few minutes before eleven, there was a click on my window that caused both me and Dex to jump. I strode to my window, stroking the top of Dexter's head to soothe him before I leaned on the window sill. There were two figures standing in the driveway below.

I darted to Mykail's bedroom door.

"Mykail," I hissed. He turned to me, startled. "Mark and Clark are here. Grab a blanket. It's cold outside."

He pulled the blanket off the top of the bed while I ran to my room and grabbed my heavy coat, slipping it on as I fished for the gloves in my pocket.

Mykail and I slipped into the cold garage and then out to the backyard. Telling Mykail to wait, I darted through the side gate to the driveway, leading the two visitors around the back of the house.

"Did you drive here?" I asked as I latched the gate behind them, realizing I had not seen a car.

"No," Clark snapped playfully. "Mr. Cautious over here wanted to walk."

"You *walked* all the way from your house in this cold?" I gasped. I turned to Mark and saw that he was dressed in nothing but his normal suit. While he was not shivering, his cheeks were tinted red and his lips were stained pale blue. Worried, I led them to Mykail and then told everyone to wait, running upstairs and snatching another blanket.

Clark was talking congenially with Mykail when I returned. I walked to Mark and wrapped the blanket around his shoulders.

"Don't get sick on us, Mark."

He blinked, surprised, and then smiled and nodded, holding the blanket appreciatively. I focused my attention on Clark.

"What about you? Are you warm enough?"

"You didn't get me a blanket anyway?" Clark pouted playfully.

"Your lips weren't blue!" I laughed. "Seriously, buy him a coat." I then let out a sigh, watching the smoke appear from my mouth and disperse into the frigid air. "Okay, I wanted to talk to you about a plan."

"Yeah, a plan for what?"

"We might have gotten everyone out of the Commission, but the only way we can ensure that we're safe is to take down the whole operation, right? Otherwise, there was no point to what we did."

"Not *no* point. We freed a lot of people," Clark objected.

"Who can't live in the fort until they die," I reminded him. "Even though we have over one hundred people, we need a lot more if we want to bring down the Commission. Dana told me that the people of America have been looking up things on the internet because of the emails and pop-ups, so we have people interested. Now we just need to prove to them that the Commission is mutilating people and making them into weapons."

"But to do that, we need something that will go viral before Central takes it down."

"So we make sure to do it on a live broadcast," I declared. "Somewhere where there will be a lot of people watching the live feed from their homes. Something that will really shock people."

"The Liberation Day Parade…" Clark said. "I see."

"What do you think, Mark?"

He nodded and tapped his right ear twice. I turned to Mykail for the translation.

"Keep talking."

"The news crews are spread out, but the major, nationwide cameras are always at the intersection of Main and Delaware, right? Because that is where the parade stops for the Ankell float to perform its dedication."

"Right," Clark confirmed.

"That is where we reveal everyone. We'll get people in the parade with signs and banners as if they are just part of another organization, maybe even the group representing the Commission of the People. It's just before the Ankell float, so all the news cameras will be rolling, waiting for the dedication. That's when everyone flips their banners around to match our previous flier with their own pictures."

Mark lifted his head quickly and did some quick hand signals. They were not as subtle as some of the others he had previously used, but Mykail understood.

"He wants to know how we get everyone to escape. There is security at the parade."

"But minimal security," I pointed out. "We get everyone to scatter before the Commission vans show up. Everyone takes a different way back to the fort." I explained. "We show our message and then we run. If nothing else, it will be talked about, which is much more important than sticking around. We'll plant some regular humans and Commish Kids in the crowd to act as distractions, and we'll get them to make a scene. That will give us time to get the experiments out of the street and into the drains, where they can all split up and take different passages to the fort."

Clark's smile widened.

"So, just the experiments, then. We won't be marching?"

"No, no," I said. "We can't. The Commish Kids will have to act as though we are trying to capture them and cause a scene that makes things too confusing for people to do anything. The experiments disappear again and we will tell Dana we tried."

"Do you think we can pull it off?" Mykail asked, turning to Mark. The silent experiment was looking at his feet in the snow. He shifted his weight a few times and then nodded, looking at me with a small, but confident, smile.

"There's only one problem I see…" Clark said. "I mean, besides the risk that we actually get caught. Most of the experiments look normal. We can't have Mark, any of the others in the Eight Group, or any of the minorities in the parade. They'll be noticed before we even get to Main."

"I agree that Mark can't be seen," I said strongly. "At this point, Mark, you are our strongest ally. We need you to stay on Dana's good side and keep you safe."

"Right, so how do we convince the people that these normal-looking people are experiments of the Commission? The Commission members are going to be the only ones who know the kind of torture these people went through."

I sighed, turning the problem over in my mind. There had to be a way for us to prove that the former prisoners had been made into weapons without endangering the people who were going to be watching the parade.

I turned to Mykail.

"Mykail…could you do something for us?"

Chapter Fifty-Six

"Hey, where are you?" I asked, trying to hear Clark on my phone around the noise of the people chatting excitedly, gathered near the temporary barriers on the street.

"Almost at the intersection," Clark said. "There are a lot of news crews…is everyone in place?"

"Pretty much," I confirmed, squeezing through the backs of two people talking to their families. "It's a zoo out here."

"I forgot that this is your first Liberation Day Parade in Central," Clark laughed. "My mother was really shocked that I wanted to come here instead of watching it on television."

"It certainly seems like the better option," I said irritably. "Felicity and Dean are here. From the text, it seems they managed to get everyone set."

"Awesome."

Feeling another buzz on my phone, I glanced at the screen to read the text message. Moving past the message from Felicity asking me where I was—our designated signal to say that all the experiments had managed to sneak into the lineup without trouble—I saw another text from Sarah, asking me where I was.

"Sarah just texted me," I told Clark vaguely.

"Great."

"Now, if I can just get where *I'm* supposed to be…" I growled, becoming extremely annoyed when a large family with three kids ran to the people at the barrier and blocked my path. Grinding my teeth in frustration, I pressed myself to the wall of a bank and shimmied around the mother and father.

"You sound tense," Clark teased.

"And you *don't*," I snapped. "Why is that?"

"What is there to be nervous about?" Clark asked. "Everything will be great. The plan is foolproof."

"How is it that you can be so nervous about the first thing we did, but not this? We're basically putting ourselves out in the open here…"

"This was your plan."

"I know…"

"Besides, we may be out in the open, but before we were strolling into the lion's den, more or less," Clark pointed out. "This involves a lot less danger on our part."

"Maybe…" I said, glancing warily over one of the Officials standing by the barrier.

"Take a deep breath," Clark instructed. "We've been going over this for two weeks. It will be perfect."

"I still wish we had a little more time," I murmured. "Okay, I'll text you when I'm at my spot."

I was extremely nervous. Even though it was my plan we were executing, developed with the help of Tori, Griffin, Mark, and Josh, I was still nervous about the execution. With all the civilians, I saw increased potential for something to go horribly wrong and things to end in a bloodbath. I was not sure if the police were armed with real guns or stun guns, but if I was wrong about the type of weapon, all I could think of was how quickly the situation could spiral toward civilian deaths.

My phone buzzed with another text message.

Becca: *Hey. Im at Main. Where r u?*

Almost there.

Typing the quick reply, I wove around people and their cameras and children, trying to avoid the lines surrounding the stands for hot coffee and giant salted pretzels. Seeing the Liberation Day Parade on television was very different from being in the crowd. There seemed to be a lot more people than I had ever seen on television.

I saw the first crew of the major news stations. They were doing their opening reports about the weather and the turnout that year, explaining that the parade was going to start in approximately five minutes. I tried to avoid walking behind the reporters. I hid behind a larger man who was walking past one reporter whose camera was blocking my path, forcing me into the pack of people.

Finally, I saw the sign for Main Street. I pushed forward aggressively, eager to get to my position. I caught sight of other accomplices, who nodded silently when they saw me pass.

That day was to be our public declaration of war against the Commission of the People.

Spotting Becca near a barrier next to one of the guards, I slipped between more spectators, earning a few nasty looks from people who were trying to get to the front.

"Hey," I greeted, finally reaching her.

"Hey," she said. "Thanks for inviting me."

"Thanks for coming," I said. "It's nice being here with someone."

My phone buzzed with another text.

Clark: *Hey. I can see you! I'm right across the road from you!*

I looked up, even though I knew that it was our signal text, and saw him standing at the opposite barrier, smiling.

I took a few deep breaths, desperate to remain calm.

"Are you okay?" Becca asked.

"Yeah, I'm, uh…" I looked around us and motioned stupidly, "a little claustrophobic."

She nodded, understanding the real source of my tension.

I spared glances at every familiar face in the crowd, seeing them stationed near the news crews as we had planned, waiting for their cue.

It was their cue that was worrying me the most.

My heart was thumping against my ribs as I worried over the fact that I was putting so many people in danger and, in a sense, outing myself as being involved in the rebellion against the Commission of the People. I peeked at the holster of the policeman next to me, cold dread swirling within me.

Clark pulled out his phone and leaned on the barrier, holding his phone sideways to start filming.

I leaned over the barrier near the guard and looked down the street. A dull roar sounded as the first float began lumbering down the street, beginning the parade. The news crews announced that the first float was approaching, led by one of the many bands and dance teams performing at the Liberation Day Parade.

Taking a deep breath, I also began recording with my phone, watching as the colorful, fun floats brought a possible disaster ever closer.

I cheered with the rest of the crowd, being sure that my voice was heard on my phone camera as I continued to film the floats, dance teams, flag teams, and civilian and non-profit groups moving down Delaware Boulevard. Even though I knew what was approaching, I was captivated as the bright balloons and skilled dance teams dazzled me with the celebration of our liberation from the Washington System. I felt as though I was five years old, finally achieving my dream of seeing the parade up close.

Looking at the wide, mesmerized eyes of the children and their smiling parents around me, I almost wanted to back out on the plan, thinking in that brief moment of smiles and awe that the Commission was acceptable to keep the peace and security of those happy families.

But the loud horns playing our national anthem made me remember that I was fighting for our country as a whole. America was safe and secure but only by putting up a façade, pretending to fight for the safety and happiness of the people when it was torturing captives and creating weapons out of living beings. There was no way I could stand for that.

I steadied my camera as the band drew closer, the float of the bald eagle followed by a group of Commission members holding the national flag as they walked down Delaware Boulevard. There was a tight ball of apprehension in my stomach, seeing the bright red and blue flag with the seven stars positioned diagonally, one for each region of America and the seventh representing Central. It was a flag I had grown up worshiping, and even though I no longer believed in what our country stood for, I still bowed my head, placing my hand over my heart with everyone else, and repeated the pledge, adding my voice to the dull rumble.

"I pledge my life, my love, and my servitude to the flag of America, and to our Central Nation Values, which I hold in highest regard, as guidance within the family of our nation, unified in service, to provide peace and security to all."

I lifted my head as the flag turned the corner onto Main Street in continuation of the parade, the band following, repeating our national anthem.

My entire body went on alert as gasps and murmurs began to fall over the crowd. Quickly turning my camera, I saw white banners of thanks to the Second Revolutionary fighters switch to banners of red and black, depicting the painted faces of the people holding the banners with their names printed in bold white.

"Griffin Thomas: Level 9 Weapon of the Commission of the People."

"Tori Gilligan: Level 10 Weapon of the Commission of the People."

A few other experiments who had their large signs hanging around their necks also unfolded their cloth banner to reveal the large message painted messily in red.

STOP THE TORTURE! QUESTION THE COMMISSION!

"Those are the people on the emails…"

"What do they mean *weapons*?"

"Who *are* these people?"

"The Commission of the People is torturing people?"

And then, the part I was most anxious for happened. The band, seeing the shocked and terrified looks on the faces of the spectators, stopped playing, turning to look at the group behind them. The float depicting the final battle of Thomas Ankell against the Washington Army halted abruptly and everyone on the float blinked in confusion.

The halting of the float was the cue.

From the weak paper depiction of the former White House on the float, which was meant to burn during the dedication of the parade, a figure burst out, launching high into the air, holding a bright red flag while another banner was tied to his waist and shoulders.

"Mykail Devenchy: Level 8 Weapon of the Commission of the People."

He flew high into the air, his powerful wings pushing him higher into the overcast sky so he could circle the area and allow everyone to get a good look at him. My heart was in my throat.

Right on cue, Becca screamed, pointing at Mykail. That was the sound that caused panic. As soon as Becca made Mykail something that warranted screaming, the police officers removed their guns and took aim at Mykail. One shot rang loudly and mass panic ensued.

Commish Kids at their barriers pushed forward, knocking the Officials off-balance and collapsing the barrier, causing panicked people to flood the streets. I fell forward with the force of everyone trying to flee. Several yelled to "seize them" though I was not sure who was trying to capture whom. I ran into the street, glancing up to see Mykail unharmed and circling. The experiments began with their other duty, throwing smoke bombs in the street to add to the confusion and help us escape. No more shots were fired in the chaos of people scattering, some trying to grab at the experiments, who were ditching their signs and slipping into the crowd, acting as frightened and surprised as the spectators. Others were trying to get away from the weapons, causing more panic when they would briefly catch sight of one among the crowd and run the other direction, creating near-pandemonium.

Following the scattering groups, I followed my planned path.

I was disoriented and worried about Mykail, who was swooping lower to keep the crowd riled up and frightened. He was buying us time, keeping the confusion strong as we fled. I ran in the direction of the park, where people were darting to their parked cars, dragging their children with them. After the parking lot, the panicking crowd thinned and I ran with a few other familiar faces to the parking garage of a nearby law firm. Slipping through the thick wires of the barrier between the levels, I fell heavily into the basement level and ran toward the mechanical room after the others, leaping in and closing the door just as I heard the clank of metal.

"Come on!" Cody said, grabbing my hand. I followed his lead, crouching to feel the edge of the opening, putting my feet in first and finding the bottom of the narrow passage. I lowered myself to crawl on my elbows through the duct toward the faint light reflected off a damp wall. Trying to keep myself from bumping my head on the pipes on the side of the tiny passageway, I turned the corner, shimmying myself into the narrow space and clambering toward the open grate. I carefully extracted myself from the duct, using my upper body strength to guide my feet to the wet cement ground in the other small passage where more wires had been piped to heat the parking garage. I spotted Hope in front of me, her back pressed against the smooth wall as she approached the maintenance door. I heard Jenny and Park arguing about someone stepping on someone's foot as Cody replaced the grate behind us.

Hope opened the door and peered out before running the short distance across the alley to the open drain pipe cover, quickly dropping to her belly and sliding into the dark tunnels below the street.

After checking to be sure that no one was looking, I also darted the same short distance, reaching my hands out for what I knew would be there.

Two hands wrapped around my wrists and guided me down, carefully setting me on my feet. Once I caught my balance, I saw Josh smiling at me brightly as he reached up to help Jenny. Smiling myself, I felt Hope jump on me, squeezing me tightly.

"It was fucking perfect!" she cheered, her voice squealing as she jumped.

"It was, but we'll celebrate when we get back to the fort," I said, motioning her quiet as Jenny joined us, also grinning broadly. She gave me a high-five, as did Park. Cody was the last one into the drain pipe. When we were below the street, Josh grabbed the grate and covered the square hole, locking the metal back into place.

Too excited and adrenaline-filled to do otherwise, we ran to the fort. As we got further under the streets and to the point where we could move a little more freely in the large storm drains, we began whooping as quietly as we could manage, exhilarated and adrenaline-filled.

We met three other groups that were taking the same pipe back to the fort. They were just as excited. I was nervous about Mykail. He was in the most danger—easy to spot and very difficult to hide. Mark had been in charge of recovering him safely, and while I trusted Mark, I could not stop my worrying.

But the high energy of everyone else caused me to feel elated and drunk off the experience. I was dizzy, thrilled that we had pulled it off so well.

We part-ran, part-walked, part-celebrated our way to the fort, bursting through the door and running into the main bunker to join the other successful groups who were whooping and cheering.

I was surrounded by spirited people clapping me on the back, yelling "we did it!" from all directions. I laughed and joined in the cheering, jumping around and hugging others tightly, celebrating our first strike without care.

More groups filed in, joining the thunderous celebration. The humans who had not been involved were told everything, though no one was able to tell the story sequentially, too excited to form coherent sentences.

The Eight Group members, who had helped by assisting in the getaways, were just as excited as everyone else. I laughed as they jumped on one another like teenagers celebrating a win at a football game, boisterously bellowing their elation.

When I saw the boy with wings enter the main bunker, I ran to him and threw my arms around him, kissing him deeply, thrilled he was safe and eager to celebrate our victory with him. He lifted me off my feet, returning my kiss enthusiastically, spinning until we both were stumbling to reclaim our balance.

I stroked his face, looking into his bright blue eyes, feeling the room fade, leaving only us in existence on the whole planet.

"Thank you..." I whispered.

He took my hands in his and kissed my fingertips. "I love you."

"I love you, too."

Reality came crashing back when the humans and experiments began gawking and leering at us. I laughed and shook my head, feeling embarrassed as I confronted their smiling faces.

"Oh, shut up..." I teased back.

"Is everyone back?" Tori called.

Josh counted all the people responsible for bringing their parties back safely and nodded.

"Everyone's here!"

Another booming cheer resonated through the domed roof of the bunker.

Ichiro began clapping a rhythm, yelling out something in his native tongue that Josh quickly seconded. Both of them clapping, they began singing a cheer no one else knew. Minsoo, Hiroki, and Keiko started clapping, singing the happy chant, even sharing a bouncing, spinning dance. Mark's younger sister also joined in the revelry. While no one else knew the dance or chant, they also clapped, feeding off the happiness the Eight Group exuded. Mark, smiling broadly, added more volume to the clapping.

The others singing went quiet and Josh chanted some lines, dancing around happily in a silly manner that had us all laughing and cheering with him. Minsoo also said a few lines when Josh went quiet, picking up the obviously well-known chant.

Everyone who was singing turned to Mark, pointing at him, continuing to clap.

I looked at Mark, realizing that this would have been his part in their celebration dance. His smile turned sad and ashamed as he dropped his head.

Josh ran to Mark, yanking him into their circle and standing behind him, taking his wrists and moving his hands as he dropped his voice deeper, imitating Mark's part.

Mark was smiling so much his eyes were closed and he doubled over, embarrassed but also elated. The others of the Eight Group played along and pretended it was really Mark singing and dancing his part, even while Josh made a show of dancing goofily while trying to be puppeteer to the embarrassed Mark.

It was a sad realization for me that the only thing I knew about Mark's voice was that it was deeper, thanks to Josh's imitation.

After releasing Mark, Josh got everyone to begin singing and dancing to the clapping, though most others did not know the words. It was an expression of celebration for our victory, our successful attempt at declaring war against the Commission of the People.

Even though it should have seemed inappropriate, considering the gravity of the situation, the dancing and singing seemed to be the best thing to do. So, I joined in.

* *** *

I wanted to stay longer, but I knew that I had very little time before it would be obvious that I was missing completely. My parents would be worried about the parade incident, which I was certain they saw on television, so I needed to get back as soon as possible.

The most difficult part about leaving was saying goodbye to Mykail.

Now that he was exposed, there was no way for him to come home. He would remain in the bunker with the other experiments and freed prisoners.

Mark drove me home, but dropped Clark off first, which was part of our plan. It was supposed to look like Mark had found Clark and then gone back to look for me. So, Mark drove close to downtown to lend as much credibility to our story as he could.

When we got to my house, I prepared myself to act.

I got out of the car after nodding to Mark and ran to the door, quickly unlocking it as Mark got out of the car and followed me at a much slower pace.

"Mom! Dad!" I called loudly as I stumbled in the house, breathing hard and looking frantically around.

"Lily!"

My mother darted into the foyer, her arms opening to hug me. I hugged her back, but quickly pulled away.

"Did you see it?!"

"We did, are you alright?" my mother gasped, looking me over.

"I'm fine," I assured frantically. "What—"

I stopped as I was hugged by my father.

"Who got your phone? We called and someone else answered," he asked.

"Thankfully, it was one of my schoolmates. I have it now," I said, pulling it out of my pocket to show them, trying not to smile as I recalled Ben talking to my parents briefly about finding the phone on the ground. "But, enough about that! We have a problem!"

"We most certainly do," another voice said in the archway to the kitchen.

Dana was leaning against the arch.

Genuinely surprised to see him at my home so quickly, I lost the ability to speak for a few moments.

"We were worried about you, Little Lily," Dana said. The tone of his voice made me shiver. It was cold, airy, almost otherworldly as his eyes tried to look through me. After a few moments of the intense eye lock, Dana looked at Mark, who was standing in the still-open front door, his eyes covered with his glasses and his hands folded in front of him.

"Mark, come out of the cold," my mother said, motioning him inside. He stepped nervously forward and closed the door behind him. My mother moved to him. "Thank you for finding my little girl. I really appreciate it. I was so worried."

As my father rubbed my shoulder, comforting me, my mother stared at Mark, who seemed confused.

Damn, what an actor... was the only thing I could think at seeing Mark's expression.

"Be simpler with him, Karen," Dana advised, standing straight and walking toward Mark. "He's probably the only one in the Eight Group I ever praise, so he knows a few of those words. Good job, Mark," he said to him, clearly enunciating.

Mark turned to Dana and bowed fully at the waist, remaining in the position for a few seconds before straightening, his head remaining down, his hands in front of him politely.

Dana smiled.

"They amuse me so much," he chuckled. "Sean."

I was thrilled to see Sean join us in the dining room. He walked to Dana, who jerked his thumb to Mark. "Tell him he did a good job. He's been working hard lately."

Sean stepped over to Mark and placed a hand on his shoulder, causing the experiment to look up quickly. Sean patted him twice on the shoulder.

"You did a good job," he told him. "Thank you."

Mark turned to him fully and bowed deeply again.

"Dana, we should give him tomorrow to rest," Sean suggested. "He may not need eight hours a night, but we've really been running him ragged."

"He's one of the best. We have to keep him around as often as possible," Dana said. He exchanged glances with Sean and then sighed. "Not tomorrow, it's a meeting day. He can have Sunday off."

Sean turned back to Mark, who was waiting for order.

"Sunday," Sean said strongly. He lifted his arms to cross them in an X. "You rest."

Mark opened his mouth slightly, feigning shock, and looked briefly between Dana and Sean, as though not sure of the order.

"Rest on Sunday. Stay home," Sean added.

Mark bowed again. As I thought about Mark resting, I was beginning to wonder if he got tired in the same way humans did. While I knew he had been busy helping me plan for the parade, I did not know what he did during the day while Clark and I were at school. I recalled that Dana sometimes called him back to work as Commission security, but I did not know how often he was working for Dana as opposed to watching Clark and me like a bodyguard. I was suddenly very worried that he *did* need rest and I had been blind to his exhaustion.

"Go home, now," Sean ordered.

Bowing yet again, Mark left.

"He seems to be quite the asset," my mother noted. "He's pretty attached to Lily."

"He's faithful, that's what matters," Dana said with a shrug. "I will admit, it was one of the hardest decisions giving him to the Markus family. But they are my advisors, and they need protection. I was also worried that if I kept him around the Commission with no one owning his contract, someone would steal him." Dana turned back to the kitchen. "Come, we have more important things to discuss than the chink."

I glanced briefly at my father, who squeezed me in a sideways hug and guided me into the kitchen. Sean followed us. Dana sat at the breakfast table, waiting for us to join him. It felt extremely invasive and

754

unsettling to see Dana sitting in my father's seat, but I had to keep calm and keep my wits about me. After all, I was about to spend the rest of the afternoon lying directly to Dana Christenson's face.

The leader of the Commission drummed his fingernails on the tabletop.

"I know I don't need to explain the implications of what happened this morning," he said. "This puts me in a very delicate position."

"I assure you, we had no knowledge of this movement," my mother started. "Of course, we got the emails, but that was it."

"And I believe you," Dana said, "*mostly*." His gaze slid to me. I blinked and straightened.

"*Me?*"

"You already know that I don't believe you are not involved in this movement," Dana stated, his eyebrow raising.

"That is a very heavy accusation, Dana," my father said, though it was obvious that he had already heard the opinion.

"This was a heavy crime," Dana responded. "This has gone from an anti-Central group who were only engaging in relatively minor crime to a legitimate threat. Their appearance today at the Liberation Parade ended in shots being fired and people being trampled. Not only that, but the Commission has been openly challenged in its dealings with criminals."

"You can always say that it was a scare tactic from a domestic terrorist group," my mother suggested.

"When I first saw them on the news, that was my intention," Dana said. "And then Mykail showed up. So now, I must get creative."

"How did he get out?" I asked.

"The screws on his windows had been filed through, so the bars on his windows swung outward," Dana explained. "What I want to know is why he did not have the cuffs on his wings."

Dana's accusatory gaze fell on me yet again, but before I needed to defend myself, my mother spoke up.

"I am to blame for that," she admitted. "I have not put the cuffs on after bathing him for many weeks. He seemed not to need them."

"Well, that has been proven incorrect," Dana said sharply. "I told you explicitly to keep those on." He leaned back in his seat, falling silent as he collected his thoughts. "The other question that remains is how no one else in the neighborhood saw him. I called the Central Security Board and they are sending me all the public footage from the security cameras in the city, which is going to cost a lot of hours and manpower to sort through."

Dana glanced at me again. "Where were you when this happened?"

"At the parade?" I asked. "I was at Main and Delaware. I was filming the parade."

"With what?"

"My phone."

Dana extended his hand, flexing his fingers. After a brief hesitation, I pulled out my phone, handing it to him. He unlocked it without me telling him my password—that didn't surprise me—and went to look at my saved videos.

As the video played and the grainy sounds of the parade washed over the table, I glanced at my parents while Dana and Sean watched the video.

My father looked at me and smiled thinly, extending his hand. I met it, allowing him to take my fingers and squeeze them reassuringly. It wasn't much, but it did remind me to take a deep breath.

"Are you alright?" my father whispered. I nodded, turning back to Dana as I heard the screaming when Mykail flew into the air. Dana watched with a stoic expression, even as the gunshots sounded. Sean looked on worriedly over Dana's shoulder.

When the video abruptly silenced, Dana sighed and set the phone down on the table.

"Alright." He nodded once. "First thing tomorrow some men will remove the bars from the windows and doors. For now, we will cover all evidence that he was here. The Commission will have to make a statement in response to this."

"You aren't thinking of—"

"No," Dana said, cutting off my mother. "I cannot let my face be shown to the public. That's for my safety as well as the safety of the Commission. We will have to have two or three faces representing the Commission."

Dana looked at me briefly, smiling with dark purpose.

"Tommy," his gaze shifted to my father, "I want you to be one of those faces."

"Me?"

"I think it's important to let the people see a new face with the old ones. You will work with Danielle and Pat and you will be tasked with calming the public."

"How do you plan to do that?" I challenged. "America, maybe even other parts of the world, saw someone with wings fly around a crowded parade. You can't explain that away."

"No?" Dana asked skeptically. "The American people will believe what we tell them."

"Will they? If you say that the whole thing was a hoax, people will start looking carefully at the videos and they will question how it could be a hoax."

"Lily," my mother took on a warning tone.

"What?" I said. "I'm just saying this is not something you can explain away. People are frightened and if you tell them there's nothing to worry about, they won't calm down, they'll fight. They don't want to be calmed like children, they want *answers*."

"What would you tell them?"

Dana's gentle voice startled me and the question caused a bolt of fear to rocket along my nerves. It was a challenge bordering on an attack. It was time for me to make my move. I was locked in a dance, both Dana and I hiding a gun behind our backs as we tried to keep the other just far enough away for the weapon to remain hidden, smiling deceptively.

"Well," I started slowly, organizing my thoughts, "I'm sure this will get attention internationally, so you can't say it was an attack from another country trying to topple America because there will be backlash from other countries for finger-pointing." I thought for a few further moments. "But, if you say it's a terrorist group, then the question will come up of how they have the technology to create someone who can fly, and then why they would try to pin that on the Commission."

Dana waited patiently.

"Wouldn't it be easier to say that you don't know anything?"

"I suppose so," Dana agreed with a nod. "But that puts the expectation on the Commission to come up with answers, when in reality, I do not intend to allow this to get any bigger. I fully intend to eliminate this group as soon as possible and allow everything to settle back to normal."

"Then tell the people that," I said with a shrug.

"But if the Commission commits to such plans and statements, then that leaves us open for criticism. The people will find it strange that the Sweeps started and *then* the terrorist group suddenly appeared." Dana looked thoughtful, though I knew he was just doing his part of our dangerous dance. "It's obvious we have been looking for something already."

"But these people came from inside the Commission," my mother pointed out. "Were any of the people holding signs people who had not been broken out of the Commission?"

"No," Sean answered for Dana.

"Their pictures have been going around in the emails," I pointed out.

"Which means that the group already knew, mostly, who it was going to break out," my father added.

"The fact that Mykail was involved makes me believe that this was all the experiments," Sean interjected, speaking mostly to Dana. "There would have been no other way for him to know what was going on. An experiment had to be the one to organize this."

Dana gaze was locked on me, his eyes bright with electricity as he played the people around the table.

"Can the experiments do that?" my mother whispered, mortified. "Can they really gather and revolt?"

"It's happened before," Dana said. "But they never got this far. This is a new kind of rebellion."

"You think the experiments broke themselves out?" my father asked skeptically.

"Quite possibly, yes," Dana said. "There is one experiment, in particular, that I am keeping my eye out for. Griffin was brought into the lab that day because of a seizure and when the security system went down, he escaped with the others. Griffin would be able to do a lot of damage on his own, but he had to have help from outside to pull everything off so seamlessly."

"Do you have any leads?" my mother asked.

"I'm looking at the young people of the Commission," Dana said, looking over at me, seeing if I would be upset. I remained calm, keeping up with our dance. "They were upset after the fiasco with Miranda and Julie. It holds true that they would try to do something against me. Youngsters are rebellious by nature."

I tried not to grind my teeth at the mention of Miranda and Julie, particularly now that I had heard their real story.

"But they couldn't organize something like *this*," my mother said, shaking her head.

"Never underestimate angry young people," Dana chastised lightly. "Ask your husband. His brother was only fifteen when he started harboring people across the border, wasn't he?"

"Lily, have you heard anything from the other children of the Commission?" my father asked, choosing to ignore Dana.

"I mean, everyone was upset about Miranda, but I don't think any of us are suicidal enough to go up against you," I said to Dana.

"You might be shocked at the stupidity some people possess," Dana chuckled, reaching into his pocket and pulling out his buzzing phone. He looked at the screen before touching the receive button and lifting it to his ear. "Yes?" He fell silent, listening. "Alright, I'll be there in ten minutes."

He hung up.

"I must go babysit Leader Simon, now," he groaned, standing. My family stood as well. "I will be seeing you tomorrow at the meeting. Tommy, Monday at lunch you will come to the Commission and we will discuss the statement for a press conference. I will set one up for Tuesday."

"Alright."

After seeing Dana out, I quickly had to escape my parents asking if I was alright. I assured them I was okay and that I was just worried about Mykail and everything that had happened. Then I made a stupid excuse to get away from them by saying I wanted to take a shower.

Trudging upstairs, I closed my bedroom door and heaved a sigh.

"This is fucking insane..."

My buzzing phone caught my attention and I reached into my pocket, answering it absentmindedly.

"Hello?"

"I must say, I underestimated you," a familiar voice said with a dark chuckle. My eyes snapped wide and my breath caught in my throat. "Don't hang up," Dana ordered.

"What are you talking about?"

"You organized an elaborate reveal and actually managed to put me in a situation I'm not entirely sure how to handle. Congratulations, Little Lily. You are progressing beautifully."

"Are you still on about that?" I rolled my eyes. "I had nothing to do with the parade today. You saw the video I was taking with my phone."

"Yes, by all accounts, that's true," Dana agreed, his voice dangerous and yet soft, like water. "However, you seem awfully calm about having Mykail gone."

"What?"

"Last I was aware, you two were getting very close, and then you come to the Commission one day sexually experienced...you don't need to be a genius to connect those dots." My stomach flipped angrily. "And with how calm you are over his vanishing from your house, there are only two options I can see. Either you knew all along and, therefore, know who is organizing all this, or you were the one to put him up to it."

"For one, I *didn't* know," I snarled. "And two, I would never force Mykail to do anything."

"As a pretty young woman, you don't need to force a man to do anything," Dana said in a way that made my skin prickle. "All you need to do is give him a taste of paradise and he'll go to the ends of the earth for you. But you already knew that, didn't you, Little Lily? You're not even aware that you're doing it. That's real talent."

"Shut up. I told you, I didn't have anything to do with it, and that's that."

"That's not that," Dana said in a chastising tone. "Mykail was involved, you were involved with Mykail. You have something to do with it. Don't misunderstand, Little Lily, I am thoroughly impressed. I'm going to have to step up my game. I greatly underestimated what you were capable of."

"Is that so?" I challenged, my tone mocking.

"Yes," Dana said. "But you have also limited yourself to Central, and that will prove to be very damaging for you."

I could not stop the smile that moved across my lips.

We'll just see about that, Mr. Christenson...

Chapter Fifty-Seven

I was surprised at how much I relished in the chaos that was the Commission meeting the day following the parade. The Commission members were frightened by the appearance of the experiments and Dana had to admit that he had lied to everyone by not revealing that experiments had also been freed, which led to higher tension in the meeting room.

I gloated at the fact that I had caused such panic and that the most powerful group of politicians in the world was finally starting to realize their mistake in supporting Dana's experiments.

Dana continued to look at me from across the room. When I was not speaking directly to him or standing in front of him, I gave him a cocky half-grin.

I could hardly wait to see what the Commission meeting was going to be like the following week after phase two of our plan went into effect. Dana had been sorely mistaken when he thought we had limited ourselves to Central. He *had* grossly underestimated me.

Monday, I focused on the gossip around school. The teachers tried to keep everyone from talking about it, saying that we should not jump to any conclusions until the official statement from the Commission of the People, but it was impossible to police the teenage conversations in the halls. When I got home from my afterschool time at the Commission, my father was waiting. He bombarded me with questions about the gossip around school. I told him a little bit of what I had picked up, but overall, I pretended to be uninterested as I trudged up to my room, ignoring the workers removing the bars from the door that had once led to Mykail's room.

I missed him. I had not had a chance to see Mykail on Sunday. It had been Clark's day to visit the fort—we were alternating to keep suspicion low.

Monday night, I could not sleep, feeling an excited knot in my stomach that I could not ignore. Dex, frustrated with my constant tossing and turning, finally abandoned the bed and went to sleep under the windowsill.

I managed to get about one hour of sleep before I was rudely awoken by my alarm clock. At first, I regretted not sleeping. But once I remembered that it was Tuesday, I scrambled out of bed and dressed, anticipating what was meant to happen that day. Besides the Commission press conference, I had my own plans. Of course, there was no guarantee that things would go as I hoped, but judging by the number of people who had posted something on the internet and social media concerning the Commission torturing people, I was feeling confident that my plan would work.

I went to school as though nothing was different that day. A few Commish Kids nodded once to show that they were also waiting for the news that our plan had been successful.

I continued to watch the clock. In Mr. McDermott's class, I glanced at the clock and smiled, knowing that it was about time we heard about another shocking incident.

Felicity was the one who called attention to it. Since she sat in the back of the room, she was looking at her phone constantly, checking for any update over her social media profiles. When she finally found one, she gasped and caused me to whirl around.

"Felicity?" Mr. McDermott said. "Are you looking at your phone?"

She did not say anything for several long moments. It took every ounce of my self-control not to break out in a wide grin. I looked at Becca, Taylor, and Jill, who were smirking about Felicity being caught on her phone.

"Felicity," Mr. McDermott said again, adopting a stern tone.

She looked up quickly, her face horrified. That caused our teacher to be taken aback.

"Are you alright?"

"…it happened again…"

"What?"

"The Stanford Parade…" she slowly elaborated. "They were there…"

Even through her vague description, everyone knew what she was talking about. Quiet murmurs broke out over the room and I looked at my group of friends, trying to act just as surprised and confused.

"Okay, everyone, calm down," Mr. McDermott called. "I know that what happened on Friday was confusing, but with the amount of publicity it got, it makes sense that there will be some copy cats that will try to catch onto the tail of that fame. What we need to do is focus on what we're doing here and not buy into the fear tactics of this radical group. Felicity, put the phone away and let's get back to what we were doing."

It was the first time I had heard Mr. McDermott so serious.

When the bell chimed and students flooded into the hallway, it was clear that Felicity was not the only one who had seen the news on her phone. The students were abuzz with gossip. Taylor fished out her phone. As we stepped into the crowded hallway, she read the article to us.

"The seventy-second annual Stanford Parade honoring the beginning of the Second Revolutionary War witnessed a terrifying spectacle during the second half of the parade. A large group of people masked in Thomas Ankell guises marched in front of the dedication float with signs resembling those seen in the Central Liberation Parade. Fliers were thrown from cars, denouncing Central and the Commission of the People as murderers of the true revolutionaries, claiming that they are making weapons out of humans for the purpose of another world war.

"Pennsylvania Street was cleared immediately and several people in the demonstration were arrested, though so far police have been unable to identify any as those who were in the Central Liberation Parade. Members of the Commission of the People are scheduled to make a statement about the incident at the Liberation Day Parade at two p.m. central time…"

No one was going to class. Students were grouped near walls, looking at various electronic devices and reading the article, or watching some of the news reports that were coming in from the recently-cleared Pennsylvania Street.

"Can you believe it?" Jill whispered. "Another strike against the Commission. What is going on here?"

"But did you see the guy with wings? *Something* is going on in the Commission obviously," Taylor said. "I wonder how these people got the signs and fliers…maybe the group is a lot bigger than they thought. Maybe they are all over the country, like the Coalition or the CCLF."

"Do you think?" Becca gasped.

"Lily, what's going on with the Commission? They must be freaking out about this," Jill said, turning to me.

"It's a little chaotic…"

"Is it true?" Taylor asked. "The whole weapons thing? That they're making weapons out of…people."

"…you know I can't talk about anything that happens in the Commission."

That was more than enough of an answer.

While I was happy that Jill and Taylor were suddenly thinking more about the message we had put out to the people, I was more thrilled that the fliers had made it to the parade safely. I had been concerned that Yi Ling would be captured before she had a chance to get the fliers from the Sweeps van to the parade office. Mark had coordinated the eighteen members of the Eight Group and had found out who was going on Sweeps to other areas of the country. Using the machines in the fort, we had printed as many fliers as we had paper for and divided them among the various parades. While the parades really only lasted through the following weekend, we were sure that we would cause enough of a stir to get the people rallying behind our movement.

I was more anxious to see how Dana had my father and the others handle the press conference, since they had only two hours after finding out about what happened in the Western Region to think up what to say in response.

When I got to where Mark was standing, I smiled and lifted my hands up to him. He hesitated and then grinned, giving me a high-five. Clark joined, also giving me an enthusiastic high-five before we were driven to the Commission.

For the first time, I was not nervous about Dana calling me in to talk to him. I was not entirely sure that he would, considering that the press conference was just finishing and it was possible he went with my father and the others. Clark seemed to feel the same way. He was not anxious at all as we went through the security checkpoint, which was still extensive—in ways more so since the parade. Even Mark was thoroughly patted down before being allowed in the basement of the Commission.

I was trying not to smile at the chaos we had created.

A part of me cringed when I pulled out all my late homework, briefly catching glances at the horrible grades I had received. The former perfectionist student I had been hated seeing the bad marks. But a bigger part of me was advocating that school didn't matter and I needed to focus on the revolution.

My phone buzzed on the table. I had never gotten a message or call inside the Commission that I did not plan on. Clark seemed surprised as well.

I saw a text message scroll across my screen.

Come to my office.

The number associated with the message was 5—Dana's private cell phone.

"Dana is telling me to go to his office."

I studied Clark's worried expression.

"What about?"

"I don't know," I said. "I don't think I'm in any trouble."

"How did he react to Mykail being at the parade?"

"He was at my house by the time I got home," I recounted. "He was pretty upset and he's convinced that I'm involved somehow."

"What did you tell him?"

"That I wasn't involved," I said strongly. "But, he's convinced."

"He hasn't taken you in…" Clark murmured, his voice strained with concern.

"He can't prove anything," I said simply. "I don't think I have anything to worry about. There was no way in hell I could have been at the Stanford Parade today."

Clark seemed more hesitant about me going to Dana's office than I was. I was excited to go. I was curious to see how Dana had reacted to the next phase of my plan.

"I'll be fine," I assured, walking out of the room. But Clark wasn't the only paranoid person I had to get past. Mark was also wondering where I was going.

"Dana wants me to go to his office," I told him, forgetting that he wasn't supposed to understand me and becoming confused when he cocked his head to the side like he didn't hear me. After a few confused seconds, I remembered where we were. "It's okay," I said simply.

I started walking away when Mark grabbed my arm, causing me to whirl around. I watched the various worried expressions cross over his features. While I had always been impressed with and admired Mark's careful nature, I was beginning to think he was *too* paranoid.

Finally, glancing around briefly to be sure no one else was nearby, he mouthed something to me.

Don't play with him.

I nodded, walking away when he released my arm and turning through the now-familiar halls that made up the lower level of the Commission of the People. I took a deep breath before I knocked on Dana's office door.

"Come in."

Dana was seated at his desk, Sean standing behind him, both looking at Dana's computer.

"Little Lily," Dana greeted. "Come in, come in."

I stepped to the other side of his desk, glancing at Sean. For what felt like hours, the three of us stood in silence, Dana watching the screen of his computer while Sean looked nervously between Dana, the screen, and me. I wanted to see what they were watching, but I felt that if I moved, Dana would pounce.

Finally, he spoke.

"I assume that you already know what happened in the Western Region today," the leader of the Commission said suddenly.

"…yes," I said. "Some kids read the report at school. It spread around the school like wildfire."

"I can imagine," Dana mused distractedly. He sighed and leaned back in his chair, glancing briefly at Sean. "That will be all, Sean. I will see you later tonight."

Sean bowed his head and turned, walking around the desk and to the door, hesitantly leaving.

Again, Dana and I were locked in silence.

Dana reached to his mouse and clicked a few things before turning the volume up.

"Come see," he offered.

I walked around his desk and nervously approached his seat. I leaned my hip against the desk, my eyes focusing on the reporter on screen.

"And now for the latest on the incident that happened in the Western Region earlier today. At the Stanford Parade on Pennsylvania Street, the group who called into question the practices of the Commission of the People at the Liberation Day Parade in Central made another appearance. A large group of approximately sixty people wearing Thomas Ankell masks marched in front of the parade dedication carrying the same signs seen at the Liberation Day Parade. While there was no sign of the winged man that appeared at the parade in Central, people still believe this was from the same radical group. We're going to Cindy Gregg who is on the scene at the cleanup of Pennsylvania Street."

The video cut to a younger woman with beautiful thick brown hair and bright green eyes, standing among a crowd of people while officials set up barriers and began gathering the signs and banners dropped in the chaos.

"Thank you, Diane," Cindy said. "As you can see behind me, Pennsylvania Street has remained closed after the police came in and arrested approximately forty of the members of the group who disrupted the parade. There has been no evidence yet to suggest that these are the same people as the Liberation Day Parade, and the police are refusing to give information on those who were captured, though they did reveal that several of the people are still at large in the city."

"Cindy, have you spoken to any of the people there? What is the general sentiment?"

"Yes, I have spoken to them, and the general sentiment right now is shock and confusion. Many are not sure what to make of this sudden rise in what possibly could be a rebellion, or even domestic terrorism. Many were unable to see the press conference of the Commission of the People and are still unsure what to think about the information that these groups have on the Commission of the People, or its validity."

"Thank you, Cindy, we will come back to you in a few minutes," Diane said as the camera cut back to the main studio. "The press conference being held by representatives of the Commission of the People is still underway and is being broadcast on local PBC networks, but here is what representative Thomas Sandover had to say earlier in the conference."

The camera showed a previously recorded clip of the press conference where my father stood at the podium next to Clark's mother, and another one of Dana's advisors.

"The Commission of the People is working very hard to gather information on who these people are and why they are using these fear tactics on the American people. At the moment, our information is incomplete, but the members of the Commission of the People want to assure the people of America that there is currently nothing to fear from this group of radicals."

"What about their message that blames the Commission of the People for torturing their captives and creating weapons out of them?" one of the reporters called. "What is your response to the claim?"

"The Commission of the People was shocked at the implications of these messages. While we understand that the Commission of the People has a notorious reputation, to openly accuse us of mistreating and altering humans is an absurd and unfounded accusation and a fear tactic to create instability within the public."

"Do you deny, then, that the Commission is torturing criminals in its custody?" another reporter asked from the back of the room.

"Yes, I deny the claims against the Commission of the People. There is no weapons testing. There is no torture. The purpose of the Commission is to keep the people of America safe, and that is what we always strive to accomplish."

"Mr. Sandover, in a time like this, it seems surprising that the appointed leader of the Commission of the People, Dana Christenson, has not made an appearance or a statement in response to these incidents. What can you tell us about Mr. Christenson's whereabouts at this time?"

"Dana Christenson has not come forward for the reason of his safety," my father said. "He is working very hard to find this group of radicals and remove them from the public in order to restore peace of mind to the American people. As such, with the way this group has been targeting the Commission of the People, it was a unanimous decision that our leader, Mr. Dana Christenson, remain out of media and public view for his safety and the preservation of the Commission of the People through this time."

"He's quite handsome in that suit," Dana mused as the camera cut back to the main reporter. "Isn't he?"

"Don't get any ideas," I warned.

"What do you mean?" he asked innocently, glancing at me as I sat on his desk, crossing my legs and glaring at him.

"Keep your hands off him. I won't have you seducing my father the way you've seduced so many men of the Commission."

Dana shrugged and leaned forward, pausing the video. "If I want him, I'll have him. It's as simple as that."

"The hell you will."

Dana turned his chair and looked me over with a crooked smile.

"Well, here we are again, Little Lily," he said. "You caught me by surprise. That doesn't happen very often."

"I'm sure it doesn't," I chuckled. "But I had nothing to do with the thing at Stanford."

"No, of course not." Dana grinned, tilting his head dangerously to the side.

I sighed heavily. "You're never going to believe me, are you?"

"How can I?" Dana barked a laugh. "You don't believe it, yourself." He leaned back in his chair and sighed, rolling his neck around. "Even if you are guilty, which I know you are, if *you* believe you're innocent, you can make others believe it as well."

"Tell that to all the innocent people convicted of crimes they didn't commit..." I scoffed.

"Well, the belief that someone is guilty can be stronger than one person believing they're innocent, but to be fair," Dana held up his hands in a shrug, "is anyone really innocent?"

I huffed. "So, I can't convince you that I'm innocent, but if I confess to anything, then you take me in and I become your slave." I clicked my tongue against the roof of my mouth. "I'm not seeing a viable option..."

"You already have a preconceived notion that you'll be my slave when I take you?" Dana challenged, his eyebrows high. "Interesting...it's wrong, but still interesting."

"Then what *do* you want from me?"

Dana's smile widened.

"Well, to be honest, I thought you would do something stupid that would cause me to take you in already, but you seem to have exceeded my expectations. I thought I would need to train you a little, but as I have said, you surprised me."

"Train me?"

"You don't need to worry," Dana assured gently. "You've already done wonderfully. Like I said, I need to step up my game." He tilted his head. "I did not think so many people would get behind you so quickly. After Liberation Day we were monitoring all streets, planes, anything entering or leaving the city and saw no fliers or signs being sent to the Western Region. We found no electronic trace—so far—of files being sent to be printed there…you have planned this well…"

I could not help but smile.

"You are getting sneaky," Dana whispered.

"How do you think they got the fliers?" I asked innocently.

"To be honest, considering the resources most likely available for this domestic terrorist group, I am genuinely stumped." Dana tilted his head to the side again. "What do you think my confusion means?"

"What do you mean?"

"What angle am I not considering?"

"You could be ignoring how much the people disapprove of what the Commission does," I said. "The Commission was controversial to begin with. And then you abused the power you had and the people now know you are creating weapons out of people."

"No." Dana shook his head. "I think I am underestimating the resources available to this group." He grinned darkly. "Whoever they are…"

Dana leaned forward, resting his hand on the exposed skin of my ankle above my sock. It took all my willpower not to flinch away from his fingers. His pointer and middle finger traced random circles over the bones of my ankle as his eyes traveled up my calf, over my thigh and up my body to finally rest on my breasts, which I realized too late I was accenting by having my arms crossed.

But I boldly remained as I was, teasing him.

He licked his bottom lip before capturing it in his bottom teeth and finally shifting his eyes up to my face.

"My, my," he breathed, "you're getting bold…"

I slowly moved my head, tilting it, allowing only the smallest of smirks to touch the corners of my mouth.

* *** *

The entire week had been filled with frantic whispers and speculations about the terrorist group. I listened to the gossip with dark glee, feeling like chuckling every time I heard the flustered hypotheses of the news stations and the students on campus. When eyes were turned on me, I instantly fell into my role, feigning my concern over the situation and offering my own half-cooked ideas about the motives of the rebel group.

Meanwhile, I was sharing secret glances with the other Commish Kids, who were also enjoying the chaos.

Friday at Archangel was far more enjoyable for me, and it must have been noticeable because I was attracting a lot of attention. I had done my rounds, hearing how different kids had heard stories from their parents, trying to collect information about how others were reacting to our growing revolution. My favorite whispers were ones like "do you think it's true?" and "what if it is true and the Commission really *is* making weapons out of people?"

The smile would take over my whole face and I would fade quietly into the crowd to enjoy the feeling.

I felt powerful, nearly invincible. Without fail, the plan was working, and Dana himself was stumped. Clark shared most of my enthusiasm, but I could tell he was not feeling it as acutely. And Mark only offered the smallest smile to show that he was happy we had made progress. But he was still as cautious and careful as ever.

For me, Friday night was a time to celebrate my power.

After getting worked up over the rumors around the club, I made my way to the middle of the dance floor, feeling as though nothing could touch me. Assimilating perfectly with the pulsing of the dancing crowd, I swayed, feeling the beat throb around me, moving my body. My eyes closed, only opening every now and then when the sensations became overwhelming. There were eyes on me, mostly male eyes, as I moved with the music, my hands falling over my body as I danced, enticing people to come closer. If I had had rational thought in that moment, I would have wondered about my attempts to seduce those around me. Every move was a message to come closer.

And they did.

Several boys approached, dancing with me while the girls looked on with contempt and disgust. I ignored them entirely, but I did not focus on any of the boys, twisting and spinning away from one to end up in front of another who was just as interested. I flitted around them as if I was an apparition.

Nothing could touch me.

But something finally did.

There were hands that settled around my hips from behind, but I knew they were not the large hands of the Commission leader, so I had no reason to startle. This was someone I could have some influence over.

I turned around and smiled, seeing Devon glaring at the other teens backing away.

He turned to me and smiled, though he seemed on edge and surprised.

"Well, you're in a good mood tonight," he noted warily. "Or are you drunk?"

"Drunk on the beat, maybe," I laughed. I closed my eyes and laughed harder. "That was really lame."

"Yes, it was," Devon agreed with a chuckle. "Don't stop, though. It's alluring."

I placed one hand on his shoulder as the song changed to a different beat, using him as an anchor to move my hips with the slower, heavier bass.

"There's something...different about you," Devon noted, watching me as though he had never seen anything like me. That did nothing more than feed my fire. I bit my lower lip as I grinned playfully.

"I know." I pressed myself to him teasingly. "It's amazing..."

"You must be drunk," Devon chuckled brokenly. "Do I need to smell your breath?"

In that moment, I did something that surprised me, but even the shock at my playful behavior was not enough to stop me.

I fisted the shoulder of his black sweater and leaned close, rolling on my toes to press my mouth to Devon's ear.

"Wouldn't you rather taste it?"

Devon's entire body stiffened immediately and I smiled, slowly lowering myself until my heels hit the floor with a click that was inaudible over the sound of the bass. Devon was staring at me with gawking eyes, his mouth open as I chuckled.

"What?"

"You shouldn't say things like that," Devon whispered, swallowing hard.

"Why not?"

"You're with Clark."

I looked coyly around.

"I don't see him anywhere..." I purred.

Devon started to lean forward and I felt my power and influence grow. Just as he was within range of kissing me, I circled away, turning a full three hundred and sixty degrees and smiling devilishly.

"But you're with Jill," I told him. "Better be faithful to her, or you're going to be in a world of hurt."

I slipped easily into the crowd and up to the balcony, smiling at my game. It was easy and intoxicating. Clark walked up to me, worried.

"What were you doing down there? It looked like you were grinding with Devon," he said. I laughed lightly and placed a hand on his cheek before walking to the plush chairs at the back of the balcony.

"It's just dancing. No reason to get jealous."

He followed me as I sat heavily, sighing and fanning my neck with my hand.

"What has been up with you lately?" Clark said. "You're acting…I don't know, *weird*."

"Weird?" I barked a laugh. "How so?"

"You're just…not yourself."

"I'm fine," I said, leaning closer as he sat next to me. "Loosen up, Clark. We've done something that no one would ever think we were capable of. We achieved something that could change the world. Enjoy it!"

"We haven't changed anything," Clark hissed, glancing around worriedly and lowering his voice. "And until Dana is out of the picture, don't get cocky."

"I'm not getting cocky," I defended sharply. "I'm enjoying myself. Is that alright?"

Clark sighed and turned away. I watched the changing emotions on his face before I rolled my eyes.

"Clark, what's wrong? Am I upsetting you somehow?"

"Kind of," he said. "You're just acting differently and I don't know if I should be worried."

"Why would you be worried?"

"Because I don't want you making a careless mistake," Clark said, his voice strained. "Just remember…you're not only risking your life, but mine as well. And Mark's, and Josh's, and Tori's, and—"

"Alright, alright, I'll be careful," I groaned. "I'm sorry if I upset you. I was just enjoying my Friday."

And after five minutes of being on the balcony, I went back to the pulsing crowd of teenagers to enjoy the high once more, trying to dispel the indignation I felt at Clark's chastising.

When I got home, my entire body was on fire, more invigorated by the dancing than exhausted. I ached for something more, something that was no longer accessible. I was longing for Mykail.

I had missed him many times since he had gone to live in the fort, but that night was different. That night, my need was far more carnal than the loneliness of missing my boyfriend. I needed to feel his touch on my skin, his lips against mine, I needed to drink him in…

With my heart pounding against my ribs and every brush of the fabric against my skin fanning the flame, I tried to tell my parents that I was tired and wanted to go right to bed.

I closed my bedroom door and leaned against it, wondering how to alleviate the heat within me. I let out a frustrated groan and moved to the bathroom, kicking off my heels before unzipping my dress, letting it fall to the tile as I moved to the shower. I pressed the setting button to start the water before going to the vanity and looking at myself in the mirror. My cheeks were flushed but, otherwise, I could not see any sign of not being composed, other than the dark hunger in my eyes.

I pulled the pins from my hair, letting the rest of my curls tumble down my back and over my shoulders. Even then, clad in only my bra and panties, I felt powerful.

Slowly removing the final articles of clothing, I stepped into the shower.

I allowed the hot water to beat over my skin. The steam made it hard to breathe but that did nothing more than arouse me further. When I was no longer able to bear it, I went to the seat of the shower, closing my eyes and running my hands over my shoulders and neck before dropping them to my breasts, feeling the rapid heartbeat and the coursing hot blood through my body.

I leaned my head against the tile and remembered the first time Mykail and I had showered together. I remembered his hands on me, working my flesh into sweet, heightened tension…the way his mouth peppered kisses down my torso and over my thighs before paying attention to the area between my legs, where I so desperately needed to feel him…

My hand drifted down my belly, sliding with the water droplets to rest at the same spot, my eyes still closed as my fingers brushed over the sensitive flesh.

I imagined him kissing me sweetly, how gentle his hands were as he handled me…

I let out another frustrated groan, my hand stilling as I tried to hold onto the image of Mykail. But it was not enough. My mind turned to another fantasy. Mykail was still kneeling between my legs, but he grabbed my arms, which were crossed over my chest, and pinned them next to my hips, capturing my mouth hungrily in a kiss.

Mykail was much taller and broader, and my fantasy moved away from the shower into a familiar office as I sat on a large, dark mahogany desk, still fully dressed, but pinned under the strong arms of the man with me.

I felt one hand leave my wrist and move to my ankle, gently caressing the skin in small circles before pushing my skirt over my knee to bunch at my waist as I panted with need, my head rolling around uselessly on my neck. The large hands dipped under the back of my skirt and pulled my hips, scooting me to the edge of the desk as my legs wrapped around his waist, anchoring him to me, grinding against him.

He remained still, letting me move on my own before one of his hands traced up my side to my blouse. With a sharp tug, three of the buttons popped off and scattered with clicks on the desk's surface.

His hands moved into my shirt, pulling my bra down and freeing my breasts, causing me to let out a carnal groan and push them forward, yearning for his touch.

"My, my, you're getting bold…" his voice chuckled.

I whined, wanting to feel his hands on me but loving the teasing, never knowing where his touch would fall next.

"That's it…" He had a grin in his voice. His hand moved to tangle in the hair at the base of my neck and pull my head forward until my mouth locked with his, both of our tongues battling for control. I breathed him in, arching my back to bring us closer, though he still was so far away, purposely keeping contact minimal.

"Slow down…I'm going to train you."

The words were like bombs that exploded over my skin, causing a moan to push out of me as my belly tightened. I was in such need I was sure I would die unless my fantasy touched me.

He did, but it was not slow and tender in the fashion of memories. It was sharp, commanding, dominating me in every way.

I choked on the groan in my throat and pushed my hips harder against my hand as I moved my fingers desperately.

In my fantasy, it was his fingers, and he was moving them inside me, crooking them to stroke my inner walls, causing lightning to rocket through me. My back arched and my hips moved in time with his fingers. They began pushing into me harder and faster, my entire body threatening to explode with pleasure. I felt the pressure building deep within me, ready to hurl me into the clouds.

When his mouth locked with mine again, I was thrown high into the air, my entire body bowing with the force of my orgasm before falling limp against the seat of the shower. I felt my body pulse around my fingers and I let out whimpers, feeling sated but unsatisfied. I purposely did not think about what my fantasy could mean about my mental state. I was bound tight that evening, and my brain had been acting of its own accord.

I could not be held responsible for the fantasy. Not that night.

Chapter Fifty-Eight

It would have been a far more entertaining Commission meeting if Dana had been present, but he was with Leader Simon, trying to find out if there were going to be any more reveals that weekend.

I guessed that the two simultaneous incidents earlier in the North-East Region had truly frightened Leader Simon. There was an anticipation that everyone could feel, yet no one was prepared. It was a big weekend for parades, being the time our country celebrated the Second Revolution in all its glory. Everyone was anxiously waiting for news that there had been another sighting of the terrorist movement.

My parents had been watching the news that morning, their expressions creased with their concern.

I was listening intently as I was making myself a snack of cheese and crackers. I had been pretending not to be interested, but when I heard that breaking news was coming in from the North-East Region, my entire body went to attention.

"Lily!" my mother called. "Come quick."

I abandoned my snack and ran into the living room, turning to the male anchor's confused face on the screen.

"We have received news that the Washington March Parade suffered an incident this morning. Participants in the parade showed sentiments for the strange movement that has been surprising the country by claiming that the Commission of the People is taking their prisoners and making them into weapons. As the congregation, holding the same banners and fliers seen at the Liberation Day Parade, moved down the street, spectators broke through the barriers and crowded Jersey Lane, demanding that the Commission of the People open their doors to an investigation of the allegations…"

I was smiling too much to notice the horrified expressions on my parents' faces.

Later that afternoon, another report came in.

"We bring you this clip from a local news station in the North-East City of Castleton," the main anchor said before the shot cut to another station reporter.

"Daniel, I'm here on Georgia Avenue, where the parade has just gotten underway. People are excited to see the special guests this year. RM celebrities such as Prescott Faraway and the singer Lydia are both present in today's—"

There were gasps and cries behind the reporter followed by people screaming "there they are!" The anchor whirled around, motioning the camera closer. The cameraman jogged forward and captured the parade moving down Georgia Avenue, holding the banners of my revolution and the pictures of the people currently living in Fort Daniels.

There was even someone in the middle of the crowd who had fake wings, leading the chant.

"We want answers!!"

Everything was going even better than I could have hoped.

Four strikes against the Commission of the People and we were already getting a response. I was riding a continuous high.

After the Commission meeting, where little was accomplished because everyone was too flustered to figure out how to handle the increasingly worrisome situation, I was feeling confident that our movement would gain enough followers to make a difference before the Commission could make a move to eliminate us—especially since it seemed that the Commission was completely ineffective without their leader present.

I trailed behind my family as they joined one of the groups at the end of the meeting. Everyone was brainstorming the best way to handle the growing support before they had another revolution on their hands. I was careful to listen, in case I needed to be a few steps ahead of their plan.

But Clark distracted me.

"Hey," he greeted, his eyes cast down as he approached.

"Hey," I repeated, looking him over. "What's wrong?"

"Nothing," he said unconvincingly. "Listen, I was wondering...the zoo is holding a charity event tomorrow and I was wondering if you wanted to go with me."

I blinked, confused.

"Don't worry, Mark will drive us," he completed.

"Oh, of course," I said, realizing we were going to the fort. My heart soared at the thought of seeing Mykail again.

"Okay, we'll pick you up tomorrow at nine," Clark told me. "The event is all day, so be sure you ask your parents if it's okay."

"They're not going to care."

Clark opened his mouth to say something, but he stopped and shook his head.

"Okay, I'll see you tomorrow."

He walked away. I stared after him, confused about his odd behavior and wondering why he seemed so annoyed with me.

The following morning, I went downstairs to have breakfast and told my parents about Clark and I going to the charity event at the zoo, which I had looked up online the previous night to be sure I had enough knowledge to answer their questions.

Their questions had nothing to do with the event.

"Lily, are you sure that wandering around on a date is appropriate, given the situation?" my mother asked in a parental tone, her eyebrows high.

"Situation?"

"The Commission is being attacked by a group of terrorists, a group that managed to break into the Commission and release these weapons. And you have been acting as though you're happy about it."

"Well, I am," I said nonchalantly.

"Lily!"

"You should not be pleased about this, Lily." My father shook his head in disapproval. "This is very dangerous for all of us, and for the country. The entire world is getting nervous. Dana has been in meetings all week with foreign leaders to assure them that he has the situation under control."

"Does he?" I asked.

"No," my father said sharply. "But you have to understand that the Commission has sold weapons to foreign governments. If the Commission is revealed, then there is a strong chance that these other governments will find themselves in trouble, and that could lead to a full-scale world war."

"Well, Dana shouldn't have been involving the other countries," I quipped. "Of course, now that I think about it, that was probably his plan. He wants to see the world fall apart."

"Don't say such things," my mother scolded. "This is a very delicate situation and Dana is doing the best he can to keep a lid on it."

"You know that I have never agreed with the Commission. I'm happy this is happening. Maybe it will make some changes and shut down the Commission for good."

"You know nothing," my mother said angrily. "The Commission may not be a clean organization, and there may be some things that are not seen as part of the moral path, but let me tell you something, young lady, the Commission is necessary in today's world. Without it, the entire world would have come crashing down and you would have been born in a nuclear winter." My mother stood and grabbed my plate, even though I was not finished eating, and turned to the kitchen. "You just think how fortunate you are that the Commission has given you such a secure world to live in."

I groaned and rolled my eyes.

"Whatever."

I went upstairs to grab my coat and scarf, pulling them on as I went down the stairs to the front door.

"Lily, I never said you could go with Clark," my mother called.

"Like I need your permission." I rolled my eyes, walking out the front door, slamming it behind me.

I still had fifteen minutes to wait, so I sat down on the icy front step of the porch and waited for the familiar black car to roll up to the curb. I was not necessarily angry at my parents—I just felt as though their opinion didn't matter. I knew what I was doing and, with the way the people were reacting and supporting us, it was obvious that the entire country had been nervous about the Commission, particularly with the reactivation of the Sweeps.

I knew I was doing the right thing for the country—the right thing for the *world*.

My mother and father did not bother coming outside to talk to me. I sat in silence until I saw the car turn the corner onto my street and park in front of my house.

Too excited to notice anything else, I darted through the crisp, clear air to the car and got in as Mark was about to open the door for me. He sat back in the car as I settled in, smiling at Clark.

"Morning," I greeted.

"Good morning."

"Wow, you seem off," I noted. "What's wrong?"

"Nothing. I just didn't sleep well."

"Why not?"

"Don't know," he muttered. "My mind was too busy, I guess."

"Oh," I said, not knowing how else to respond. I turned to Mark to dispel the awkwardness. "How about you, Mark? Doing well?"

He nodded once.

The car felt tense. I tried not to let it get to me, turning to look out the window, watching the city pass by as Mark drove toward the zoo. There were a lot of cars and buses in the parking lot during the charity event. Mark parked the car near the back of the parking lot and got out, opening the door for us. I huddled into my coat, feeling the chill of the air at the higher elevation. As Mark removed his shoe, pulling out the container with his tracers, I was startled by a familiar voice behind me.

"Clark! Lily!"

I rounded to see Becca jogging toward us with a large smile across her face.

"Becca!" I grinned, hugging her briefly when she reached us. She smiled, shifting her feet around.

"Wow, it's freezing today!"

"Thank you for coming, Becca," Clark said, nervously looking at his feet. I smiled at his shyness around the girl he liked, trying not to think about the more complicated network of relationships that was occurring within our group of friends.

"No problem."

"Did you ask her to come here?" I asked, confused.

"Yeah," Clark said, reaching into his pocket and pulling out a plastic bag, showing his tracers. "She agreed to be our cover. This is kind of her test to win Mark's trust."

I turned to Mark, who had just closed the driver's door and turned to face Becca.

"Are you Mark?" Becca asked.

He nodded once.

"It's nice to meet you." Becca extended her hand. I was not sure if her trembling was due to being nervous or cold. Mark hesitated, making all of us anxious, but he eventually removed his hand from his pocket, taking hers and shaking it once.

"You can't speak?" she asked awkwardly. He shook his head, making the situation that much more awkward. Mark was wary of Becca, I could tell. I rolled my eyes and laughed, leaning into Mark, bumping him with my shoulder.

"It's okay, Mark," I assured. "She's a good friend. You can trust her."

Mark forced a smile and nodded. I could sense that he did not trust her. His distrusting nature was starting to annoy me.

"It's okay that he doesn't trust me," Becca said. "I mean, you guys have to be careful. But I'm just going to keep those in my pocket and spend some time with the animals."

I grinned, reaching into my sock, pulling out the little bag of the tracers and handing it to Becca. She put both of our tracers in the zipped pocket of her coat.

"There," she smiled. "I don't need to have Mark's?"

"No," Clark shook his head. "He's supposed to stay in the car while we're here."

"Okay," Becca said. "Well, I'll just be in there," she motioned to the zoo behind her. "I'll be in the café when I'm finished, so you guys can find me there when you get back."

"Thank you, Becca," Clark murmured. I hugged her again. As she walked to the bustling entrance of the zoo, the three of us went the opposite direction.

"Mark, you can trust Becca," I insisted. "There's no need to be worried."

"He's just being careful," Clark defended. "Have you forgotten what a dangerous time this is for us? We can't get careless."

"We're not being careless," I scoffed. "It's Becca."

"We just need to be careful, okay?" Clark repeated in an annoyed tone as he trudged ahead of me on the trail. I hesitated before jogging to catch up to him.

"Hey, what's been up with you?" I snapped. "You're acting like I did something wrong."

"No, you haven't," Clark said, turning to fix me with a sharp look. "So don't start."

We fell silent for the trek to the cave passage. I was getting annoyed with how everyone was acting as though we had done something terrible. I did not understand how they could not see what an accomplishment it was to gain more support from the American people.

There was a warm welcome waiting for us at the fort. Everyone turned when they saw the door opening and let out a cheer, rushing toward Clark and me. The energy of the fort made me smile and renewed my determination. Everyone was still talking in amazement about the response we had received, thrilled with the growing attention and the additional demonstrations around the country.

Tori gave me a hug and then Griffin came up to me, hugging me tightly, lifting me off the ground.

"How have you been, kid? Steering clear of Dana?"

"Trying," I laughed.

"Well, we have someone who really wants to see you." Griffin winked. "But, we kinda figured you didn't want an audience."

I laughed. "Thank you."

Griffin cleared a path for me through the crowd of whistles and playful teasing. Normally, that would have made me embarrassed, but I was too excited to see Mykail to care about the jibes.

Tori led me down a hallway of storage rooms and brought me into the ammunition room. She turned to me with a grin.

"Just stay on the right wall, the left one has the grenades."

"Alright," I laughed. I had been in the ammunition room a few times before, and was always annoyed with how little light there was around the cases of bullets and grenades. That time, the dim glow fell on pristine white feathers.

"Just come to the main bunker whenever you feel like it," Griffin said behind Tori as she closed the door, shutting me in the room with Mykail.

I ran to him and threw my arms around his neck, my mouth locking on his as he stumbled to steady himself, his arms wrapping around my

780

waist and holding me close. We kissed passionately for several long minutes before I finally pulled away, my breath as heavy as his.

"I missed you," he whispered.

"I missed you more." I pecked him on the lips. "I was about to go insane without you."

"Really?" Mykail laughed as I pushed on his chest, making him step back, turning him until he was against one of the larger stacks of crates.

"Yes. I was about to go find someone else I needed you so much," I teased.

"Don't even joke about that," he chuckled airily. "I would have to come steal you back if you went with anyone else."

"Oh really?" I ran both my hands up his abdomen and to his chest, pushing him harder to pin him. "What would you do to win me back?"

"Anything I had to," he murmured, leaning forward and kissing me in a lingering lip-lock before breaking away and smiling. "Would you be willing to take me back?"

"Oh...I think I might..." I grinned devilishly. "You already know so well what I like..."

He smiled proudly before taking a deep breath and cringing slightly.

"Lily...let me go," he said with a broken laugh. "You're pinning my wings."

"I know," I said, keeping one hand on him as I unbuttoned my jacket with the other hand, revealing the deep V-neck sweater underneath, a large pendant resting in my cleavage to draw his attention. I had fully planned on jumping Mykail when we had a moment alone, and I wanted to leave no room for him to refuse.

His eyes fell to the pendant and his pupils dilated. He licked his lips before looking back at me, his eyes dark with purpose.

I let him go just long enough to shed my coat before I pushed him back against the crates. He winced and tried to push forward.

"Lily, I'm serious. My wings..."

"I know it hurts," I said, leaning closer. "But a little bit of pain every now and then is pleasurable, isn't it?"

His eyes fluttered shut. I was sure he was recalling the nights we had been a little rougher with one another and the excitement we had both felt at small jabs of pain.

I wrapped both my arms around his neck, directing his head to the exposed skin under my collarbone. He let out a breath of relief as the strain on his wings lessened and kissed the large pendant before his hands wrapped around my sides, holding my ribcage as he kissed the exposed skin.

My breath came short and heavy and before long, I was bored of the slow foreplay. I turned him away from the crates and pushed him onto the floor. He caught himself on his hands and looked up at me as I pulled the sweater over my head, dropping it to the ground and shimmying out of my jeans and shoes. I straddled his lap, kissing him as he leaned back on his wings, his hands now free to grab at my thighs.

My hands skimmed down to his pants, working them open and eagerly finding the hot flesh I desired.

His mouth broke from mine and his breath hitched in his throat.

I smiled at how easily he was aroused by me. It was just another part of my power trip, knowing I had such a profound effect on him.

The thought that we were in the fort with other people nearby did nothing more than excite me. I was in control entirely and Mykail willingly followed.

Our hunger was eventually sated and we remained still, shuddering, still connected as we sat in the middle of the ammunition room, our eyes closed and our breaths labored.

"Wow..." Mykail finally breathed. I chuckled breathlessly. "That was really..."

"Amazing?" I completed, opening my eyes to see his pleased expression.

"I was going to say bold, but yes, absolutely amazing," he agreed. He wrapped his arms around my waist and lifted me, sitting upright and stretching his wings, which had been supporting him through our entire reunion. "I like it when you're aggressive."

"Me, too."

"But..." a sheepish smile took over his face, "please don't pin me anymore. It really hurts with the wings."

"Okay," I agreed, kissing him. "I won't do that again."

We took our time composing ourselves. I should have felt embarrassed walking into the main bunker again, considering everyone knew what had just happened between Mykail and me, but there was no part of me that was ashamed. I felt amazing, powerful, and beautiful. I easily mingled with those eager to talk to me, leaving Mykail to trail behind.

At one point, Mykail went to speak to other people while I listened to some of the stories Tori was telling me about the preparations made for our next move.

When there was a lull in the conversation, I felt a hand gently tap my arm. Mark was behind me, his glasses off, revealing his serious, yet sad, eyes.

"Hey, Mark," I said, worried. "What is it?"

Mark lifted his hand, his palm to the ground, and bent his fingers, as if waving, before he began walking away.

"Wait, what?" I turned back to Tori. "What was that? Is he leaving?"

"No," Tori chuckled. "He wants you to follow him."

I followed Mark to one of the rarely-used hallways off the main bunker. He led me to one of the heavily-locked doors. I tried to remember where the door led, but it had been so long since I had explored the fort that I had forgotten a lot of the rooms. Mark heaved the door open with little difficulty before descending the staircase, the single light above flickering incessantly.

I immediately remembered the room at the bottom of the stairs. It was a large room that seemed to have had no purpose. It was a cavernous space that echoed and always gave me the creeps. Halfway down the stairs, when I realized where we were going, I halted.

"Mark, why are you taking me down here?"

He turned, his eyes filled with a sad and worried emotion that I could not quite fathom. His jaw clenched and he opened his mouth as if he was about to speak, but he let out a quiet breath before climbing the few stairs that separated us and reaching a hand out, palm up.

I looked between the hand and Mark's expressive, dark eyes.

After I placed my hand in his, he led me down the rest of the staircase to the other door, which was already open, pulling me into the cavernous room. I stopped, surprised to see Griffin standing next to a table near the door. He also looked extremely serious.

"Griffin?"

I jumped when Mark slid the door shut behind me and the sound echoed through the room. I was becoming frightened.

"Come over here, Lily," Griffin coaxed.

I forced my almost-shaking legs forward. Mark followed, though he moved to a trunk that had been placed against the wall behind the table.

"You both are making me nervous…"

"Good," Griffin said. "It will keep you alert." Griffin turned to Mark, who was crouched in front of the chest, gathering items in his arms. "Don't worry, Lily, we're not going to hurt you. Mark and I want to teach you something." He extended an arm around my shoulder, pulling me toward the table. It was only then that I noticed there were plastic milk jugs in the far corner of the room. One was suspended from a rope near the back wall.

Before I could ask what was going on, Mark was at my other side, holding his gun out in front of me. His finger pressed something on the side and the magazine slipped out. Placing the full magazine on the table, he pulled the top of the gun back and tilted it sideways to let the bullet slip out of the chamber. I was frozen, staring at a weapon I had never been so close to.

When Mark had completely emptied the gun in front of me, he held it out for me to take. I stared stupidly for a long moment before looking up at Mark, whose eyes were no longer sad. They were hard and cold.

I turned to Griffin, who also sported a very serious expression.

"Go ahead," he urged.

I turned back to the black metal. I touched the handle, closing my fingers around the cold gun and lifting it from Mark's hand. I was surprised by how heavy it was and quickly tightened my fingers to keep it from slipping.

"Alright, first rule," Griffin said, stepping to my other side and placing his hand over mine, pointing the gun down at the table. "Don't point a gun carelessly. Don't aim it at anyone, even if it's empty. Particularly don't aim it at either of us because we know how to disarm you before you can blink."

I shivered at the words.

"This is the safety." He pointed to a switch near the back of the gun. "S means the safety is on, if it's red," he flicked the switch to show the painted red, "then it's live." He put the safety back on even though the gun was not loaded. "Here is your hammer. This is a double action, so that means that when you fire a shot, it cocks the gun again so you can keep firing." He stood behind me and his large arms wrapped around my shoulders, lifting my hands with the gun. "This hand is the one you will pull the trigger with, go ahead and rest your finger there," he moved my finger into position. "Now, this hand," he grabbed my other hand and put it around the gun, "will help you stabilize and aim." His hands went to my shoulders and turned me at a slight angle. "Use your core," he told me, tapping my belly. His head dropped to my shoulder, and he pointed at the two ridges on the top of the gun. "Here's your sight. When you aim, try to line up the ridge at the end of the barrel between this sight." He backed away. "Okay so far?"

I nodded silently.

Griffin picked up the magazine on the table, turning to show me the numbers on the back as I lowered the gun, taking special care not to point it at anything other than the table. "This magazine is full. You have fifteen rounds. You're going to try and hit that target."

"This is target practice?"

"This is a lesson in how to use a gun," Griffin corrected. He turned to Mark, who handed him protective headphones. "Put these on. You don't want to damage your ears. The gun is loud enough as it is, but it echoes like hell in here."

I put the gun down and grabbed the bulky headphones, carefully slipping them over my head before pushing one side back to hear Griffin.

Griffin took another pair of the headphones from Mark and put them around his neck. "Pick up the gun and the magazine and load it," he said, watching as I shakily picked up the gun and magazine, turning it and putting it in the gun carefully. Griffin reached over and hit the bottom to lock it in place. "Good, now take the safety off and pull the hammer back with your thumb."

I followed instructions cautiously.

"And you're live," he said, pulling the headphones over his ears as Mark did the same. "Take your time to aim and try to hit the jug."

Mark reached forward and pushed the headphone back over my ear as I took a deep breath, trying to keep my hands from shaking. I closed one eye and tried to line up the ridges as Griffin had told me, pointing at the jug. My shaking hands caused me to continue moving the gun, particularly as my finger curled around the trigger. I took another deep breath, tightening the pressure on the trigger.

Suddenly, both my arms bent and my wrists suffered a sharp jerk as the bullet left the chamber and soared to the left of the jug, embedding in the wall. I was shocked at the amount of recoil the gun had and how hard it was to aim. Nervously, after getting the nod from Griffin, I took aim again.

Mark approached me and his hand went into the inside of my right elbow, bending my arm before readjusting my left hand to support my right. His hand went around my back and pressed on my shoulder blades while his other hand pressed flat to my stomach, causing me to lean forward. He readjusted my shoulders before stepping back.

Focusing on the target again, I took careful aim.

Pulling the trigger once more, I was still surprised by the jolt of movement, but I was not shaken by it. The bullet hit much closer to the jug, but was low. I took aim once again, remembering to bend my arm, lean forward, and angle my shoulders. I pulled the trigger. That time, my shock was due to something else entirely.

The side of the jug ruptured and water ejected in all directions. The water sloshed over the ruptured edges as the jug swung back and forth from the force of the shot.

I should have been proud that I hit the target, but there was a greater part of me that was horrified. While I knew plastic and water was not a good representation of human flesh, realizing how the bullet had decimated the plastic made me think of what would happen to a person.

Mark placed his hand on my wrist and slowly lowered my hands, turning the safety on before taking the gun out of my hands, pulling out the magazine once again and emptying the chamber, setting the components on the table.

Griffin took my shoulders and pulled me away from the table, removing his headphones. I did the same, turning to him, my heart racing and my hands trembling. I thought firing the gun would make me feel more powerful, but it didn't.

It frightened me.

"Good job, you hit it," Griffin congratulated. I watched Mark walk to the jug, untying it.

"What…what would that do to a person?" I whispered, my voice weak.

"Nothing much different."

We watched silently as Mark walked to us with the jug. Mark held out the plastic. I was surprised that, with all the water that had exploded from the container, the damage was clean and precise. The side had blown out from the displaced water, but it looked as though someone had cut the plastic with a knife.

"Lily, it's important that you know how to fire a gun and protect yourself," Griffin said. "The truth is, Mark and I were getting worried. You seemed to be getting a little too confident with what's been happening lately. Actually, it's nothing to celebrate. A rebellion has bloodshed. People get hurt and people die. And when we start getting support is when we become a threat to the people with the really big guns."

I looked between Griffin and Mark.

"You have to humble yourself, and remember that every life is precious. You were upset because of the way the experiments were treated. So don't contradict your care for people by getting careless and forgetting how easily someone can be killed."

I looked at the jug and swallowed hard.

"I'm sorry…"

"We're not scolding you," Griffin said. "But...Mark and I...we've both killed. And that is something that changes you forever. We want you to understand that a rebellion is not without pain and blood."

Griffin wrapped one arm around me.

"We just want to look out for you, keep you in line," he teased, his tone growing light. I smiled before wrapping my arms around as much of him as I could.

"Thank you," I whispered sincerely.

After he released me, I turned to Mark, who was watching with a slightly-happier light in his eyes.

"You, too," I said, opening my arms. He smiled shyly and stepped back, shaking his head. "Oh, come on, we've hugged before. I'm going to hug you whether you want to or not."

Mark retreated another step, laughing silently.

"He doesn't like to be touched," Griffin noted with a chuckle.

"Well, generally those people," I said, jogging to him and hugging him tightly, "are the ones who need hugs the most."

Mark only hugged me back briefly before backing away. I laughed at how shy and awkward he was, such a change from who he had been when he brought me to the room. I glanced between them. "Seriously, thank you...I guess I really needed a lesson."

"We all do every now and again," Griffin said with a wink.

"So...I'm curious about something," I started. "Who shoots better out of the two of you?"

"Ah, we have not found out, yet." Griffin grinned at Mark. "You promised we would compete. I guess now is the time."

Mark nodded and walked back down the room, tying a new jug to the rope. I watched with a smile, trying not to look at the ruptured jug on the ground behind me. Mark returned to the table after fixing the target.

"Ten rounds?" Griffin asked. Mark nodded and motioned to the gun on the table. Griffin easily put the gun together, checking how many rounds he had. He placed his headphones on and took aim.

In quick succession, he fired ten shots, moving the gun as the jug swung with the force of impact. After Griffin lowered the gun, he pulled it apart and set it on the table, removing his headphones as Mark went to retrieve the target.

"Damn," Griffin groaned. "I know I missed at least three."

I was still blinking in surprise at how many times I saw the jug jolt from another bullet passing through it. When Mark returned to the table—tying another target up beforehand—we crowded around the mangled plastic and counted the bullet holes.

"Six..." Griffin groaned. "Not bad..." He was obviously not happy with his accuracy. "It's hard to guess which way it's going to swing. But this is a nice gun," he said, lifting the empty weapon and studying it. "Is this Commission issued?"

Mark shook his head.

Griffin's face broke into a wide grin.

"You stole it?"

Mark shook his head again.

"No shit, you bought it on the black market? Unregistered?" Griffin gawked. Mark nodded. "Damn, you've got some balls, Mark."

Reaching to his belt, Mark pulled out a full magazine, taking the gun from Griffin. I felt a ball of excitement ricochet around my abdomen.

Putting on his headphones, Mark aimed carefully. He took a breath and slowly let it out, pulling the trigger for the first time before he completely exhaled. In the same rapid way as Griffin, Mark shot ten rounds, but on the fifth round, the entire bottom of the jug fell to the ground, leaving the swinging top empty and causing it to spin when Mark hit it with the sixth shot. When he had fired all ten, both Griffin and I had our jaws wide open.

"Did you ever *miss*?" Griffin gaped.

Mark nodded, settling the headphones around his neck with a sigh. He held up two fingers, disappointed.

"Holy shit, Mark..." I breathed.

"Holy shit? That's it?" Griffin laughed. "I would say, what the *fuck*? You really are some kind of ninja."

Mark smiled, looking a little cocky. He turned his body and aimed once more, ignoring his headphones while Griffin and I quickly scrambled to put ours back on. Mark fired one more shot. The handle where the rope was tied snapped, causing the rest of the jug to fall to the floor.

"Oh, well, now you're just showing off..." Griffin groaned with a smile.

Chapter Fifty-Nine

Tuesday brought more good news for the rebellion. As I was getting ready for school, my mother called me downstairs. We had partially-reconciled when I had returned home. I had apologized to Clark, my parents, and even Mykail after my time at the shooting range, humbled by the experience. And even though I was aware of my behavior, I was still annoyed at my mother for trying to change my opinion about supporting the rebellion.

I leaned on the back of the couch and watched the newest report.

"Students of the North-East Military Institute Number Seven, which mostly focuses on tactical and technological military advancement, joined with new recruits of the nearby military base in Connecticut Recreational Park in protest to the aversion of answers the Commission of the People representatives had at the press conference discussing the Liberation Day Parade incident."

The shot cut to show many people on the browned grass of the large park, most in military uniforms. One man stood on a car and was speaking into a megaphone at the crowd in front of him.

"The Commission of the People was established to balance the population, to keep America safe, and no one can deny that they have done their job well, but it was not the responsibility of the Commission to take control of the military!"

There was a rally of cheers.

"Washington had control of the military! The Washington President rolled out the troops and slaughtered students our age. That is what started the Second Revolution.

"Now, the Commission of the People has begun developing weapons, weapons of which we do not know the capabilities. The Commission completely disregarded the questions about the one who had wings and flew over the crowd! The development of such technology shows a complete disregard for humans, for the military, and for what our families fought for in the Second Revolution!"

Another round of cheers sounded.

"Will we let the Commission of the People become the next Washington?!"

"No!!!"

"This is getting out of hand..." my mother murmured shakily.

"The protest is still ongoing. The students say they will not go to classes until they are certain that the Commission of the People no longer has a hand in the military," the anchor's voice explained over the various shots of the extensive protest.

"I think it's time Dana Christenson stops hiding behind the Commission and explains the truth about the Liberation Day Parade and what the Commission has really been doing with their prisoners. We no longer need the Commission of the People, but instead of slowly fading, the Commission is beginning to take over the country. I say that, until we have answers, every American should halt their support of Central. Military men and women…be prepared. If they won't give us answers, we'll storm the Commission and dismantle it brick by brick!"

Even I was disturbed by the anger of the group.

Everyone was talking about the protest at school. Becca and Jill were engaged in a heated discussion about the possibility of an attack on Central. I tried to keep up with the conversation, but I was getting swept up in the frantic atmosphere, my breathing becoming short and labored as the panic swelled within me. Commish Kids were being hounded by other students. Between my first and second classes, a teacher had to break up a fight where three students jumped Ryan and began kicking him, demanding that he tell them if it was true that the Commission was trying to take over the country.

It felt like the anger we had instilled in the people was about to backfire. By now, all the Commish Kids who were in Third Tier were involved in the revolution, but because of Dana's influence, we had to remain quiet about everything. We were setting ourselves up to be targets.

Things were spiraling out of control.

The tension of the school was not at all eased by the teachers. They were silent, refusing to talk about the occurrences of dissent. Every time a student asked, teachers would not even acknowledge they had heard the question.

That seemed to exacerbate the problem.

I was cautious and nervous walking to Mr. McDermott's class. I felt as though everyone was looking at me, ready to attack and beat answers out of me. I quickly slipped into the classroom, but was still surrounded by the whispering of worry.

Mr. McDermott had barely started class, asking everyone how they were doing, before he was asked: "Should we be worried about the people attacking Central?"

The class fell silent, the air thick with tension. Mr. McDermott froze, his eyes looking among the students. We waited, wondering if he was going to shrug off the question or if he was going to answer.

He finally let out a deep sigh and placed his copy of *An Angel Without Wings* behind him on the desk, crossing his arms.

"I know that the news has been frightening as of late," he started. "I've been asked not to give you any incomplete information, but I think it's important to discuss what's happening." He looked at his feet briefly and collected his thoughts. "I do not think there is an immediate threat to Central, no. I think that, if what this group has said about the Commission is true, then it would not take much to get the people to attack."

"We don't even know that this is true about the Commission," Katie called from the back. "Why is everyone so quick to believe that the Commission is trying to take over the country?"

"Well, I don't want to frighten you, but in many ways, the Commission of the People is more powerful than the Central office. It's already controversial and frightening, so to think that an organization that powerful is trying to gain more power is terrifying. It hasn't been that long since the revolution, and people, particularly in the military, have family who have spoken of fighting in the Second Revolution and how they had to turn on their own government and fight for what they believed was right. The people are still afraid of a government system that is too strong, and they want to stop any attempts at seizing control before it's too late and we revert back to what we were before the Second Revolution."

"But we only saw the weapons once. It could have been a hoax, or something to just try and rile everyone up," Katie continued.

"True," Mr. McDermott agreed. "But we're already making the problem worse." He leaned back on his hands. "Let me tell you about something. When the Americans had their guns taken away, there was a huge uproar on both sides of the issue. It had always been a hot-button topic, but concerns were raised as people continued to cite school shootings and mass-killings that had occurred in the past. It became something that was almost accepted. Someone would walk into a school, just like ours, pull out a gun, and start shooting and when they were about to be caught, or they were finished with what they wanted to do, they would kill themselves. Try to imagine that for a moment…"

The students were looking at the desks, staring at the wood grain.

"Do you know what made it worse?" Mr. McDermott asked. "The way we unintentionally glorified these people. They got their names on the news, they got a place in history, notorious as it may be. For some, that was all the motivation they needed. How many of you have ever shot a gun before?"

I looked nervously around the classroom. No one raised their hands, so mine stayed down.

"Okay, well, I do not advocate giving guns back to the populace, but I do not think guns are dangerous. People are dangerous, and people with radical thoughts and ideas are extremely dangerous. When we give attention to these radical thinkers, we give them more power. I don't know what the truth is, but the best thing we can do is not engage these people, and wait for the Commission and Central to decide the course of action."

"But what if the Commission really is trying to take over the country?" Jacob pressed. "What if they really are making weapons out of people? *Torturing* people?"

"I don't know…" Mr. McDermott said. "I am waiting for the truth just as much as you are."

* *** *

"I'm getting worried," I whispered, pulling the blanket tighter around me.

"I understand that," Griffin said, looking at the ground, where our large flashlight was shining upward into the dark canopy of the trees. The core strategy group was meeting in our usual spot in the park, trying to decide the best course of action for all of us. Clark, Tori, and I were huddled under one blanket while Josh and Mark were under another, and Griffin had one to himself.

"Dana is calling meetings," Josh said. "I don't know who, but there are many people coming to meet with him."

"Don't do any snooping that's going to put you in danger," Clark warned.

"I agree," Tori seconded. "You're our inside information."

"The Eight Group is getting nervous," Josh said. "Dana refuses to put up a defense around the building, but says he'll use us if needed…"

"What does that mean?"

Griffin looked at the two members of the Eight Group worriedly.

"You mean if the building is stormed?" he asked. When they both nodded, Griffin turned to me. "If the building is stormed, Dana will let people come inside, and he will order the Eight Group to pick them off one by one in the upper floors to keep the basement Commission area safe."

"That sounds like him," Tori groaned with disgust. "Griff, what do you think about the military involvement?"

"They're pissed, and that's understandable. In their position, I would have been, too. But I hacked the military system last night, and Command is telling officers to keep the others quiet. Three of our leading generals have been called to meet with Dana."

"Then Command knows the truth?" Tori muttered.

"It would not surprise me."

"It's really amazing…" I whispered.

"What?"

"Dana." My eyes remained locked on the ground. "He owns these people. He lets people know what he's doing, gets them involved and, as soon as he does that, they're stuck. He can reveal them at any time as being privy to the Commission's dealings and then they're the next target. Same with the foreign leaders." I closed my eyes and shook my head. "He has the entire world on strings…"

"Dana is a formidable force, but we have the advantage for the moment," Tori said. "He's confused and does not know how we managed to get as far as we have. While we have that advantage, we need to use it."

"What are you thinking?" Griffin asked.

"I think we need to show ourselves again," Tori declared. "We need to show the people that we were not a fluke. We need to stoke the fire."

"Put Mykail out in the open again?" I asked, worried.

"We need to clarify the weapons aspect," Griffin said. "Most don't understand what we meant by saying we were weapons of the Commission. Mykail is the only visible proof…" Griffin looked at Tori. "Maybe we need to be the proof, as well."

"What do you mean?" Clark asked.

"We need to find a way to show people that the Commission has been altering humans. We need to prove our powers."

I had been dying with curiosity to know what everyone's different abilities were, but had thought it would have been rude to ask.

"How?" Josh questioned.

"Well, some will be more obvious than others," Griffin admitted. "But for others, like Tori, it will be more difficult to prove…"

"Well, what if instead of showing powers, everyone tells their stories?" I suggested.

"We can't be in one place long enough to do so." Tori shook her head. "We have to be quick."

"We can be in one place for a long time," I disagreed. "The internet. We've already been using it. There has to be a way for us to post videos of everyone telling their stories. It gives us a face, but keeps us directly out of harm's way."

"We have to be careful about that, too," Josh said. "We have to film outside of the fort."

"And away from any possible entrances," Tori added. "With technology, they could probably find where we were if we did anything in the fort. We can't risk it."

"I think next week, we should do the videos," Clark seconded. "Everyone can prepare their stories, and it can be the humans also, talking about the treatment they suffered with the Commission. We won't be able to send it out like the emails, we can't risk sneaking into the Censor Board again, but maybe the fort has something we can use to upload the videos."

"We have a few programmers," Tori said. "We'll see what they can accomplish."

"In the meantime," Griffin sighed, "we lie low."

Mark raised his hand, grabbing our attention. He turned to Josh and motioned a few things before Josh straightened.

"Oh, right," he nodded. "He was thinking that we could have Mykail appear a few times on his own."

"What do you mean?" I said nervously.

"Just quickly, enough to remind people that he has real wings," Josh explained. "Like fly through town and then disappear again."

I turned to Mark, who was already looking at me, waiting to see my reaction. I sighed heavily and my hands tightened around the blanket. I looked at the ground, turning the idea over in my head. I knew this was a critical time in our movement against the Commission and I wanted to trust the experiments with their ideas, but I was worried about Mykail being hurt or captured.

"Will you be sure he's safe?" I asked, looking at Mark.

He nodded, keeping eye contact, promising me.

* *** *

Friday, a large group on Massachusetts Avenue—where there was a large military base—in the North-Midwest Region in the city of Jefferson's Point was flooded with people, holding signs and demanding answers about the winged man at the Liberation Day Parade. Many were holding signs that demanded Dana show his face and explain what was happening in the Commission of the People.

The worry had died down at school, but at the end of the school day, something happened that I had never experienced before in my life.

It was twenty minutes before the end of the last class when the intercom system in the school rang out through the classrooms.

"Code Red. The school is currently in Code Red."

Everyone looked around worriedly, unsure of what the statement actually meant.

Our teacher blinked at the intercom box and then turned to the class.

"Okay, those in the back row, close the blinds. Everyone move to this corner of the room, sit on the floor and remain quiet."

Not believing what was happening, I hurried to the corner as our teacher locked the door and took a towel out of the storage cabinet, laying it across the threshold. I shared worried looks with my classmates, all of us jumping when the lights were turned off, the room lit only by the slats of sunlight barely visible through the gaps in the blinds.

Sitting in a confused huddle, most students pulled out their phones, searching social media and the news to find out what was going on outside that caused the Code Red. I watched my teacher move around the room, counting heads and going to her computer, submitting her attendance to the main office to account for who was in her class.

"Oh my God..." Madison, one of the girls who normally sat in the back of the room to sleep, gasped. Everyone turned. "The angel...he's back."

"What?" we all said simultaneously.

"Stay quiet," our teacher warned quietly.

"It says that the city is on lockdown because the angel was spotted flying around the downtown office buildings. Witnesses say that he was holding a red flag and had a banner behind him that said: 'Rally Against the Commission.'"

I was a little worried that two revolutionary activities in one day would send the country into dangerous panic—since the city was frightened enough to put the schools on lockdown—but I was also a little pleased to hear that everyone was calling Mykail the angel and not the monster or the weapon.

We were trying to make him our figurehead, and the way people perceived him worked to our advantage. I was trying to keep myself from smiling, but thinking about how Dana must be reacting to Mykail's sudden reappearance made me giggle. I tried to pass it off as a cough before people questioned my reaction.

"Do you think he's real?" one boy whispered.

"What do you mean? Of course he's real!" another groaned.

"I know that, moron, I mean…do you think that the Commission put wings on his back and made him into a weapon? Or do you think that the wings are fake?"

"They're real," one girl said strongly. "I was at the Liberation Day Parade and the way he was flying, it was like watching a bird. I don't think animatronics could make wings move that fluidly or allow him to fly as easily as he did."

"But…*how*?" one girl hissed.

"I'm thinking more about him as a person," another girl mused. "The group said to stop the torture of the Commission, so he was made this way against his will. That means that there's more of them, that the Commission has been making people into test subjects. Their guidelines state that they can do nothing but humanely treat their prisoners and return them to their native countries if it is applicable to the situation."

"Well, they're obviously violating those laws," one boy growled. "My grandmother always said that she knew the Commission of the People would get too powerful and try to take over the country one day."

"Are you part of the terrorist group?" Madison teased.

"No," the boy said. "But I don't disagree with what people are saying. Do we really still need the Commission?"

"What do you think, Commish Kid?" another boy snarled, glaring at me. I was startled by how quickly the conversation swung to me.

"What do you mean?"

"Do you think we need the Commission still?"

I looked at the expectant faces surrounding me, worried they would attack me if I did not give them the answer they wanted.

"To be honest, no," I whispered, pretending as though I didn't want anyone else to hear. Everyone leaned closer, interested. "I don't know if this is really something that's been going on in the Commission, but it would make sense. A lot of people, even in the Commission, don't know what Dana Christenson does."

"Really?" they gasped.

"We're forced to sign a non-disclosure agreement before we even enter the building. So, who knows who could have done this."

"Holy shit, that's scary…" one boy said. "Even some people in the Commission don't know?"

"So you don't know if the angel was really made by the Commission?" Madison pressed. I shook my head. I had, at least temporarily, cleared the names of some of the Commish Kids.

We were in Code Red for an hour. When we were finally released, there were people on their phones calling parents and friends, asking them what they knew. I did not call my parents. I went around the side of the school to see if Mark was waiting.

Clark was already at the car. He motioned me over and I jogged carefully across the icy asphalt.

"Are you alright?" he asked.

"I'm fine. You?"

"I'm fine." He opened the door for me, and I glanced briefly at Mark, who was still sitting in the driver's seat, watching both of us. I assumed from his presence that he had successfully kept Mykail safe and hid him at the fort again.

When I slid into the car, Mark reached back, handing me a business card. There was a scribbled message on the back.

Call Sean. #4.

"Is everything okay?" I asked worriedly. Mark nodded and smiled to reassure me.

Deciding to trust Mark despite my nervousness, I pulled out my phone and called Sean.

"Hello?"

"Hello, Sean, it's Lily Sandover," I greeted awkwardly.

"Oh, hello," Sean said. "So, you're with Mark. Good. I'm assuming you know what happened this afternoon?"

"Yes."

"We're putting the city on lockdown and searching for Mykail, so Dana wants you both to go to your homes and stay there. No one is allowed to leave their homes until we can be sure the city is secure."

"Wait, really?"

"Yes, and, obviously, we need Mark, so can you tell Clark that I'll be borrowing him for the rest of the day?" Sean asked.

"Um…sure," I agreed. "Is it that serious?"

"The people are frightened," Sean admitted. "We're trying to find him quickly. If you hear anything, let us know."

I hesitated, surprised and worried. Sensing my concern, Sean sighed on the other end of the call.

"I know Dana thinks that you're somehow behind all this but, call me old-fashioned, I believe in innocent until proven guilty."

Again, I was stumped at how such a caring person could be working for Dana.

"Will you tell Clark?" Sean asked.

"Yes, I will."

"Thank you."

"And Sean?" I started. The words stuck in my throat. I felt extremely guilty about the lie I was about to tell. "If I hear or see anything, I'll call you."

"Thank you, Lily," Sean said, a smile in his voice. "Have a good afternoon."

"You, too," I said mechanically. "Bye."

I hung up the phone and turned to Clark, trying to breathe around the tightness of my ribs.

"What did he say?"

"We're supposed to go home and not leave. They're searching the city. And they need Mark, so Sean says he's borrowing him for the rest of the day," I relayed. Mark started driving. I leaned forward. "Hey, are you sure everything's okay?"

Mark nodded with a smile and gave me a thumbs-up. I decided, with how cautious Mark was, things had to be alright if he was reassuring me.

I was surprised to see my parents waiting at home for me. They asked if I was alright, and then would not let me escape to my room, telling me to do my homework in the living room. They had closed all the windows and locked the doors, as the news was telling everyone to do until the Central had declared the city safe. There was reluctance from the military to help in securing the city and finding Mykail because many of the lower level men and women were sympathetic with the growing rebellion, and that slowed progress.

What really made me smile was when there was a knock on our door and we saw that someone had been sent to search our house.

"Oh...come in, please," my mother said, motioning the two suit-clad men inside. They stepped in and removed their glasses. I tried not to smile at the familiar faces of Hiroki and Minsoo.

"We're here for search," Hiroki said with a fake, thick accent.

"Please, go ahead," my mother agreed, motioning them further into the house. They walked through the house, even looking in closets and pantries as we remained in the living room for them to deem the house safe.

"The Eight Group is checking the Commission houses?" I asked as casually as I could manage.

"Makes sense," my father said. "After all, they would not be surprised at the experiments in everyone's homes."

"Every home but ours," my mother sighed. "I hope they catch him soon, before this gets out of hand."

"Mom…if they catch him, Dana will kill him."

"At this point, it's understandable. It'd be better if they kill him on camera to prove that he's gone. Maybe that will calm people down."

"How can you say that?" I gasped.

"I cared about him just as much as you did," my mother defended.

I sincerely doubt that… I barely managed not to say.

"But he is dangerous to the stability of America. And he betrayed us. He betrayed our trust. We have to look at the bigger picture."

I bit my tongue hard enough to taste blood.

Our house was cleared and Hiroki and Minsoo left. The city was later deemed safe, though no one had found Mykail.

The following day was the Commission meeting.

As it had been the last few times, there was a lot of talk about how the "situation" needed to be contained. Dana stood at the front of the room and listened to the babble for over an hour before he finally spoke.

"Alright, I have heard what you have to say, now let me tell you what we are going to do," he started. "Right now, we will admit to looking at the possibility of improving human strength, but nothing more. We will state that this information was in the most basic state and we had not started testing, but somehow the information leaked, and the terrorist group used that to formulate an attack on us.

"As for Mykail, I understand the concern and I agree that we need to catch him as soon as possible. But as far as the Commission is concerned, we have absolutely no idea where he came from," he continued with a sharp tone. "We will only react to him when he appears publicly. We will not search for him in ways that the public can notice. We will shrug and say we have no idea where he came from, but we will not rush to cover anything up. A hurried response will lend credibility to the idea that we created him."

Dana sighed.

"There are many foreign nations getting nervous. They are watching us very carefully. There are many that know of our program and are beginning to see a threat to their credibility as leaders. As you know, we have sold many of our successes to foreign dignitaries and that makes them conspirators. We do not need an international scandal so near the completion of the Machine of Neutralization project."

My stomach flipped. Somehow, I had completely forgotten about Eina.

"Sir," one of the men in the front called, "if you plan to mass-produce the Machine of Neutralization, how can you allow the people to know that we were only in the beginning stages of such a project?"

Dana glanced at me and my blood ran cold. There was something devious and dangerous in the eyes of the leader of the Commission of the People.

"I'm working on that," he said. "I have an idea, but we will see if I even need to use it."

* *** *

Due to the panic of the city, Mark refused to take us to the fort on Sunday. While I didn't blame him, I was upset that I would not get to see Mykail. Instead, I stayed home and caught up on homework, thinking about other things the rebellion needed to accomplish. I felt as though the revolution was teetering on a cliff. The frightening thing was I knew where it was going...

I saw the bloodshed coming at me rapidly. I knew things were going to get violent and all I could think about was the way water spilled from a ruptured jug. It would only take one bullet and we would be at war with Central...in a bloodbath with Dana Christenson.

I was standing there, looking at it just before it was about to begin. I could feel the oncoming war in my bones.

That night, I dreamt I was in the echoing, cavernous room with the gun laying on the table in front of me. Dana was on the other side of the table, a gun already in his hand, smiling darkly. I turned briefly to see Mark, Griffin, Tori, Clark, Mykail, and hundreds of others behind me. I turned back to Dana, confident in my army.

Dana tapped the gun's handle with his forefinger, smiling.

"Well?"

I picked up the gun, put it together as I had the previous week, and pointed it at him.

"I think it's only fair that you understand the concept of the game," he told me. "You move your pieces, and I'll move mine. You shoot me, and I'll shoot you."

I aimed at his heart and pulled the trigger. The gun had no recoil, and the bullet soared through Dana's chest, causing his shoulder to fall back with the force of the blow. But he straightened and raised his gun.

"My turn."

The gunshot was loud and I flinched. The bullet hit me. I felt the cold air that soared through my chest, but I did not fall. Blinking, I turned and saw Griffin lying dead behind me. The others were staring ahead, unblinking, as though Griffin had not died at all.

Frightened, I turned back to Dana and shot the gun as many times as I could, hitting him, knowing I needed to kill him before he killed anyone else. His body jerked and jolted as it was riddled with bullets, but he remained standing, smiling darkly, unable to fall, too strong and deeply rooted.

When the clip was empty, I pulled the trigger uselessly as I saw Dana raise his arm to aim at me.

The cold air hit my body like a train as he fired bullets with the same rapid fire. I felt my body move, shivering and shaking from the cold, but I did not fall, either. There was not enough force to push me down completely.

When he stopped firing, I was terrified to turn around.

As much as I screamed at myself not to, I turned.

The bodies littered the floor of the room, soaking the cold concrete in blood as it eased out their wounds. The ungraceful heap of mangled limbs and glassy eyes made my panic swell.

"What a mess you made…" Dana tutted.

I jolted awake, trying to find my breath and come back to reality. Every time I blinked, I saw the dead bodies. In a panic, I leapt out of bed and turned my lights on, looking around the room frantically.

In that frantic and terrified moment, I wanted to stop the revolution.

Throughout Monday, I replayed the dream, trying to convince myself that it was just a nightmare and not a premonition. When I heard that Maryland-Tuckett University in the Western Region, a school mostly dedicated to humanitarian efforts and aid to Third World countries, had called the Commission out on inhumane treatment and becoming the next death concentration camp, I realized the ball was rolling too fast to be stopped.

I was fearful of what I had set in motion.

I tried to block out the chatter around school about Mykail and Maryland-Tuckett University calling for investigation into the health and care of the criminals the Commission kept, but every time I heard snippets of the conversations, I saw another dead body. It was another strike against Dana, and he was going to strike back soon enough, like a taunted predator.

That was the first day I felt that we were already at war.

At the end of the day, I was exhausted and worried about the rapid progression of events. Clark noticed, but he seemed to be feeling the same way. We did not speak as we were driven to the Commission, and the stoic Mark did not provide any insight into how he was feeling about the growing tension.

We went through Commission security silently and got into the elevator without a word.

However, when the doors opened, instead of being greeted by the normal silence of the Commission of the People, we heard chatter. Mark was just as surprised as us. He carefully stepped out of the elevator, his hand at his hip to grab his gun if necessary.

Carefully opening the door to the meeting room, all three of us were surprised by the sight.

The room was full of people, men and women dressed professionally and all with an intimidating air about them. On one side of the room there were two large groups of men and women donning military uniforms, decorated with medals and ribbons, their hair short and slicked back. Through the rest of the room, there were people of many different races, all with translators and advisors at their shoulders. There were foreign ambassadors and even a few foreign leaders I recognized, such as the Prime Minister of France, and the President of the Korean Peninsula.

And there was Dana, standing at the front of the room with Sean stationed behind him. Dana saw us and grinned. His gaze caught the attention of everyone in the room, who silenced and turned.

It felt as though the whole world was staring at us.

"Ah, Little Lily and the gang," Dana said in a chastising tone. "My apologies, I guess I should have told you that I was having a meeting today and that you didn't need to be here. Sorry about that. Mark, take them home."

Mark hesitated only a moment before he bowed at the waist and ushered us backward, closing the door to the meeting room.

Nausea overwhelmed me. The miscommunication had not been accidental. Dana was flaunting to me that he was already planning his next move against me.

Chapter Sixty

The following day, Carolina High School in the South-East Region organized a walkout, claiming that they were refusing to learn material approved from the Commission of the People when the Commission was torturing the people they were capturing.

There were whispers around our school of doing the same thing.

Again, it felt as though everything was going too fast.

I was having nightmares about people dying, about our revolution failing and Dana somehow winning in the end. I tried to tell myself they were only dreams. Besides, that same Tuesday, I had other things to worry about.

Saying I was going on a date with Clark, I left the house, running away after my mother started talking about condoms and safe sex. Knowing she thought I was having sex with Clark made me cringe. Then I blushed because of the sex I had been having with Mykail *without* protection.

Mark took both Clark and I to the agreed abandoned warehouse by public transportation, walking us from the bus stop to the location. I vaguely remembered how to get to the factory we had seen when trying to decide where to base our operation. We decided to complete our project in the basement so that any lights through the broken windows would not attract attention.

By the time the three of us got to the basement, Peter, a medical school dropout, and Bethany, an art student, had set up the lights and camera facing a chair. Tori and Griffin were there as well and greeted us warmly next to Hiroki, Ichiro, Rin, and Minsoo. It had been a while since I had seen some of the members of the Eight Group, so I hugged all of them.

Griffin was the first to sit in the rickety chair and speak to the camera. Everyone present watched quietly, listening to his story once again. Griffin also told the camera what his abilities were. As far as I could tell, he was the perfect fighter. He had enough strength to lift cars with ease and even throw them. He had reflexes fast enough to avoid most direct attacks and was able to see with great precision in the dark. His hearing was superb and his aim was also impressive. He only needed to sleep for about an hour a night and did not need as much food or water to stay in peak condition. He was an ultimate warrior.

Griffin also said that he had metallic plates under his chest that expanded and contracted with his ribs and were bulletproof to anything but a straight shot, protecting most of his vital organs.

When he was finished explaining, removed his shirt, turning sideways and taking a deep breath, causing his chest to expand, showing the plates move under his skin, protruding to make his ribcage look like slats on a shutter. I stared at the display unblinkingly until Griffin let out his breath and replaced his shirt.

After Griffin, Tori told her story and explained her abilities.

She had all the capabilities Griffin had, only she seemed like the improved version, with metal plates along other vital points and the ability to operate for days at a time without sleep. She was also smaller and could be hidden more easily than the large Griffin. She was the perfect, manufactured soldier, particularly since she did not need a gun to fire a bullet at the speed of a gun. She had enough muscle power in her hands to shoot a bullet with her fingers, something she proved on camera.

When Griffin and Tori were finished, Peter and Bethany glanced at their list, asking for the next few people. Rin and Minsoo went to gather them, while Mark and Clark joined Griffin and Tori to discuss something. Instead of following them, I turned to Hiroki and Ichiro.

"How have you been?"

"Busy," Hiroki laughed. "But good. You?"

"Eh, haven't been sleeping well, but that's to be expected, I guess." I shrugged, downplaying my nightmares. "So…um, do you guys need to sleep? And eat?"

"Yes," Hiroki said. "I think we all need about one or two hours of sleep, but we don't need to eat as much. Maybe once a day."

"Has Mark been taking care of himself?" I pressed. "I don't want you to lie for him. I feel like he's the type that would ignore sleeping and eating."

Hiroki laughed. "Don't worry, we watch out for him," he assured. "And I know you sometimes think that Mark is being a little too careful and paranoid, but trust him. He knows what he's doing."

"He learned his lesson…" Ichiro mumbled with a snort.

Startled by the icy tone, I straightened. Hiroki rounding angrily on Ichiro and scolded him in their native tongue, though Ichiro looked away, ignoring Hiroki.

"What does that mean?" I asked worriedly.

This time Hiroki smacked Ichiro on the back of the head, causing the other member of the Eight Group to let out a whine and say something back to Hiroki, who replied sharply. Ichiro bowed his head before walking away. The other member of the Eight Group sighed heavily.

"Sorry, he's just..." Hiroki shook his head again. "I think the phrase is 'he's just like that.'"

"It's fine, but..." I looked back to see Mark still with Griffin and the others. "What did he mean? Did Mark get in trouble?"

"Yes...but he meant...well, we all learned our lesson," Hiroki said. "This isn't the first time Hyunwoo has gone against Dana. He knows better now how to be careful."

"You mean when he got his voice..." I did not complete the sentence. I glanced back at the leader of the Eight Group. "Why would Dana mutilate him like that?"

"He didn't just mutilate him," Hiroki whispered. "Hyunwoo was the one who organized the experiments to rise up against Dana four years ago. We got close enough for Hyunwoo to attack. He tried to kill Dana. But there were not enough of us, and we tried to take over the Commission from the inside, which failed...Hyunwoo is the one who paid for it."

Hiroki took a deep breath and looked at the ground, leaning against the wall behind him.

"Dana didn't just take his voice...he *humiliated* him. He broke him down and made us watch as punishment. Dana had the scientists beat Hyunwoo with pipes before he was on the table...they waited for him to stand before beating him down again until...until he just couldn't get up anymore..." Hiroki's voice was tight with pain and I could tell by the look in his eyes that he was reliving the experience as he recounted the story. "And every time we would look away, Dana would shock us and make us look."

My hand was already at my mouth, tears blurring my vision.

"When Hyunwoo couldn't get up anymore, they put him on the table, put his head in a vice, and burned his face. Dana still wanted Hyunwoo to be able to work after the torture, so they didn't hurt his eyes...instead they put the cigarettes in his mouth and on his tongue, they made him swallow them. Then they urinated on him. We had to watch this happen...there was nothing we could do." Hiroki swallowed hard and lifted a hand to wipe away the tears. "They laughed when he vomited...they teased him when he was screaming as they started cutting into his neck without numbing him...the things that they did to him...they weren't just taking his voice, they were breaking him."

Trying to hold my own tears back, I turned to look at Mark once again. He was listening very intently to what Tori was saying, completely unaware that I was learning of the horrific torture that left him without a voice.

"But they didn't break him..." I barely managed to choke.

"They almost did," Hiroki disagreed. "When he was recuperating, he wouldn't move, he wouldn't look at anyone…he wasted away in that cell, no matter how we tried to reach him." Hiroki took a deep breath. "But, as always, Woobin understood him and finally got through to him, helped him stand up again. Hyunwoo finally came back to us…and even after all that he's fighting."

Hiroki drew in a deep breath.

"Every time I think about what we want to accomplish and think it's too much, or that I need to give up, I remember what Hyunwoo endured, and how he still is turning to spit in Dana's face." He laughed. "Hyunwoo was always quiet and calm…but when you get him angry, he is a force of nature."

"What did Josh say to him?" I asked. The experiment shrugged.

"I don't know. Hyunwoo has…always been a little strange, even when we were growing up. Not in a bad way, he was just different. The only one who ever understood him was Woobin. They lived in houses next to one another, so they spent more time with one another than with the rest of us. Woobin was always at Hyunwoo's house because his own father kept trying to kill him. It was safer with Hyunwoo."

"*What*? Why?" I gasped, horrified.

"Woobin was another mouth to feed," Hiroki said. "When you're a hidden society like we were, children are not a blessing. They're dangerous to the safety of the community and to resources. So, Woobin spent time with Hyunwoo to escape his father. That's why they're so close. They always have been."

"Where is Josh now?"

"He should be here soon," Hiroki answered. "Lily," he called my attention, "Hyunwoo would not want you to know that story about his torture. I only told you because I think it's important for you to understand that Mark has learned the hard way, and you can trust him to be very careful. Trust his judgment and understand where it's coming from."

I sighed.

"The truth is, lately…I've been thinking that what we're doing is wrong…that it's going to get people killed and that it's not worth it," I murmured. "I wanted to talk to Mark about it, but he's sacrificed so much for this."

"Just because he's invested in this revolution doesn't mean you can't talk to him," Hiroki chuckled.

"I know…but…" I thought for a moment before lowering my voice. "A lot of this is my doing, my idea…and I don't want everyone to know that I'm having second thoughts. And talking to Mark alone, I think, distresses him because he can't converse easily."

Hiroki nodded slowly. "He can't even talk to Eun and I know that's devastating to him."

I hesitated. "Does he think we can win?"

Hiroki was silent for a long moment.

"If I had to take a guess," he finally said after my stomach had tied itself into knots, "if he didn't think we had a good chance, he wouldn't be doing this right now."

The door at the top of the basement stairs opened and Minsoo and Rin descended into the room with Sophia and Alexandra. Tagging behind the entire group was another familiar face.

"Look who we found!" Rin laughed.

"Josh!" Tori greeted. I also tried to smile, but I was still rattled by the story of Mark's torment. Josh waved to everyone with a big smile and when he saw me, his grin widened and he came over to us first.

"Hey, Lily," he said, hugging me around the shoulders with one arm. I smiled, trying to swallow the tight ball in my throat. "How are you?"

"Okay, you?"

"...fine. You don't sound okay." He pulled away and turned to face me fully. I tried to hide my face. "Are you crying?"

"No."

"You look like it," he said. He looked between me and Hiroki. "What is it?"

Hiroki said something I could not understand and Josh hesitated before turning back to me.

"Oh..." he whispered. "Don't tell him that you know," Josh said, his hand tightening on my shoulder. I shook my head and sniffed, trying desperately to keep the tears from overwhelming me. Josh rubbed my shoulder.

"I knew it was bad...but...I never thought..." Once again, I sniffed and swallowed hard. Josh hugged me again.

"It's okay," he said, his hand rubbing my back. "It's over. He's alright."

"How did you...what did you say to him?" I asked, backing away to look at Josh. The experiment sighed, making a face, trying to figure out how to explain.

"Hyunwoo is...he's really simple in a complicated way," Josh started, struggling with the words. "That was the first time he was...not good anymore." He turned to Hiroki, frustrated, speaking quickly.

"Oh. He wasn't able to help anyone. He was the one needing help."

"He had to think about himself," Josh continued. "He always thought about himself by how he helped others. But then he was…" Josh was at a loss for words.

"Helpless?" I whispered. Mark's best friend nodded, his eyes sad.

"He thought he had failed everyone," he added. "And he thought we would be angry with him."

"But, he's your leader. Surely he knew that you wouldn't do that to him," I said.

"He is our leader, but only because we follow him," Hiroki agreed.

"Hyunwoo never said 'I am your leader.' He just had ideas and the brains to make them work," Josh elaborated. "And he put everyone before him. He did not understand that we had to take care of him when he was hurt, and it was too much for him. He wouldn't let anyone in."

"Hiroki said that you guys watch out for him," I said. "You make sure he eats and sleeps."

Josh nodded. "That's why I'm here. I brought food." He looked at me with his eyebrows high. "Are you hungry?"

"No, thank you."

"Are you sure? There's a lot."

"I'm sure."

Josh hugged me once more and then turned, calling to Mark, who turned quickly and followed his friend up the stairs.

While I was pleased to hear about the way the others of the Eight Group took care of Mark, my stomach was still churning. As Sophia began filming her message, my brain detached and I thought about Mark being beaten with pipes, humiliated and burned, screaming in pain as his throat was sliced open. The tears were burning my eyes again. While a part of me was strengthened by realizing that Mark had endured the torment and was still fighting, a bigger part of me was terrified. Hearing the brutality used in torturing Mark made the reality of Dana's power that much stronger. Someone who I thought could never be taken down, could never break, had been beaten and humiliated to the point of almost giving up on life, and we were poking at that same volatile creature that had already caused so much damage.

More than before, I was convinced we needed to stop what we were doing.

I tried to keep a smile on my face and stay strong in front of everyone. I laughed at Josh teasing the others to get the emotions in their voice, telling everyone to act like puppies looking for homes. I forced a smile every time Griffin and Tori looked at me with a pleased grin at our progress. I spoke with Clark about how we were going to circulate the videos. But my head was a mess of scattered and frightened thoughts, contemplating calling off the revolution.

* *** *

The following morning, during rush hour to school, I was shocked by the city coming to a dead halt when Mykail was spotted once again. This time with a banner reading "watch our stories."

Through the three-hour delay at school, I had nothing to do but sit in the school hallway and fume. One week previous, I would have been thrilled at how much attention we were getting, but with my current mindset, I was furious. It was the first time I found myself angry at Mark. I was upset that he would put Mykail in immediate danger once again, so soon after his other appearance. I was upset that he was causing the ball to roll faster and bring the reality of our revolution closer.

My lack of sleep and frightened thoughts caused my emotions to overpower rational thought and made me forget that I had agreed to the plan with Mykail the previous evening.

As the halls began filling, chatter of the angel and questions from the students filled my ears, echoing in the large hallways and amplifying the noise. I angrily stormed to one of the courtyards, ignoring how cold it was and covered my ears, crouching to the ground and trying to control my breathing. Everything was spinning out of control, as if I was already surrounded by gunshots and the groans of my dying friends.

I was swimming in thoughts of other options. I could find a way to sneak the experiments and freed humans over the southern border, where they might be able to find a way to live their lives. Perhaps I could go to Dana and admit my fault, causing him to take me in and leave the others alone. I felt trapped, frightened, and that I was about to lose my grip on reality. I had created a movement that was too big to control, and it was growing bigger by the day.

I did not talk to Mark that afternoon but I could tell he was worried. Even through his glasses as he drove us to the Commission after school, I could see him glancing at me through the rearview mirror. I tried to assure Clark that I was just catching a cold and had a headache, which was a stupid excuse for my weird behavior.

The Commission was a mess when we showed up.

Office aids were running around the halls, yelling at one another to call different people and different countries, frantic. I blinked at the chaos, stupefied.

"What the hell?" Clark hissed.

Mark placed a hand on both of our shoulders and nodded once before walking down the hall, telling us silently that he was going to gather information.

Listening to the rarely-seen office personnel yelling, we found a conference room and sat, looking at one another worriedly, knowing it could not have been Mykail's appearance alone that caused such a racket.

With nervousness tying our insides into knots, we waited for Mark to return.

For two hours, we waited. The longer we waited, the more nervous we became. We dared not discuss what could have happened, but Clark and I shared nervous glances, showing that both of our imaginations were working overtime forming possibilities.

Finally, Mark returned, but he remained outside the door, staring up into the corner of the room from the glass panel in the door.

I glanced in the same direction and saw the camera, so I stretched, pretending that I was rolling my neck around so as not to appear as though I was also watching the camera.

For three agonizing minutes, Mark waited outside.

When he was sure it was safe, he walked in. As soon as he opened the door, I looked back at the camera to see the dim red light was off.

Mark extended a hand-written note to us.

"The Hampshire Peace Fund lost 96% of their backers because it was controlled through the Commission. Now, thirty-four programs in other countries have no funding. The Commission is trying to find a way to come up with the deficit without stopping the programs which would cause international panic."

I passed the paper to Clark as I turned to the leader of the Eight Group.

"Does this have to do with the rebellion?" I whispered. Mark nodded once and took the paper back from Clark before scurrying out of the room and out of sight.

I turned to Clark.

"The Hampshire Peace Fund?" I whispered. "I didn't know the Commission controlled them."

"All the money has to pass through the Commission to get to other countries. The Commission just monitors how the money is distributed based on need," Clark elaborated. "This is bad. If those programs are cut, the international community will get even more nervous."

"Does that mean that the rebellion could have international support?"

Clark shrugged. "Unlikely, but I guess it's possible."

On our way home, we swung by a café where Clark and I got a coffee for appearances and went to the table in the corner, to join Melody and Dean.

"Hey!" Melody smiled broadly. "What are you two doing here?"

"Just getting something warm to drink," Clark laughed. "It's freezing outside."

"Come sit down," Melody beckoned.

I sat awkwardly, trying to keep my head on straight as I thought about the Hampshire Peace Fund, wondering who else knew about the financial crisis.

"Are you ready for that test in Angermann's class?" Dean groaned, nudging Clark. Clark groaned and rolled his eyes.

"Hell no."

"I borrowed Peter's notes. Do you want to look them over?" Melody asked, reaching into her bag and pulling out a notebook. My stomach flipped, knowing that the 'notes' were actually statistics of who had seen the videos. We had posted twenty-three videos the previous night after Ben, Paula, and Melody programmed over one hundred accounts and uploaded all the videos to each of the accounts from government computers. Melody had skipped school to stay in the fort and monitor the views on the videos.

"Sure, thanks," Clark said, sounding nervous.

Melody opened the notebook and turned to the correct page, showing it to both of us. We leaned over the paper and scanned the numbers.

Many of the videos already had over forty thousand views. All but three of the videos had been downloaded twenty thousand times and re-uploaded about four hundred times.

We're doomed... was my initial response.

"Wow, Peter takes some really good notes," Clark chuckled.

"You can borrow them, if you want," Melody assured. "Feel free to mark all over them, as well."

I carefully ripped out the page, knowing that Mark had asked to see the statistics. I was half-tempted to keep the statistics away from him out of spite. I had no logical reason to be angry at Mark, but I was worried and confused and that was quickly turning into anger at the man who was currently running everything.

I handed the stats to Clark instead, allowing him to give them to Mark when we got in the car.

Mark glanced over them with a smile on his face before driving me home, being sure to burn the paper and push it into the storm drain when the numbers were unintelligible.

The following day, my body was screaming with cramps as my period took its harsh toll. I had never had difficult periods, but I immediately understood why other girls complained so much. I guessed that stress had something to do with the cramps, but all it did was irritate me more when I had to go to the bathroom after every class.

During lunch, I was hit with nausea and dizziness, so I went to the bathroom and sat in one of the stalls, cringing, waiting for the painkillers to take effect. Unfortunately, in that quiet room, there was nothing I could do but stew.

I knew I needed to speak to Mark more than anyone. Mark was running the operations outside the fort while the experiments remained hidden as the hype around their videos skyrocketed. I was certain that if I told Mark that I thought we should stop the revolution and he agreed, we could all wait for the fuss to die down before sneaking everyone over the border and going back to our lives as though nothing happened.

I was losing sight of what had made me so angry against the Commission. There were so many reasons I could think of, but nothing held the same power anymore. Everything just felt dangerous, unnecessary and, overall, pointless. I was distressed by my sudden change in demeanor, but I was frightened by the idea of so many people dying because we decided that we did not like what the Commission did to criminals.

I wanted to smack myself and scream that many of the people we had broken out were not actually criminals, but victims of circumstance or even falsely accused. While those thoughts were present, they were suppressed, muted by the storm of fear ruling my mind.

I groaned and stood, grabbing my backpack and walking out of the stall, stepping to the sink and washing my hands, trying to ignore the pangs in my abdomen.

The door opened and another girl entered the bathroom. I barely knew her from my biology class, only knowing that she sat in the front and annoyed everyone with her opinionated demeanor.

Emily stopped when she saw me and I glanced at her through the mirror.

"Lily," she said, walking to the sink next to me.

"Hello, Emily," I said, my eyes dropping to my hands.

"Did you see the videos? The ones about the experiments of the Commission?"

"Yeah, I saw them," I said, walking to the paper towel dispenser.

"Well?"

"Well what?"

"What do you have to say about them?" Emily demanded. "You're in the Commission, so you know if it's true or not, but you're not saying anything."

My fear became more acute. Every instinct was telling me to get out of the bathroom.

"Look, I don't know everything that happens in the Commission, and even what I do know I can't talk about. They make us sign an NDA."

"When the security of the nation is at risk, that shouldn't stop you from coming forward," Emily growled. "Tell me, is it true that the Commission is making weapons to take over the country?"

"I'm sorry, I can't say," I said, throwing the paper towel in the trash before starting to leave.

I was violently pulled by my backpack. I lost my balance and fell heavily to the tile floor, jarring my back.

"No, no," Emily said darkly, looming over me. "You don't get off that easy."

"What the *fuck*, Emily?!" I snapped, scrambling to my feet.

"It's about time you fuckers in the Commission give us answers," Emily snarled. "There is a threat of a civil war and you all are avoiding answering."

"We *can't* answer," I repeated sharply. "I told you. We signed an NDA."

Emily smacked me. With how angry I was, I wasted no time smacking her back. She stumbled, grabbing my hair and pulling, trying to drag me to the ground. I grabbed her shoulders with a shout of pain and tried to push her into the wall.

We both jolted when her back hit the tile wall and a thud resonated from where her head connected.

She released my hair but her hands went around my neck, turning us both and slamming me into the side of the sinks. Ignoring the pain, I lifted my knee into her stomach.

Emily let out a choked gasp and curled forward, grabbing her stomach. I stood in front of her, my breath short from anger. She glared, cringing around her injury, before she grabbed the front of my uniform blazer, pulling it sharply and causing one of the buttons to snap off. I was pulled toward the nearest stall, stumbling in, but managing to catch myself on the back of the toilet, turning around quickly and slamming the door into Emily's face as she tried to come after me.

She fell backwards and I pinned her down, though her nails began scratching at my face and neck, creating hot lines of pain across my skin as I tried to control her flailing arms. Finally managing to scratch me near my eye, she flipped us so I was laying on my back on the floor with her on top of me. She slammed her hips against my stomach and knocked the breath out of me.

"Just fucking tell the truth!" she demanded, backhanding me once before her hand closed around my throat.

"Okay, okay, okay," I gasped. "Yes, the Commission is making weapons, but Dana is watching all of us really closely, so we can't say anything or he will kill us."

Emily released my neck, though she remained on my stomach, making catching my breath an arduous task.

"Why not tell someone? I mean, he can't do anything if the public knows," Emily said, perplexed. I wanted to smack her and scream at her to get off of me and that she didn't know anything about Dana. I heaved a few breaths and closed my eyes.

"We're trying…the rebellion, it's organized by members of the Commission…but Dana doesn't know that, yet. If we tell anyone before we have support, he'll kill us all…then he'll just continue to do what he's doing now…"

Emily was still, thinking the information over.

"Emily…get off me…"

"Oh, sorry," she said, scrambling away. I coughed and turned on my side, ignoring my disgust at being on the bathroom floor as I struggled to breathe.

"Are you telling the truth?" Emily asked suspiciously.

"Yes," I said. "Please, *please*, don't say anything. Try and tell the others to stop attacking the Commish Kids. They're all helping, but we need to stay hidden, or Dana *will* kill us."

"But…what are you planning?"

"I don't know, we're still working on that," I half-lied. "What has everyone been saying about the rebellion? Are they in favor?"

"If what you're saying is true," she said. "Most don't know if they can believe it, though."

"Yeah, I wouldn't have believed it either if I hadn't seen it," I agreed, my diaphragm trying to resume the function for breathing. "You can't breathe a word of this."

"But…what if people want to help?"

"People want to help?"

"Yes," she said. "I've already heard a bunch of people talk about sending messages to the rebellion pledging their support and asking what they can do to help. If they knew that it was really the Commish Kids, then—"

"No, Emily, *no*," I snapped. "You have no idea what Dana is like."

"Dana Christenson?"

"Who else?" I growled. "He has already threatened to take everyone in and turn them into weapons. No one can know, yet."

"But people want to help. *I* want to help."

"Well…" I sighed, not sure what to tell her, particularly since I had been spending the better part of the week thinking about ways to *stop* the revolution. "You know Clark?"

"Clark Markus? The little dorky kid with the glasses?" I barely suppressed my wince at the description.

"Yeah, him," I said. "Talk to him. Tell him I sent you to talk to him but tell no one else. We have to figure out how to safely involve other people who aren't inside the Commission."

"Okay," Emily agreed. "You have a lot of support, trust me."

"Yeah…I'll keep that in mind…" I groaned, rubbing my throbbing face.

Chapter Sixty-One

Mark looked as though he was about to have a heart attack when he saw me walk to the car that afternoon. Everyone had been fussing over me, asking me what had happened to my face. I told them that I got into a little fight with someone and that I was alright. No one really believed me and Becca and Jill almost dragged me to the nurse, though I adamantly refused.

Mark, on the other hand, was not as easily convinced.

When we got to the Commission, he led us to a conference room, but as soon as I set my bags down, trying to hide my wince, Mark's hand was around my wrist. I jerked it from his grasp, angry at him for no reason I could logically explain. He hesitated, staring at me with a confused and worried expression before he held his hand out.

I did not take it.

"I'm fine, Mark," I insisted sharply.

He shook his head, and turned his hand over so his palm was facing down, beckoning me to follow. I rolled my eyes but followed, hoping he would at least lead me to some painkillers, which I would not have refused.

I trailed behind him to the empty break room. Mark pulled out one of the table chairs before grabbing a first aid kit. I listened to him rifle around a drawer before returning to the table and sitting in front of me, finding an antiseptic wipe and bringing it close to my neck.

I backed away and glared. He stopped immediately and shied away, confused and upset by my response.

"I said I was fine, Mark."

For several long moments, we stared at one another. He set the white cloth down and stood, motioning for me to wait as he left the room. I rolled my eyes, angry, turning my attention to the first aid kit, sifting through the contents for painkillers.

To my luck, at the bottom, there was a package of two small pills marked "Painkillers." I tore open the package, gathered the two pills in my palm, and put them in my mouth, walking to the sink and dipping my mouth under the faucet, taking a few sips of water to down the medicine.

As I was wiping my mouth dry, the door opened and a familiar face entered the room in front of Mark.

"Miss Sandover?" Sean asked, concerned. "What happened to you?"

"Nothing," I assured, trying not to glare at Mark for bringing Sean. The head of security walked to me and lifted a hand to take my chin, moving my head around to see the scratches across my face and neck.

"You were obviously in a fight," he said. "Here, sit down."

Throwing a quick glare at Mark, I sat. Sean looked over the first aid kit already on the table and then looked between Mark and me.

"Why didn't you let Mark treat you?"

I did not answer, dropping my head. There was a pang of guilt about my idiotic behavior. But every time I saw Mark, I was reminded of my insecurities and my desperate need to tell him how I felt. Being mad at him and keeping him at a distance was easier. I barely looked at Mark, who had his hands folded in front of him, his eyes focused on the ground, clearly distressed about being unable to ask what was wrong.

Sean grabbed the antiseptic wipe, lifting it to my face as I cringed away from the sting.

"He might seem a little intense, but he's really quite gentle," Sean said. "And he knows what he's doing."

"I know…"

"Besides, he cares about you." Sean gently dabbed close to the scratch that had barely passed under my eye. I flinched. "When he can't help you, he gets distressed."

I remained silent.

Sean continued to clean the cuts around my face and neck as my gaze remained locked on my lap, feeling horrible in many different capacities.

"Was there just a lot of scratching and hair pulling?" Sean tried to tease. I shook my head. "What else?"

"She slammed me into the sink, and she sat on me so my stomach really hurts."

"Okay, stand up for me," Sean instructed, standing as well. When I was on my feet, he gently touched my stomach, feeling where I was tender before moving to my back, poking and prodding my ribs and spine. I hissed in pain and tried to move away from his hands.

"When your bruises heal, it would not be a bad idea to see a chiropractor, but it doesn't seem like anything is wrong internally. Just take painkillers and try to avoid heavy exercise," Sean suggested. "Of course, if the pain gets worse, go to the hospital immediately."

Sean rifled through the few remaining packages in the first aid kit.

"Did you already take something for the pain?"

"Yeah."

"Good."

817

"Thanks, Sean," I said, watching him clean up. "But...shouldn't you be with Dana?"

"Believe me, it's nice to get away for a while," Sean grumbled. "He's in a weird mood. I haven't seen him like this before."

"Like what?"

Sean sighed and shook his head.

"It's hard to explain unless you've known Dana for a long time," he evaded. He fell silent for several moments before turning to me, surprised that I was still waiting for an answer. "What?"

"Are you going to elaborate?"

"I don't think it's a good idea..." he admitted, closing the first aid kit and replacing it in the drawer.

"Why?"

Sean placed both hands on the counter and hung his head. He finally turned to look over his shoulder.

"Because I don't want to frighten you or start any rumors," he said. "I'm with Dana for at least twelve hours every day. Sometimes...I think I'm just a little hyper-sensitive to him. I'm sure I'm over-thinking—"

"Sean...you're scaring me more," I laughed brokenly. "Do you think Dana's about to do something drastic?"

"Always." Sean barked a laugh. He turned around and leaned on the counter, looking at the floor. "Remember something, Miss Sandover, he was tested on. He was made into a weapon. He has an instinct in him that most of us would never have." He looked at Mark. "It's a calculating, manipulative, and dark nature," he mused. Mark's eyes were wide with confusion. I wondered how he could keep that expression while knowing exactly what Sean was talking about, implying Mark understood that same weapon instinct. "Down here, Dana is nothing more than an animal in a cage. This whole thing...it's like someone left the cage door open and he's finally allowed to hunt. He's...he's acting like he's in his element, and knowing how bad he can get, yes, I am worried."

I was silent, feeling my heart thunder against my ribs.

Sean sighed and stood straight, placing a hand on each of my shoulders.

"Miss Sandover...can you promise me that, no matter how you feel and no matter what happens, you'll stay out of his way?"

"But...we can't just let him run wild like that," I said, swallowing hard to make my voice stronger.

"We don't have a choice," Sean said. "Promise me."

I hesitated, not because I was thinking about how to respond to him, but because I was trying to stop myself from pleading with Sean to tell me how to stay out of Dana's way, asking him how to reverse the damage I had already done.

Reluctantly, I nodded.

"Thank you." He relaxed a little. "And remember, stick close to Mark. He'll take good care of you."

Sean released my shoulders and walked to Mark, patting him on the shoulder as he walked by on his way out of the break room.

Now, Mark and I were stuck in an awkward silence, staring at one another. If I didn't know better, I would have thought Mark was frightened to be alone with me.

I bent my head, starting toward the door. Mark flinched away as I passed. The action broke my heart. I stopped in my tracks and turned to him, trying to keep the tears from showing in my eyes or choking my voice.

"I'm sorry, Mark," I whispered. "I just need a little time."

That was all I could say.

Friday, I was exhausted from a disturbing nightmare about being an animal in a zoo, waiting for the vet to euthanize me. It was stressful to be stuck behind the bars with no room to move. I was half-asleep through the whole day, feeling claustrophobic in the classroom and wanted nothing more than to run out into the cold February air, and scream at the sky until I couldn't breathe.

A few times, I nearly did.

I kept my ears open for any news. As expected, something happened—there was no longer a quiet day in America. Everyone was abuzz with rebellion, fear that the Commission was going to take over the country. Because of that, rumors spread and what the Commission thought they covered up with the Hampshire Peace Fund had been leaked.

Realizing that finances were now involved, people swarmed banks to withdraw money, causing panic that the banks would collapse. Virginia Street in Central was crowded with people trying to get into the main branches of the banks. Mark was stuck in traffic as police tried to guide us around the chaos. My face was pressed against the window, studying the people banging on the windows, yelling at people in line, or on the phone, hurriedly discussing what they felt was necessary to keep their money safe.

It seemed like the people were going to create a problem that the government would have to swoop in and solve, strengthening the people's idea that they needed the government's help.

As we drove along the back roads to the Commission, I saw posters and graffiti all promoting the "Central Angels."

The rebellion was permeating into every corner of society.

* *** *

Despite the way his demeanor changed once other Commission members began arriving for the meeting, I could not get the image out of my head of Dana throwing the pocket watch into the air and running to catch it, egging Sean to play a game of keep-away.

Dana was playing like a child in the quickly-filling meeting room, despite everything that was going on around the country. I could have written his behavior off as Dana just being insane, but there was something deadly about it. It had been obvious from the beginning that Dana was enjoying our dance, but the game made me think that the battle between the Commission and the rebellion gave him a reason to play, a reason to act like an amused five-year-old.

He was not at all worried.

The others in the Commission of the People did not share the same playful attitude. They were terrified by the bank situation, thinking that the entire country was going to collapse in what the media was calling "The Month of Monsters."

"At this rate, our greater fear is with the public, not the terrorist group," Mr. Baker said sharply at the front of the room once the meeting was underway.

"I agree," a woman whose name I did not know seconded. "Mr. Christenson, if we do nothing but sit back and wait, the country will fall. The banks are unable to pull everyone's money. We're looking at another great crash! How can you do nothing?"

"Let me ask you what you think I *should* do," Dana challenged.

"Tell the people the Hampshire Peace Fund pulling out is just a rumor," she snapped desperately. "Make the banks secure. That should lessen the panic."

"No," Dana said. "The fewer lies, the lower the chance we will have to contradict ourselves in the future. It's better to shrug and say we don't know, or even say nothing. We're already the target of distrust. Digging down is not a good way to get out of this hole."

"But we can't just sit back and wait to see what happens," another man protested strongly.

"You're right," Dana agreed. "Which is why, until further notice, I am disbanding the Commission meetings."

There was no outcry at the proposition, only silent disbelief.

"Now, before everyone pitches a fit, let me explain my decision," Dana started, raising his hands peacefully. "At the moment, this suspension is only for three weeks. The offices will remain open and operating, but the Saturday meetings will cease. The security staff has already caught several American citizens trying to spy on the building, so obviously, we must limit the amount of activity outside regular hours. Until things calm down, we need to be mindful of appearances. Until further notice, for three weeks, the Saturday meetings will not convene."

"Why? Are you going to try to run things on your own?" Dean snapped. I would have glared at him to be quiet, but I was curious about the answer.

"Yes," Dana said easily. "Not the way you're thinking, though. I will be meeting with the military leaders, foreign ambassadors, and trying to calm the international community down. At the same time, all of you won't waste our collective time sitting here, arguing about our next move. I'm giving you a break. Get out and hear what the people have to say. Put everything into perspective. Unless things change, we will meet in three weeks and go from there."

Again, we sat in still, stunned silence.

"Any questions? Comments? Concerns?" Dana pressed, looking around the room. No one could say anything. "Great, if anyone needs me, of course, they can still reach my advisors. If it is a real emergency, you can contact either Sean or myself. Enjoy your three weeks off. If anything changes, I will call you."

No one moved, not sure if they should leave. Awkward glances were thrown around the room.

"That's it. Show's over. Thanks for coming," Dana said with a laugh, motioning for everyone to leave.

Two seconds passed before the first person stood. When he was on his feet, others also stood, grabbing their jackets and bags, murmuring with one another about the oddity of Dana's decision.

My mother and father were also confused. I, on the other hand, was frightened. I would no longer have insight into what Dana was doing unless I spied on him after school. And it was entirely possible that he would tell Mark not to bring me to the Commission after school anymore as well.

As soon as I saw Dana make a beeline for our table, I knew he was going to tell me that I wasn't going to be going to the Commission anymore.

"Karen, Tommy," he greeted. "Little Lily," he nodded to me, his tone changing when he said my name. I stared defiantly at him. "I hope you are not concerned about this decision."

"Well, a little bit," my mother said with a weak laugh. "I mean, this is a little strange…and we do feel slightly responsible."

"Responsible?" Dana echoed. "Whatever for?"

"The whole thing with Mykail…"

"Oh, Karen, do not be concerned," Dana said, placing a hand on the side of her face. "I do not blame you at all for Mykail's involvement with this group. You saw from the beginning that he disliked me. It comes as no great surprise that he would sympathize with this movement."

"But if we had just been more careful…"

"It might not have stopped him," he said. "Mykail was a powerful experiment, and he was very smart. Generally the quiet ones are the ones you have to watch out for, and I should have thought about that more. I do not blame you."

"Thank you, Dana," my mother whispered.

He smiled at her before turning to my father.

"Tommy," he started, "I thought you did so well at the last press conference that I want you to become one of the speakers for the Commission."

"Are you holding another press conference?"

"No, no, not yet. Right now I have everyone working on getting those videos off the internet. When that's complete, I will try to think of a beautiful way to spin it so that you can tell the people everything is fine. You are a very eloquent speaker, Tommy. It's a very attractive trait."

"…thank you, Dana," my father said, averting his gaze to his feet.

"And, of course, Little Lily," he said, turning to me. "I was hoping I could speak to you privately."

"Dana, we really need to get home…" my father protested.

"There is no need to be concerned," Dana assured. "I am merely going to ask about the rumors circulating the school. Nothing more."

Dana put a hand on my shoulder and led me to that same dreaded hallway as my father watched us anxiously.

My panic was reaching a new level. I wanted desperately to stop the revolution, and I was beginning to think I should just tell Dana I was involved, hopefully allowing me to spare some lives. The more I thought about confessing to the leader of the Commission, the more terrified I became.

I jumped when the latch on the door clicked shut.

"Here we are again, Little Lily."

"I'm coming to dislike our little chats," I told him.

"Really?" he asked, genuinely perplexed. "That wasn't the impression I got from our last encounter."

I cringed internally at the thought of sitting on Dana's desk as he ran his fingers over my ankle. I managed to pass the discomfort off as an annoyed sigh.

"What do you want?"

"There are a few things I need to discuss with you," he said, stopping a few paces in front of me. "I know that even if I ask you about the rumors in the school, you won't tell me anything solid. However, there is something very important I need to discuss with you." He reached out and gently tucked strands of hair behind my ear. I flinched away. "You really are beautiful…"

I smacked his hand away. "What do you want?"

He looked me over briefly and then blinked his eyes slowly, his entire demeanor changing with the miniscule movement, causing him to ooze honey and charm from every pore.

"Are you alright?" he asked. "Your entire being seems tense and troubled."

"I'm fine."

"You're not very good at lying," Dana smiled. "There is nothing wrong with being frightened by everything going on. It is always unsettling sitting on a precipice."

"A precipice?"

"I know you can feel it," he whispered, reaching both hands out and cupping them around my shoulders. His thumbs moved over the fabric of my sweater, putting pressure against the skin and flesh over my joints, the sensation biting to the bone. "You can feel the tension in your bones, the apprehension that makes your hair stand on end…It's an intoxicating drug, isn't it? Doesn't it make you excited?"

"You're crazy." I shook my head, shaking free of his grip and trying to push past him to leave. "I don't have to listen to this."

He grabbed my wrist and pulled me back, turning his body to put his back to the wall and turning me to face the emptiness of the hallway.

Before I could snap at him to release me, his lips were against my ear, his breath rushing in like water to assault my senses.

"Don't run away from it, Little Lily," he breathed, the varying tones of his voice tingling over my skin. "You've come so far. Don't back away from it now…"

"What are you—"

"This tension, this anticipation and empathic link you feel with the people, it has its hooks in you. Give in to it…follow it to its conclusion…"

"You want me to look forward to the world falling into chaos?" I growled.

"No." He pressed his face against my hair, his breath ghosting over my scalp. "I want you to embrace it, fall with it..." He took a deep breath, his arms locking around my stomach. He pulled me closer. "You've wanted to play this game, and now that you're in it, you can't back out just because you're frightened." He pressed a gentle kiss to my temple. "Just let yourself fall into it."

He tipped back on his heels, holding me tight. He began falling backward as I panicked, trying to free myself from his embrace.

We both jolted as his shoulders hit the wall, stopping our fall abruptly.

A few silent and still seconds later, I sighed and shook my head, leaning back to look at him.

"You're one of those people who loves destruction, aren't you?"

"It is the only thing that is constant in society other than fear," he said, pushing us upright and finally allowing me to move away. I turned slowly, trying to figure out how best to craft my confession.

"Dana..." I started, "what if I told you I *was* involved in the revolution?"

"It wouldn't surprise me in the slightest." He grinned. "*Are* you telling me that?"

I studied his expression carefully, noting the glint in his eyes. There was something about his expression that confused me, that made me feel like he was disappointed in my confession. I replayed his words in my head, how he told me not to back down from our competition just because I was frightened...

Seeing the look in his eyes, I began to replay the news reports, the immense support that we had against Dana...Considering how far we had already gotten, my only fear was in taking that last step.

Stepping off the precipice, as Dana had said.

My mouth spoke before my brain could command it what to say.

"No," I said. "That wouldn't be much fun, would it?"

Dana's disappointed glint disappeared, his smile becoming pleased.

"No, it wouldn't," he agreed. "But say that you are involved...there is something I need to tell you."

"What?" I asked, crossing my arms.

"The rebellion is about to have massive problems, and it has nothing to do with the Commission or me. All of the problems are going to come from inside."

"What do you mean?"

"The rebellion is playing with loaded guns," he explained. "As you know, the successful experiments are often sold or used, such as the Eight Group." He cocked an eyebrow at me. "Did you ever wonder why there were experiments waiting in the wards?"

I just stared at him, schooling my expression, though my heart was picking up pace and a nervous flutter was spreading through my abdomen.

"They're either not complete, or they can't function without medical help," Dana said. "These are experiments that need assistance. They need medical attention. You should know this from Mykail. If I can't get to him, then it is entirely possible that his body will begin fighting against the wings and it will kill him, slowly and painfully. He is not the only one who needs attention like that."

"Then what you're saying is that the weapons the rebellion has are going to eventually work against them?" I scoffed. "They'll get sick and die?"

"More or less," he confirmed. "Therefore, if you are involved— and I'm not saying you are—I would suggest you think very strongly about how you're going to care for these experiments when you do not have the resources to do so."

"I guess that's something that the group has already figured out," I said, trying to shrug through a lie as best I could. In reality, I had never put thought to the experiments needing medical attention, and the sudden thought that we had been neglecting the needs of our most powerful allies caused my lungs to constrict painfully. "After all, they've been doing fine so far."

"No, the people have been making the most fuss," Dana disagreed. "The experiments have only appeared once in public, and then they made those trivial sob-story videos…otherwise, they have been largely out of sight."

I tried to resist grinding my teeth together in frustration. There had been a lot of talks about other ways to get the experiments out in the open, but with my current doubts about the revolution, I had been heavily opposed to all ideas presented. I knew we could not continue to keep them hidden if we wanted to succeed, but I was unsure how to proceed safely.

"Anyway, that's what I wanted to talk to you about," Dana declared, putting his hands in his pockets. "And Little Lily," he added, "remember what I said. Embrace what's coming…because it will be your fate."

* *** *

Monday was another day of terror for the country as York & Brothers, the most powerful investment company in infrastructure and development across the country, cut funding for the government. All day, politicians and news crews alike were talking about how, without York & Brothers, it was entirely possible that America would have to resort to borrowing money from other countries to keep up with the maintenance, stability, and basic needs of the people. Most speculated that the international community would be unwilling to provide financial aid to America with the rumors circulating about the Commission's experiments and the tensions that were making the country so unstable.

I could not grasp the severity of the situation at all.

I had problems within my own world—specifically with Mark.

The leader of the Eight Group was obviously worried about even looking at me after I had been so harsh to him through the previous week. Since I had found the courage to stand up against Dana and tell him that I was not involved—even though he knew that I was—I felt nearly ready to discuss my insecurities with Mark. However, seeing him so worried around me, looking away as if he was a dog I had kicked too many times, I was beginning to feel as though I needed to mend our relationship before I spoke to him about such sensitive material.

It was harder than I expected.

Tuesday night, after Mark brought me home from the Commission, I had planned on speaking to him, but backed out at the last minute, kicking myself for my cowardice the entire cold walk from the car to the door.

My parents were talking worriedly about the trouble with York & Brothers while I sat at the dinner table, listening half-heartedly. I never understood investments or the reason why this would be such a problem for the country, but everyone who was older than twenty seemed to understand the gravity of the situation.

I went to my room and paced like a moron for three hours, something that had become my nightly routine. I went through hundreds of scenarios where I could approach Mark and talk to him, tell him what was wrong and how I felt, but it was more difficult to get the experiment alone than I expected, which was my first major barrier.

As I was sitting on my bed, trying to find some peace of mind that would help me fall asleep, I watched Dexter blankly, who had finally gotten annoyed with my nervousness and moved to his spot on the windowsill.

Dex turned his attention out the window, his ears perked up and his forequarters low.

Confused, I stood.

"What is it, Dex?" I whispered, walking to him and cupping my hands around my eyes as I pressed my face to the window. Near the end of the driveway, passed the darkened windows of the kitchen, there was a figure clad in a simple black suit, hands in his pockets, walking back and forth in the same spot, bouncing on his heels to fight the cold.

"...Mark?"

I grabbed my heavy coat, pulling it on over my pajamas, and slipping on my boots, making my way downstairs to the garage, where I slipped out of the door to the backyard and around the side of the house.

When I opened the gate, the person near the corner of the house turned. I tried to see if it was Mark, but I could not make out any features in the dark.

"Mark?" I whispered, closing the gate behind me and walking cautiously over the ice, listening to the snow crystals crunch under my feet.

"No," a voice chuckled, also cautiously stepping to me. "Sorry, just me."

"Josh," I said, hugging him as he wrapped his arms around me. "What are you doing here?"

"Sorry for standing outside your house," he chuckled guiltily, his lips blue from the cold, his hands deep in his pockets. "It is probably creepy."

"A little," I laughed. "Is everything okay?"

"Yeah," he said. "Well...I think..."

"What do you mean, you think?"

"Why did Hyunwoo ask me to check on you?" he asked slowly. "Why did he tell me he could not talk to you? Well... I mean...he can't talk, but he couldn't...um..."

"I know what you mean," I said, refusing to meet his gaze.

"Did he...do something?" Josh pressed. "Because I know sometimes he can be intense, but he would never hurt you. He loves you."

"I know," I whispered, my voice pained. "He didn't do anything. I'm just...I'm a little worried. There's a lot of things going on, and it's happening really fast..."

Josh nodded. "But...what did *Hyunwoo* do?"

"Nothing," I repeated, pinching the bridge of my nose. I could feel Josh's eyes trying to pry the answer out of me. "I just..."

"I don't have a sister," he told me with a chuckle, "so...I don't understand women. But I think you should talk to him, regardless."

"Is that what he sent you here to tell me?"

"No." Josh shook his head. "He just wants you to be okay...he worried that you'd do something bad to yourself."

"Oh, no," I gasped quickly. "I'm fine. I'm just...trying to wrap my head around everything."

Josh hugged me again. I rested my head on his shoulder. Despite him being so thin, hugging Josh made me feel safe.

He pulled away and grinned.

"It's cold," he whispered. "You should get inside and sleep."

I nodded with a grin and turned, carefully jogging to the backyard gate. When I reached it, barely managing not to slip on the ice, I turned back to Josh.

"It's cold!" I repeated with a laugh. "Go get warm!"

As I turned to unlatch the gate and go back to the warmth of the house, Josh called to me again.

"Lily!" I turned back quickly. "Talk to Hyunwoo."

I nodded, assuring him that I would, and then quickly moved into the house, running up the stairs and waving to Josh from my window as he waved back, walking backwards. I could not help but laugh when he slipped and fell, though I was sure to watch him run across the street to his car to be sure he was not hurt.

* *** *

I had every intention of finding a way to pull Mark aside and tell him I wanted to talk to him that Wednesday, but something captured my attention as soon as we got to the Commission. Unlike when the Hampshire Peace Fund pulled away from the Commission, no one was running around, desperately trying to figure out how to deal with the sudden dilemma, but there was a small group of people, walking quickly, whispering to one another.

"How do we shut them down? If we shut them down, then the people will know it was us," one woman hissed.

"What choice do we have?!"

"First the paper, now this..."

The group disappeared and I turned to Clark, wondering if he knew what they were talking about.

"I saw the thing in the newspaper, but...I don't know what else happened."

"Wait, what happened in the newspaper?"

"There was an editorial about the rebellion," he said vaguely. "I'll show you."

Once we found a conference room, Clark pulled out his computer. Mark seemed hesitant, wanting to see what we were talking about, but knowing he had to keep appearances in the constantly-monitored hallways. The leader of the Eight Group ended up standing outside the door, occasionally throwing looks over his shoulder at us.

Clark pulled up the website for the Central Daily and showed me the editorial about the rebellion, talking about how strategic the group had been at unveiling themselves and how it put the Commission of the People in a very difficult position, where they could neither confirm nor deny what the members of the rebellion had claimed about them. Because the Commission was in such a difficult position, the editorial said that it was important for the people to find out the truth on their own.

"That's good..." I said.

"Let's see what else is going on..." Clark whispered, opening up another tab and searching the latest stories.

After a little bit of searching, we found a live-stream titled: "Carolina Media CEO Denies Commission Censorship."

Clark clicked on the video and we both anxiously waited for it to load. When the picture finally came on, there was a gaunt man with brown hair sitting at a desk.

"—ays that he will no longer support the quote 'sneaky manner' that the Commission of the People is using to handle the problem with the rebels. He says that Carolina Media is now dedicated to bringing the people of America news about the rebellion without the interference of the Commission of the People."

Clark and I looked at each other in shock.

We watched in dumbfounded fascination as the live stream showed footage of the parade reveal, the different demonstrations across the country of people supporting the quest to unveil the secrets of the Commission, and even replaying some of the highlights of the videos we posted of the weapons showing their particular abilities.

The fear came back, consuming me.

The whole world was watching what was happening in America.

Rather than me taking the step off that precipice, I found it crumbling underneath me, threatening to plunge me into the abyss of war with Dana Christenson.

I did not use that day to pull Mark aside, deciding to wait. I wanted to walk around Fort Daniels again, feel the energy there and see if I could clear my own thoughts before I went dragging Mark into my troubles.

Therefore, Friday, instead of going to Archangel, several of the Commish Kids went to the fort. The Commish Kids wandered and talked with the people in the fort as if they had been friends for years. Those we had broken free seemed to harbor no grudge against anyone in the Commission other than Dana and the scientists. Everyone treated the Commish Kids with immense respect, enjoying their company and talking congenially despite their affiliations with the institution that had imprisoned them.

To me, it made sense that the Commish Kids were more comfortable in the fort than with others our age.

With the exception of some, the Commish Kids were only putting on strong fronts and angry exteriors in school because they were trying to find a way to deal with the reality of what they knew about our government and the way it tortured people and ran the country from underground. They felt powerful in the school, but when it came to Dana, they were powerless and frightened.

I also spent a lot of time walking around, saying hello to people and asking them how they were doing, keeping everything casual. I was trying to gain energy from them, not feeling confident in our revolution and hoping to recapture my motivation.

However, the more I walked around and saw the smiling, happy faces, the more I remembered my nightmares about everyone in the revolution dying, their faces pale and eyes glassy, robbed of the spirit and happiness that I saw around the fort.

Seeing how lighthearted everyone was, I saw no reason for the revolution anymore.

I was ready to call everything off and find a way to get everyone out of the country.

I spotted Mark across the bunker. He was watching me, straightening when my eyes landed on him. Drawing in a deep breath and deciding I could no longer avoid him, I walked across the bunker toward him.

"Hey, Mark," I said as I approached. He nodded once, his eyes looking everywhere but my face. "I want to say I'm sorry...for everything...it's just been a lot to process."

Mark glanced at me worriedly and I sighed heavily, biting my bottom lip as I looked at the floor.

"I wanted to ask you something," I started, certain that he was feeling just as awkward as me with the conversation. "Dana said that most of the experiments need some sort of medical care…can we take care of that? I mean, I don't know if he was lying, but…"

Mark nodded slowly, reaching into his coat and pulling out a small note pad and pen, scribbling a note.

"The Eight Group steals what they need from the lab for now."

"Oh, good," I said. I had been hoping that we would need to figure out how to help the experiments, giving me time to talk to Mark and find a way to mend our wounded relationship. I stood stupidly by his side, waiting to find something to say, my mind remaining stubbornly blank.

Someone came to my rescue.

"Hey!" a voice boomed. I turned quickly to Josh, who was walking over, his arms open.

"Hey, Josh."

"How are you?" he asked, backing away from our hug.

"Okay," I said, not sure what else to say. He looked between the two of us, pointing a finger.

"Have you two talked, yet?"

"Ah…no…" I admitted, looking nervously at Mark. Josh was still for a moment, watching as we both focused our gazes on the ground, feeling as though we were being scolded.

"Okay." Josh nodded once. He grabbed both of our hands, pulling us roughly to the dry-supply room. Josh pushed us inside and then turned on the light. "Talk," he ordered sharply, closing the door, leaving us alone in the dim room.

I looked away from Mark's eyes, not sure how to begin. I was about to open my mouth when the door opened again and Josh haphazardly threw in a pad of paper and a pen.

"You will need this," he called.

Mark fumbled to catch the items before taking two steps toward the door that latched shut. He sighed and rolled his eyes before stooping to pick up the fallen pad of paper. He straightened the distorted sheets and placed it on one of the crates next to us, setting the pen on top.

I stared at the two harmless objects, realizing the action meant he wanted me to talk first.

He turned to face me, his eyes full of warm understanding and concern. Slowly, he stepped forward and wrapped his arms around my shoulders, holding me in a tender hug. For a few moments, I could do nothing but stand completely still, surprised. Then I wrapped my arms around him, closing my eyes and relaxing into the hug, tears trying to spring to my eyes.

He continued to hold me, communicating the sentiment the only way he still could. I could feel him telling me he was there for me, that he wanted to know what was wrong so he could help.

The tears refused to be pushed away.

What had felt like years of troubled thoughts and fears about the revolution finally bubbled into a stream of steady tears that had Mark holding me tighter. I sobbed, unable to even try to regain control of my emotions.

I do not know how long it was before I finally found the strength to pull away from him, my hands going to my face to wipe away the tears and snot running down my face in the least attractive way possible. Mark kept his hands on my shoulders, patiently waiting for me to lift my head.

Finally steadying myself, even though I knew how horrible I looked, I glanced at him.

"I'm sorry…" I whispered. "I'm alright."

He continued to stare, waiting for me to continue.

Sniffing and clearing my throat for the umpteenth time, I took a stuttered breath and locked eyes with him.

"I'm scared, Mark," I said. "I don't…I don't think we should do this anymore. Dana is more powerful than any of us…and all I can see is him killing everyone if we go up against him. The Commission is too big, and too many people are going to get hurt." I swallowed hard and looked at the ground, thankful that Mark's hands were still around my shoulders, holding me steady.

After a few seconds of me standing, staring at the ground, Mark moved his hand to hold one finger in front of me, telling me to wait as he grabbed the notepad and pen, sitting against the crates and beginning to write.

I watched him focus on the paper in front of him. After several long minutes of me standing there and staring at him like an idiot, I finally moved to sit next to him.

Several more long minutes later, he finally let me read what he wrote.

"This has never been a fight against the Commission of the People, Central, or Dana. This is a fight against everything that the Commission and Central have come to stand for. Both promote the ideology of 'us versus them.' Both demote the idea of humanity to being right and wrong, evil and righteous, powerful dichotomies that blind everyone to the one truth that we are all human. Regardless of what we look like, whether we were born male or female, who we love, what higher power we choose to believe in, we are all human. Every one of

us can feel love, joy, pain...We all know that when a human is in love, they are happy. When a human feels joy, they laugh. When a human is hurt, they cry. Empathy is the strongest bond that people have to one another. So the harm people do to one another is not the thing that tears society apart, it's apathy and indifference that bring ruin to a nation's people.

"When we start to lose contact with our fellow humans, lose the ability to understand their pain, we become something that's not human or beast, but something far colder, like metal, incapable of feeling, incapable of everything that makes us human. When we turn a blind eye to those who are suffering because we think it has nothing to do with us, it harms us even more as a collective people, because as soon as we stop seeing one creature in pain as being worthy of our time, we lose sight of the people around us and then we quickly lose sight of ourselves and the power we have inside to change things for the better.

"While Dana tortured and hurt the people on the table and made them into machines and weapons, he has done nothing more than awaken the strength of the human spirit. Because those people did not break to his will. They still had faith in their humanity, still held on to the love they remembered from their mothers and fathers, and the joy they got from their friends and loved ones. They remembered that they were human because of the people who brought them up to be human.

"The problem comes from the bigger family: the government. When the government acts like the parents bringing up a society, deciding what's best for the people, it already oversteps its bounds. At this point in civilization, the government cannot be a stable establishment. As soon as it becomes rigid, the problems of the world change, and continue to change until the government cannot accommodate the difference other than through bloodshed.

"America may have needed help, it may have needed the Second Revolution due to this very problem, but the administration it tried to put in place to keep the same cycle from repeating only caused more harm by turning people away from those feelings that hold people together. The Population Cleanse and Central were the extremes that people wanted when they were angry, and that extreme cut off their empathy because the only thing people felt at the time was anger and fear. And they were right to be angry, but they were angry at the wrong people. They were angry at the people who they believed were causing the problems, the people who made them unsettled because the government did not want to change to accommodate the changing society.

"The people of America are just as guilty as Dana. The people inherently knew what the Commission was doing, that it could be capable of more devastation than the Washington System ever could manage. To cope with that, the people tried to cover the whole sky with their hands, tried to ignore the problem that was just behind it. Right now, Dana is doing the same thing. He is insisting that people prefer to live in ignorance, when it's obvious with the support we've been getting, that people are angry at what the Commission has done and no longer believe in its cause.

"The only reason this is working so quickly is because it is so soon after the Second Revolution. The people have heard stories from their families, they remember the carnage and the uproar. It still affects them directly, and there is still a fire that can be stoked. If we had tried in two more generations, the feelings would be lost to complacency, apathy, and ease, and it would be easier to turn away from what was happening, because they would be completely disconnected with it, just as they are disconnected from other humans.

"But if you look around the bunker and see how easily these 'criminals' come to trust and care about those around them, you see that they are not disillusioned with the idea of society and structure. They only know what it means to be completely human—raw and unfiltered, unable to rely on anything other than those who were in the Commission with them. There is a transformation that happens through the pain on the table. It cleans out the infection of modern thought, society, the 'us versus them' dichotomy, and brings them to a pure understanding of what really matters, what humanity, as a whole, has lost sight of.

"The people need to get back to what it means to be human, what it means to interact with another person, to connect in the most basic way. Not to get together and talk about politics and social unrest and philosophies that they have no interest in changing themselves because that is where people disagree and where apathy is born to avoid unpleasant confrontation. That is how we grow apart as humans. Every human can agree on much more than they can disagree on. They can agree that they are lonely, that they want at least one other person to be with, to love, because there is nothing more important than feeling that bond with another human being. Why not extend that feeling of love and care to the people of the world? Instead of that connection, people put in houses and cars and promotions and paychecks to fill the emptiness, which in the end takes all the energy and love away from where we want it—and need it—most.

"This revolution will be violent. Revolutions are. But this is not just a small group of people making a fuss and trying to cause trouble. We are fighting for the very right to live. The right to be human, to live and love as we were meant to. We're not just fighting for the people in the Commission, we're fighting for the people of this society, and the people of the world who are trying to find a way to do the same."

I looked up at him, fresh tears in my eyes. While the note had been bold and daring, his eyes were gentle. He felt everything he had written so strongly that I was able to feel those emotions within my own chest.

While there was a fear at realizing that this was far bigger than anything I had originally expected, there was a sense of purpose and pride in what we were doing that was far more profound.

Mark wrapped an arm around my shoulders and brought me into a side hug. As I fell against his side, I felt myself turn around and lean back, allowing myself to tumble off the precipice.

Chapter Sixty-Two

The tension had reached a fever pitch. I felt it all Saturday night as my parents and I sat at home, watching the news in anticipation, listening to the talking heads prattle on about the Rhodes of America Annual Parade the following morning. Everyone was expecting the experiments of the Commission to show up at the parade, though there was no proof that they would make an appearance.

"Lily," my mother whispered, "I don't want you going out tomorrow. Just stay home."

"Mom, Clark and I have a date tomorrow."

"I don't care," she said. "Cancel it."

That sparked the next world war in my house. I told her that I was going anyway and that I *hoped* something happened at the parade. When I was sent to my room, I slammed the door and sat by my bed, my entire body tense with fury. Even Dexter was afraid to approach me.

It was a sleepless night. I ran through the plan in my head, tried to see if there were any faults in what we planned, replaying countless scenarios of what could happen.

It's going to happen tomorrow...

There was a cold apprehension sitting in the marrow of my bones, chilling me far deeper than my body could feel. There was a feeling in the chilly night air of that last night of February. The Month of Monsters was over. Something had to give. The pressures of the Commission of the People, the tensions of the people who were anticipating the parade the following day—because they knew what would happen—and the people who felt the fear in their bodies, but tried to ignore it, trying to take comfort knowing that the government would clear up whatever mess was coming their way.

Something had to give.

The following morning, I snuck out of the house before my parents woke, sure they would try to keep me under house arrest. I took the bus to a coffee shop near where the parade was to start. There were a lot of people in the area, setting things up for the parade, bundled in their jackets as they tried to fight the cold first day of March.

I watched from the window of the almost-empty café, my hands wrapped around my warm mug, trying to take in the crisp, fresh feeling in the air to clear my mind.

But the clouds overhanging Central, threatening more snow, matched the looming darkness that sat within my chest.

Eventually, my phone buzzed from Clark sending me a message that he was on his way to the café. I sighed when I looked at the message, trying to think of how I was going to explain my empty mug when he got there.

Deciding not to chance an explanation, I asked for a refill shortly after he sent me the text to make it look as though I had not already been there for two and a half hours.

He showed up shortly thereafter, huddled in his jacket. He smiled at me weakly, showing that he was feeling just as nervous. After getting his coffee, he sat across from me, sipping it slowly.

Other than greeting and reciting the formalities of seeing one another, we were silent, waiting for the hour to come.

I wanted to ask Clark if he thought we should call off our plan. It had crossed my mind multiple times to run to the spot where our people were leaving the fort and tell them to stay, that there was something wrong about that day, but I had managed to stop myself, reminded of what Mark had said and how we all knew the bloodshed was coming.

If that was what it took to get the Commission dismantled and allow people to live as humans, then the violence was something we had to accept.

"Should we go?" Clark suggested, looking at me with the same apprehension across his features that had turned my stomach into knots.

We walked in tense silence out of the café to the spot in the parade where other Commish Kids were sitting with a few other familiar faces that we smiled and nodded at once.

A few minutes later, while we were waiting for further instruction on where we were in the parade, Diane walked to me.

"Lily, it's Griffin."

I took the phone from her hand and put it to my ear.

"Griffin," I greeted quietly.

"Hey, Lily," he said. "We're here."

"Oh, good..." I said, turning to look down the street at the skyscrapers that lined the boulevard. "Good..."

"Everything alright down there?"

"Yeah, everything's fine," I said, trying to mask the worried tone in my voice. "Just a little nervous."

"Don't worry," Griffin said. "Everything will be fine."

I agreed quietly and then handed the phone back to Diane.

"Hey, you guys are the group from Central University, right?" a flustered woman asked, running to us.

"Yeah," Daniel confirmed.

"Great, this float is going to move and then we're going to signal you to go after they have already made a good distance. You need to make sure to keep at least five car lengths between you and them, okay?"

"Why?" Clark asked.

"The whole damn army is lining the street. They want clearance to interfere if there is a problem," the woman groaned, rolling her eyes and rushing to the next group.

Everyone turned to one another, eyes wide.

"The *army*?" Clark hissed.

"We didn't plan for the army to be here," Joey said. "What do we do?"

"Look, for all they know, we're just university students," I told them strongly. "They aren't going to have memorized over one hundred faces to spot anyone here. They're going to remember the experiments."

"Yeah, but Mykail—"

"Is going to be flying above us," I cut Peter off. "He will draw attention away. We act just as planned and we get the hell out if things go south."

There was no more conversation as the parade officials ran up and down the line, telling everyone to be prepared to move.

Our late entry into the parade as the honor students of the university who were trying to get funding for charity work made me cringe when we filled out the application and then made me roll my eyes when we were accepted. The Rhodes of America Foundation, which provided scholarships to all majors in universities, needed more people in the parade. Four groups had backed out after the demonstrations around the country.

I wondered if the Rhodes of America Foundation asked for support in keeping the parade safe, or if the army decided to be there of their own volition.

Once, when I was seven years old, I participated in a dance recital. It was something that my mother made me do like most girls my age. I did not want to do soccer or any of the other sports offered, so my mother told me I had to go into some form of dance, claiming it would help me with my coordination and presence. I practiced, awkwardly stiff and not at all interested, and when the recital came, the thought of performing in front of all the people in the audience, even though it was only the parents and families of the girls dancing, made my heart beat so fast, I was sure I was going to have a heart attack and die before I stepped out of the wings.

I had not felt that type of terror since. Since I was older, the fear I had at moving to Central, at going to the Commission, at meeting Dana and planning the revolution against him, was more mature, more complicated and caught up with different thoughts about how I needed to act appropriately within society and the situation.

But when I saw the float in front of us move, the fear was more acute, more childish in the fear of having all those eyes on me, just as I had felt walking out onto the stage when I was seven.

The woman ran up and snapped at us, agitated, ordering us to move forward when the float was the appropriate length away.

I slinked into the middle of the group of humans we had broken out of the Commission, grabbing a section of the large flag that was part of our simple parade set up. Clark walked next to me, holding his sign with three others that listed the name of one of the charities that Central University was affiliated with.

We began the walk down the crowded boulevard.

I glanced at the faces gathered on both sides of the street, remembering when I was in their position for the Liberation Day Parade and how nervous I had been thinking how everything could go wrong. This time, the fear was different—*raw*. There was a threat that I would be in direct danger if Dana saw me in this group. Same with Clark.

It was a risk we both had decided to take.

I saw the green uniforms lining the barricades as we drew closer to the center of the city. I had always imagined the military to have large rifles, even though I knew that those guns were only used for ceremony in modern times. The men who lined the streets had two smaller guns strapped to their legs, just within reach.

I lost track of how my feet were hitting the ground, too focused on my surroundings to realize where I was walking, using the edge of the flag to guide me, hoping the others knew where they were going. I was watching the buildings pass, trying to be discreet as I looked at the others in the group, the spectators, the military, and the street signs that were crawling by, bringing us closer to the building where Griffin, Mykail, and Cody were waiting.

Finally passing the street where Mykail was set to make an appearance, Clark and the others dropped the other section of the banners, showing the organizations who called themselves charity organizations and scholarship providers—particularly in science and medicine—but actually gave money for the research that was provided by the Commission experiments, a list of industries given to us by Josh.

From where I was in the parade, I could not hear the shock that the people had seeing us at the parade. Looking at their faces, I saw that they were not surprised at our appearance, but at our message. Rather than whisper quietly, several people began yelling, congratulating us for exposing the organizations. Large groups of people pushed closer to the barriers, voicing their support and expressing their anger at the Commission of the People.

A small group looked up and saw Mykail leap off one of the buildings, spiraling toward the parade, spreading his wings and changing his direction at the last moment, flying forward, low enough so everyone could read his message.

"Abolish the Commission!"

Just as I felt myself smiling at the cheering surrounding us, my nightmare seemed to come true.

Gunshots echoed between the buildings and everyone jumped, turning to the men in uniform, most of them pointing guns at the rapidly moving angel. Mykail spun around a corner and soared high into the air, over buildings, evading skillfully as the gunshots reverberated off the towers of steel and glass.

My eyes followed Mykail, the whole parade halting as many of the military men began shouting orders at one another not to let Mykail out of sight. My attention was diverted to other angered voices.

"Don't fucking shoot him!"

"You're just a dog of the Commission!"

My gaze focused on a group grabbing three of the military men, all of whom had their guns drawn, and pulling them into the barricades. The people were yelling, storming into the streets, trying to take down the military men who were still aiming at the experiment circling above the parade.

Several in our congregation dropped what they were holding, wondering how to react to the sudden, unexpected chaos.

There was another gunshot, much closer to where we were, and I dropped into a crouch, looking around as horrified screams sounded. My eyes settled on the young woman on the ground, completely still, a pool of blood forming around her.

"Let's go!" Clark yelled, grabbing my arm and pulling me away. I followed his lead as our group tried to escape the riot. With the chaos in the streets, it was impossible to move as a large group, and when the military saw us fleeing, many of them pursued.

"Split up!" Ben bellowed.

We scattered, Clark pulling me as we ducked between some office buildings.

I was disoriented, focused on the screaming and gunshots. My heartbeat was deafening and it was impossible for me to catch my breath. I heard the angry blades of a helicopter moving over the parade-turned-riot. My heart plummeted.

"Mykail..." I gasped.

"He's fine!" Clark snapped. "We have to go!!"

I had to be dragged through the remainder of the alleyway, and Clark finally managed to get me close to the river, peering out from around the side of the building before squeezing my hand and walking onto the promenade, pulling me close, trying to act as though we were just a couple walking, unaware of what was going on several blocks away.

My eyes were distant on the ground as we walked. I was trying very hard not to collapse as I processed how quickly everything had fallen into panic. I looked up when I heard a loud boom that startled me and several people around us. Both Clark and I stopped and turned in the direction of the noise.

I glanced at Clark, my eyes filling with panicked tears. He nodded, squeezing my hand and quickly moving to one of the sports bars in the area. Once inside the restaurant, we saw that everyone in the building was watching the various screens all around the establishment. The news was trying to show reports of what was happening in the downtown area.

My hand was over my mouth when I saw the pile of smoldering, distorted metal in the park on the street where the parade had been taking place. Around the fiery helicopter wreckage was a large group of young men and women, likely university students, who were cheering. Military personnel were pointing their guns at the young adults, ordering them to get on the ground.

"This is the wreckage of the military helicopter that crashed after trying to interfere in a riot that broke out at the Rhodes of America Annual Parade. The helicopter was called in after a winged man that has come to symbolize the terrorist movement against the Commission of the People was seen flying over the parade. The winged man pulled the two pilots and gunner out of the helicopter and then crashed the aircraft, jumping free of the wreckage and evading capture. There is no information yet about the well-being of the personnel manning the helicopter."

Every eye in the restaurant was glued to the screens, breaths held, watching the replays of the carnage.

I could do nothing but stare in horror.

It was our doing.

We had created chaos.

I knew at least one person had died because of it, recalling the brief glimpse of the woman dead on the asphalt.

That realization sat heavy on my chest. The people had finally snapped, and they had sided with us against the Commission, against the military, against the Central Administration because of what we had told them. We had changed the opinions of the nation and, after today, it was going to be a domino effect. Just as had happened with the Liberation Day Parade, people across the country were going to watch what happened and they were going to show their anger alongside their countrymen.

While there was a part of me that understood that meant more vandalism and more death, there was a strange sensation deep within me, licking at the walls of my stomach and causing my skin to prickle.

I felt powerful again. We could win this fight against the Commission of the People.

The rebellion had turned into civil war.

Chapter Sixty-Three

Getting in touch with everyone after that fateful Sunday was extremely difficult. The school had been closed for the week because the capital had declared a state of emergency due to the riot. I watched the news religiously, even though it meant I had to sit with my infuriated parents, who were scolding me over and over again for going out when something so horrific had occurred.

So far, they had failed to see me on the news, which was a very good sign for my safety.

But I was full of anxiety. Because school had been canceled and my parents were keeping such a close eye on me, I was unable to see Clark, Mykail, Mark, or anyone else in our group. On Tuesday, after I had spent all day watching the news and hearing the increasing number of dead and injured in the riot, I was frantic to know if we had lost anyone in our group in the chaos. I texted Clark and asked him if he saw the numbers on the news of the people who had died. When he responded that he had, I asked him if he knew who any of them were.

He did not reply.

Around eleven that night, I got a text message. Tense from the entire day, I scrambled to my phone, tripping as my feet were caught in the sheets of my bed and causing Dexter to meow in frustration. I was surprised that my cat even bothered to sleep on the bed with me anymore. I had been having such horrible nightmares that he would always move to his own bed at some point in the night.

I glanced at the text message from Clark.

"Sorry about not getting back to you sooner. My mom had me running errands with her."

I stared at the text message for a long moment, wanting to call Clark and scream at him for no particular reason. It seemed like too simple of an excuse to not text.

I stopped and turned to the window. Quickly making my way to the cold glass, I glanced out and saw Clark standing in my driveway. He waved at me.

When I got out to Clark, his teeth were chattering, his lips blue.

"How long have you been out here?"

"Too long…" he admitted with a chuckle. "I got here about an hour and a half ago, but your parents were still awake. I was creeping from over the neighbor's fence until I saw the lights go out." He shivered, his teeth chattering.

"Come into the garage," I said, pulling him through the side gate and to the back door of the garage. I would have brought him into the house and up to my room, but I was already in enough trouble with my mother. I didn't need to have a boy she believed to be my boyfriend in my bedroom so late at night.

"Are you okay? Where's Mark?"

"I don't know," Clark said. "Sean called him yesterday and he disappeared. I saw the car outside for about an hour this morning but it was gone around ten."

"Is everything okay?"

"My mom says it is," Clark said. "She said that Mark was working with the other security personnel and the Eight Group on some clean up stuff from the parade."

"Do you know if we lost anyone?" I whispered, my voice tight.

Clark cleared his throat.

"We did lose Jackie," he admitted. "She was killed when she tried to escape. From what Mark said, her body was taken to the Commission after her identity was confirmed." Clark shivered, forcing his teeth to stop chattering. "Mark also said that Josh made sure to contaminate the evidence they found from the autopsy that could lead to them finding out where she was living for the past two months."

I let out a long sigh and shook my head.

"We are seriously lucky to have Mark and Josh," I said. "Poor Jackie…" I pinched the bridge of my nose and shook my head, closing my eyes as I thought about the beautiful brown-haired, green-eyed girl who had been brought into the Commission because she had been found transporting drugs across regional lines.

"Yeah…but at least she didn't get taken back to the Commission alive," Clark said quietly. "I'm sure Dana would have done much worse to her then."

"That's true," I said, trying to take comfort in the fact, though it did not ease the pain. "So out of the nine that have been declared dead, only one was ours," I murmured. Clark said nothing, looking at the ground awkwardly, his shivering slowly coming to a halt.

"It's something we knew would happen…" he whispered.

"I know," I said. "What about you? How are you doing?"

"I'm alright. My mother is furious at me, but I think it's just that she was afraid I was going to get hurt when the riot started."

"You didn't tell her that we were there, did you?"

"No, no," he assured. "I told her what we agreed on. That we had a date, but we were away from the area."

I sighed, relieved, but also remembering the current drama within my family.

"My mom is pissed, too." I rolled my eyes. "She's forbidding me from leaving the house for anything other than school next week."

"Yeah...Mark has been absent, obviously, but he did tell me that he didn't want to take me to the fort for a while. He wants everything to calm down. He told me that everyone was alright apart from what happened to Jackie. A few were nicked by bullets, but Peter, the med-school guy, is treating them."

"Good thing we have a medical room at the fort," I said. "Well, when you see Mark and he has a moment, I really want to talk to him."

"Okay, I'll tell him."

We were silent for several long moments. I finally shook my head.

"We did it...we actually started a revolution..." I muttered. He laughed brokenly, nodding, also looking at the cement at his feet.

"Yeah...we did."

"Feels a little too simple, doesn't it?"

"Just a little."

"So," I continued, clearing my throat, "are you still sure? You know, about...the next step?"

Clark looked up and swallowed hard before nodding, looking frightened, but not hesitant.

"Are *you*?"

"I've been ready for a while," I chuckled. "I'm pretty sick of this act."

"But are you really ready to say goodbye to this part of your life?" he pressed.

"Of course." I was steadfast in my decision.

* *** *

On Friday, the city had calmed down and cleaned up from the riot. The number of people dead was at a solid eleven, and the number injured was at seventy-two. Of course, the media would not let go of what had happened and continued to replay terrifying footage of the chaos, showing people being beaten down, people dancing around the fiery crash of the helicopter, and the sheet-covered bodies of the dead being hauled into different ambulances.

It was called the "Rhodes Parade Massacre." Our group had solidified our title as domestic terrorists.

The most violent reaction to what was going on was from the international community. As far as the other countries were concerned, the powerhouse of the world was now in civil war and it was entirely possible that America would crumble. Countries were scrambling to figure out political powers and financial standings. There were conferences and meetings across the globe as the world prepared for our war against the Commission of the People.

While the city was cleaned up by Friday, the chaos had moved into my house.

Late that night, my mother called me down from my room. I begrudgingly obeyed. We had been at each other's throats the entire week and my father was disappearing, adding credence to the belief that he was having an affair and upsetting my mother further, which just made me more indignant toward her and her habit of venting her anger on me.

But she was still my mother, so I obeyed when called.

She was sitting at the kitchen table, her laptop in front of her and her eyes filled with tears. I hesitated before climbing the three steps into the kitchen.

"Mom? What's wrong?" I asked, becoming very frightened that something had happened to my father.

She took a deep breath and cleared her throat, clicking a button on her computer and turning the screen to me.

"This was taken on the day of the parade..." she muttered, her voice tight.

My gaze fell on the screen as I sat in the chair next to her. I watched the unsteady camera move around the float in front of our group and a strong wave of nausea passed over me. I watched in horror as my face appeared on the screen, next to Clark, holding the long, white banner. My eyes were glued to the screen, watching the banners drop, the camera turning upward to Mykail, following him, and then turning back to us as the people began to attack the military personnel shooting at the experiment. The camera stopped on a blurry frame where my face could be seen in the bottom left corner.

There was nothing I could say. I turned slowly to my mother, who was letting her tears flow.

"How could you?"

"How could I? How *could* I? You're really asking me that?" I snapped. "Mom, I have been telling you for months that I don't agree with the Commission, that I hate what they're doing, and that I support this revolution. You think my opinions have suddenly changed?"

"You're involved in this group?" she choked.

"Yes."

"For how long?" she whispered. "Since before Mykail escaped?"

"He didn't escape," I told her simply. She closed her eyes and let out a breath as though my words physically struck her. Her jaw was clenched tight as she tried to breathe evenly.

"I didn't want to believe it..." she mumbled. "How could you do this? To the family? To me and your father?"

"Since when is this about you?" I said. "You know, Mom, this is a hell of a lot bigger than our *appearances*. Dana and the Commission are building weapons out of people and torturing and enslaving other people! There was a time when that really bothered you...when you wanted nothing more than to get out...then all of the sudden you get a taste of Dana's cock and all you want is—"

My mother's hand lashed out and slapped me, effectively shutting me up, though it did nothing to calm me down. It enraged me further.

"You insolent little girl," she snarled. "We don't live in an ideal world. We live in an ugly world with some ugly truths. That is something you just have to accept and live with, not put yourself in danger to try and upset people with information that they don't need to know."

"If I don't, then who will?" I growled. "Would it be better to wait until the Machine of Neutralization is done? Should we wait until Dana mass-produces those things and they take over the world? This is so much bigger than anything else that has happened to this country. We are trying to stop a mad-man from playing God!"

"That mad-man is the most powerful man in the world, so as far as you are concerned, he *is* God!" my mother bellowed. I stood quickly to face her. "You are putting yourself in unnecessary danger!"

"Mom, do you have any idea that Dana was molesting me when I was at the Commission after school?" I spat. "Did you know that he was telling me he was going to take me in the back and test on me? That he assaulted both me and Clark? Are you telling me that it's okay to take that kind of abuse because he's Dana fucking Christenson?"

"Yes."

I blinked, my jaw dropping.

"You mean as long as it doesn't affect *you*..." I said. "As long as I'm the perfect daughter you always wanted me to be and you don't have to hear the ugly truth."

"Don't you dare think that you know how I feel," my mother growled, pointing her finger. "You are young and stupid and you know fuck-all about anything that is going on because you are selfish enough to think that just because *you* are uncomfortable, the country needs to rebel."

"I can't believe you!" I yelled. "Who the hell *are* you?!"

"Things change, Lily," my mother told me sharply. "People change, but you can't go fucking up the entire country because you are upset with Dana."

"Oh my God, Mom, I keep telling you, Dana is only part of the problem!" I said, exasperated. "You always taught me to stand up for what I believe in, to fight for what I thought was right, regardless of what everyone else says! You taught me to be strong, to watch out for others who could not take care of themselves, and then as soon as I start doing that, you turn around and stab me in the fucking back! You have no one to blame but yourself for this!"

She pushed me so hard I fell to the ground, my whole body jolting with pain as I caught myself on my elbows, avoiding a painful crack to the back of my head on the hardwood. But before I could regain my bearings, my mother was on top of me, slapping me violently across the face and causing my head to fall back. I tried to curl up and get away from her hands as they continued to beat over my body.

"How dare you blame me for what you've done?!" she screeched. "I would never have raised my daughter to do something so fucking stupid!"

I wanted to yell back at her, but I was too busy covering my face and trying to get away from her flailing hands. She grabbed my wrist and ripped my hands away from my face, her nails digging deep gashes in my arm. I let out a choked cry of pain and tried to pull my hand out of her grasp, but I was immediately blindsided by her other hand smacking me flat on the front of my face, pushing my head into the ground as she put all her weight onto my skull.

"Mom! Stop it!"

"What? Now I'm your mother? I thought it was entirely my fault that you were such a selfish bitch! I thought that you didn't know who I was anymore!"

There was legitimate fear in my gut that my mother was about to kill me.

Suddenly, a deep voice washed over me and brought me intense relief and a new sense of panic.

"Karen! What the fuck are you doing?!"

My father hauled my mother off of me, though she was kicking and fighting, her feet connecting with my ribs as her nails ripped away the skin on my wrist. Her other fist pulled at my hair and lifted me off the ground as I struggled to get free of her.

"Get the fuck off me!" my mother screamed, continuing to kick and curse.

"Karen! Stop it! That's your daughter!"

"Shut the fuck up, you cheating son of a bitch!" she screeched, turning her anger to him, shoving him away. I dared to glance at my mother from the ground, seeing the red flushing her face, the way her entire body was tense and agitated, ready to attack anyone nearby like an infuriated animal. "You think I don't know that you're going out and fucking some little bitch?!"

My father stared at her for a moment, surprised.

"So you attack Lily?"

"Your fucking daughter has gotten herself mixed up in the fucking terrorist group!" she bellowed, pointing a trembling finger at me. "But, I guess that if you're willing to throw away our marriage for some whore, then you're throwing away our daughter as well, so it shouldn't matter to you!"

"Of course it fucking matters! And you were the one who threw the family away when you fucked Dana!" my father retaliated. "So how dare you accuse me of infidelity?"

"Of course, everything comes back to me! It's all my fault!" my mother cried. "It's my fault that you're cheating, it's my fault that our daughter is part of a fucking domestic terrorist group. Well you know what, fuck *both* of you! I have done everything I could for this family, and you're going to just throw it back in my face like that?"

"You're fucking insane!" I gasped from the ground. "What the fuck? Did Dana's dick make you catch his crazy or something?"

"Don't you dare," she kicked me hard, once in the stomach and then in the back after I curled up, "talk down to me, you little whore!"

"Karen, stop it!" my father snapped, grabbing my mother and pulling her back, keeping her foot from connecting again. I watched as my mother jumped and fought against my father's grip like a wild animal, trying to claw at him, screaming loudly before all her defenses crashed and she broke down crying, doubling over in her husband's arms, sobbing loudly.

"I want to die…I just want to die…" she moaned pathetically.

I forced myself to my feet, holding back my own tears. I ran to the door, grabbing my big coat and scarf, sticking my feet in my boots, not bothering to pull them on completely as my father called loudly for me to come back.

I slammed the door behind me. I shuffled across the street to the retaining wall for the neighbor's front lawn, sitting down to pull on my boots properly, zipping up my jacket and wrapping my scarf around my neck. I fished in my pockets for my gloves only to find that they were gone. Trying not to let the frustrated and frightened tears overwhelm me, I also realized I had left my phone behind.

Deciding I did not care enough to go back to my house, I began walking in the cold night, moving through the dark streets, watching my feet pass over the sidewalk as I moved around the neighborhood. I found a park devoid of people and strolled among the teeter-totters, slides, and the sand pit to the swings, where I sat for only five seconds before completely breaking down, crying so hard I was groaning in pain from the sobs that tore my chest apart. I shivered, my teeth chattering from the intensity of my pain and the cold air that bit into the tears running down my face. I curled around my bruised and throbbing stomach and cried through the radiating pain from the injuries, remembering the look on my mother's face as she kicked and hit me, seeing the unbridled hatred in her eyes.

It was an indeterminable amount of time before I stopped sobbing and finally found the strength to sit straight on the swing, shivering in the bitterly cold air.

It did not feel safe to go home, so I made my way toward the bus stop, trying to think of where I could go, but I was halfway to the nearest bus stop when I remembered that I did not have my phone or my wallet, which meant I did not have my pass for public transportation. Cold, exhausted, and starting to feel the pain of my mother's attacks, I grumbled, trying to decide where to go so late at night. I had no sense of time, but with how cold the air had become, it was obvious that it was getting close to eleven.

Turning around, I began the long, freezing walk to the only place I could think to go.

When I approached the large, white house, staring at the pristine columns around the front door, I was disappointed to see the lights off. Looking around the immense driveway, trying to think of where else I could go, the frustrated tears began to flow once again. I sat on the top step of the Markus' porch, trying to figure out the best course of action around the tumbled and terrified thoughts inside my head.

My eyes were slipping shut from exhaustion and shivers wracked my body so violently it almost made me sick.

I faded in and out of consciousness, overwhelmed. I thought I hallucinated the headlights turning into the driveway. The humming of an engine and the growing intensity of the headlights made me blink to complete awareness, seeing the car round the circle in front of the house, coming to an abrupt halt at the steps.

The driver's door opened and I felt tears come to my eyes once again, this time from the all-encompassing wave of relief.

"Mark…"

He was immediately crouched at my side, his arms around my shoulders. His eyes were wide with concern as he guided me upright, my shivering and frozen body refusing to stand without assistance.

He led me around the side of the house to a smaller door, unlocking it and motioning me inside. I stepped into the dark room but stopped immediately, not knowing where to go.

Mark closed the door on the cold night air and turned the light on in the pantry where we stood. He opened the other door for me, turning the light on for the kitchen and ushering me to sit at the heavy, dark wood table. I lowered myself into one of the chairs as Mark hurried to do something behind me—I assumed by the sounds he was heating something over the stove.

I remained huddled in the chair, shuddering and cringing.

Mark was at my side a few moments later, looking me over as he sat in the chair next to mine. He tenderly pressed my swollen right cheek before scanning me to gauge the severity of other injuries. He caught my gaze, silently asking about the extent of my injuries.

My vision blurred from the tears that had come so many times that night.

I unzipped my jacket, slipping it from my shoulders, Mark helping when he saw me struggling from the pain in my right shoulder. He caught sight of the gashes in my arm and gingerly rotated my arm to examine them. Motioning for me to wait and draping the coat over my shoulders to keep me warm, Mark disappeared from the kitchen.

I remained in the large, quiet room, trying to listen for any other sounds within the house. The only sound came when Mark returned with a first aid kit. He set the white box on the table before returning to the stove. Defrosted enough to turn my body, I watched the experiment take the copper kettle off the burner and pour steaming water into a cup he had already prepared, covering the cup with a cloth and bringing it to the table, setting it in front of me. He turned my chair and sat in front of me, opening the first aid kit.

I cringed as he treated the cuts tenderly. He glanced at me briefly, the unspoken question in his eyes.

"...my mom..." I answered, averting my eyes, feeling the tears return, though I tried to push them away, tired of crying. "She lost it. She just totally fucking lost it..."

Mark paused and I could feel his gaze on my face as I tried to keep the tears at bay. I bit my lip and closed my eyes.

"If I hate her so much...why does it still hurt that she said and did all this?" I murmured, my voice cracking. "Why am I so upset about her wanting nothing to do with me…when I…when I want nothing to do with *her*?"

He did not move to comfort me other than his thumb moving over my wrist, subtly letting me know he was there to listen. I hiccupped as a sob tried to force its way past my barriers. I lifted my other hand to my face and pressed my fist against my forehead, trying to get my emotions under control.

It felt like forever that Mark was watching me, waiting for me to continue.

Finally, one of his hands gently touched my hand, pulling it away from my face. I cleared my throat and took a deep breath.

When I was no longer on the verge of tears, Mark placed bandages around my arm, pressing gauze to the scratches before wrapping the wounds. When he was finished, he moved to the freezer and pulled out an icepack, wrapping the compress in a towel and gently pressing it to my face.

I held the cold pack to my aching cheek, cringing in discomfort. Mark resumed his seat in front of me, pointing to my face and then my arm before looking at me expectantly.

"…she kicked me…" I whispered. "My stomach…and my back…my right shoulder really hurts…"

Mark stood once again and moved around my back, feeling around my right shoulder as I winced in pain. He let out another sigh and rubbed my shoulder gently before retrieving another cold compress, holding it to the ache as he felt around the rest of my back, being gentle when he found a place that made me flinch.

He lifted my shirt off my shoulder, moving my bra strap and, as gently as he could manage, placing the compress under the strap to hold it to my shoulder.

He then moved to my stomach, trying to get me to sit straight as he felt around my abdomen, intensely focused on where I was hurt. When he stopped poking at me, he retrieved a bottle from a nearby cupboard, opening it and bringing two pills to me, putting them in my free hand before uncovering the cup of warm tea.

"…thank you, Mark."

We sat in silence as I drank the tea, taking the icepack away from my face every few minutes and seeing how long I could keep it away before Mark lifted my hand to its position again.

Before I knew it, my eyes were sliding shut and I began to wonder what I would do for the rest of the night. I did not feel safe going home, but I was unsure if Mark would take me to the fort.

Seeing my exhaustion, Mark removed the icepack from my shoulder, taking the one in my hand and setting them both on the table. He motioned for me to follow him. Standing with more effort than should have been necessary, I trailed the leader of the Eight Group through the kitchen door and into the dark dining room, through the foyer, and toward the hallway under the stairs.

Turning a sharp right under the stairs, we entered a narrow hallway with one door on each side. Mark opened the door on the left and flicked the lights on before stepping back to allow me inside. Hesitantly, I stepped in, surprised to find myself in a bedroom with a tiny window to the outside. There was a bed in the far corner with a nightstand and next to the table was a simple chair.

I walked into the bare room, looking at the quilts and blankets on the bed, the walls devoid of pictures or color.

Mark went to the nightstand and set down his keys and phone.

"This is your room?" He nodded slowly and motioned to the bed. Not sure what he was asking, I hesitated. He pointed at me and then put his hands under his face, telling me to sleep, before motioning to the bed again.

"What about you?"

Mark shook his head, motioning to the bed again before walking to the door, turning to smile once at me before closing the door and leaving me alone.

I stood still for several long moments before my exhaustion got the better of me and I moved to the bed, pulling the sheets back as I toed off my shoes. I climbed under the blankets, pulling them tight around me. The bed was not comfortable, but I was too tired to take notice. I turned onto my side and stared at the wall, replaying the entire confrontation with my mother, thinking over her words, as well as mine, the way my father had more or less confessed to being unfaithful, the way my mother told me indirectly that I meant nothing to her…

I tried not to let the tears take me again, clearing my throat and blinking my eyes, trying to get to sleep before I was overwhelmed anew.

As my eyes were beginning to drift shut, I heard the door open. I remained still, listening carefully, knowing Mark had returned, hearing how quietly he tried to close the door. I heard him tiptoe to the bed and carefully drape something—I assumed my jacket—over the foot of the bed before stepping back and turning off the light.

I was still, my back facing him, wondering what he was doing. He had not left the room, which made me too curious to fall asleep.

When my eyes had adjusted and I was unable to hear movement from the experiment, I turned on my other side, closing my eyes and pretending to shift in my sleep. I counted to sixty before opening my eyes again.

Mark was sitting in the chair, his arms crossed and his head dipping forward as his eyes began to close. His eyes opened and he lifted his head, fighting the sleep threatening to claim him.

I felt guilty dropping in on Mark and then taking his bed when it was obvious that the experiment was exhausted. I had forgotten about Clark telling me that Mark was being called into the Commission to help with the cleanup of the riot. I wondered when the last time was that Mark had slept.

I was about to say something but I saw his eyes slide shut and his head went forward, dropping to his chest. I remained silent, my mouth open to speak. I decided not to disturb the experiment just to fight about him sleeping in the bed.

Before I knew it, sleep had also claimed me.

Though not for long.

There was a gentle touch on my shoulder, shaking me, forcing me back to the conscious world. My head throbbed, foggy from the lack of sleep and crying. I tried to move my arm to rub my eyes, but cringed and let out a sorry sob of pain at the sharp sensation in my shoulder.

The hand moved away and I blinked my eyes into focus. Mark stared at me worriedly before glancing over his shoulder. I turned in the same direction and saw a familiar face in the doorway.

"...Dad?"

My father moved further into the room and sat on the side of the bed, smiling sadly as Mark retreated.

"I'm so sorry, Lily," he said. "I don't know what came over your mother..."

"Well, whatever it was, I don't want to be around her," I groaned, forcing myself to sit up.

"I understand." He sighed heavily and placed his hand on mine, as though he was about to tell me some bad news. "I think your mother had a mental breakdown...so I took her to the hospital. She's going to stay there for a week or so."

I blinked stupidly, surprised that my father would check my mother into the mental ward. He cleared his throat.

"I don't want you to listen to what your mother said," he told me strongly. "Okay? You are the most important thing to us, and...even though you are having difficulty with what's going on...sweetheart, what you're getting involved in is dangerous."

I looked at the blanket on the bed, acutely aware of Mark watching near the door.

My father gently placed his hand against my hair.

"We'll figure things out…" he assured. "So what do you say we go home?"

I tensed. Even with my mother gone, I felt safer with Mark than in my house. I turned to the experiment, seeing the conflict in his eyes. He was stuck, unsure if he should show that he knew what my father was saying and find a way to make me stay, or continue with his act and be obedient to my father's wishes.

My father also looked at Mark and smiled, standing.

"You really are something," he said, reaching a hand out to the experiment. "Thank you for taking care of my little girl."

Mark looked at the hand, before slowly taking the hand, bowing almost fully at the waist.

"Dad…I would rather stay with Mark…" I protested weakly.

I tried not to notice how hurt my father was at the words. He turned and smiled, trying to hide the pain.

"So you can see your boyfriend in the morning?" he teased. "I don't think so. You're not old enough to be having sleepovers, yet."

I rolled my eyes and looked at Mark for help. He looked just as concerned.

My father turned back to Mark and patted him on the shoulder twice, causing him to flinch away.

"Don't worry," he said. "She's safe." My father walked back to me and picked up my coat, waiting for me to move. "He's really protective of you, isn't he?"

Seeing no other option in my exhausted state, I extracted myself from the blankets and sat on the bed while I put my shoes back on. I took as much time as I could, reluctant to return home. Finally standing, my father held my coat out for me, which I put on, cringing in pain as I moved my bruised body.

I walked past Mark, reaching my hand out to touch his arm.

"Thank you…" I whispered.

Chapter Sixty-Four

With my paranoid mother gone, I could go out on the weekend, though my father still wanted me back before it got dark. He only brought up my interaction in the terrorist group once on Sunday before he left for his meeting with Dana.

I wanted to text Clark back after he asked if I wanted to meet and talk about why I had been at his house, but my face was bruised and I was moving stiffly, so I did not want to bundle up and fight the cold while I still felt so miserable. I did not answer him. I figured it was easier than coming up with an excuse.

I was uncomfortable, out of place, and I wanted to leave.

It was something Clark had discussed with me. We knew that being in the parade would put us out in the open as people allied with the domestic terrorist group, the Central Angels, but leading the double-life at school with the revolution was becoming impossible. We were both waiting for the right time to run away and live in the fort until the revolution came to its conclusion.

When my father returned home, we ate dinner in silence. I asked him what his meeting with Dana was about, but he just said it was about the press conference to do with the riot, since it had become international headlines.

But I could see tension in his body that worried me.

I went back to school on Monday and moved through the hallways as though I was not really there, observing the school life through the eyes of someone else. I was staring out the window, watching the melting snow as winter crawled to an end. I got a lot of questions about the bruises on my face, but I told them I slipped on ice and fell really hard, which got a lot of laughs.

Becca seemed to be the only one who could see the dilemma in my eyes.

Tuesday, at the end of the school day, she ran up to me before I went around the side of the building to meet with Mark.

"Listen," she whispered, "if you need me, for anything, you can always call." I smiled and looked at my feet before hugging her tightly. As I pulled away from the hug, I chuckled and shook my head.

"You might regret saying that…"

"No," she said. "I'm rooting for you. You're my hope."

I swallowed the tears and nodded, walking away from her before I broke down.

Mark was not the one waiting. Hiroki waved to me and I quickly ran to him, frightened at not seeing Mark. Dana had not had Clark and me at the Commission for over a week, which made me completely blind to what the leader of the Commission was doing. Seeing Hiroki as our driver made me nervous.

"Hello, Lily," he greeted.

"Hi," I said quickly. "Is everything alright? Where is Mark?"

Hiroki looked at his feet and my hand went to my mouth, frightened that something horrible had happened to the leader of the Eight Group.

"He's fine, he's fine," Hiroki said quickly when he looked up and saw my horrified expression. "He's just really busy right now."

"Don't *do* that!" I gasped, slumping.

"Sorry," he said. "I'm supposed to take you to Clark's house, right?" I nodded. "Then I'll talk to both of you there."

After hearing him say that, I wanted to grab Clark, run to the car and then tell Hiroki to drive as fast as possible. I nervously waited with the other experiment, watching the direction Clark would appear from, anxiety eating away at my belly.

When we finally did make it to Clark's house, Hiroki pulled us away from the house to one tree on the far end of the property. Reaching into his pocket, he turned on his scrambler.

"I only have a few moments, so listen carefully," he started. "Mark says that there is a lot of movement of the local Sweeps teams. He is unable to find the plans for these teams and it's making him nervous. Right now, he's trying to discreetly gather information, and he'll let you both know as soon as he finds out what's going on."

"Does he think the fort is in danger?" I whispered.

"He doesn't know, yet," Hiroki said. "Just be alert. He will let you know what he finds out."

Hiroki had to leave quickly in case Dana was tracking how long his car was out front of Clark's house. He drove away as Clark and I looked nervously at one another.

Later that night, I found a note on the refrigerator from my father, telling me he had a late dinner meeting and asked me to make myself dinner. I tried not to think about my father having an affair. It was bad enough when my mother cheated on my father with Dana, but now I felt betrayed by both parents because of their infidelity to one another. It broke my heart to see my family tear apart in so short a time.

I ate little, my appetite non-existent. I then went to my room and tried to get some sleep.

I was awakened suddenly when I couldn't breathe. I shifted uncomfortably in my sleep before jerking awake, panicked when I realized there was a hand over my mouth. I saw a suit-clad figure standing over me, his finger lifted to his lips.

"Don't scream," he whispered. "It's just me."

"*Josh*?" I hissed when he removed his hand.

"Lily, you need to get ready to leave."

"What? When?"

"Soon," Josh said. "Hyunwoo thinks that you are the target of the Sweeps."

I blinked, struck dumb. My mind raced as I thought about what Dana had said about not wanting me to give up, about wanting to continue our game.

"Are you sure?" I asked, sitting up.

"Hyunwoo thinks so."

"Why?"

"Dana was talking to your mother," Josh said. "And then he saw a map of your neighborhood."

"My mother's in the hospital..."

"I know. But you don't have time to think about that now. Tomorrow, pack, get into a fight with your father, and run away."

I stared at him.

"*Tomorrow*?"

He nodded and leaned down, hugging me.

"Get out of here as soon as possible," he whispered. "It's the best way to keep you safe."

I did not bother to figure out how Josh had gotten into my house to pass on the frantic message. I had no hope of going back to sleep. My mind was jumbled and terrified with the idea of the Sweeps coming for me. I thought about running after Josh and telling him to take me to the fort that night, but as I thought about the haste with which he passed the message on, I realized that he was not alone and was worried about being caught. I had to pretend I knew nothing to keep the Eight Group members safe.

I was also confused. I thought that Dana wanted to continue our game, that he did not want me to be caught until he had had his fun. Did he change his mind? Or was it true that my mother called me in and asked him to capture me?

The thought of actually leaving home finally crossed my mind.

Of course, I had been thinking about it for a long time, talking to Clark about running away, but hearing that the following day was my last with my father, in our house...that hurt more than I anticipated. I swallowed hard as the tears gathered in my eyes.

I looked at Dexter, sleeping in the bed by the window.

I got out of bed and walked to him, gathering him in my arms though he went limp, indignant about being moved. I brought him to my bed and held him tight, listening to his purring as I curled myself around him. He shifted to a comfortable position before closing his eyes again. I let a few tears run down my face as I thought about leaving my family, including Dexter. I wondered if he would wonder where I went...if he would miss me...

I thought of my father, who was so willing to look past the parade footage and tell me that everything was going to be alright, that the family would figure things out...the father I had always felt so close to, even during the strange distance that had come between us since the Commission of the People became a part of our lives.

I thought I had made peace with the idea of leaving, but it was obvious I had not.

The following day, I was an emotional wreck, looking at everything with a nostalgic eye, noticing little details that I was sure I would miss. I tried to interact with my friends as I realized those were the last memories I would have of them, though I was so emotionally unstable that I almost cried every time someone said something funny or made me smile.

Becca noticed my emotional state and continued to give me hugs, but she did not attempt to ask what was wrong.

There was a large hiccup in the plan Josh proposed, however.

My father was not home that night.

I found another message, saying that he was busy again and he apologized by note once more.

That made me extremely nervous.

I went upstairs and threw some things into a bag, looking around my room, trying to decide if there was anything else I needed to bring. As I was glancing at everything, a strange sense of peace came over me. I didn't need any of the little things in my room. They were trinkets of the life I no longer embodied.

I went to Dex and hugged him tightly, wishing I could take him with me.

Then, it was a long wait for my father to come home so I could start a fight with him. I grabbed the backpack with some clothes, my phone and wallet, and the cash I had been slowly pulling out of my allowance and saving, just in case. I sat in the living room, waiting.

I fell asleep before I could help it and woke up two hours later, looking at the clock in the living room that read one-thirty in the morning.

A ball of disgust rose in my throat as I thought about my father with his mistress, whoever she was. Angrily, I snatched my backpack and stormed through the house, turning off the lights on my way to the front door, ready to leave regardless of what my father thought the reason for my disappearance was.

I stopped, though, when my hand was on the doorknob and looked back into the large house, glancing at the family pictures on the walls and the large dining table where we would have dinner…it was incredibly painful to leave that part of my life behind.

Taking a deep breath and preparing myself, I turned back to the door.

I moved the lock one millimeter before I froze.

I heard mumbling on the other side of the door, hushed whispers of three or four men.

My blood ran cold.

The Sweep team was there.

I carefully and quickly moved away from the door, slipping my backpack over my shoulders and crouching low as I moved through the kitchen, stopping to glance at the glass doors leading into the backyard to be sure that no one was there. When I saw no one, I darted toward the garage before thinking better of it and running upstairs, turning toward Mykail's old room and listening to the sounds of the house. I was certain that the Sweeps team had surrounded the house. I decided that as soon as I heard them come into the house, I would wait for them to converge on my bedroom and then run through the open upstairs layout, down the main stairs, and out the front door, praying I was fast enough to evade them.

I moved backward through Mykail's bathroom, keeping my steps and breathing light as I strained to listen for the doors opening. I made my way into the other guest room and finally into the hallway at the top of the main staircase.

That was when I heard the click of the deadbolt moving out of place.

I slinked into my parent's bedroom, dropping to the floor and crawling under the bed, pulling the bed skirt down just in time for me to see boots coming up the stairs in front of me. I saw four sets of black boots go into the bathroom and another four sets come toward me. I was worried my frightened heartbeat would give my hiding spot away.

It was obvious that the men already knew the layout of the house with the way they split up through the open layout, making sure I had no chance of slipping past them.

I watched the boots move, quiet "clears" being muttered as they moved further into the massive room. When I saw only the heels of their boots go to the hexagonal room between the bathroom and bedroom that my parents had turned into an office, I crawled out from under the bed, remaining in a crawl until I was out of the room, where I scrambled to my feet and swiftly moved down the stairs, seeing a clear shot to the open front door.

I reached the bottom of the stairs and darted to the door, but a set of arms wrapped around my stomach and pulled me to a screeching halt.

"There you are," a familiar voice chuckled. I whirled around and, to my horror, recognized the face of the one holding me. Dana grinned broadly as I tried to struggle, my arms flailing enough for him to be forced to catch them, though he took advantage of the opportunity and put me on the ground, settling over my hips and pinning my hands above my head.

"Do you really think fighting me is going to accomplish anything?"

"Get the fuck off me!" I snapped, trying to move my hips to free myself, though his larger size gave him the distinct advantage.

"Now, now, I'm here to take you where you belong," he said with a malicious grin.

Barely managing to wiggle my wrist out of his grasp, I used the heel of my hand to push upward into his nose, just as I had been taught in my self-defense class as a freshman, but the motion did not have as much strength as I needed. It stunned Dana, but it did not break his nose.

I managed to squirm enough in his distraction to nearly be free of him, but Dana moved off of me, his legs circling my waist and pulling me so I was resting on top of him, his legs keeping me confined.

"I can do it this way, too," he said. "I'm versatile."

"You said that you wanted to keep this game going," I said, straining to pinpoint the boots of the team moving through the house.

"The game ends when I say," Dana said. "You really don't get it, do you? Every little aspect of your life was planned so you would come to me. So you would get to this point. You think you're in control of this, Little Lily, but you have been moving exactly as I wanted. *I* appointed your father. *I* brought you to this house. All to get you to this point. I did it all for you. Now it's time to really see what you can do…"

Ripping my hands free of his grasp, I linked my fingers together and straightened as much as I could, turning my elbow and jamming it as hard as I could against Dana's inner thigh with enough pressure for his legs to loosen.

When I had just enough room to move, I backed away and lifted my knee into his groin.

There was no pain on his features, but there was surprise, and his legs did release me. I scrambled to my feet and flew out the door faster than I had ever moved in my life. Other members of the Sweep team were patrolling outside and, when they saw me running, they pursued, a few of them getting into the cars and peeling out of my driveway.

I darted the short distance to the park and did the only thing I could think of. Removing my backpack, I held it above my head and jumped into the icy waters of the tributary ditch that had been decorated to look like a creek. Feeling my breath leave as if I had been kicked, I tried to force my lungs to work as I moved with the current, waiting for the first tunnel, trying to swim past the sound of the tires screeching as my muscles locked in the frigid water.

I was sure I was going to freeze to death, or be caught by the Sweeps team, before I finally found the first tunnel that dipped under the road. Sticking my hand out, my nails scraped the cement wall, searching for what I hoped was there. I was not sure if all the tributary tunnels had an excess flow chamber, like the one I knew from downtown that led to a passageway for Fort Daniels, but I prayed luck was on my side.

Amazingly, my hand latched onto a lever and abruptly stopped my drifting body. My frozen fingers were barely able to catch the metal and I had to force my legs to stand strong in the waist-deep waters. I tried to remain strong against the current of melted snow, looping my backpack around my neck, using both hands to grab the upper lever of the two-tiered flow chamber. I put all my strength into opening the grate enough for me to throw my backpack inside and slide in after, only able to pull the grate partially shut behind me.

I remained in the slightly damp, musky cement area for only ten seconds before I forced myself to clutch around in the dark for my backpack, reaching inside with frozen fingers and scraping the bottom for my phone. I used it as a flashlight to look for a means of getting out of the tunnel. I crawled through the pipe and tried to gracefully drop into the main drainage pipe that would lead to the larger tunnels under the city, but my frozen body tumbled down and my shivering muscles gave out.

Holding my phone with my teeth, I pulled my drenched clothes off my body, trying to keep myself moving, jumping up and down to get my blood pumping. When the wet fabric was away from my skin, I pulled out one of the sweaters and a pair of jeans from my bag, also pulling off my wet socks and placing dry ones over my numb toes.

Dressed in dry clothes, I grabbed my backpack, moving my arms around to get blood flowing to my fingers again. I gathered the wet clothes and began walking, without shoes, in the cold pipe, using the compass on my phone to head in the direction of downtown.

By the time I reached the familiar tunnel system, my body was not nearly as cold, though I still lacked feeling in my fingers and toes.

I always kept an ear out for the Sweep team, but was sure I had lost them.

When I came to the door that I knew would lead to the rest of the revolutionaries, I picked up speed, eager.

Once inside the last hallway with the door closed behind me, I half-ran to the end of the corridor and pulled the heavy door aside, finding myself in the lit hall of the ammunition rooms leading into the main bunker. There was a dull murmur from the main room, and I clambered toward it.

Griffin caught sight of me first and a big smile took over his features.

"Lily!"

Tori ran to me excitedly.

"We've been waiting for you!" she said. I smiled at the happy faces around me, including one that I had not seen in what felt like years. Mykail wrapped his arms around me in a tight embrace.

"I'm so glad you're here safely," he breathed. He pecked a kiss on my lips before looking me over, running a hand through my still damp hair. "What the hell happened?" he chuckled.

I laughed, but was unable to answer, feeling too many complex emotions wash over me as I looked around the bunker.

This was my family, now.

"You're shivering!" Tori laughed.

"Come on, we'll get you some blankets and warm you up," Griffin declared.

* *** *

While I had escaped the Sweep Team, that was not the end of the horrible ordeal. I was unable to sleep, despite feeling comfortable as I lay with Mykail for the first time in so long.

I needed to go back, needed to confront my father, needed to close the door on that section of my life properly before I could dedicate myself entirely to the revolution.

Naturally, I could not tell anyone where I was going, so I told them that I was going to go to Clark's house just to make sure he was still there.

I traveled on the bus back to my house, surprised at how out-of-place I felt in the almost-empty vehicle. The previous night, I had barely managed to evade the Sweep Team of the Commission of the People, and it seemed unreal that I was able to get on the bus without being hounded once again. I was constantly looking over my shoulder, making sure I was not being followed, paranoid.

There was no guarantee that my father would be at the house, but I hoped he was. I walked to the house, overwhelmed by its enormity. I made my way around the back and into the garage. Using my key, I unlocked the back door and peeked inside. Both cars were present.

My father was home.

Taking a deep breath, I stepped to the door into the house. Before I could think better of my actions, I entered, listening for sounds of my father.

Someone was unloading the dishwasher, so I walked toward the kitchen, keeping quiet as I moved through the house that felt foreign, despite having been there twelve hours previous as a resident.

I ascended the three stairs into the kitchen and saw my father bent over the dishwasher, placing the clean plates on the counter.

I took a step forward and made sure to make noise on the hardwood floor. He hesitated, stopped in his stoop before slowly turning. He looked as though he had not slept at all, his eyes dark and bloodshot, sunken into a pale face.

"Hey," I said stupidly.

"Lily…"

"I'm sure you have a good reason for vanishing last night," I said coldly. I fixed him with a hard stare. "Why didn't you just turn me in? Why did you back out like a coward and let the Sweep Team come to take me?"

"Lily, you shouldn't be here…"

"Obviously," I snarled. "But you at least owe me an answer."

"…I don't have one," he admitted. I nodded, looking at my feet, trying to think of what I wanted to say.

"Mom called me in?" I asked.

"She did…" he confirmed. "She thought you were out of control…that you couldn't be brought to reason…"

"She did? Or you both did?" I snapped. "Because it's obvious you didn't step in on my behalf last night."

"Lily, what you're doing is wrong. It's dangerous to everyone, including yourself," he said, stepping toward me as though he was trying to calm me down.

"And you thought I needed to learn that the hard way?" I asked. "You figured it was best to just have me disappear and then never hear from me again? Let me guess. Now that the Sweep Team came through and I'm a wanted criminal, Mom's coming home so you two can carry on having your separate relationships within your marriage."

"Lily…"

"No, you know what, Mom was right," I said, the tears starting to choke me. "You really did give up on me…*both* of you did."

"I wish there was something I could say," he murmured, his voice tight with agony, "but the truth is, there is nothing I can say. I know what I did, and as much as it hurts me that my daughter is wanted by the Commission of the People for being involved in domestic terrorism…I know I did the right thing."

I blinked.

"The right thing?" I whispered. "You did the right thing? Supporting a system that hunts people down and turns them into weapons, or tests on them until they die? That's the right thing?"

"You're part of the group that is causing panic across the country." He shook his head, as though the statement in itself validated his decision.

"So are you," I growled. "You think the Commission doesn't cause panic?"

"It's not the same."

"Yes, it is the same," I snapped. "You know, I shouldn't be surprised, really. It runs in the family. Grandfather turned in your older brother for going against the Commission and now you are doing the same to your daughter."

"What my brother was doing was far nobler than what you're doing," my father retorted. "Yes, Liam disapproved of the Commission, but he discreetly moved people out of the country. He didn't parade around the streets flaunting what he was doing and getting people killed!"

I stared at him, hurt by the words. The man I looked up to for going against the Commission, for being impervious to all the tests the Commission put him through, was someone I had now betrayed for trying to do the same thing he had done.

I could say nothing, the tears falling down my cheeks as I clenched my jaw tight. My father's eyes were also welling with tears. He sniffed once and pointed a finger at me.

"I won't report that you were here today…" he said. "But you are dead to me now, Lily Sandover."

He might as well have taken a knife to my heart. The words struck me harder than anything I had ever known before. My father was denying my existence, denying everything that he had taught me about standing up for what I believed in.

He was killing me.

I turned and left, closing the door on the life I had always known, leaving a part of my soul in the house with my father, crying at the physical and emotional pain that tore through me.

End of Part 2

To be continued in:

Inside
Part 3

More Works by K.J. Amidon

Inside
(Written as Kyra Anderson)
Inside – Pt. 1
Inside – Pt. 2
Inside – Pt. 3
Inside – Alternate Part 3
Inside the Commission

The Coalition Trilogy
(Written as Kyra Anderson)
Forged Under Fire
The Rising Tide
With Banners Raised

The Significant
(Written as Kyra Anderson)

The Significant Expanded Story
(Written as Kyra Anderson)
The Degenerates
The Deserted

The Faith
(Written as Kyra Anderson)
The Faith
The Sacred

The Dimension Guardian Series:
The Realm of Beasts – The Guardian Tournament
The Realm of Darkness – Blind Ambitions
The Realm of Humans – Fate
The Realm of Light – Imbalance
The Realm of Demons – Scars in Time
The Realm of Exile – Continuum

The Roadside Paradise Series:
Into Oblivion
Wander the Lost
Until Dawn Breaks
Hiding from Sight
For Fools
Challenge Gods